PRAISE FOR

Spindlefish and Stars

A *Booklist* Editors' Choice

A *Kirkus Reviews* Best Middle Grade Book of 2020

★ "Bewitching, beautiful, and bewildering. Immensely satisfying." —*Booklist*, starred review

★ "An epic tale of abandonment, travel, secrets, family, and the meaning of art....Exquisite in detail....A tapestry, both humble and rich." —*Kirkus Reviews*, starred review

★ "A lyrical debut exploring the nature of destiny and sacrifice....The narrative voice makes this enchanting story feel like an all-new myth built from classic material." —*Publishers Weekly*, starred review

★ "Offers a...measured view of the unavoidability of pain and the beauty of kindness as well as commentary on the persistence of powerful stories through art." —*The Bulletin*, starred review

"Expertly written, full of beautiful imagery and elements of Greek mythology. An engaging and inventive novel." —*School Library Journal*

"Both r̶   ̶rsive
story tha   nd the
v̶

SPINDLEFISH
AND
STARS

SPINDLEFISH
AND
STARS

CHRISTIANE M. ANDREWS

Ⓛ Ⓑ
LITTLE, BROWN AND COMPANY
New York Boston

Little, Brown and Company
Hachette Book Group
1290 Avenue of the Americas, New York, NY 10104
Visit us at LBYR.com

Originally published in hardcover and ebook by Little, Brown and
Company in September 2020
First Trade Paperback Edition: October 2021

Little, Brown and Company is a division of Hachette Book Group, Inc.
The Little, Brown name and logo are trademarks of
Hachette Book Group, Inc.

The publisher is not responsible for websites (or their content)
that are not owned by the publisher.

The Library of Congress has cataloged the hardcover edition as follows:
Names: Andrews, Christiane M., author.
Title: Spindlefish and stars / Christiane M. Andrews.
Description: First edition. | New York : Little, Brown and Company, 2020. |
Audience: Ages 8–12. | Summary: "When Clo's father goes missing, she
takes the mysterious items he left behind and journeys across the sea to find
him, but is stranded on a strange island and must learn to spin fish into
yarn to unravel the secret of all that has happened"– Provided by publisher.
Identifiers: LCCN 2020012167 | ISBN 9780316496018 (hardcover) |
ISBN 9780316496025 (ebook) | ISBN 9780316496056 (ebook)
Subjects: CYAC: Missing persons–Fiction. | Voyages and travels–Fiction. |
Tapestry–Fiction. | Fantasy.
Classification: LCC PZ7.1.A5327 Spi 2020 | DDC [Fic] –dc23
LC record available at https://lccn.loc.gov/2020012167

ISBNs: 978-0-316-49603-2 (pbk.), 978-0-316-49602-5 (ebook)

Printed in the United States of America

LSC-C

Printing 1, 2021

FOR OLIVER ROBIN

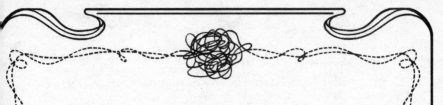

IN WHICH THE BOYISH GIRL DIGS UP HER TURNIPS

O NCE, ON THE FAR END OF THE VILLAGE IN THE LAST OF the crumbling homes, lived a girl. *Perhaps a girl*, the neighbors said; at any rate, she was not pretty. She kept her dark hair shorn as tight as a lamb's in spring and wore a boy's dirty tunic and leggings and boots, and when she was not with her father, which was often, she skulked in the shadows of the buildings or at the corner of her house, where she dug and poked in the dirt around a miserable patch of turnips and straggly weeds. She never smiled or offered a *hello* or *bonjour* or *guten morgen* or *ahlan wa sahlan* or *privet* or a greeting in any language, no matter how many times the neighbors showed her their own rows of yellow teeth, and when they tried to stop her to make her speak—*to mind her manners*—she

would scuttle away, bounding out of their grasp, and disappear with a bang behind her own front door.

A shame, one neighbor would sigh.

The child needs a mother, another would add.

How about you? a third would suggest.

This always made them all laugh, great heaving, spittle-laced laughs, for as much as the motherless boyish girl set the neighbors' tongues to flapping, the thought of anyone marrying *that man*, the gray and wizened, stooped and shuffling little man who called himself her father, was too much for any of them to bear.

Oh, he has one foot already in the grave! the first would hoot.

Just one foot? the second would sputter. *I think there's a leg and an arm in there as well!*

Ah, if he only had a fortune, the last would cry, *the first gust of winter would make his widow rich!* This thought, of course, silenced them for a while. But no, he could not be rich. Whatever work he did, it was daily—or, rather, nightly: he would depart each evening before the sun sank below the mountains and arrive each morning just as the town began to shape itself out of the darkness. There was no leisure. And night work...whatever it was—emptying the chamber pots or sweeping the stables or loosening the grime that clogged the gutters along the streets—was filthy work. Rank, lowly work. Work that smelled. Work best done in the dark. Work that did not fatten a man's purse.

But it mattered little how much the neighbors talked, or how often the girl—for she was a girl, shorn hair and short tunic and all—darted into the shadows to escape their eyes, or how often her stooped and aged father trudged past on his way to his dark duties. For there would come a day, there *always* came a day, when the father would not return, and the girl, after having swept the stoop and plucked the last small turnips *and* the weeds from the little garden and tied them in a sack, would clamber over the village wall and disappear into the fields and then the forest, never to return. Sometimes, one of the neighbors, up at dawn and yawning at the window, would see the girl perched on the wall, ready to jump, and would ask, *Now where*…but the neighbor would scarcely form the question before letting herself forget all about the child and the old man. That he was too old and she too boyish was really all there was to talk about, and when they were not there, well, honestly, what was the point in calling them to mind?

So Clo, wall-jumper, turnip-grower, corner-skulker, lived a life in the shadows. But those moments before they left the village, the ones where she perched on the wall and prepared to launch herself off into the wilderness, small bag of turnips and weeds and household things in hand, those were the moments she most treasured. The sun, just rising

above the edges of the hills, would be staining the sky a faint pink; the village, just beginning to wake up, would be quiet and still, except, perhaps, for the distant noise of a cart trundling along the cobblestones; and Clo, relishing the silence and the air at the top of the wall that carried the scent of dew and pine and not the steaming, fetid odors of the town, would feel her pulse quicken at the thought of the journey that awaited. Her father would meet her at the edge of the woods, his pockets heavy with breads and pastries and cheeses he had pilfered from the kitchens and his bags strapped to an ass he had pilfered from the barns, and the two would set out, tramping for days upon days through bright fields and dark forests and glimmering mountain heights.

These travels, thought Clo, and not the towns that interrupted them for a scattering of months at a time, made up their real life. For it was only then, walking under the thick shadows of trees or at the edges of windswept moors or even in the gloom of dank and terrible swamps, that the worry and fear that lined her father's eyes faded, and Clo, sensing his relief, allowed her own face to relax into a smile that–had the villagers seen it–might have caused them to reconsider the word *pretty*. No, even then, they would not have said *pretty*, but *pleasant*, yes. They might have called her smile, at least, pleasant.

And so it was such a smile that Clo should have worn

that morning that found her again on the wall, swinging her legs and taking in her first deep breath of non-manure-scented air. Having heard the tower bells chime five and having not seen her father come through the front door—*Were they meant to leave today?*—she had rushed to wrap up their scant belongings and pluck the garden and sweep the stoop and clamber the wall. But once there, about to push off into the damp morning air, she felt, instead of joy, a small, uncomfortable seed of foreboding. She delayed a moment, frowning, wondering. Her father had not given her any warning. Usually, he offered her some notice that their town days were drawing to a close: *Clo, I am nearly finished—a fortnight, perhaps*, or *Clo, the steward is, I think, suspicious; take care to heed the bells these next weeks*. But this time, he had said nothing.

No matter. They had been in this particular village for many months, as many as they had ever stayed at another. Even the grandest manors had only so many moldering baubles for her father to polish: he would certainly be finishing his work. Clo glanced back. There was their crumbling house with its freshly swept stoop, there was a neighbor staring slack-jawed through a window, there were a few faint curls of smoke rising from chimneys about the town. She narrowed her eyes at the goggling neighbor. *My father does not, does not,* she protested silently, *have three entire limbs in the grave. And he does not,* she added, glaring, frowning, *sweep the*

night soil from the privies. She turned away, looking toward the open field. She would not miss this dreary hamlet and its gossiping inhabitants.

Tightening her grip around the bag of turnips and things, she pushed off, landing lightly in the muck that laced the wall, and set off at a trot through the fields. She kept her eye on the forest edge; her father would have left the manor under cover of dark, and he would be waiting now—with pastry-laden pockets—for her to arrive. *Or he should be.* She felt again that uncomfortable seed of foreboding, now a bit larger than before. A seed perhaps splitting and beginning to sprout. She could not see her father's silhouette or the silhouette of a stolen ass anywhere beneath the trees. She began to run, the sack bouncing against her side. The line of trees rose and fell with her gait, and though she scanned and scanned, she still could see no form of man or donkey.

"Father!" she called when she had drawn close enough to distinguish one tree from another. Perhaps he was in the woods, resting on a bit of moss or leaning against a log. "Father!" Perhaps he had closed his eyes for a moment and fallen asleep after his long night of work. "Father!" She raced along the edge, calling into the shadows. "Father!"

She stopped. Only silence and the gentle sweep of leaves. "Father!" she tried again and strained, listening.

He was not there.

Clo looked back at the town. The village gates, though

open, were empty. The wagon tracks leading to them were also empty. No donkey, no man. Her father was not here, and he was not simply delayed.

One last time: "Father!"

Only the *shush-shush-shush* of the trees answered.

Clo sat, leaning back against the rough bark of a pine. The seed of foreboding that had split and sprouted and taken root now blossomed thick and bitter.

What to do?

What to do?

What to do?

Clo, wall-jumper, turnip-picker, corner-skulker, was not a hand-wringer, but in the many many times and in the many many ways they had fled a village, never had her father failed to meet her. *Always*, he had made her promise, should the morning bells ring five without his return, she should leave the town. "*Do not stay*," he would instruct her. "*Do not tempt fate by delaying. You must not stay.*" And *always*, he would promise in kind, he would meet her at the forest edge under the tallest pine. "*Always, Clo. Always.*"

Never had he told her what to do should she find herself there alone.

Shush-shush-shush, the trees said. *Shush-shush-shush*.

"Always," Clo whispered. She folded her hands on her lap. "Always."

WHEREIN THE POCKMARKED SWINEHERD CURLS HIS LIP

Fʀᴏᴍ ʜᴇʀ ᴘᴇʀᴄʜ, Cʟᴏ ᴡᴀᴛᴄʜᴇᴅ ᴛʜᴇ sᴋʏ ꜰᴀᴅᴇ ꜰʀᴏᴍ ᴘɪɴᴋ to gray and gradually brighten into a pale, washed blue. The town, in the distance, came to life: little figures—men and oxen and sheep and horses—moved in and out of the gates, and the murmurings of the village—shouts and cries and clatterings—came now and again on the wind. With increasing agitation, Clo heard the tower bells chime six.

Then seven.

Then eight.

Then nine.

At ten, the sun had grown too strong, and she backed a little into the forest, settling herself against a mossy stump. Here, she could still see the village and the paths that wove around it, but in the shadows, she felt less desperate. So she

would wait. What else was there to do but wait? He would come. *Always*.

By now, thought Clo, if her father had come home, they would have already breakfasted together. She would have warmed yesterday's cold crust over the fire, sliced the onions thin. He would have asked her how she slept—*Clo, did the rats keep away?*—and she would have fibbed and said they had. By now, he would already have fallen into a deep sleep on his pallet on the floor, and she, surely, by now would already be outside picking weeds from their garden. She squinted hard at the little town, imagining herself there scratching in the dirt around the tubers, yanking out rogue shepherd's purse and goosefoot, scurrying to the well and back for water, tending to her seedlings, going about her morning as it should have happened.

At eleven, the trees stopped saying *shush, shush, shush* and fell into a quieter, steadier *sssssss*.

Not much later, Clo's stomach began its own rumbling monologue, complaining that, in her mistaken anticipation of pastries from her father's pockets, she had not eaten. She untied her sack and, looking over her collection of turnips, took the smallest of the little crop. She rubbed it clean on her tunic and ate it like an apple. Afterward, her mouth felt dry and puckered; she smacked her lips and swallowed and wished desperately she had something to drink, but her father was the one who always carried the skins of water. *Always*.

9

At two, full of midday heat and the steady hum of insects, a stillness settled over the town: the little figures in the distance were resting. Clo watched an emerald beetle climb steadily up a tree trunk until it disappeared into the leafy canopy.

By five, when the sun was beginning to dip in the sky, Clo's little plant of foreboding had itself gone to seed. She felt within her a whole garden of dread rooting and sprouting and twisting its vines.

Smoke was now rising from the village cooking fires. Clo thought of the suppers she usually prepared—working quietly around her father's sleeping form—to share with him before he went to work: a simple, thin soup, a hunk of bread. She imagined herself pulling from the embers the loaf she had shaped, ladling out the steaming broth and its soft scraps of potato and turnip into their bowls, hiding from her father that she was giving him the meatiest pieces. Though she was now too full of anxiety to be hungry, she thought of the comfort of those foods with longing.

By the time the bells tolled six and lights from the village showed against the deepening sky, Clo, who was not a hand-wringer, was, in fact, wringing her hands in earnest. She twisted her fingers and bit her lips and stood and paced and stared at the town. *Should she return? Should she remain? Should she go on? What had become of her father?*

Her feet padding steadily across the carpet of needles and moss and leaves, she reconsidered his goodbye to her the evening before. *Had there been anything amiss?* No...not amiss. Not exactly amiss. She had been sewing by the fire while he shuffled about, wrapping his brushes, his rags, his potatoes, his pots, and placing them in his can. She had shown him her poor attempt at patchwork—*I'm trying to mend your winter tunic, Father*—and he had sighed, looking over her stitches—*I'm afraid the cloth is too worn to hold together, lambkin.* He had kissed her as he always did on the crown of her head, the pale bristle of his chin scratching her brow. *If only I had stronger thread for you, my daughter, that tunic might see another winter. But all the same, you are good to try. Good to try to keep us warm as the days grow shorter.* His smile had been small. He had pulled his cloak over his narrow shoulders, fastened its dark button. *Good night, my lambkin, my daughter so full of care. Good night, Father, good night.*

As she wrung her hands and paced to and fro, a flash of movement on the village wall caught her eye. Clo stopped, squinted. A little figure wobbled atop the stones. The figure swayed, then tumbled, and was lost against the darkness of the structure. Clo stared.

In a moment, she caught sight of the figure moving across the field. It was striding quickly but unevenly, as though struggling under a weight. It did not, Clo thought,

have her father's gait. Though she did not share—*fully* share—the townsfolk's opinion of her father as a gray and wizened, stooped and shuffling old man with a leg and an arm and a foot in the grave, she could not help but admit that he moved more… *hesitantly* than he once had. She frowned, her little garden of dread stirring again. Yes. *Hesitantly.* Especially in recent months. This figure, moving with long legs and impatient speed, could not be her father. It was, however, moving directly toward her.

Clo stepped back into the shadows of the trees.

The figure continued its quick advancement. It *was* burdened; as it drew closer, Clo could see a pack slung over its shoulder. And it was a boy. A boy a bit older than herself, perhaps fifteen. He was tall and thin and, thought Clo, when she could finally see his face, mottled with angry pockmarks. His nose was as large and bulbous as a branch of cauliflower.

She stepped behind a thick trunk, hoping he would not see her.

It did not matter that she hid; he came straight to her.

He circled the tree and stopped in front of her. Pushing a shock of bright red hair from his eyes, he stared at Clo, his eyes traveling up and down her person. His lip curled. Just slightly. A slight sneer. She pressed her spine against the tree trunk.

"Are you Clothilde?" he said, though his words, stretched

through thick accent and boyish mumbling, sounded more like, "Art tha Clatil?"

Clo, who had not spoken to anyone but her father in many months, said nothing. The boy smelled like a swineherd, and his boots, mud- and muck-covered, suggested the same.

The boy dropped the pack he was carrying.

"If th'art Clatil," he said, his lip still curling, "thy father said I'd find a lass with all the beauty of th' stars and sun here beneath th' tallest pine, but"—he paused and ran his eyes over her again—"th'art but a nipper as spindle-shanked as I've ever seen."

Clo still said nothing, but her hands, at the mention of her father, trembled slightly. She curled her fingers into her palms to hide her agitation. The boy noticed her small fists and laughed.

"If th'art Clatil, thy father has given me a silver coin for a letter and a parcel to deliver. So"—he removed and held aloft a square of paper—"art tha Clatil?"

Clo's eyes narrowed and settled on the note pinched between the boy's long, dirt-stained fingers.

"Clatil? Clatil? Art tha Clatil?" The boy waved the letter back and forth above Clo's head. She grabbed for it. The boy, laughing again, moved it swiftly out of her reach.

"Ah. Th'art Clatil. Hold, and I'll read it." The boy moved the paper to the end of his nose and narrowed his eyes at it.

He huffed, then squinted, and huffed again, and finally murmured out, "Me-yiy dee-arrrrre-esss-teeeee seee-lllow—"

"Give it here." Clo jumped and snatched the letter from the boy's grasp. She scanned the text anxiously. It was in her father's hand, but scrawled and smudged—not written with his usual care. Inkblots bloomed over and obscured some of the text.

"Canst tha read?" The boy was incredulous.

"Of course I can read." The text swam in front of her.

He gawped at her. "How did tha come to learn? How did a lass like tha come to learn?"

"My father taught me," she murmured. Of course he had taught her. He'd held her at the table on his knees while she traced the letters with her small fingers and learned their sounds—*C-L-O, yes, lambkin, that's your name.* He'd made sure—when he could—she'd even had books to practice with—*Try this sentence now.* Yes, *of course* she knew how to read.

Clo shook the letter as though to loosen the distraction and tried to steady herself enough to focus on the words. *My dearest Clo*, the letter began.

The boy watched, bemused. "So th'art a spindle-shanked *and* a clever lass. I've not met a lass who could read, and most lasses do li'l more'n scrub pots an' do stitchin'—"

"Stop talking, will you?" The boy's garbled chatter muddled her brain. She shook the letter again.

My dearest Clo,

Forgive me. Fo⬛⬛⬛⬛*ust*
travel alone. I w⬛*re not so. Yo*⬛⬛*.*
⬛*e brave. The ticket is a promi*⬛⬛
⬛*ago to*⬛*ther. It will give you*
safe passage, and w⬛⬛*e, bring y*⬛
⬛*ever sh*⬛*gone. Follow the* ⬛⬛*.*
⬛⬛*s to the harbor to Haros,*
I ⬛⬛ *will find you. W*⬛⬛⬛⬛
certain, be voyag⬛⬛*ether* ⬛⬛*aft.*

The canvas is for ⬛⬛⬛*e last I*
⬛⬛⬛*much* ⬛⬛⬛⬛*ou.*
You ⬛⬛⬛*perhaps e*⬛⬛⬛
⬛⬛*n* ⬛*save me.*

I hope you will come to understand.

⬛⬛*ow I love you. So much my daughter.*

Y⬛⬛*e beauty of all the stars.*

> *Alw*⬛⬛*ays, always,*
> *your loving fa*⬛

Clo read and reread the letter, cursing the ink smudges
and rubbing her thumb at them as if she could erase the

splotches and leave the text beneath. Of its sense, she only understood *forgive* and *canvas* and *travel alone*. And *save me*.

The garden of dread that had been growing all day twisted again, the blossom hot at the back of her throat. She swallowed. ——*n–save me. Can save me? Cannot save me?* Which was it?

"Where is my father?" She spun to face the boy. "Where is he?"

"Th' last I saw him, he was crouchin' in th' pens, like he was a sow rootin' in th' straw. And he grabbed me like this"–here the boy hauled at his own collar–"when I come in, and he said I'm t' have a silver coin for safe deliverment of this"–he pointed to the letter in Clo's hands–"and this." Here the boy, kneeling and untying his sack, lifted a bundle, which he dropped at Clo's feet.

It was her father's cloak wrapped and knotted around a heavy parcel.

Kneeling in the leaf litter, Clo worked at the blue woolen knots. The words *crouchin' in th' pens* made her fingers shake so she could not loosen the fabric; the wool, pulled too tight, did not want to give way.

"He said I'm to take from th' lass some wood'n matter. Hast tha got wood'n matter? It's for th' payment. 'Be sure,' he says, 'to take the wood'n matter.'"

Clo, desperately trying to open the parcel, did not look up. The boy was speaking nonsense.

"Wood'n matter. I'm to take it back or–or tha'll not get this." The boy wrenched the cloak-wrapped parcel from Clo's hands.

"I have no wood!" Clo tried to grab the parcel back.

"Woooood"–the boy stretched his mouth grotesquely around the words–"aaaaan maaaaaaattteeer. He says tha'll be carryin' it, and I'm t' have it." The boy hesitated. "It's for my payment. Mine."

"Look." Clo stretched out her arms. "I have no wood. *No-thing wood.* I have my clothes. And"–she gestured to her small sack–"some turnips. And…ah." Understanding came with unease. *Why had her father promised this? Didn't he need it for his work?* Clo hastened to the bag of turnips and things. "Here." Pushing the turnips aside, she lifted the wilted bundles of garden weeds from her sack and handed them reluctantly to the boy. She did not like to give these away; she had grown them for her father.

"Wot's that, then?"

"Your wooden matter."

The boy looked skeptically at the shaggy plants. "'S not."

"I promise you. If my father promised it, this *woad* and *madder* is exactly what you are meant to have–it's worth… several coins if you sell it at the market. Now return that package to me."

The boy tossed her the cloak-wrapped lump and, relieved

of his burden, turned to go. But he took only a few strides in the direction of the town before he stopped.

"Is't true wot they say on him?"

"Is what true?" Kneeling over the parcel, Clo kept working on the knotted cloak. *What village gossip had this muck-boy overheard? That her father scraped the night soil? That he had three entire limbs in the grave?*

"Well, th' cook, he said he knew thy father soon as he saw him arrive at th' house offerin' his service. Recognized him right away."

Clo kept her gaze on the bundle. *Her father had been recognized?* Still, this was no cause for panic.

"That's right. Th' cook, right away, he said, 'That's th' thief did steal from my last master.' He told the steward, 'You watch him; he's a chiseler and a thief.' An' wouldn't tha know, there *has* been a theft. Just today th' house is all a-tumble with it. Jewels missing out of th' lady's chamber." The boy, raising an eyebrow at the parcel Clo was still trying to open, paused to gauge her reaction, but if he saw how her lip trembled or how her hands grew still at the word *thief*, he did not let on.

"My father's no *jewel* thief." Clo chose her words carefully.

"Well, and here's th' thing. The lady's maid, she argued with th' cook. She said *she* knew him, too! 'That's no thief,' she said. She knew him when she was a girl, she said. 'A famous dra'tsman, he is,' she told th' cook. 'Painted all th' lords n' ladies. Lived in th' great house. Painted my mother,

too,' she said, 'even though she was just a washerwoman, God rest her soul, and he painted a wee one for me, too.' And she'd had a locket, even, and she showed it to us, and lo if there weren't a tiny biddy there, lookin' so red-cheeked and lively she were almost breathin'."

At this, a loud *Ha!* burst from Clo. *Living in a great house? Painting lords and ladies?* "That's definitely not my father," she said, her voice firm and certain. She rocked back on her heels to gaze directly at the boy. The swineherd waited a moment, watching, but she shook her head. "Stories. Only stories."

"Lot o' stories. In th' stables, there's no muck to shovel without th' pigs to make it." But shrugging, the boy turned to go.

Kneeling again over the package, Clo tugged violently at the wool; the knots would not come free.

"Wait!" she called after the boy.

He kept walking.

"Wait!" Clo darted after him into the field.

"An' wot, then?" He stopped, turning. "An' *wot*?"

She could not look at the boy. "My father—was he all right? Was he hurt?"

"He was hidin' in th' pens. I'd not call that right."

Clo hesitated. "Do you know... where is he now?"

The boy glanced down at the wilted plants in his hand. "N-no." He shrugged and looked away uncomfortably. "But

I'm sure he's gone on. I'm sure th'art to go on." Gesturing to the parcel, he turned again to go.

"Wait—just one more thing."

"I've no time t' wait." The boy turned so he was walking backward. "Wot? Wot?"

"What's a *Haros*? Do you know what a Haros is? A town? A person? It was in the letter."

The swineherd shook his head. "I've heard of no such things."

"Well, what's a harbor, then? Do you know?"

"Tha canst read, but tha hast no idea o' *harbor*?" Still walking backward, nearly tripping, the boy doubled over laughing. "And tha thinks me ignorant. All here knows th' harbor. Th' harbor? Th' sea? Th' water that's full o' salt and has no edge?"

Clo shook her head.

The boy frowned and waved at the woods before turning away. "A day's walk through th' woods," he called over his shoulder. "An' tha'll smell't afore sightin' it."

Clo watched the swineherd stride across the darkening fields. In all her travels, in all the mountains and valleys and highlands and lowlands she had ever crossed, never, *never* had she seen a water that was full of salt and had no edge. Clo, wall-jumper, turnip-eater, letter-reader, felt her world shift to include the idea of *sea*.

It felt as large and deep and dark as the word *alone*.

PERTAINING TO THE UNWRAPPING OF A STINKY CHEESE

FOR A LITTLE WHILE, AFTER THE MUCK-COVERED SWINE-herd had disappeared, Clo continued to sit under the pine. She read and reread the ink-splattered letter and worked despairingly at the woolen knots on her father's parcel while night thickened around her.

She turned the word *sea* over and over in her mouth.

She thought of returning to the town and finding her way to the barns and the swine among whom her father was said to have crouched, or of sleeping there, at the edge of the forest, and seeing what morning might bring. But the urgency of her father's note—its hasty scrawl, its ink splatters—and the story of the cook, the worry that her father might have been recognized, compelled her to go.

A day's walk through the woods. A night's walk?

Follow the ~~■~~.
~~■■■■■~~ s to the harbor to Haros,
I ~~●●●~~ will find you...
~~●●●~~ n ~~●~~ save me

She would go to the harbor. The sea. If there was nothing there—no Haros, whatever that might be—if she could not find her father, she would return. It was a day.

She gathered her belongings and entered the dark of the woods.

Under a thick slice of moon, the forest was more gray than black—shades of darkness that suggested rather than defined forms. Clo followed the space in the darkness, the gray ruts of the wagon path, easily enough. The words of the swineherd, *crouchin' in th' pens*, hurried her along.

Another girl—wall-climber or no—or another boy—turnip-picker or no—really, most any inhabitant of the town might find the night of the forest too dark to enter. Too full of the shufflings of unseen creatures and windshook leaves. Too full of teeth and claws—of wolf, of bear, of bands of thieves. But Clo, wall-jumper, turnip-bearer, letter-reader, was not scared of the dark. Not truly. She had spent too many nights under the stars on her journeys with her father. The dry rustlings of the forest, even those of wolves and bears, had ceased to startle her long ago.

And the rustlings of thieves? Thieves with flashing

teeth and flashing nails and flashing silver blades? Clo had journeyed too long and to too many distant lands *with* a thief really to be frightened of them.

Her father was not, Clo knew, of the knife-wielding brand of thieves. He did not crouch in the shadows and take poor travelers unawares. He did not threaten violence, frighten the innocent, terrorize the populace. He took only from those who had much...and most never noticed their loss.

Who would miss a pocket's worth of pastries? A sausage link from the smokehouse? A sack of grain from the storerooms? Who would begrudge a father and his daughter a meal? Even a half dozen meals?

Who would notice the loss of an obsolete almanac or a well-thumbed primer? A chronicle left collecting dust? Who would berate a father for wanting to give his child some schooling?

Who would mind that he led away the oldest or lamest or stubbornest ass in the barns? No one would be sad to see those querulous beasts gone.

Of course, that wasn't all...

Clo frowned and touched the cloak-wrapped package she was carrying. *His thievery was not always so trifling.* He always took one. At least one. A canvas. Some painted thing he found. Some piece of art he could sell. He could not help himself.

Clo tried to push away her misgivings. His work *otherwise*

was honest. True. Above suspicion. A humble cleaner with his brushes and pots, an unassuming servant who kept to himself in the corners.

She thought of how he would present himself at the manor house whenever they arrived in a new village. *At your service,* he'd announce, bowing as deep as his crooked body would allow. *Restorer of all decorative arts.* He'd sweep his hat over the stones. Servile. Unassuming. *For your lords and ladies, I can remove the dirt, the grime, the grease, the dust, the ash, the soot. I can erase cooksmoke and water stain, mildew spot and errant smudge; I can repair the yellowing of whites, the fading of pinks, the crackling of age. The smears along the ceiling frescoes, the tarnish on the gilded platters, the graying hues of family portraits—all can be made fair and bright and new.*

Yes, honest night work, Clo thought, feeling the cloaked package in the dark again. *Mostly* honest, careful, modest work by candlelight. While the masters and servants of the house slept, he'd remove the grime that collected over years and years by wiping bread or potatoes across the painted surfaces, gently, painstakingly cleaning every detail. Or sometimes he'd mix a bit of color—steeping the woad leaves and madder roots that she grew for him in her garden or grinding a bit of lime or charcoal—and dab where paint had flaked away. "Honest night work," she said quietly into the dark. Honest gardening. She was proud of the plants she grew.

They were not really thieves.

All about her, the woods were silent. The path opened in gray space ahead of her.

The harbor.

She hurried on.

Clo worried she might grow tired, but the farther she walked, the farther she seemed from sleep. Her sack and her father's parcel both were hooked over her shoulder, and with each step, they *shush*ed against her in a rhythm that said *always, always, always.* The *always* carried her deeper and deeper into the woods: it was just that sound, and her steps, and the grayness.

An hour passed, then another, and another. Her mind rested in a way that it would not have had she stopped: she was walking because she was supposed to walk. She felt full of the quiet and the dark. *Always,* *shush*ed the bags. The moon, fragments behind the branches, sank deeper in the trees.

Only when a faint gold light began to rise and give shape to the forest did Clo start to tire and begin to wonder whether she had in fact fallen asleep, whether she was now dreaming of walking rather than actually walking. But by then, something in the air had changed. The woods were heavy with dew and the scent of pine, but there was something else as well. Clo could almost taste it, almost feel it, a stickiness on her skin. She sniffed. Something like salt—*Did salt smell?*—was thick in the air. *You'll smell't afore sightin' it,* the swineherd had said. *Was this the smell of sea?* The idea hurried Clo forward. *Asea, asea,* *shush*ed the bags at her quick steps.

In the half-light, the woods were opening up. The spaces between the trees grew larger, the light between them now more pink than gray. Clo's legs ached with weariness, but still she rushed forward, the thought of *sea* and the thought that she might find her father there propelling her on. Overhead, a great gray-and-white bird flitted in the treetops. It gave a shrill cry—to Clo, a sound like rusty metal—and was gone. *Seaseasea*, thumped the bags against her.

The woods gave way to nothingness—*no, not nothingness*, pale blue sky and pale blue water on and on and on. *Water that has no edge.* Clo stared. She could not see where water or sky ended; each simply seemed to become the other. When she finally lowered her gaze from the horizon, she saw she was on a ridge, high above a town. Little houses perched alongside the water, and boats floated near the shore. Small figures, men with buckets and nets, moved between the boats and the buildings in a steady, busy pattern.

Cautiously, Clo followed the cart path down to the village. *Harbor*, she murmured. Having always skulked in the shadows, she found it easy now to slip into the town's darker spaces, just out of sight of the figures carrying salt-stinking buckets and barrels and sacks from the boats to the shore. If any of the men, men as thick and sturdy and opaque as the barrels they carried, saw her, they saw only a disheveled boy, dirty and burdened, no different than any of the guttersnipes and urchins who scrounged in the town.

Clo, disheveled guttersnipe, slunk to the water's edge. From here, the water was not a pale, flat expanse, but dark green with ripples and flecks of foam. It curled up the rocks, broke, retreated, curled again. Kneeling, Clo placed her fingers in a little pool at her feet and then touched her fingers to her tongue: *full of salt*. She dropped her bags and sat, feeling exhaustion settle over her limbs.

The sound of the water, its steady roaring, surprised her. It seemed to echo the sound inside her head now that she had done what her father's letter asked her to do. She had reached the sea, she had reached the harbor: What was she meant to do here?

Pulling her father's cloak-wrapped parcel onto her lap, she tried to undo the knots again. But the wool, damp from the night of walking and the salty air, seemed even tighter. *If only she had a knife*. She ran her hands along the rocks where she sat until she felt a sharp edge: a white shard, like a crescent moon. She pressed it into the fabric below one of the knots, pulling, sawing. The fabric split and came away.

Clo felt a pang of regret for having cut her father's cloak, but she reassured herself: it was only a small corner, part of the bottom edge. She could repair it for him later. She pushed aside the bundled fabric; it opened and opened. To something orange. Something rank. A wheel of cheese.

A wheel of cheese?

Clo pulled the gap wider and raised out of the cut folds

an enormous golden round. Its rind was dark and mottled, almost marbled, and its pungent smell cut through even the briny air.

Clo put the cheese down carefully on the rock beside her and stared at it, frowning. It was not unusual for her father to sneak provisions from the kitchens or the storerooms, and they had carried such wheels with them on their journeys before. *But why would he send her this?* How long would she be alone? How far was she meant to travel? How much cheese could she, Clo, spindle-shanked guttersnipe, eat?

The cheese smelled like despair.

Hoping this could not be all her father had sent, Clo reached again into the folds. She found a small square wound all about with rags, as though it were bandaged.

With growing dread, she unwound the scraps of cloth.

No. She pulled the wrappings over the object again.

Had anyone seen?

She looked around. Satisfied that the barrel-men were concerned only with their barrels, she lifted the rags once more just enough to see the object beneath.

It was a painting. *Of course it was a painting.* Fruit. A cluster of grapes, their dark skin marked with silver bloom and water drops.

It was not, as far as her father's usual thievery went, a terribly remarkable painting. Usually, he took pieces that were *obvious* in their value. *Look, Clo,* he'd say, his fingers

hovering reverently over a newly pilfered prize. *The brush-work. The use of color. Masterful.* The value would be obvious enough that the painting fetched a good trade or a hand-ful of coins when he was finally ready to sell it. Though these grapes were well painted, beautiful even, the painting seemed too small to earn much—it was scarcely larger than her hand.

But its frame...

Usually he only took the canvas.

And this frame...

Her stomach turned.

Clo had never seen what might be called a jewel; she had never known *ruby* or *emerald* or *pearl* beyond their names, but here, she was sure, decorating the flowers carved in the wood, were *rubies* and *emeralds* and *pearls*, deep red and green and silvery gems glinting even in the slanting morning light.

Don't worry, Clo, her father always said to her when he unrolled his stolen canvases. *They won't even notice it's gone.* He would reassure her: *It was hanging in a forgotten corner. It was tucked in the shadows. It was stowed alongside a nest of mice in a cupboard. Don't worry; it won't be missed at all.*

But this...surely *this* would be noticed. Surely this was the swineherd's *jewels missing out of th' lady's chamber.*

What was she meant to do with this? She looked back at the barrel-shaped men. *Was she meant to sell it? To them?* She felt ill. She rewrapped the rags around it.

One last object remained in the cloak. Reaching into the wool again, she felt a leather corner, a soft edge. "Oh...oh, no...," she whispered. She knew what this was even without seeing it, and she withdrew it with trembling hands. *Her father's notebook.*

This book was part of his very person: he never parted from it. And here it was, tucked beneath a wheel of reeking cheese.

No, my lambkin. She could almost hear her father's voice in the leather. *You mustn't touch this.*

No, my dove. No, no. This is not for you.

The simple leather book—the only thing her father had ever kept from her. She ran her hand over its cover, thinking again of the rage that had come when, once, as a small child, she had crept up behind her father with the book open on the table in front of him.

He had been drawing, or trying to draw. Clo, silent, hardly breathing, had watched him try to outline the profile of a woman. His gestures were awkward, hesitant; the drawing, too, was awkward, hesitant—more a lopsided collection of angles and corners than a woman. But Clo, a child, had been delighted.

She had reached over him to touch the lines of the sketch. *Is that my mother?*

Why she had asked this, she did not know. Even then, small as she was, she knew it was the wrong question.

He had snatched the book away.

Clo, confused, had asked again. *Is that—*

But white, red, trembling with a rage that seemed to overwhelm his small frame, her father had not answered.

This is all I ask of you, he had finally said. *All I ask, Clo. This is not for you. I forbid it.*

The depth of his fury—his widened eyes, his shaking voice—was enough that she never touched the book again.

Even now, feeling the book still forbidden, she held it gingerly in her fingertips.

This was all. A wheel of cheese. Her father's notebook. And a stolen painting that was surely the reason her father had been *crouchin' in th' pens.*

Clo felt the earth tilt a little under her.

Hesitantly, she turned over the notebook. It was tied, as her father kept it, with a band of leather. A slip of paper had been tucked under the band. *Clo,* it read, and then, in smaller letters beneath, *be brave.*

She worked the paper out from under the leather and unfolded it. Heart sinking, she saw at once it was not a letter from her father. She saw nothing familiar or expected at all.

What was this? How could she even begin to understand this? Her head swam. She felt as though something were unspooling deep within her.

The writing was strange, stretched, not her father's dense, neat script.

No. a113

Place: _Kotum_.

Date: _16/Jan_.

Received from: _Cam_ the sum of _in trade_

The poffeffor of this ticket fhall be

intitled to paffage from _Glorm Har-br_

to _Jumor_.

Whole number of perfons:

_1_ adultf

_1_ children

1/2 paffage only! was scrawled and underlined in the corner, next to a wavery signature, _CMDRE Haros_, and a thick gob of red wax with an imprint of an oar. Clo ran her thumb over the raised impression on the wax.

Haros? Haros? The words of her father's ink-splattered letter came back to her: *travel alone. Passage? Passage where? Or half paffage where? What, who was Haros? Where was her father sending her?*

Clo felt something tighten on her shoulder. "Girly," said a voice next to her ear.

Clo jumped. Startled, confused, she could only think that the sea must have grabbed her.

"Girly," said the voice again. "Yer wit' me."

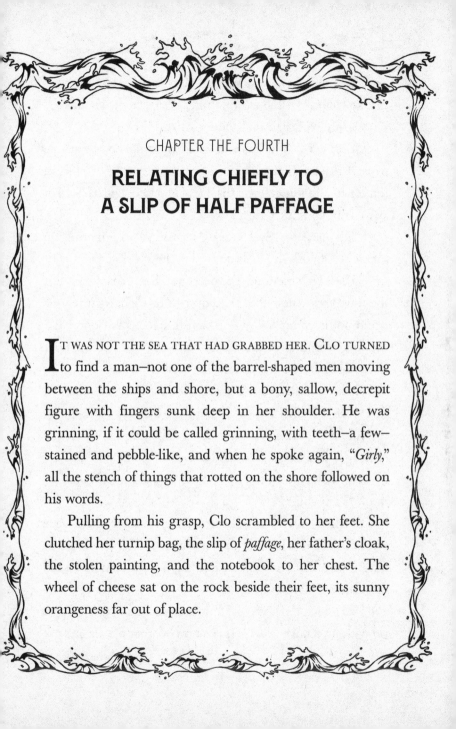

CHAPTER THE FOURTH

RELATING CHIEFLY TO
A SLIP OF HALF PAFFAGE

I T WAS NOT THE SEA THAT HAD GRABBED HER. CLO TURNED
to find a man—not one of the barrel-shaped men moving
between the ships and shore, but a bony, sallow, decrepit
figure with fingers sunk deep in her shoulder. He was
grinning, if it could be called grinning, with teeth—a few—
stained and pebble-like, and when he spoke again, "*Girly*,"
all the stench of things that rotted on the shore followed on
his words.

Pulling from his grasp, Clo scrambled to her feet. She
clutched her turnip bag, the slip of *paffage*, her father's cloak,
the stolen painting, and the notebook to her chest. The
wheel of cheese sat on the rock beside their feet, its sunny
orangeness far out of place.

"Ah, now, girly." A laugh rattled from the man. "No need to take fright. 'Tis the way of things. Yer t' come wit' me."

Clo shook her head, backing away. "No."

"It is, it is." The man laughed or coughed again. He paused to spit, half turning away. A gray line of phlegm remained dangling from his lip. He lifted and flicked it away with a knuckly finger.

Clo raised her eyes from the phlegm shimmering on the rock. "No," she repeated. "I'm here…I'm here with my father. He's coming. To meet me." She glanced toward the town. She knew she could outrun this fellow; surely he could not keep his footing on the slick rocks for long. Still, the lingering impression of his bony grip on her shoulder unnerved her. She stepped farther away.

"No, no, girly. You've got it wrong. See there"–he nodded at the bundle she was clutching–"you've got passage on my ship. I see the ticket there in yer little fingers. That's the seal–I see it. The oar, it is, no? It is. Yer t' come wit' me."

Clo looked from the *paffage* paper to the pebble-toothed man. "Your ship?"

Pinched and weather-beaten as it was, the man's face did not hold much room for anything besides its lines and crags, but still it seemed to Clo that, at her question, a kind of sadness shifted over it.

"To which I'm bosun." He spat again. "An' you'll not get on without a hurry. Departure's now–t'other passengers are

34

filing on already. An' if you miss th' boarding, well, you'll not enjoy th' wait for our next docking. Why, I've got a family now"–he jerked his thumb toward the ships–"that's been resting here for months waiting for Cap'n Haros. So, girly"–he nodded at the wheel of cheese–"gather yer things and follow."

Clo, who had begun to back away, started at the name. "Haros?"

"Ay, Cap'n Haros, girly. An' he's not much for waiting, bein' as it is what it is an' *he* is what he is. You'd best come along now."

A knobby finger was beckoning her forward. Clo did not want to follow this man, this stringy, sea-rot-smelling bosun-man, but he had said the name *Haros*, the word from the letter, and Clo, as adept as she was at staying in the shadows, at seeing her way through a forest at night, could not think how else she was to find *Haros* in this town filled with boats and barrel-shaped men.

With the man watching, with her hands trembling, Clo wrapped her belongings in her father's cloak: the wheel of cheese, the sack of turnips, the painting, the notebook. She kept the odd slip of *paſſage* in her hand.

The man's little line of pebbles grinned again. "That's good." He nodded approvingly. "An' come along."

Scrawny and bent as he was, the man moved with surprising grace over the rocks. Hugging her cheese-shaped

35

bundle, Clo followed uneasily as they made their way through the boats. The vessels loomed over them. The barrel-men, shouting, stomping, lugging their goods, took no notice of the two figures. Even when the bosun, pausing, sank his hand deep into one of the casks and pulled out a briny pig's hoof, which he popped into his mouth with a wink at Clo, no one so much as blinked at them. Clo felt the men might have walked straight into her if the old man had not taken her by the shoulder and guided her through the crowds.

"Here, here, girly," he said, by turns pushing and pulling her. "Here, here." He led her past fluyts and schooners and sloops and clippers—though to Clo they were only *boats* and *boats* and *boats*, some larger, some smaller—to the far end, where a small dinghy bobbed and pulled against its rope. *Rowboat*, thought Clo, taking comfort in at last knowing the name of something.

"I've got one for you." The man pushed Clo ahead. "She's got passage an' everything. All formal-like."

Stumbling forward, Clo found herself staring up at a wild, tangled gray mass—something like the nets the barrel-men pulled and carried, something that might have been dragged along the shore. It was matted and damp and flecked here and there with bits of sea-things. It was attached to a chin. A man. The shape of his face hidden beneath the

36

hairiness, he looked down at Clo with eyes that seemed far too bright. Clo lowered her gaze.

"Passage?" The beard waggled in disbelief. "Let's see, then."

Clo felt the slip of paper pulled from her hand.

The bearded man grunted. "Half. *Half.*" Reaching over Clo, he slapped a thick palm against the bosun's forehead. "*Half passage.* You should have left her, you boil-brained limpet. *Half.* You brought me a *half passage. Half.*" Each utterance of the word *half* sounded like bellows at a fire. He glowered at Clo. "How's that, then? How came you by half passage?"

"I…"

"Yes?"

"I don't…I'm not…" Clo could not seem to form sensible words in the presence of this greasy-bearded figure. "It's…my father, he…"

"Never mind. However you came by it, you have it, and we shall have to accommodate it. Take her." He waved at the dinghy. "Row her out. Put her…put her in the locker. We cannot have the others with a half passage. But bring them, too." He gestured over his shoulder at a small family huddled by a stack of ropes and barrels. "Our departure is already too much delayed."

The pebble-toothed man took Clo by her shoulder again. "Come on then, girly." He pushed her toward the

dinghy. "An' come on, you lot," he called to the huddling family. "It's yer time, too."

"Are you Haros?" Finally finding her tongue, Clo turned back to the bearded figure. "Do you know my father?"

"Girly." Pebble-mouth pushed her again. "He knows everyone."

"But"–twisting in desperation, she wrenched herself free of the bosun's fingers–"are you Haros? Do you know my father?"

Haros, if he was Haros, gave a slow nod.

"Yes, you are Haros? Or yes, you know my father?"

"Girly–" Clo felt herself gripped again, but the Haros-figure held up his hand and stepped forward. He loomed over Clo, his gaze lingering over her shorn hair, her leggings, her boots. Again, his eyes seemed too bright.

"I know the knave," he said finally.

Clo felt her cheeks grow hot. "*Not*–" she began, but the man nodded firmly.

"Knave," he repeated. "I know his tricks. His thievery."

The bundle under Clo's arm felt suddenly heavy. She flushed again. "Well," she said. "Well. It may be…" She hesitated, unsure. "It may be he has something for you." She made her words firmer. She raised her eyes. She had seen her father sell stolen paintings before. "Something he wants to trade with you. Or sell to you. It's valuable."

She removed the rag-wrapped painting from her bundle and peeled back a corner. The frame glimmered in the light.

The beard cracked widely at the mouth. Plucking the object out of Clo's fingers, the Haros-figure lifted the rags and guffawed loudly. "I see it! The thievery! *Hah-hah! Haw-haw!*" He twisted a pearl deftly from the frame and held it to the light. "*Hah-haaa!*" he laughed again, flipping the pearl into the ocean. He returned the rags and frame to Clo. "Worthless."

Clo's cheeks burned. "But—"

"Worthless!"

"But perhaps he means to buy passage on your boat with it!"

The Haros-figure gestured at the bosun and turned his back to Clo. "The knave has been on my manifest these many years."

Clo felt herself propelled along the dock. She turned, struggling.

"Your manifest? Is he a passenger on the boat? Is he to come on the boat?"

"Of course yer father'll come, too, girly," the bosun said, pushing her onto the rocking dinghy. "You've no need to worry on that."

Clo allowed herself to be guided onto one of the rowboat's low benches. Her mind worked feverishly as the bosun began to row them out into the open water. *Manifest.*

She repeated the official-sounding word. He was on the manifest. He would meet her. She was meant to meet him on the boat. *Certainly. Always.*

Across from her, gray-faced and mute, sat the little family the bosun had been instructed to take aboard. A boy, a girl, a mother, a father. They stared at Clo, expressionless.

The sounds of the shore died away as they pulled farther into the water; after a time, it was just the echoes of shouts and the sound of the oars in the waves, a gentle splashing. The little boy coughed, a sad, empty-sounding *hee.*

"No more o' that," said the bosun with a phlegmy grunt of his own. "Jus' habit now."

A pale something dangled from the little boy's fingertips. Clo watched the wind tug it away so that it fell on the damp floor of the boat. She picked it up. *A lacy handkerchief.* She held it out to the boy. "Here," she said.

Somber-eyed, the boy looked at the handkerchief but did not take it.

Clo tried again. "You dropped this," she said quietly. The delicate lace fluttered in her fingers.

The boy did not take the handkerchief from her. No one from the family took the handkerchief from her. They stared blankly ahead while Clo, cheeks burning, held out the offending square.

"Ah, well. If they don't need it now, I do," said the bosun, grabbing the lacy cloth and running it under his nose.

Discomfited, Clo turned away from the family's vacant gaze and hugged her bundle closer to her chest. Only one or two large ships floated here; the water stretched wide and open around them.

Water that is full of salt and has no edge, she thought.

She felt herself full of salt.

She rubbed a knuckle across her eyes.

The manifest. Many years. It was an official document. She was meant to be here. Her father must have arranged it so. She slipped her knuckle across her eye again, then raised her chin. *Manifest.*

"That's us." The bosun tipped his head in the direction of the largest boat. "The three-master there. She's a beauty, no? An' a good voyage she'll give you, too."

Clo followed his gaze, her skin prickling with cold.

No, *beauty* was not the word she would have used to describe the ship. A dark shadow rising out of the water, its sides greasy and scabbed with barnacles and seaweed, it listed as though it were already half sunk. Even without knowing anything about the harbor or the sea or the vessels used to navigate it, Clo could imagine no *good voyage* coming from that gloomy craft. *No*, she thought, *not this boat. This can't be right.*

The gray-faced family turned their heads just enough to look. Nothing—no flicker of emotion or knowledge crossed their faces.

Hee. The little boy coughed an empty cough again. *Hee.*

Clo, turnip-lugger, wall-jumper, found herself now a boat-climber; the bosun maneuvered the little dinghy under a rope ladder that draped over the side of the ship and instructed his passengers to climb it. The family ascended ahead of her, and as Clo waited her turn in the bobbing dinghy, she wondered at the ease with which the mother and children in their skirts—for the little boy, too, was in a lacy, delicate gown—ascended. Even the father, who carried a small trunk, moved seemingly unimpeded. But when Clo grasped the rungs, the ladder swayed and tilted under her weight. Panicked and trembling, she was sent swinging against the side of the ship. The bosun yelled from below, a man leaning over the edge of the ship yelled from above, but Clo could not control the thing, and the two men were obliged to balance it for her, pulling it tight against her motions. She reached the top breathless and shaking. A trio of straggle-bearded crew members grabbed and pulled her into a somber line of passengers where the staring family also waited.

"Girly," Clo heard from below. "Move not a whit. Boys, she's not with the rest. She's..." The bosun clambered onto the deck. "Ah, never mind what she is. You can take that lot to the cabins. A whole family there, that is. I've got this 'un." He took Clo again by her shoulder. Scarcely knowing what she was doing, Clo allowed herself to be shoved along the deck and into the innards of the ship. "Here, here, here.

Through here, girly, now here, take these stairs, mind yer head, an' down here, 'nother stair, bit farther, down this passage, that's good, mind the beam, duck a bit, an' down here, through this bit now, an' here we are."

They were standing in a dim, cramped corridor. Clo could make out little of what was around them—just the narrow walls and a small, thick door that the bosun was now, with a jangle of keys, unlocking.

"Here you are. Yer half passage." He pushed open the door, revealing an even more shadowy and cramped space. "It's the locker. You'll have t' share it with some ropes and tools and such, but it's yer own fer now. And yer voyage is not too long." His mouth, drooping along its line of pebbles, looked almost apologetic.

Clo cast her eyes desperately around the chamber. Things were mounded everywhere inside it, and ropes snaked and coiled everywhere over the things.

"You'll be needin' a light, I gather. And maybe somethin' t'eat? A half passage has got t'eat, I suppose. An' to drink. I'll see to it to remind the captain. Here"—he gave Clo an almost-gentle shove so she was now fully inside the room—"I'll be bringin' you somethin' soon as I can. But we're settin' sail in a moment, and I've got to shut this behind me. Can't have you wanderin' the ship. Upsettin' fer t'others. All right, then, girly." His mouth sank deeper into regret as he pulled the door after him. "Closin' up now."

"But my father?" Clo pleaded, calling through the narrowing gap.

The closing door halted on its arc. From the other side, she heard, after a pause, "I've got no knowledge of that, girly, but Haros said he's to come."

The door finished closing, and Clo was plunged into blackness.

With the departing footsteps, she heard him mutter again, lower, "An' they always do."

Breaths too shallow, Clo swayed in the darkness. All around her, she could hear water lapping against the boat, and the floor rolled in time to its sound. Reaching out, she grasped at what she could not see and tumbled into what she thought must be coils of a rope.

The floor rose and fell, rose and fell. Her heart thudded heavily, a rapid, off-kilter knocking of fear. Her fear was not of the dark nor of the dank, salty smell of the things around her, but of the unknown...all that was unknown: her father, his whereabouts, his state, the boat, its captain, her destination...all the mystery that had been unfolding since the bells had rung at five the morning before and her father had not come home. *"Why didn't you come?"* she whispered to the fatherless dark. *"Why aren't you here?"* A sob filling her throat, she hugged her knees to her chest, but she could not stop the tears from coming. *"Where are you?"* She rocked herself as she wept.

In the blackness of the little room, with the floor rising and falling and the waves chucking against the walls in a warm liquid rhythm, her heart and then her breathing steadied and slowed, and her fear and anxiety began to ebb in the monotony of the motion.

Her eyes fluttered closed. Or else the darkness closed around them; she could not tell.

The floor rocked, *gentle, gentle, gentle.*

The water sloshed, *sleep, sleep, sleep.*

The darkness and the rhythm of the boat lulled her into a kind of dreaming that was also a remembering: she felt as she did when, as a small child, her father carried her on his back when their travels grew too long for her toddling legs. Cheek resting on his shoulder blade, calmed by the rocking of his stride, she would drift in and out of sleep. She remembered being carried by him through the forest shadows; she felt even now she was being carried by him through the shadows.

"Lambkin." A dream. A whisper. "Are you asleep?"

Clo felt his shoulder blade against her cheek, felt her own warm breath against the wool of his cloak. "No, Father."

"I need to put you down, lambkin. Can you walk for a time?"

"Yes, Father."

Above them, the shadows of trees.

Her father limped. They walked slowly.

"Where are we going this time, Father?"

"Another village. Somewhere else. Perhaps better. Would you like me to tell you a story as we walk along?"

Her feet padded softly on the forest floor. "Oh, yes."

"Once, Clo, once upon a time there lived a spider who spun webs so delicate and beautiful, they seemed made of starlight."

"I remember this story, Father." Her hand was small inside his. "This is the story about the spider who wished to be a moth, and when she spun herself a pair of wings to wear, she became trapped in her own web."

"Yes, that's the one."

"Please don't tell it."

"Why, lambkin?"

"It's sad. It makes you sad."

His hand tightened around hers. "Yes." His voice was soft. "I suppose it does." He cleared his throat. "Would you like me to tell you a different story, then, Clo?"

In the half-light of the forest, her father looked strange. Some kind of veil or rag seemed to have fallen over his face; the lines around his cheeks and brow had grown darker, deeper: his eyes more shadowed. Hidden.

"Father?" She wanted to reach up and pull away the tattery thing. *Where had her father gone?* "Father." She tugged on his arm. She wanted him to stop.

He knelt beside her. "What is it, lambkin?"

She placed her damp palm against his cheek. Her little fingers brushed his brow. His wispy hair. "Why are you so old?"

"Oh. Oh, lambkin." He wrapped her in his arms. He took her face in his hands. "I'm not old at all, lambkin." He made himself a little straighter before her. "Why, I'm not yet even thirty."

He smiled. The tattery curtain lifted.

He ran his hand over the wrinkles that sloped across his cheek. "Though my face is not so *lovely* as it once was…" He grinned. He teased. "Though fate has made my skin more *uglified*…" He winked. "My hair more *grizzled*…my gait more…*peculiar*…" He tapped her nose. "I promise I am still a young man."

"Really, Father?"

"Truly. Not yet thirty. It is just my poor fortune to look…*three times that*." The rag drifted for an instant across his eyes again. She reached to push it away.

"Ah." He laughed. "Would you like me to carry you again?"

She hesitated.

"Lambkin. I promise I am strong enough to carry my own daughter."

"No, Father." She raised her chin. "I want to walk."

"Well, then. Should I tell you another tale—perhaps the one about the boys and the frogs now?"

"Yes, Father." She took his hand.

"Once, Clo, once there were some boys playing by a pond where there lived a small family of frogs...."

They walked through the shadows of trees. Her father's voice rose and fell, rose and fell. Her own steps rose and fell, rose and fell. The story drifted through the air as they walked and walked and walked through the forest and into the darkness settling around them.

In the darkness, rising and falling, in the dark of the ship, rising and falling, the floor of the ship, rising and falling, rising and falling, Clo finally slipped into a profound, dreamless sleep.

Only a *fffa*- fluttered on her lips.

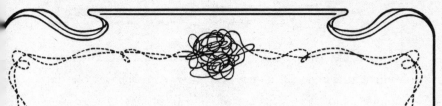

IN WHICH THE PEBBLE-MOUTHED MAN APOLOGIZES

WHEN CLO AWOKE, SHE WAS JUMPING REPEATEDLY OVER the village wall, *no*, falling repeatedly over the wall, *no*, being thrown repeatedly over the wall, *no, no, no*; she was in the dark and in her bed and being shaken by her father, *no*, by angry villagers, *no*, by hounds that had been set on her, *no—the smell, the smell—the sea, the sea, the salt*, she was underwater, *no*, in a net, *no*, in the belly of a fish, *no, in a ship, a ship…*

When Clo awoke in darkness, in terror, the gentle rocking of the boat had given way to violent roiling, up and down and up and down, movement that sent her thumping against the things in the dark, and the lappings of the waves had turned into crashings at which the boat creaked and groaned.

Reality came back to her in a sickening wave. Grief and dread rose in her all at once—she knew where she was. She did not want to know where she was. *Her father. Haros. A ship. A ship.*

She stood shakily, feeling that she needed to get out of this terrible, wallowing darkness, but on her feet, still in blackness, the buffeting grew worse; she could not keep her balance. And standing, she was suddenly ill—her stomach churned with the violence of the waves.

"Oh…"

She retched. But as she had neither eaten nor drunk in many hours, the retching was empty and terrible.

"Oh…"

She collapsed back into the ropes. If only the crazed rocking would stop. The ship rose…and crashed…and rose…and crashed. Clo curled herself into the darkness.

"Stop. Please."

She could not hold any thought in her head except her desire for that movement to end. How long it went on, how long she lay trying to quiet the nausea rocking within her and willing the rocking outside to end, she could not say, but after a time, she became aware of a voice.

"Girly? Girly?"

Clo opened her eyes. The bosun stood at the door.

"Girly?" He raised a lantern. "You've got a bad look about you."

Clo opened her mouth to speak, but all that came was the sound *Uh*.

"Come on, then, girly." The bosun took her by the wrist and pulled her into a standing position. "The water here's a bit rougher than we usually take, and with you deep in the bow, yer feelin' the worst of it. This locker's not called *the hell* for nothing, though none of us usually much notices. Can you hold this?" Pushing her cloak-wrapped bundle at her, he maneuvered her into the passage. "Haros says yer t' come on th' deck. Others're all down below, an' they don't get the same sick. 'S been a while since we've had a half passage. The air'll help, it will."

Rocked and wobbling, barely able to stay upright, Clo was obliged to lean on the bosun for balance. His sea-rot breath fanned over her, and she turned away, afraid she would retch again. She desperately wanted to be anywhere, anywhere but this dark, crashing room. She had to get out.

"Come, then, girly, yer in a bad way. Jus' a bit farther now. Up those stairs, an'—"

A whiff of air entered from above.

"Oh…" Releasing the bosun's arm, Clo clambered up the stairs. *Air, she must have air.* Reaching the top, she took a long, deep breath. *Air.* Another breath. *Air, salt, and wind.* A shade of nausea evaporated.

"All right, then, girly. There you go." Coming up behind

her, the bosun prodded her to step onto the deck. "There you go."

Still rocking, the world came into focus. Everything, Clo saw, was swathed in gray: gray tatters of mist that shifted and slid over the sky and sea, with only the roiling waves breaking across their form now and again. Clo felt the enormity of the rocking world around her, the immensity of the distance they had traveled.

"Where are we?" Her voice cracked in distress. "Is my father here? Has he come?"

Turned away, the bosun did not seem to hear.

Clo pulled on his sleeve. "Where is my father?" she cried over the wind. "Where are we?"

"Take this." Without answering, the bosun pushed something firm and woodlike into her hand. "Ship biscuit. Scrounged it up for you. A bite or two'll help settle yer stomach. And help smooth out yer teeth, too."

Her stomach churning with dread—*Where was her father?*—Clo did not want to eat. But with the brown cracker now in her hand, she nibbled—then gnawed—at its edge.

"An' some water. Look there." He pointed. "Ladle in the bucket. Keep it on the deck t' catch the rain when it falls."

She had not realized she was thirsty, but seeing the bucket, she rushed desperately to it. Grabbing the ladle, she drank greedily: gulp after gulp of water. Salt- and oak-tasting

water. She could not drink enough. *When had she ever been so thirsty?* It felt as though she had not drunk in days. Weeks.

"Apologies for forgettin' you, girly. Didn't mean to leave you there so long."

"What do you mean?" Clo ran the back of her hand over her lips. "I only slept for a bit, I think." She drank again, watching the bosun over the ladle.

"Ah…" The bosun looked uncomfortable. "So you slept, then? Felt like you slept? That's good." He looked out over the water. "Nearly there now. The waves'll tell you that—always fiercest drawin' close."

"Nearly there?" Clo looked apprehensively into the grayness surrounding the ship. She could see no sign of land. "Nearly where?"

"Yer half passage. 'S why the captain called for you to come up. He'll need us to row out soon as he gives his signal."

"Is my father here?" Clo struggled to hide the unsteadiness in her voice. "Or there?"

"I've got no other half passage now, girly." Working on the knots of a rope that lashed a dinghy to the rail, the bosun frowned. "That's not to say he won't come. He'll come sometime. I can promise that. But yer half passage is on yer own now."

Clo, considering the bosun's words with ever-growing

alarm, gnawed again on the biscuit. It did not taste like *promise*. Or *always*. It tasted hard and dry and bitter.

"I'll take you there, o' course. Haros was of a mind to leave you to the swabbies, let one of them row you, as we'd had no plans for a half passage, an' when they all refused, he thought he'd leave you to yerself, but yer a slip of a thing, and leavin' you to row through that"—he nodded at the waves—"well...half passage or no, it's a fearful thing."

"I'm not a slip of a thing." Clo felt her face grow hot. She thought of the wall-climbing and wall-jumping and field-running and forest-trekking and *dark* and *alone* and *brave*, and knew she was not *a slip of a thing*. Still, looking into the waves that tossed and pushed and sent the three-masted ship rocking and heaving, she knew she did not want to be left alone in them.

The pebble mouth lifted a bit, then collapsed. "Ah, but you are. Full passage, well, not much we can do for that, but half, well, I can at least make this last part a mite easier on you, girly. For I'd a daughter once, no slip was she, but I'd not let her row alone here if I'd a say in it." His mouth slumped more as he nodded toward the front of the ship. "An' that there, girly, that's Haros's signal fer you now, I'm afraid."

Clo glanced toward the bow, where a lantern was now swinging in the dark.

Beside her, the bosun muttered under his breath, "Yes,

yes, I see you, old man." Untying a final knot, he gestured to the dinghy he now held aloft with rope and pulley. "Right then, girly, in you go."

Clo, feeling her own gray sea of doubt and fear roiling within her, hesitated. "But *where* are we going? I don't know *where* we're going."

"Wellaway, girly, it's the only place a half passage goes. The island, it's a mite, a tip, maybe, better'n full. Neither here nor there. Take it an' be glad. But if you don't go now, we'll lose our chance. See Haros still swinging that light? He's taken us all he can, and he's not the patient sort, so if you want yer half passage, an' you think yer father's got a half passage comin' too, go, girly. Go now. Haros can keep the boat here just so long."

Clo opened her mouth to protest again, but the bosun shook his head. "If we delay, I cannot take you. Yer ticket will not matter. You'll be full passage, and there's no return for that."

Clo glanced from Haros's light to the the bosun offering his hand to help her into the dinghy. Her mind raced. *Her father had given her the ticket. He'd know where to find her.* She did not want to go, not a single bone in her body wanted to go, but she would have to.

Clo, wall-jumper, biscuit-nibbler, father-seeker, now forced herself to clamber over the side of the boat and into the dinghy. It was not the one she had arrived in; it was

smaller, with only a single bench for the rower. It swung wildly. Her heart swung with its motion.

"On th' floor now, better t' be on th' floor, there you go, an' here's yer things, hold tight to them, all right, then." Still holding to the ropes, he heaved himself into the dinghy and settled himself on the bench. "That's it. Now"—he raised his hand in the direction of the flashing lantern and began lowering the boat into the waves below—"Don't mind the wet or the waves. A bit of time is all it is an'—ach!" He stopped the dinghy's descent. "I'd nearly fergot. An' smashed to bits we'd be! Here!" With one hand pulling hard against the ropes, he reached beneath his jerkin and removed a slip of paper. Clo recognized it as the *half paffage*. He shoved it at her. "Take it. Take it! Make sure you hold it—don't let the wind or waves—"

"What?" cried Clo. There, so close now to the churning water, she could hear only the crashing voice of the sea.

"Don't let the wind or waves rip it from yer hand!" the bosun shouted as the little dinghy plunged into the waves. "Hold tight now, hold tight, girly!"

The little boat, a speck on the surface of the sea, a speck on the waves that rose and crashed beneath and above and around it, was lifted and thrown and tossed and whirled into what Clo thought must surely be oblivion.

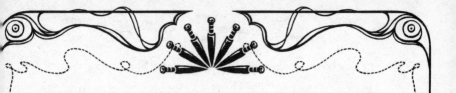

IN WHICH THE PEBBLE-MOUTHED MAN IS SORRIER STILL

C LINGING TO HER WOOL-WRAPPED WHEEL OF CHEESE AND the slip of *half paffage*, Clo pressed herself against the bottom of the boat. Waves, cold, a cold so deep it seemed unearthly, broke over the dinghy again and again. Clo felt herself drenched through, and in the stuporous cold and in the violent tossing of the boat, she thought she surely must be already at the bottom of the sea. *She must be drowning. How could this not be drowning?* But in flashes, she saw they were still in air, upon the waves. The bosun, pulling hard on the oars, rowed them up the gray mountains of water and guided them down their frothing cliffs. Between waves, she thought she glimpsed his line of pebbles open in a wide, delirious grin, thought she heard him howling out a song, but the water crashed again and again, and she could hear nothing but its roaring.

She was not drowning. Was she breathing? She braced herself against the boards. She clung to her cheese. She shivered and tasted salt. Her eyes were blurred by water and wind. Over and over the boat climbed or was cast up the walls of water and was plunged into its seething ravines.

And then suddenly, plummeting down one last wave, pitching over a few last breakers, they were through. They had found the edge of the fog, the edge of the storming sea. The calm was immediate. Behind them, the water continued breaking and churning, but ahead of them, the sea stretched into a flat, rippling gray expanse.

"Ah, there we are. All right, girly? I told you that's a fearsome thing. Not fit for any man. Now, I've not had to row that in a good many ages—not so many half passages—but that, *that's* the test of any boatman. And a test of yer nerves, too, eh?" The bosun gave Clo a crooked smile. "The rest is easy going."

Clo, still shaken, nodded. She sat up carefully, looking with horror at the waves they had just come through. She felt the word *sea* in her mouth and understood the depth and violence of *water that is full of salt and has no edge*.

The bosun, far from looking weary, appeared younger, reinvigorated. Even his teeth, grinning, looked more like teeth than pebbles. "An' there, well, there's yer port."

Clo whirled around. Dead ahead was an island. *No*, not so much an island as a cliff rising straight out of the water—stone, steep, straight cliffs of stone. No trees, no green grew

anywhere on its ledges; its gray shape was simply darker than the sea and sky surrounding it.

"Ach, an' there's the same tidesman. Never leaves, that one. See 'im standing there?" He gestured with his chin.

Following his nod, Clo saw a small figure standing at the edge of a line of stones that extended out into the sea. He was dwarfed by the towering cliffs behind him.

How could this be her destination? Stomach sinking, Clo scanned the waters. Behind her, the walls of waves. Ahead, the island of cliff and stone. And beyond, nothing. *Nothing.* The gray water. The gray sky.

"Do you sing, girly?"

Clo shook her head, incredulous the bosun could even think of music in this bleak place.

"A bit o' music is good for th' travelin'. Good for passin' th' time."

The bosun rowed ahead, singing in rhythm with the strokes of the oars:

> *Merrily, merrily rowed he on*
> *across the frothing sea;*
> *the waves did toss his little boat*
> *as on and on rowed he.*
> *He rowed until his back grew stiff*
> *and his arms could row no more,*
> *but there at last before the bow*

he saw a distant shore.
The shore he reached was still and dark,
as dark as dark might be;
no light or wind or sound or shade
could he hear or see.
"So I'll sleep," the man did say,
"sleep here on this bleak shore,"
and down he laid his heavy head
and slept forevermore.

Clo, shivering, half listening, watched the cliffs draw ever nearer. Approach changed nothing: nothing grew on those jagged walls. *Walls,* thought Clo. Walls that could not be climbed or jumped. The little figure at the base, the tidesman, did not move. The boat, without waves to jostle it, slipped easily over the water. So smoothly did they glide across the expanse that Clo did not notice when they finally floated to a stop.

The bosun stopped his song and stared silently at the little wisp of a thing in front of him.

"Here you are, girly. 'S the end, I'm afraid."

"What?" Clo turned her eyes from the cliffs to the bosun. "What do you mean? The shore is far over there. We're still in the sea."

It was true. The bosun had stopped his boat a good distance from land.

"Wellaway, it's as far as I can go." The bosun rubbed

the bridge of his nose. "Not permitted to take you farther. And look, 's not deep here."

Clo peered into the water. Under its gray sheen, she thought she could make out a shimmering pebbly bottom.

"But I can't swim," she said, then blushed furiously. Clo, who was comfortable living in the shadows and who was not afraid of the dark, had never, not once in all her years of traipsing mountain and forest and moor and bog, ever immersed herself in water—except to sit in a shallow pool or large bucket to bathe. And this she did only infrequently.

"Nor I! But here it's a walk; it's not above yer head, girly, I promise. Walk right up to the island. Hold yer little parcel there on yer head. Water's calm; you'll have nothing to trip yer feet, and you'll not go under."

Clo looked at the bosun with an expression she would not have recognized in herself, but he saw that her eyes were desperate and pleading.

"Girly," he said softly, standing in the boat. "I hate to do it. But I can't take you back. It's yer half passage. And"– he pulled her, wobbling, to her feet–"I've got to row myself back to Haros. Here." He took the cheese parcel from her arms. "I'll hold this. Now climb out over the edge—that's it. I've got the balance there...."

Clo, without being fully aware what she was doing, allowed herself to be lowered over the edge of the dinghy and into the water.

A sharp intake of breath. *The cold, the cold!* The cold was filled with panic and terror. The water came up to her chin, and she rose on her toes, desperate to keep her head above the water.

"No!" she cried. "No—it's too deep! Too deep!"

"Ah, girly. Yer all right, yer all right. Here, hold yer parcel on yer head to keep it dry. That's right, that's right. There you are, now just walk ashore, a few minutes in the water is all." The bosun sat down into the boat and picked up the oars.

"Don't leave me!" The words burst from Clo; she had not thought to say them, but now that she had, she felt her entire being behind them. "Don't leave me!"

She stared desperately at the man in the boat. His lank hair, his pebble mouth, his arms and chest, everything seemed to sag at once.

"I'm sorry, girly." A pull on the oars. "I am." Another. The boat was moving away. His face was as gray as the sea.

"My father!" Clo called after the dinghy. "My father!"

Five, six, seven strokes, the boat moved into the distance.

"My father!"

. . .

"Please!"

. . .

The sound of the oars died away.

OF A PIPING AND A MURMURING

I N THE WATER, ON HER TOES, LITTLE WAVES SLIPPING AROUND her chin, Clo shivered. She could no longer see the bosun; he had disappeared into the line of roiling waves.

"Please," she whispered again to the empty expanse. "Please."

This could not be what she was meant to do.

She looked toward the island. The small figure, the tidesman, was still standing, immobile, at the end of the line of rocks. He seemed a rock himself.

Willing herself to walk forward, she felt the cold heaviness of the water pushing against her every step. Her feet, seemingly far, far beneath her, seemingly not her own, slipped again and again on the stones below.

She rose slowly out of the sea: her shoulders, her chest,

her waist emerged. She took the cheese bundle from her head and clasped it in her arms. The tidesman—now she could begin to see his features, his leaden face, his craggy nose—stared blankly as she approached. Behind him, Clo saw with some relief, stretched a thin beach, a pebbly bottom to the cliffs that rose ominously above it.

"*Tekcit!*" the tidesman cried as she neared his rock. "*Tekcit!*"

Clo halted knee-deep in the sea. Frigid as the water was, the air felt even colder on her skin. Her teeth chattered uncontrollably. "Take it?" She looked at the craggy man.

"Tekcit!" he barked again, his voice flinty and sharp.

Though Clo saw his mouth move, his face seemed rigid. "I…What…" She shook her head, attempting to clear the confusion of cold. *She had to get out of the water.* Shivering, numb, she stumbled toward the shore. Collapsing on the dark rocks, she curled into herself for warmth.

The tidesman strode up to her, gesturing vigorously at her cheese bundle. "*Tekcit!*" Reaching down, he snatched the slip of *half paffage* from Clo's fingers. Until Clo felt it being removed from her hand, she had forgotten she was still clutching it.

"Oh…but…"

Unfolding the damp document carefully, he bent his hooked nose above the crease and nodded sharply. He

handed the paper back to her and turned away, waving over his shoulder at the cliffs. "O, go. No. *No.*"

"What? Go where?" Clo cried in dismay and confusion, but the stony figure was already stalking back to his post on the rocks. Clo looked from the man's weather-beaten profile to the slip of *paffage*. "Oh…" The ink on the paper, she saw, had run and smeared. Though the phrase *half paffage* was still clear, everything else was illegible smudge. *Except at the fold.* Here the ink had pooled and shaped what looked like new letters. *Soporta. Soporta?* An inky swirl. It meant nothing.

Shivering, Clo worked frantically at the knots she had tied in the cloak. It fell from the cheese and the rag-wrapped painting, and she pulled the fabric, its scratchy warmth, tight around her. She sat, teeth still chattering, looking from water to cliff and cliff to water. She could see nowhere she might go, nor could she see the bosun's boat anywhere in the sea.

The cloak under which she now huddled smelled faintly like home, faintly like her father. She sniffed deeply. There were the scents of woodsmoke and honey, of stew and bread, of warmth and comfort. And there was the scent of pine. And salt. And dark. And alone. And the awful odor of the cheese. She felt a sob rise in her throat.

"No," she whispered fiercely. She stared hard at the wheel of cheese, her sack of turnips, and her father's notebook

crushed beneath them. *"Always."* She gathered the things into her arms. *"Always."*

Standing, she took a last look at the tidesman—he kept his face turned to the sea—and made her way across the beach. The wall of rock rose straight and menacing, a sheer gray face of stone. But drawing closer, she saw, hidden in the crags of the cliffs, stairs that rose sharply, crookedly, up and up and up.

Hugging the cheese, the notebook, the turnips, Clo began to climb. And climb. And climb. The stairs wound into cracks and fissures in the cliffs; the dark stone loomed above her.

She counted a hundred, then another, and another. The scent of cheese, uncloaked, was everywhere, and at every breath, she tasted its thick scent. Another hundred. She stopped to rest. Far beneath her, she could see the tidesman on his rock, the flat expanse of the gray sea, the distant line of crashing waves. She lifted her head, trying to find where the staircase ended.

On and up she went, smelling the rank cheese, feeling now fully warm, almost hot, under the wool of her father's cloak, its hem dragging behind her. From time to time, she thought she heard above her the clattering of stones, the noise another's step might make. Now and then, she even thought she heard a faint melody, a gentle piping. But each time she stopped to listen, there were only silence and the

sound of her own labored breaths. *Where was she going?* She could see nothing but the cliffs, rising ever higher, and the stairs winding through them.

Finally, though, perhaps halfway to the top, she began to hear what she was sure were voices—a murmuring through the stones. She strained to make out what they were saying, but it was just a mumbling, almost as though the stones themselves were talking.

Mrmrmrm. The voices grew louder the higher she climbed. *Mrmrmrm. Mrmrmrm.*

Clo climbed on, her chest tight with apprehension and the effort of the ascent.

Mrmrmrm. Mrmrmrm. Mrmrmrm. The voices now were loud enough to bounce off the cliff walls. *Mrmrmrm. Mrmrmrm. Mrmrmrm,* they echoed.

And then the stairs ended. Clo, eyes on her feet, saw suddenly space instead of stone—an opening nearly as wide and tall as a door. She halted. The cliffs stretched up and up and up; she was still far from the top. But the steps ended at this crevice. Kneeling, half holding her breath, Clo peered into the gap. It was not deep. She could see the bottom a few feet below. And the floor—it was not stone. Not *just* stone. Cobblestone.

Clo hesitated, then dropped carefully into the fissure. She passed through an arch of stone. The space around her grew larger and brighter. She glanced up. The cliff walls

67

rose straight above her, but now she was on the other side of them, *inside* them, in some hollowed-out area—almost as though the top half of the core of the island had been scooped out and lifted away. The murmurings grew louder.

Here was a town. A narrow street. Little stone huts.

Clo gripped her wheel of cheese, the sack of turnips, the notebook, the painting.

Mrmrmrm. Here were people, gray-faced and jabbering. Old, old men and women, aged and bent and prattling over baskets and carts. For a moment, on first glimpsing them, Clo saw in their crooked forms her father's own hunched shape—but *no.* These people were not like him. Their agedness was such that they seemed more like damp wadded rags or crumpled scraps of paper that had been fashioned into people, and yet, unlike her father, they moved with vigor and ease.

Seeing her, their chattering grew hushed. They stared and stepped aside as she walked down their narrow street. *Mrmrmrm.*

The cliff walls rose straight over the diminutive town and framed a gray circle of sky. The light that reached the street was pale and dim.

Mrmrmrm. The people pointed and nodded and whispered to one another in tones too low for Clo to hear.

Walking steadily, Clo cast her eyes desperately over the crowd of ancient people, the baskets, the carts, the huts, the

doors. *What should she do? Where could she go?* She followed the narrow street up its gentle slope, trying and failing to make herself small. Clo, who had lived her whole life in the shadows, found here no shadows in which to hide. There was only the single street hemmed in on all sides by the little shacks, themselves crammed in a motley jumble of doors and walls and windows against one another.

Her heart pulsed through her feet. Her legs. Her arms. Her head. Her eyes.

What was she doing here?

The people followed, pointing, whispering. In the windows of the huts, she saw faces flash and disappear. She clutched the cheese more tightly.

Mrmrmrm! Mrmrmrm! The whispering grew more urgent. *Mrmrmrm!*

Clo felt a hand touch her elbow. She whirled around.

The eyes that met hers were watery and gentle, but Clo drew back all the same. Touching her elbow again, the figure pointed to a hut at the end of the street and opened wide her palm at the path leading to its door.

"Here?" Clo asked, the word dry in her mouth.

All the crowd nodded. More hands pointed. *Mrmrmrm,* they whispered.

Apprehensively, Clo approached the little door. She raised her hand to knock. Behind her, she heard the murmurings rise in excitement.

Mrmrmrmrmrmrmrmrmrmrmrmrmrmrmrm.

Clo closed her eyes. She held her breath. She rapped once, twice, three times.

The door swung open.

An old woman, her face shriveled and shapeless as a dried apple, her eyes nearly lost in the rumpled cheeks and brows, her mouth chewing and chewing and chewing, peered up at her.

Something like a smile half lifted the blousy cheeks. She raised her hands to Clo's shoulders.

"Emoclew, rethguaddnarg," she said.

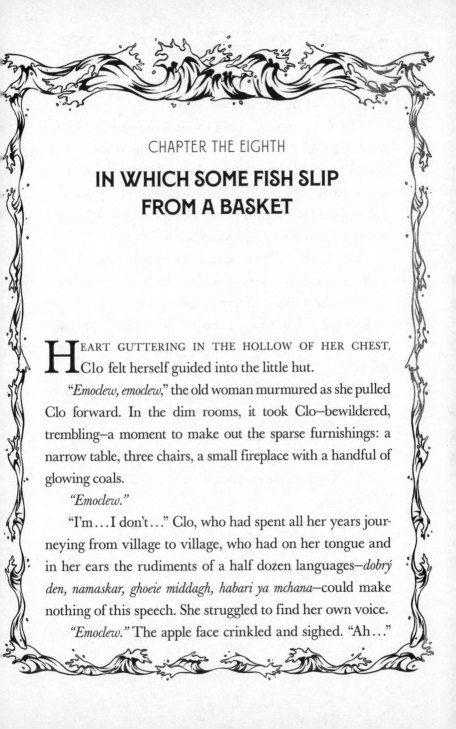

CHAPTER THE EIGHTH

IN WHICH SOME FISH SLIP
FROM A BASKET

Heart guttering in the hollow of her chest, Clo felt herself guided into the little hut.

"*Emoclew, emoclew,*" the old woman murmured as she pulled Clo forward. In the dim rooms, it took Clo—bewildered, trembling—a moment to make out the sparse furnishings: a narrow table, three chairs, a small fireplace with a handful of glowing coals.

"*Emoclew.*"

"I'm…I don't…" Clo, who had spent all her years journeying from village to village, who had on her tongue and in her ears the rudiments of a half dozen languages—*dobrý den, namaskar, ghoeie middagh, habari ya mchana*—could make nothing of this speech. She struggled to find her own voice.

"*Emoclew.*" The apple face crinkled and sighed. "Ah…"

She reached and pulled Clo nearer to her and touched her shorn lamb's hair. *"Rethguaddnarg, emoclew."*

Clo, feeling the woman's hands move gently over her head, recoiled. "I don't...," she said again as the woman placed her palm against Clo's cheek. "I don't know if I'm supposed to be here. There was a boat, a half passage.... I'm supposed to meet my father, I think.... Do you know... have you seen a man... he looks like me, a little...."

The crinkles fell away, and the woman's mouth gave over to its empty chewing again. The beads of her eyes, deep in the creases of brow and cheek, flickered over Clo. *"Emoc, rethguaddnarg. Ew evah neeb gnitiaw."* She pulled Clo, not ungently, across the room and through another doorway.

"Ruoy moordeb, ruoy rebmahc top." She gestured around the chamber. Here were a low bed, a small table, a jug, a bowl, a window cut into the stone of the wall. The woman spread open her hands and held them, palm up and empty, at Clo. *"Rethguaddnarg, emoclew."* *Chew, chew,* went her lips and cheeks.

"Is my father—" Clo tried again, feeling she *must* make this strange woman understand, but the old woman gestured impatiently.

"Uoy tsum tser retfa gnol slevart." Nodding, she stepped out of the room and closed the door behind her.

For a few moments after the woman left, Clo stood

quietly, not moving, not exactly thinking. She sat on the bed and placed her cheese and things beside her.

Her mind buzzed uncomfortably. *Was this to be her room? Did her father know this woman? Would her father come for her here?*

In the past, when she and her father had traveled from village to village, the finding of a home had always been the last of their tasks. There would be the arrival, the inquiry, the securing of service. Often they would sleep at the edge of town, on pine boughs in the woods or hayricks in the fields, until her father had found a little hut that had been abandoned or that he arranged as payment for his work. And it would be left to Clo, after the hut was theirs, to gather straw and leaves and to stuff and shape their mattresses.

This bed, the *fact* of this bed, seemed to offer some reassurance. Perhaps this was what her father had meant for her. He had sent her on ahead. He had made sure she would have a place of comfort. He would be following later.

And the mattress...it was softer than anything she had ever slept on. She reached under its covering. It was stuffed with a fine, silvery fleece, almost more light and air than wool. She rubbed a shimmering tuft between her fingers and leaned back into the cushion.

A mattress and a bed. She had never slept in a bed. Not really. Once or twice, when their walls were too thin to keep out the damp, or when the rats woke them one too many times from their sleep, her father had lifted her little

mattress from the floor and set it on the table so she could sleep dry and rat-free while he was away at night. And her father had told her of beds—beds fine and elaborate and curtained and gilded, with cushions plush with thousands upon thousands of feathers.

This was neither a table transformed into a bed nor a gilded masterpiece, but, thought Clo, she would be glad not to be tucked up against the stone walls and floor and the cold that would surely creep along them. At least, while she was here. For however long that would be.

Standing, Clo crossed to the window. The opening was thick, carved out of the stone that shaped everything. Through its glass panes, she could see pale gray sky and pale gray sea, stretching on and on into the distance. No boats, no birds interrupted the expanse; only there, far into the gray water, she could see the line of crashing waves the bosun had rowed her through—a rim of white. It was eerily quiet: in this little room, she could hear nothing—no wind or wave or bird or voice—nothing but the shuffling footsteps of the woman behind the closed door.

Leaning closer to the glass, Clo looked straight down as far as she was able and realized, with a dizzying start, that this little home was part of the cliff walls; it had simply been carved into them. This must be, she thought, the back of the island, not the side she had climbed.

She scanned the sky for sun or moon, wondering if

evening was approaching. The light from the sky was a dull and steady gray—flat, with no glimmer behind the clouds to give a hint of time. She sat back down on the bed. It could be morning, or afternoon, or evening, but her eyes felt heavy, and her body, after the waves and the climbing and the fear and the uncertainty, felt heavier. She would close her eyes, just for a moment....She removed her father's cloak and pulled it over her like a blanket. She listened to the pulse of her heartbeat against the softness of the mattress. *Clothilde*, it said. *Clothilde*.

Clo awoke in the terror that something was consuming her: something was sitting on her, something was pushing sharp teeth or claws into her shoulders again and again. It was dark and heavy and furry and piggish...*an animal...there was an animal on her, an animal eating her*...Clo screamed and pushed the thing; it dug into her, and Clo grasped the thick bulk of the beast and threw it off. It backed into a corner of the room, hissing and snarling. Scrambling to sit up—*What was that thing?*—Clo grabbed the first thing she could reach—*the bag of turnips*—and, still staring at the hissing thing, groped blindly with her fingers for a turnip globe. She hurled it, and the animal made noises more horrible still, *rowl*ing, howling, beastly noises. Clo took aim with a second turnip.

Before she could throw, the door burst open, and the little apple-faced woman entered in a flurry. *"Feihcsim, feihcsim,"* she said, rushing to the beast.

"No!" Clo waved at her to move. "It's dangerous! It's wild!"

But the woman knelt over the beast and raised it maternally in her arms. *"Feihcsim,"* she soothed. She turned to Clo, still poised to chuck her turnip, and wagged a crooked finger at her. *"Feihcsim."* She patted the thing gently, and it let out a rumbling.

Clo stared at the animal—its fat paws, its long tail, its dark mottled fur—with horror. The noise it was making—*it was purring*—suggested it was a cat, but if it was a cat, it was the largest, most beastly cat she had ever seen. It looked more boarish than cattish, thick and rough with a squished bristly face.

The woman released the beasty-cat, which hissed again at Clo before slipping from the room. The woman gestured to Clo that they should follow.

Standing, folding her father's cloak, glancing out the window, Clo could not tell how long she had slept. Her body felt old, immensely old, as though it were a thread that had been stretched so tight it had begun to unravel. But the light was the same outside as when she had arrived: no sun rising or setting, no moon anywhere in the sky—just the same grayness.

Waiting next to her, the woman made a little clicking

noise of disapproval. She pinched at the fabric of Clo's tunic, and the lines of her face creased into deeper displeasure. Clo looked down: her tunic and leggings were dirty, perhaps, but not much dirtier than usual. Cheeks burning, Clo tugged at her tunic hem, but the woman merely shook her head and guided Clo into the front room.

The table had been set with three bowls and three spoons, and the coals in the fireplace had been coaxed into a brighter flame. A large kettle hanging over the fire billowed out small clouds of steam. Clo watched the little woman shuffle around the hissing, burbling pot, stirring and muttering to herself, while the beast-cat sat in the corner swishing its tail and licking its hoofish paws. From time to time, the woman would lift a slippery piece of something from the pot and toss it at the animal, and it would crouch over the food, devouring it in violent, growling, squelching bites.

"Can you tell me," Clo finally said, "when the next boat is arriving?"

The woman lifted a ladle from the pot and took a small sip. She gave no sign she had heard Clo.

"The boat? The next boat?"

The woman flipped another slippery morsel out of the pot and onto the floor for the cat.

"I think…my father, he sent me here. He gave me a ticket. A half passage. He must be coming. I know he'll come. My father? Do you know him? My father? *Mon père?*

Moi otets? Vater? Pabbi? Baba? Papa?" Clo pronounced the word slowly, loudly, in all the languages she knew, hoping one might catch the woman's understanding.

But at this final repetition of *father*, the ladle hit the pot with an angry clang, and the woman flapped her hand dismissively at Clo.

Clo sighed in exasperation. *How could she make this woman understand?*

Whatever was in the pot did not smell of any kind of stew Clo knew—no pungent herbs or meat or roots. If she had to say, she'd say it smelled like *cold*, but with the red coals and boiling broth, she knew it was anything but *cold*. Still, the air seemed to smell and taste like *snow*, like *ice* or *wind*, empty and stark. Though she knew she ought to be hungry, she felt nothing for whatever was bubbling in the kettle.

A knock on the door set the apple-faced woman into a flurry again. She tossed the cat another slippery morsel, wiped her hands on her shift, ushered Clo into a chair, and crossed to open her front door. A figure—as tall as the apple-faced woman was short—ducked inside. He was as old as the little woman, but where her skin rucked and rumpled, his was stretched as thin and translucent as vellum. He almost seemed to crackle as he walked. The man lowered the basket he was carrying. It was, Clo saw, full of fish: hundreds and hundreds of black-eyed, silver, shimmering fish. One or

two, slipping out and skidding across the floor, were quickly captured and devoured by the cat.

"Rethguaddnarg." The old woman's face crinkled as she lifted a palm toward Clo.

Placing his fingers under Clo's chin, the man raised her face to look at his. Up close, she could see a pulse flickering under his skin at the edges and hollows of his bones; with each little flicker came a rustling sound, like the whispering of dried husks. *Let go,* she thought, shrinking from his touch. *Let go!* She tried again to pull away, but the man's leathery grip held her. His eyes darted over her hair, her tunic, her leggings. "Ah." He nodded, releasing her. He sat in the chair next to Clo's while the woman brought the steaming pot from the fire.

She ladled the stew first into the old man's bowl, then into Clo's, then into her own. The stew—the *soup*—was thin and gray. The man slurped his eagerly; the woman, too, after sitting down, ate quickly. Clo looked into the gray soup. Lowering her spoon, she watched the liquid shimmer and shift. She thought she saw the flash of fish scale, the sliding of fish eye. The liquid moved like clouds. And there was the smell, the smell of ice and wind and cold. *No. She could not eat this.*

She pushed the bowl away.

The woman pushed the bowl back toward Clo. *"Rethguaddnarg."* The word carried a note of anger.

"No." Clo's stomach turned. She nudged the bowl away again. "No, thank you."

The little woman and the tall man glanced at her and then at each other over their spoons. Their gaze was full of the shimmering movement of the soup. Light and shadow swam in their eyes.

Their spoons clinked against their bowls. Between bites, their voices rose.

"*Era uoy erus siht si ruoy dlihcdnarg—*" the man began, before Clo lost track of his garbled speech.

"*Fo esruoc siht si ehs ohw esle dluoc ti eb—*" the woman began her reply. Their gibberish was animated, almost angry. They gestured at Clo with their soup spoons.

In the avalanche of unfamiliar words, Clo stared at the table, at the floor. She had never, she thought, felt so alone. The beastly cat sidled alongside her chair. It flicked its tail. It fixed its piggish eyes on her.

Clo felt the animal's hunger.

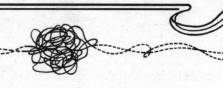

REVEALING THE CONTENTS OF A FORBIDDEN NOTEBOOK

AFTER THE OLD MAN AND WOMAN HAD SCRAPED THE last silvery pools from the bottoms of their bowls, and after the old man, seeing Clo's still full and shimmering bowl, had emptied it into his own and eaten it in quick, slippery bites, and after the table had been cleared and the dishes licked clean by the cat, and after the old man had departed with a small nod of his head, Clo walked back into the little chamber that was—she guessed—her own.

Outside, the gray was the same gray it had been when she arrived, the same gray it had been when she woke with the cat kneading her. In the next room, she could hear a steady tapping, hushing noise—the old woman shuffling about. *Had she just served dinner? Breakfast?* The sky offered no answers.

She sat on the bed. There were the sack of turnips, her father's notebook, the wheel of cheese. Its smell had grown ranker, even more despairing. Digging her fingers into the rind, she pulled away a hunk of its odorous flesh and chewed slowly, staring at the notebook.

The book her father always carried with him. The book he never let from his sight. The book he forbade her to touch.

Forbidden. The *forbidden* notebook.

She rubbed her cheese-rimmed fingernails on her tunic and picked up the book.

How many times as a small child had she taken hold of the cover, run her fingers over it, entranced by its softness?

Father, may I see?

No, my lambkin. Even now she could almost hear her father's patient voice. *This is not for you.*

May I hold it? May I carry it for you? I'll keep it safe, I promise.

No, daughter. You mustn't touch this.

How many times had she seen him, when he thought she was asleep, turning its pages in the firelight? How many times had she ruffled the leaves with her little fingertips or pulled at the knot, wondering what her father kept inside?

Father, would you show me the pages?

Taking the book away, he would move it always out of reach. *No, my dove. No. This is not for you.*

And the terrible time she had come upon him drawing in it—his unbearable fury: *All I ask, Clo. This is not for you. I forbid it.*

She remembered the awkward image of the woman, the lopsided jumble of angles her father had sketched. In memory, the woman had grown even more angular, more lopsided, a grotesque scratch to which she had given the name *Mother.*

Clo fingered the knot on the leather band. She did not want to disobey him.

Still…he had given it to her.

Perhaps he had left something inside to tell her why she was here. When he would come.

Taking a deep breath, she eased away the knot and opened the cover.

For a long moment, Clo stared at the pages in confusion. Then she flipped them, quickly, frantically. Nothing here made sense.

Across the first pages were scattered small sketches—parts of things, of people: a hand, a nose, a garden wall, a horse's mane and bridle, a bit of lace. Here and there, a whole person would appear: a lady before her looking glass, a hunter with his hounds at heel, a cook with his arms about a kettle, a musician with a lute cradled to her chest. But these images were not lopsided scratches of chalk: their

lines were light, fluid. Full of confidence and grace. Even unfinished, incomplete, these drawings . . . the people . . . they almost seemed to breathe.

Clo's head swam. The images showed a talent her father did not possess. A life that could not have been his.

At least, she did not know him this way.

She tried to imagine him living among these people, surrounded by flowers and music and feasting. She tried to imagine him sitting, sketching, capturing the musician, the cook, the lady, the hunter. The drawings were warm, intimate, unhurried: her father had shared his days with the people he had drawn. *Could these really be the work of his hand?*

Disconcerted, Clo turned the pages more slowly. The father she knew had trekked with her across wasteland and wilderness, had called a crust of bread and turnip dinner, had shooed the rats from his pallet of straw before sleep. What did he know of feasting and finery?

She missed him, she desperately missed him, but did she know him? Know him at all?

Her father was a cleaner. A restorer of all decorative arts. But he was not himself an artist.

Of course he loved art, Clo thought reluctantly. That she knew. She glanced at the rag-wrapped painting. He loved it too much. Far too much.

She continued flipping through the notebook. Whole years passed in the sketches. She saw her father's life open

up before her—a life that, if not of leisure, was of a comfort she had never known with him.

Clo had loved their life in the shadows, had loved their life of tramping through fields and forests. But this had always seemed to her a life of necessity. *Why would her father have left a world of comfort behind? To live a life of . . . cleaning? And chiseling . . . thievery?*

"Father," she murmured. *"Where are you?"*

The door opened, and Clo, startled, slapped the notebook shut and tucked it behind her back. She looked up to see the old woman in the doorway, the basket of slippery fish in her arms. The cat wound around the woman's legs, watching the basket greedily.

"Rethguaddnarg." Her voice sounded like a question. Chewing emptily, she held out the basket. *"Eht gnidrac,"* she said finally. *"Eht gninnips."*

Clo stood, wondering what the old woman wished her to do. *Perhaps she wanted payment for her lodging?* Clo glanced at the rag-wrapped painting still on the bed.

"My father . . ." Removing the wrappings, Clo held out the painting. "This may be meant for you. . . . My father may have sent this. . . . He sometimes trades paintings he . . . finds. He may mean to trade for . . . board? Room and board? Look." She raised the painting toward the woman. "It's valuable. The frame—"

At the sight of the painted grapes and the gem-encrusted

frame, the woman's nose creased in disgust. *"Sselhtrow."* Shaking her head, she pushed the basket of fish toward the girl. *"Eht gnidrac."*

"Just the jewels–" Clo started to protest, but out of the corner of her eye, out the window, she caught sight of a flash of white, a motion in the water.

She raced to the window, looking into the gray expanse below.

A boat. *A boat!* Just there, sailing right below. Clo's heart leapt; she leaned, straining to follow the vessel's progress, but it sailed too close to the island cliffs beneath her. She saw its entire body, then just the tip of its white sail, then nothing. She rattled the window latch; it would not open.

"A boat!" she cried, turning to the old woman. "I saw a boat! My father is coming. I'm sure of it. I should go.... If it's him, I have to meet him! I have to make sure he finds me."

Sighing under the weight of the fish, the old woman shook her head and tried again to put the basket in Clo's arms.

"No." Clo pushed back. "You can have the painting, but I can't help with these...fish. With the gutting or scaling or cooking or whatever it is you want me to do with them right now. There's a boat." Swinging her father's cloak over her shoulder, grabbing his notebook, she rushed past the old woman.

"Rethguaddnarg..." Heavily lidded, almost hidden, the woman's eyes followed Clo out the door.

The town, its cobblestone streets and little stone huts, was now silent and empty. Gone was the crowd of elderly, crookbacked men and women who had swarmed after Clo with their murmuring. Doors were shut and windows dark; only once Clo thought she saw a flicker of movement behind a pane of glass, but when she turned, all was still.

Clo retraced the path she had come, following the street to its end, where she clambered up the opening to the cliff path. The descent, with its views of the sheer drop and the open air and the rocks and water below, seemed more treacherous than it had on her ascent, but Clo rushed as quickly as she dared down the stairs. Between the rocks, she caught glimpses of the tidesman and the open sea, yet strain as she might, she could not see the sail of the boat that had passed under her window. Still, she was certain. *Her father was coming.* Her feet thudded on the rocks, a jubilant noise of *boat, boat, boat.*

From time to time, as she hurried down the cliff, she thought she heard another set of footsteps behind her, but whenever she stopped to listen, she heard nothing but the wind moving through the stones. When she scurried on, the noise started after her again.

"Is someone here?" she finally called.

Silence. And then, so faint it might have been nothing but a breath of air, a long hissing. "Ssss…"

"Someone is here?"

The soft hissing again. "Ssss...Y-yessss."

"Who is here?"

Silence. Stones. Wind.

Disconcerted, Clo continued to pick her way down the stairs. But now she listened anxiously for whatever might be behind her, above her, on the cliffs.

Steps. The scraping of stones. Someone was following her.

Was it one of the rumpled villagers? The parchment-skin man? She thought of the way he had gripped her face in his leathery fingers.

Alarm growing, Clo hurried as fast as the treacherous path allowed. But the thudding behind her kept pace. At last, seeing a small outcropping, she edged off the stairs and onto the ledge. Backing away as far as she was able, she stood quietly, trying to steady her breath. From here, she could see a wide, boatless expanse of sea. She closed her eyes against the dizzying distance. The steps came more clearly now: hesitant, then quickening.

Step. Step. Scrape. Step.

Pressed into the rocks, half holding her breath, Clo waited.

CHAPTER THE TENTH

DESCRIBING THE *PLIPP*ING OF STONES

THE SCRAPING NOISE RUSHED ALONG THE STONES. It was just above her. Beside her.

She turned her head carefully.

She almost laughed.

It was a boy. A boy no older than she. Portly. Pale. Dark, dampish hair.

She watched him hurry past. "H-here…I'm er…h-here…," he murmured, passing without seeing her. He thudded down the stairs, trailing his fingers on the rock walls.

Clo waited a minute, then stepped carefully back onto the stairs. She resumed her descent, now following in the boy's wake. But she hadn't gone more than a few dozen steps when she rounded a corner and found the boy stopped, his arms folded over his soft belly.

"Yh–…Wh-why are you ff-following me?" the boy stammered. He was breathing heavily, and his face was waxy and damp, an almost bluish hue.

"I? Following you?" Crossing her arms, Clo scowled at the boy. "You were following *me.*"

The boy chewed his lip, considering. "Are you a yo–… are you a b-boy?"

"Are *you*?"

The boy might have blushed if his pallid skin could have held that hue. Instead, his moon-shaped cheeks grew a little moonier, and he dropped his eyes and held out his hand. "I'm yrr–…s-sorry," he said. "But no b-boys ever come. Or l-lr–…*girls.* No girls ever come either. T-ts…" He paused. "Just me."

Clo glanced at his outstretched palm. "I have to get to the shore." Pushing past the stammering boy, she started down the stairs again. "I saw a boat. My father may be on it."

"A t-ta–…a *boat*?" The boy followed after her. "Where did you ee–…see it?"

"From a window. I saw it sailing."

"On…*N-nno*…Your father…is he a nn–…a ff–…fisherman?"

"No," Clo huffed. "He's no fisherman."

"Eh–…the boat you saw…it's the d-d–…island fishing boat. Your father t-tno–…won't be on it."

"How do you know?" Clo whirled toward the boy standing a few steps above her. "Did you see the boat? Do you know my father? He *is* coming. He *will* be here."

The boy dropped his gaze again. His moony cheeks slumped.

They continued in silence down the rest of the path, the boy following a few careful measures behind Clo.

When they reached the narrow beach, the tidesman turned his head briefly before resuming his stiff position on the rocks.

"Is there a boat arriving?" Clo called to him.

The tidesman, still and quiet, did not acknowledge her.

"Has there been a boat?" Clo called more forcefully.

The tidesman's arm swept over the sea in a gesture that encompassed all its emptiness.

Standing on the little beach just out of reach of the water, Clo scanned the horizon, the distant line of crashing waves. The longer she stood, the more despondent she grew. She felt the emptiness filling her. *No sail, no boat.*

No Father.

She sat. Digging her fingers into the beach, she shifted handfuls of pebbles back and forth. This shore was nothing like the harbor where she had first sat unwrapping the cheese, still hoping and believing her father might be nearby. There, the water crashed with force and energy, foaming up the rocks, roaring all around her. Here, it

sloshed gently, lifelessly, more like water borne in a bucket than water pulled and rocked by tides. It made no more noise than a pale splashing, a pathetic lapping.

Clo tossed the small gray and black pebbles one at a time into the water. They *plipp*ed brightly, too happily, watery circles expanding out and out around the splash. *Water that is full of salt and has no edge.*

Clo was conscious of the boy standing a little distance behind her. He scuffed his feet in the stones. Clo's pebbles *plipp*ed and *plipp*ed. After a long while, she heard the boy sit and shuffle in his clothes, and then a thin melody began to rise. Clo glanced back. The boy was holding a small broken flute to his lips and piping softly, barely audibly, his tune spreading in the air around them like the watery circles from the stones.

Clo did not think she could bear the emptiness of the sea against the boy's bright tune. "Stop that, will you?"

The boy fell silent.

After a longer while, a hundred or so *plips*, Clo, keeping her face turned to the unchanging horizon, spoke. "When do the boats come?"

"The g-g–... fishing boats?"

"No, the boats with passengers. The boats with passengers to the island."

The boy scooted forward in the sand, only a step or two behind Clo now. "I don't... w-wo–know."

92

"Well, when was the last time a boat with passengers came?"

"Ss–...y-yours."

"Before mine."

"Sometimes, I see a ttt–...b-boat pass beyond the w-waves." In the corner of her eye, Clo saw the boy's hand gesture to the distance. She pitched another stone into the water, and the boy continued anxiously. "Uu–...Y-you should not throw the sea coal, the k–...b-black stones, they are for the s–f-fires...sea coal..."

Clo hurled an entire handful of pebbles into the sea. *Plipplipplipplipplipplipplipplipilipplipplipplip.* She turned on the boy. "When do they come? When did you last see a boat arrive?"

"Tttt–Ton...*Not,* not since I dev–d–...." The boy's moons puffed and billowed. He buried his head in his arms.

Turning back to the ocean, Clo whipped stone after stone into the sea, hurling them farther and farther into the distance until she could hardly hear their splash.

Behind her, the boy took a deep breath. When he spoke at last, his words were slow and measured. "No boats have come since I arrived here. I've never seen a boat come. Or leave. Only sss–y-yours."

A clamminess settled at once all over Clo's skin. She shivered. *Surely this was wrong.*

Clo shifted so she was facing the boy. He looked at his

hands, then raised his eyes—full of the sea and the gray of the sky—to meet hers. "And when did you come?" Clo asked. "How many days or months or..." Clo felt the heaviness of the word in her mouth. "How many years ago?"

The boy shifted pebbles beneath his fingers. His mouth opened and closed. "I don't know how to rre—...answer."

"Well." Clo looked up at the cliffs that towered over them, at the gray sky that was the same gray, the same sunless gray. "How old were you when you arrived?"

A pucker formed on the boy's forehead. He considered. "E-ev—...El—...Tw-twelve? Ss—...spa—...*Perhaps* I was twelve?"

Clo smiled. A smile that even the boy—with the damp hair and moonish cheeks, who had not seen another boy or girl since he had arrived at the island and who seemed, at best, flustered and confused by every word Clo put to him—recognized as warm. Warmhearted. Full of relief and light.

"Well, you can't be *much* older than twelve now," she said, still smiling.

"N-no..." He sounded unsure.

"So you can't have been here very long."

"I es—...su-suppose," he said, adding quietly, "It see—seems long."

"So another boat must be due again soon."

The boy didn't answer, but his shoulders lifted with all the slow imperceptibility of the water rising and falling along the shoreline.

Clo turned back to the horizon. For a long while, she stared at its unchanging gray lines. The boy, she felt, was watching her: she was conscious of his eyes on her back, his nervous shifting. Finally, he asked a careful question.

"Do you have a…a *name*?" he asked.

"Clo."

"Clo." The boy pronounced her name slowly, turning it over, *Cuh-low*.

She *plipp*ed a few pebbles into the water. She heard him say again, softly, "Clo," and again, "Clo."

"And yours?" she thought to ask the still-whispering boy after a few minutes.

"E–…M-mine?"

"Your name?"

"Ye…Th-they call me *boy*. Just *boy*."

"Well, that's not a name."

"N-no."

"What do your parents call you?"

Clo heard the boy dig into the pebbles behind her; the crunching of stone covered a smaller sound, a little breath like a sigh. She turned.

"No parents?"

The boy shook his head.

"Well, what *did* they call you? What name did they give you?"

The boy's face looked paler and damper than ever. His lip quivered over the word. "Ca- Carus. I k–...th-think. Carus."

"That's not a name either. That just means *dear one*. Like my father calls me *lambkin*."

Eyes downcast, the boy again busied himself with the pebbles on the beach; his fingers, Clo saw, were prunish with the wet of the shore. She glanced at her own: dry. *Why was this boy so thoroughly damp?*

"Lambkin," the boy at last said quietly, his lip still trembling. "I don't think my re–...f-father called me anything like that."

Clo wished she could stop the boy's chin from wobbling so. "Perhaps your name is Cary?" she offered hopefully. "That is a name I know."

A faint trace of color flashed across the boy's cheeks. "Y–...Ca-Cary." He smiled gratefully at Clo. "Yes, Cary. That ts–...must have been it."

Clo nodded. In her life in the shadows of villages, she'd had no need–no real need, she'd told herself–of the company of other children. She had known and watched and even silently mocked the ones who had scampered in the streets or hung on their mothers' skirts or dabbled in the puddles and gutters while she swept the stoop or poked

the turnips or waited for her father to return in the dawn. She did not like the way they whispered about her father–*vagabond, night soil man, invalid*–the way they pointed at him when he walked down the street in the evenings with his buckets and brushes, the way they stared at *her* even, wide-eyed and openmouthed and runny-nosed, pointing at *her* while she knelt over her plants in the garden. Even when she had recovered a ball or a knucklebone that had gone tumbling away from one of their games, and she'd brought it to them, holding it out on the flat of her palm, they had shrunk away from her, gawping and whispering, preferring to lose their game piece than take it from her. No, she'd had no need of their company; their raucous laughing, their petty squabbling grated on her ears.

She did not, she thought, really need this boy *Cary* either. But he was quiet, and, she had to admit, she liked the way his smile fluttered in a quick line from moony cheek to moony cheek.

Standing, the boy Cary shook away the pebbles that clung to his clothes and skin. He offered Clo his hand again, but at her doubtful glance, he tucked it behind his back.

"Y–...Li–...." He shook his head. "They will be gn–... wa-waiting for me. I'm to help the fi-fishermen unload the boat. I always help da–...u-unload the catch."

"I'm not leaving. I want to watch for a boat. I mean to stay until dark."

Cary's eyebrows lifted in surprise, but he nodded and turned to walk toward the cliff.

When he had just started ascending the stairs, Clo called after him. "Cary!"

Cary's voice, when it reached her, came with the echo of the cliff walls. "Se–Yes?"

"What did your boat look like? The one that carried you here?" She waited for his answer, wondering if he would describe the same gloomy craft on which she had traveled.

A pause. Cary was now too far in the stairs for Clo to see him. "O–...No boat."

"No boat?"

"They de–...fi-fished me out of the a–...out of the s-sea."

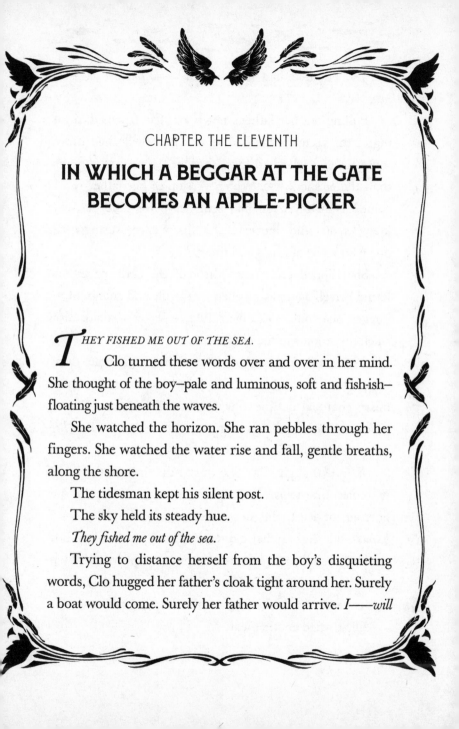

CHAPTER THE ELEVENTH

IN WHICH A BEGGAR AT THE GATE BECOMES AN APPLE-PICKER

*T*HEY FISHED ME OUT OF THE SEA.

Clo turned these words over and over in her mind. She thought of the boy—pale and luminous, soft and fish-ish—floating just beneath the waves.

She watched the horizon. She ran pebbles through her fingers. She watched the water rise and fall, gentle breaths, along the shore.

The tidesman kept his silent post.

The sky held its steady hue.

They fished me out of the sea.

Trying to distance herself from the boy's disquieting words, Clo hugged her father's cloak tight around her. Surely a boat would come. Surely her father would arrive. *I——will*

find you. The note had said this. *He would find her. He would come.*

Pulling out her father's notebook, Clo frowned, thinking of the sketches she had seen. The *he* who had drawn those images, who had lived that life, seemed so different than the *he* she knew. Which version of her father would come? Which version had sent her here? The one who knew of rats and thievery...or this one, the stranger, the one who knew of feasts and finery?

She flipped once more through the early pages and found herself again astonished by the life and energy of the images. She could *almost* hear the lute player's ballad, *almost* smell the blooms in the lady's vase.

The small sketches gave way to more elaborate drawings. The first of these, a full page, showed a woman in misty charcoal outline. She was standing against a wall, vines and blooms clambering up the stones behind her. *Beggar at the Gate*, her father had written beneath.

Beggar? thought Clo. She traced the lines of the image with her fingertips. The woman was not beautiful—her portrait, at least, did not obviously exclaim, *Ah, here is beauty!*—but the way her expression, her eyes, her lips, hovered between joy and sorrow gave her an appearance of wisdom that was beautiful. Her hands were empty; her head was covered. She looked too regal to be a beggar.

Clo turned another leaf.

Apple-Pickers, read her father's note across the next illustration, a sketch covering two full pages of an orchard at harvest. Men and women carried fruit in baskets or tucked up in aprons. The people and the trees had been drawn quickly, with little detail, so as to give an impression of the overall scene, but one woman, perched on a ladder and laughing as she was reaching for the fruit, had been so carefully rendered Clo could almost hear her laughter echoing around her. She peered more closely at the figure. Despite the joyful smile, the woman's eyes were still shaped with sorrow. She was the beggar at the gate, now no longer a beggar.

The next several pages were dotted with sketches of a young man with a fine nose and fierce gaze: these grew more and more detailed and exact until a finished image finally took shape of the young man in an elaborate lace ruff posing with his hand on the hilt of his sword. Clo pulled at the collar of her own tunic; she could not imagine wearing such an absurd, starchy creation around her neck. *Study for MB Portrait*, read her father's script beneath.

Then another two-page illustration: *Wedding Feast*, her father had titled it. A trio of musicians with bagpipes stood at the edge, playing to tables filled with men and women and children, raising cups, lifting spoons, talking with wide gestures at one another. The scene was chaotic, noisy, jubilant; the image had no center. But in the far corner, holding

a jug, stood the apple-picker, the beggar at the gate. Again, she had been drawn with more care and detail than anyone else in the image, even the apparent bride and groom. She was looking directly, Clo realized, at Clo's father drawing her, and she was smiling, a wide, warm smile.

Had her father felt this happy when he attended this feast? Clo tried to imagine him there. *Had he danced to the bagpipes? Even danced with this woman?*

More small sketches followed—a lady with a child resting on her lap, a wagon brimming with hay, a washerwoman hanging clothes to dry. *A washerwoman!* Clo thought wryly, remembering the swineherd's story of the lady's maid and her laundress mother. And then Clo turned to a page that brought her up short.

It was a scene of home life: the woman again. Her father had drawn her sitting before a fire, a drop spindle dangling from her hands. Her lines were soft, indistinct, almost cloud-like. She was gazing, as before, at Clo's father, but here she seemed to be looking beyond him, across a great distance, her expression again caught between joy and sadness.

Her dress was stretched over her middle. She was with child.

Spinning, her father had chalked as the title, but it was not this word that took Clo's breath. It was the smaller, hasty letters he had penned beneath, a smudge of ink that read *Spinning for Clothilde*.

For Clothilde.

Clo stared for a long time at this image and at the words her father had written in the margin.

The woman was a stranger: Clo felt nothing for this cloud portrait she felt ought to be called *Mother*—except perhaps the pain of absence, of not-knowing.

Clo traced the chalk lines with her fingers, searching for anything familiar in the image. *The cheeks? The chin? The nose?* She rubbed her own cheekbones, the bridge of her own nose. Perhaps the nose. *The same sharp edge.*

Why had her father never told her anything about this woman?

Tell me about my mother, she used to beg when she was very small. *What was she like?*

Not now, lambkin, her father would always answer, his voice strange. He would turn away; he would begin some task with his hands. He would wash his brushes, slice an onion, stir the coals. *Not now. One day.*

But once, she had pestered him. All afternoon. They had been traveling, walking through the woods, and all day, over and over, she had pleaded. *Father, tell me.* She had pulled on his hand, wrapped her arms about his middle, hopped up and down by his side. He had been patient. *No, no. Not now, lambkin. Let me tell you a story instead.* Finally, she had stopped asking. But later, as evening settled and they stopped to gather kindling, she had asked again. *What was my mother like, Father? Do I look like her? Am I at all like her?* He

must not have expected to be surprised like that, scrounging in the leaf litter, arms full of sticks.

How his face had twisted. How his chin had trembled.

He had put down his bundle. He had taken her by the shoulders. *Shh, shh, shh, shh, shhh*, he had said, a kind of quieting, a kind of comforting, but Clo, seeing her father's eyes wet, his face strange, was not comforted. *Fate took her away from us*, he whispered. *A punishment. I loved her. And still now, fate punishes me. Do you see how I am punished? Taking her was not enough. And you...I can't bear more...if you, too...when you, too...*

I'm sorry, she had said hurriedly, feeling she had done something wrong.

She had not wanted to ask again. She had not wanted to see her father's face like that again.

Clo ran her fingers over the lines of the cloud portrait. "Mother," she said aloud experimentally, seeing how the word felt in front of this image. The sounds were strange in her mouth. Lopsided. Uncomfortable.

"Father," she said, and this word felt full of sorrow... heavy and empty all at once. She thought again of the way her father's face had twisted. *Yes*, that twisting expression was how she felt now. It was grief. And love. And fear. And confusion. And...anger. Yes, even anger.

He'd sent her here alone with nothing but a stolen painting, a wheel of cheese, and a notebook that showed only how much he had hidden from her for so long.

She stared at her father's chalk strokes, wishing she could see his hand in the lines he had marked on the page with such care.

The next leaf held an unfinished sketch—a few graceful strokes that suggested the shape of a woman with babe in arms—but without details, Clo could determine nothing about the woman or child. She turned another page, expecting to see more of her father and mother's story play out, perhaps even the story of her own infanthood. But abruptly, the elegant sketches ended. The chalk figures that seemed to breathe on the page were replaced by hundreds of the grotesque angular images Clo had once seen her father draw. The lines were clumsy and heavy, carrying marks of her father's frustration. Some had been x-ed out or hastily scrawled over. Again and again, Clo saw the image of the woman, distorted and scarcely recognizable—almost monstrous. And she saw what must be her own self as a child, but again, gruesome and misshapen.

The scribblings grew angrier and more desperate as Clo flipped through the book. The last few pages had been ripped out altogether.

What had happened to her father? What had happened to the talent he once possessed?

Where was he now?

Clo closed the book and retied its leather band. In front of her, the horizon was flat. And gray. On and on and on. Endless gray.

Spinning. For Clothilde.

The gray seemed the same gray of her father's chalk. Of the cloud-woman. Of the angry scrawls. She stared at the horizon, wishing for a boat, wishing, really, for anything to break the terrible blank expanse and its terrible unsolvable refrains.

They fished me out of the sea.
Spinning. For Clothilde.

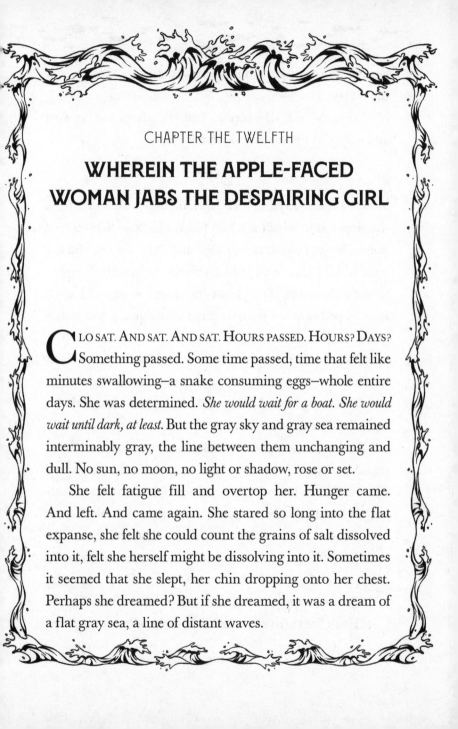

WHEREIN THE APPLE-FACED WOMAN JABS THE DESPAIRING GIRL

Clo sat. And sat. And sat. Hours passed. Hours? Days? Something passed. Some time passed, time that felt like minutes swallowing–a snake consuming eggs–whole entire days. She was determined. *She would wait for a boat. She would wait until dark, at least.* But the gray sky and gray sea remained interminably gray, the line between them unchanging and dull. No sun, no moon, no light or shadow, rose or set.

She felt fatigue fill and overtop her. Hunger came. And left. And came again. She stared so long into the flat expanse, she felt she could count the grains of salt dissolved into it, felt she herself might be dissolving into it. Sometimes it seemed that she slept, her chin dropping onto her chest. Perhaps she dreamed? But if she dreamed, it was a dream of a flat gray sea, a line of distant waves.

No ship, no sail, no dinghy, rowboat, raft, or log crossed the waves.

"Always," she whispered. And the *always* was as vast and empty as the sea and sky before her.

When a quiet, rhythmic clicking finally roused Clo from the stupor into which she had fallen–a stupor that seemed impossibly to hold days and days and days–the sea and sky were still the same dull gray. She stood unsteadily, listening to the little waves slip against the shore. *Alone, alone, alone,* they lapped at her. A dull panic enveloped her. *A boat was not coming.*

"Where are the boats you wait for?" she tried to shout at the stony tidesman, but her throat was too dry for her words to carry. It didn't matter. He did not even turn his head; he would not answer.

Behind her, she saw, a trio of villagers had arrived. Gray mantles draped over their hunched forms, looking more like misshapen lumps of clay than people, they were combing the beach silently, dropping black stone after black stone into the wide, deep baskets they dragged behind them. The steady dropping of the stones–*click*–punctuated their travel along the shore.

Clo, legs tottery beneath her, moved toward the figures.

"Has a boat arrived?" she asked the smallest of the three.

A pair of button-like eyes, dark and coppery and deep in the folds of brow and cheek, peered up at her.

"*Heee?*"

Clo tried again. "I'm waiting for my father's boat." She pointed at the sea. "When does the next one land?"

The little figure turned to the larger stone pickers. "*Tahw seod eht lrig yas?*"

The two forms raised the lumps of their shoulders. They picked their stones. The button-ish eyes blinked and turned away.

Clo's voice broke in frustration. "Can't you tell me?" Before, on her travels with her father, she had never had trouble learning a language. Wherever they had gone, she had only had to listen, and she came to understand. This... this *helpless* feeling was new. She did not like it.

"*Yhw si ehs ton ta reh krow?*" one of the figures murmured. They shuffled on, plucking their stones.

Clo spun away from the trio. At least the Cary-boy understood her. She could take comfort in that.

She looked again at the boatless expanse. Having sat for so long, she felt *not right, not like herself;* she was dizzy. Light-headed. Wobbly. She shook her head; she tried to stiffen her knees.

Perhaps boats did not land here, she thought. Perhaps the island had another harbor.

If the boat was not here, she at last determined, she would look for it elsewhere.

The island was not large. She would walk around it.

Leaving her boots and her father's cloak and notebook on the shore, she stepped tentatively into the water, the cold at once numbing the bones of her ankles. Pushing on, she waded out, trying to follow the wall of the island around its visible edge—*Was there a harbor around the corner? Another place for a boat to moor around the cliff?*—but as soon as she moved from the beach, the pebbly bottom dropped away. She found herself quickly up to her waist, her chest, her chin in the frigid water.

Standing on her toes, she struggled to keep herself upright. The icy water lapped about her lips. She felt herself slipping. "Help!" she cried, a salty burbling. Fanning her arms desperately, she caught herself on the cliff wall. She found her footing again.

She looked back at the shore. The stone-pickers still combed the beach. The tidesman still stood at his rocky post. No one seemed concerned that she might have gone beneath the waves.

Shaken, she turned back. She tried the other direction, maneuvering around the tidesman's jetty. Again, the sea-floor dropped away. Chest-deep, shuddering with cold, hand on the cliff wall, Clo stood staring into the water—*there* was the bottom, rocky and gray, *there*, a step forward, was drowning—just darkness and shadows falling into the deep.

Water that is full of salt and has no edge, she thought bitterly. She could not walk around the island.

As she stood staring, shivering and numb, she heard a voice calling in alarm. She glanced up, strangely grateful that one of the stone-pickers had finally noticed her near drowning.

No, it was not them. Hurrying past the imperturbable figures on the beach, waving in clear consternation, was the moon-cheeked boy. "O-o–C-clo!" He flapped his arms. He hollered at the water. "C-Clo. T–…Wh-what are you gn–…doing?"

Still in a fog of cold, Clo turned and began to make her way back to the beach.

The boy watched her as she climbed to the pebbly shore. His cheeks puffed with concern. "Are you all th–…right?" he asked as she wrapped herself in the cloak. "E–…H-have you been here all this time? Have you been here ec–… si-since I left you?"

Teeth chattering violently, Clo gathered up her belongings. "How long have I been here?"

Cary's eyes widened. "Ll-long. Very long."

"I was waiting for a boat, but…" She gestured vaguely. Out of the shocking cold of the water, she felt herself growing faint again. She tried to right herself.

Cary shook his head, a sad *No boat*. He peered at her. "Here. Te–…Let me h-help you." He held out his hand. "You need to eat. You've been here and ev–…have had nothing. No one es–…else will come to help. The old na–… wo-woman–"

111

"I can walk," Clo said, but as she stepped forward, she swayed unsteadily.

"Let me help," Cary said again.

Clo shook her head, *No, she could walk on her own,* but as they started toward the cliff path and her steps wobbled precariously, she was relieved he was beside her.

"They fished you out of the sea," she said as they began the slow climb to the town.

"Yes."

She wanted to ask, *How did you come to be in the sea?* but she was breathless with the effort of the ascent. "How?" she at last managed.

"I...fell. I think I fell. I re-remember...falling."

"From here?" Clo pointed to the top of the cliffs.

Cary shook his head. "On...No. My re—...father..."

Even light-headed, Clo recognized the sadness shifting over the boy's face as her own. She had no breath left for questions, but she did not want to ask more. She concentrated on the climb, on keeping her feet moving up the stairs. She did not want to fall on the boy walking behind her with arms half outstretched in case he needed to catch her.

When they at last reached the village, Clo's breath had become so thin, her head so cloudy, she could not be sure she was still moving forward.

Her legs trembled. Her head swam. *Did she even remember which was the old woman's home?*

Cary guided her to the end of the street.

The apple-faced woman opened the door at his knock. *"O, rethguaddnarg."* Her face crumpled as she reached to support Clo. *"O, yob..."*

Cary stood in the doorway as Clo was led inside. "Y-you need to ta–...eat and drink," he said. "T–...Re-rest...*ehs sdeen ot tae–*" he called as the little woman closed the door in his face.

"Tis, tis, rethguaddnarg." The woman pointed to an empty bowl and spoon at the table. A pot of soup burbled above the fire.

Clo shook her head. Letting go of the old woman, she stumbled into the room she thought must be hers and sat heavily on the bed. Under the bedclothes, she felt the wheel of cheese, the sack of turnips, the painting. She reached for a turnip and ate a desperate, bitter mouthful; gagging, she forced herself to chew and swallow.

The old woman entered carrying a bowl and a mug.

"No." Clo pushed the proffered bowl lightly with her fingertips. Something slithered in the liquid. "No. I don't want it."

"Uoy tsum–"

"No!"

"Rethguaddnarg!" The woman's face grew heated and pink in its creases. She pushed the mug into Clo's hand.

Clo peered into the cup: *Water, it was water.* A few silver fish scales floated in the liquid. Clo drank gratefully, catching and holding the small, sharp scales on her tongue. When the mug was empty, she spat the silver flakes into her palm and handed the mug back to the old woman.

The old woman sighed and touched her fingers lightly to Clo's forehead. *"Ruoy seye..."*

Clo turned away from the gesture. The turnip and the water now sloshing in her stomach, she felt fatigue rolling over her. She collapsed into the softness of the wool. Vaguely, almost dreaming, she felt the old woman stroking her hair.

"Rethguaddnarg..." The woman patted her head. *"Ew detiaw rof uoy rof os gnol....Woh dalg ew era taht uoy era ereh ta tsal...ereh ot ekat pu ruoy krow..."*

Clo, shrugging the hand away, pulled her father's cloak over her head. It still smelled of home.

The woman's voice came muffled and dark through the wool.

Clo felt no surprise when she awoke to the same flat gray sky outside her window. She stared at it for a time from the bed. *Would the air here ever be anything but tepid and dull? Would it never rain? Or snow? Or grow hot? Or turn windy? Would night never come? Would the sun never rise? Would nothing ever change?*

She thought longingly of the mornings in the village, the pink stain of sunrise above the houses, the smell of woodsmoke from cooking fires, the clatter of hooves on the streets...even the voices of the gossiping old women, the raucous laughter of the children in their games....Truly, she had to admit, she missed these, too.

Clo sat up. She had rolled over onto the turnips and cheese as she had slept, and she felt bruised where the roots had pressed into her back. Lifting the bedclothes, she took a small bite of the orange wheel.

The painting, she noted, had been hung on the wall beside her bed. In the gray light, even the jewels seemed flat and dull.

She could hear the woman muttering to herself in the next room—"*Feihcsim...od uoy ees reh ereht? Woh hcum uoy tsum ssim reh...sey, feihcsim...sey, ehs si gninnips ereht, nrobbuts dlihc, gninnips daerht ni eht dlrow, tahw did ehs kniht dluoc eb enod htiw ti*"—and the cat responding with its own guttural *rowl*ing. The woman had been kind, stroking her hair as she went to sleep, but Clo felt something was...*not right*.

She patted the bedclothes, then, with increasing agitation, stood up. Cheese. Turnips. Cloak. "Where is it?" she whispered. She yanked at the sheets, shook them, threw them to the floor, shook them again. The turnips rolled across the chamber.

"Oh, where is it?" she pleaded to the empty room.

She clutched the bedclothes to her. *No*, she could not feel anything in them. *It wasn't there.* She lifted the mattress—*nothing.* She pushed aside the basin, the bowl. *Nothing.*

Clo heard again the old woman talking to herself in the other room. *"Sey, feihcsim…hcus a doog ssenekil ti si…sey, eh saw syawla detnelat…syawla gnipahser eht—"* Clo threw open the door.

The little woman was sitting at the table, her back to Clo, the piggish cat visible as flicking ears and tail hanging from either side of her lap. At the sound of the door, the woman jumped, her hands flattening on something in front of her, then clasping the something into the folds of her dress.

But Clo saw.

"That's mine! That's my father's!" Her words were sharp.

The woman stood and clutched the notebook against her bosom. Apple cheeks bright, she backed away from Clo. *"Enim,"* she whispered. *"Ym—"*

Heat prickled all over Clo's skin. "You can't have that! You can't take it! It's mine. Not yours." She rushed back into the chamber and pulled the painting off the wall. She tried to hand it to the old woman. "Here! Take this instead! Look at the jewels! The painting! Think how valuable this is! Those are just sketches you're holding. Here!"

Glancing only once at the painting, the old woman

shook her head and gripped the notebook more tightly. Her jaw worked furiously, a vexed and vacant chewing.

Flushed with anger, Clo attempted to wrest the book from her. "You cannot have this. It's my father's.... He gave it to me to...to hold...to keep safe." She struggled with the old woman, who bent over the book, twisting her body away from Clo. Her grip was surprisingly strong. Clo tried to fit her fingers more tightly around the cover, to work it out of the woman's hands. She did not want to hurt her, but she could not let her have her father's book.

"*On!*" the woman shrieked. "*On!*"

Startled, Clo let go. The old woman scampered into the corner.

"*On.*" Huddling over the book, she flipped open the cover. "*Ym...*" She slapped at an open page. "*Ym...rethguad...*" She ripped out the page.

Clo gasped. "No!"

The woman pressed the torn leaf against her chest. Through her fingers, Clo could see the sketch of the cloud-figure, the soft lines that carried the uncertain name *Mother*. The woman held out the leather book now for Clo to take.

"What did you do?" Clo snatched the book out of the old woman's hands. "How could you? My father's work..."

The old woman shook the paper at Clo, then tucked it into her bodice. "*Ym rethguad.*" She patted at the hidden page.

"That's my mother. I think...I think it's my mother. My father's drawing. *My mother.* Give it back. It's all I–"

The woman stretched her knobby fingers toward Clo but made no motion to return the drawing. *"O, rethguaddnarg..."* Her fingers landed lightly on Clo's shoulder.

"No!" Clo stepped away. "No! You've taken something from me. Something important. It wasn't yours to take." Her voice quivered; her eyes felt hot. After the bitter disappointment of *no boat*, after the endless gloom of sea and sky that never changed from gray, this loss was too much. "And I don't know who you are, or what I'm doing here, and I don't know when my father will come, or if he'll come, but that drawing wasn't yours. Isn't yours." Her voice hiccuped into a sob. "Give it back. Give it back!"

The old woman's face, its gentle folds, turned gradually severe as Clo spoke. She jutted her chin and pointed her finger, first at her bodice where she had tucked the paper, then at Clo. She jabbed and jabbed again, speaking haltingly but carefully a single measured word.

"Mm...mi–mine." *Jab.* The woman's finger pushed against Clo's breastbone. Swaying against the force, Clo stepped back in surprise.

"Mm-mine," the woman repeated.

Jab.

Jab.

Jab.

Clo backed first into the piggish cat, which snarled and scratched at her, then into a chair, which toppled behind her, then into the table, which finally blocked her way.

"M-mine." The woman put her hands on Clo's shoulders.

As the fingers gripped her bones, Clo understood the deep truth of the word. Somehow, in some way, she, Clo, wall-jumper, turnip-eater, water-watcher, belonged to this woman.

"Mine."

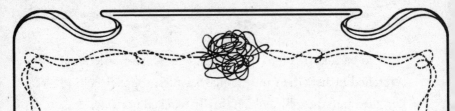

DESCRIBING A DESCENT

THE DAYS THAT PASSED, IF THEY COULD BE CALLED DAYS— after the woman had jabbed at Clo and called her *mine*— came to have their own routine. Clo would eat a bite of turnip and a hunk of cheese, then, when the last of the turnips were gone, just a hunk of cheese. She would watch out the window for boats. She would walk down the cliff and stand on the beach and watch for a boat. She would return. She would accept a mug of water from the old woman; she would catch the fish scales with her tongue. She would push the piggish cat from her bed. She would sleep. She would wake. She would eat a bite of cheese. She would watch again for a boat.

There were certain things that were *always*. Always the pebbly shore. Its gray sky. Its empty sea. Its stony tidesman.

Always gray. Always empty. Always still. But there were other things that were *often*, and still others that were only *sometimes*. Sometimes the little woman would bustle around the coals, stirring her shimmering stew. Often she was in her own room, muttering and thumping behind a locked door. Sometimes she would jabber at Clo and try to press a basket of fish or a bowl of the cold-smelling soup into her hands. Often she merely shook her head and let Clo come and go at will. Sometimes the old woman would pull a gem—a ruby or an emerald or a pearl—off the painting she had rehung on the wall and toss it to the cat to play with. Often the cat, overcome by its own gluttony, would swallow the gem and lie on its side, *rowl*ing piteously. Sometimes the boat Clo came to know as the fishing boat rounded the rocks beneath her window. Often only the waves lisped against the cliffs. Sometimes the vellum-skin man would come with a basket of fish and and sit slurping his meal at the table. Often no one knocked at the door at all. Sometimes the street would fill with the aged, murmuring villagers, pushing barrows and lugging baskets filled with fish and sea coal; often, only Clo's footsteps echoed along the cobblestones.

Sometimes Clo was reconciled to the uncertainty of her life on the island. To the absence of her father. To the necessity of waiting for the boat that would surely come. Most often she was not.

Sometimes Clo walked to the pebbly shore alone. But sometimes Cary joined her—a mostly quiet but still comforting companion. A comfortable companion. He would sit behind her, humming soft little tunes or playing on his broken flute as she *plipp*ed handfuls of pebbles into the water. And because she was often unreconciled, often unhappy, sometimes even on the edge of despair, she found herself hoping—and hoping more and more earnestly—that she would see his moon-cheeked face peering at her from behind the rocks or hear his stuttering call, *O-o–C-Clo!*

She had not, now, seen him for several days—or what she had come to think of as days, the time between sleeping and sleeping.

She had tried looking for him, walking up and down the empty village street, but all the doors were closed, all the windows dark. Occasionally, she saw a lumpish figure peering at her from behind the glass, but none of them was Cary, and no one came to speak to her. She could find no other alley or passage or even corner where Cary might have gone: the street was blind, the cliff path the only exit.

Finally giving up, she had spent what she might have called the entire morning—if there were times such as mornings here—picking her way up and down the cliff, looking to see if she had missed another set of stairs branching away, another track cut into the rocks, a path leading anywhere

else on the island...*another harbor, another village, anywhere,* but no. Though she clambered onto every ledge and rock she saw, she found no other route: the stairs led nowhere but the beach; they rose nowhere but the town. The island wall was too sheer to traverse.

"Where is the port?" she muttered as she climbed. "Where is the harbor?" she murmured as she descended. She slapped the soles of her boots against the rocks with each word. "And where did you go?" she added under her breath, thinking of the blue-cheeked boy. *There must be more to the island,* she thought. *There has to be.*

At last, though, as she picked her way up the cliff yet again, she heard a familiar trill echoing against the stones: Cary's flute. Steps quickening, she followed the sound until she caught sight of him perched on a rock, swinging his feet, waiting for her.

"Cary!" Despite the relief she felt on seeing him—relief she did not want to admit, even to herself—she spoke to him with anger that surprised even her. "Where have you been? Why haven't I seen you in all these days...in all this... *time*? Where do you go? Why do you keep disappearing?"

Cary's smile faded in the heat of Clo's words. He lowered his eyes and the hand he had raised in greeting. He tucked his flute into his pocket. "M—...I'm y-y—...s-sorry. I...th-th-thought you w—...we—...knew."

"Knew what?" By now, Clo understood that the more agitated Cary felt, the worse his speech became, and behind her anger, she felt the forming of guilt, but still she glared at him.

"I p-ple—...h-help with the g-gn—...f-fishing b-boat, n-n...wh-when it sem—...c-comes in."

"And when is that, Cary? When do the fishermen come in? What day? Monday mornings? Thursday afternoons? On the full moon? When?"

Cary's mouth sputtered emptily. His shoulders slumped.

"And when does the boat leave? When does it set out?" Clo felt all the uncertainty and frustration she had carried since arriving on the island bubbling up and spilling onto poor, wide-eyed Cary, but she could not stop herself. "I see the boat sometimes...and then I don't. I see the fish! Oh yes, I see *plenty* of fish! Always fish! Endless fish! Pots and barrows and baskets of fish! *But where's the boat?* Where does it go? Where do you go? Why are you here"—she pushed him lightly—"and then not? *Not here.*"

The sound *nnn* had become stuck in Cary's mouth. He huffed his lips and tongue around it but could get nothing out.

Crossing her arms, Clo turned away. Far below, she could see the tidesman, standing as still as he always did, staring at the sea and sky, as empty and gray as they always were. "He's always there," she muttered. "Always. Always. *Always.* But you...just sometimes. You're a *sometimes.*"

"Nnnn–Clo!" The word exploded beside her.

Cary, his cheeks two sunken moons, held out his palms helplessly. "I'm y–...sorry," he said at last. "I know you're gn–...hoping your father...I know how hard..." He trailed off, then added, "I waited for my r–...father for a long time, too. I remember waiting for him to come, and he didn't. I was alone...and no one de–...helped–"

Clo glanced at the boy. He was gazing at his feet, his lashes a dark fan against his cheeks. She did not like seeing how distressed he became as he told her how alone he had been. She did not like hearing how long he had waited...or that his father had never come. She did not want to consider that his fate might be her own–that a boat carrying her father might never arrive. *But if it doesn't come?* she thought. *If it doesn't come? What then?*

"Can you show me?" Clo said, struck suddenly with an idea. "Can you show me the fishing boat? Do you know where it is?"

"I..." Cary hesitated. "I don't think I'm de–...supposed to. I don't think they will let–"

"Please, Cary. If I see where the boat is kept, maybe I can see where other boats come in...or learn where it goes." *Or learn how to leave the island,* she thought. If her father did not come, she would have to leave to find him.

"I don't know....The ne–...fishermen would be angry if they saw...."

"Please." A note of desperation crept into her voice. "You said no one helped you. But this could help me."

Cary rubbed his brow, considering. "Well...there might...yes, I k–...think that could...yes..." He nodded, still unsure but pleased with himself. His chin dimpled with satisfaction. "Yes. Come with me." He took Clo by the arm, pulling her back toward the town.

"Shouldn't we be going to the water?"

"Yes," Cary said, still leading them up the path.

When they reached the opening in the cliff that marked the village entrance, he paused. He dropped Clo's hand. He put his finger to his lips. "Shh." He closed his eyes, listening, then, apparently satisfied, pointed. "T–...W-wait here." He put his finger to his lips again before descending into the gap and stepping out of sight.

Settling herself against the rocks, Clo listened as Cary's footsteps grew distant. Then faintly, a door creaked...then silence. And more silence. The island was almost always silent. So little wind–nothing, really, to even make a noise; even the line of waves was too distant for its roaring to carry. The water that edged the island made only the gentlest lapping noise, a cat licking its paws, a sound that carried no farther than the shore.

It took a long time for Cary's footsteps to return, but when they did, they were stumbling and rushed. Clo heard his ragged breath before she saw him–a figure struggling under a web of heavy nets.

Entangled, Cary tripped and tripped again, and as he reached her, he threw his nets down in clear frustration.

"N–...o-on," he panted, and tapped his shoulder. "I ev–...h-have to carry you." Seeing Clo's eyes widen, he waved his arm as though to pull her toward him. "They can't see you. Y–...qu-quickly. If you want to see the boat, we dl–...sh-should go now, while the villagers are resting in their homes."

Clo looked skeptically over her wheezing companion, whose moony cheeks were lit with damp, but when he patted his shoulder more emphatically, she climbed gingerly up. She felt him steady himself under her piggybacked weight.

"Now the st–...nets." He reached and began pulling the nets up and over his back and Clo. "You must stay hidden. I don't wo–...know what they would do if they saw you at the boat."

Clo tugged the nets over her. The ropes and knots weighed heavily. Though she gathered the folds up as best she could to keep them away from Cary's feet, she could feel him already struggling to stand upright.

"It's too much weight," she said.

Cary was resolute. "I can carry you."

"I don't...I don't think this is a good idea. I don't want to hurt you."

"Shh," he said, beginning to walk toward the town. "Y–...St-stay quiet."

He lurched through the gap and down the street—a jerky *step-pause-step-pause* motion that threatened to turn to outright stumbling and falling at any moment. Nearing the end of the lane, he turned to one of the smaller structures. "Shh," he cautioned again as they approached the door.

It opened at his knock.

Through the veil of nets, Clo could see one of the town's crookbacked citizens. The lines across his anvil-shaped forehead lifted in surprise.

"*Yob...? Os ylrae?*" came the muffled voice.

Cary's head bobbed. "Mmh-mmm."

"*Retne...*" The man stood aside.

Under the nets, in the dim light, Clo could see almost nothing at first, but then she realized there was nothing to see: they were surrounded by stone. Ahead of them stretched a tunnel of darkness. Around her, only the sensation of damp and cold, a mineral smell.

"*Nretnal?*" grunted the voice behind them.

"*On.*" Cary shook his head and walked forward, bumping against the walls.

"*Llew, uoy wonk eht yaw...*" A grunty laugh.

As they moved away from the man and entered the tunnel, Cary's gait grew more erratic; he swayed and lurched and gasped with each step. Clo realized with alarm that they were descending stairs. Every step felt like they were

falling, plummeting forward into the darkness. Without meaning to, she gripped Cary more tightly, and he made a strangled gargling noise under her arms.

"T–…N-not so t-tight."

Clo moved her hands away from Cary's neck and sank her fingers into his shoulders. Cary continued his unsteady descent, thumping first against one wall, then the other.

"Only the fishermen come here," he whispered. "No one de–…showed me until I had been here"–he huffed and panted–"very long…Se–…Ages."

"Doesn't everyone here fish?"

Cary shook his head. "Most. But some only collect sea coal for the se–…f-fires. Some only repair things–like baskets and swo–…barrows and nets. Everyone has a k–…task." His words came with difficulty. Beneath her, Clo could feel his legs shaking.

"Put me down," she said into his ear.

"En–…someone might see."

Shake. Step. Gasp. Lurch. The farther they descended, the stiller the air became: Clo could almost taste it, damp metal on her tongue. But then, she was sure she felt it, a light breath, a stirring, and with it, a few steps later, the darkness lifting.

On the last few steps, a figure entered the stairwell. Cary clenched Clo's legs.

In the half-light, through the lines of the nets, Clo saw the vellum-skin man standing with a lantern and rope dangling from his hands.

"*Yob.*"

The man moved up the stairs, lifting his lantern at Cary. "*Sten os ylrae? Lla deriaper?*"

"*Sey,*" Cary murmured. He halted, pressing his back against the wall. Clo squeezed his shoulders in complaint.

The man fingered the nets. Clo held her breath, trying not to move. The man paused, peering at the knots, then held his lantern high, his eyes traveling up and over the net-covered boy. Clo could see the translucent skin that stretched over his nostrils quivering as he sniffed. She regretted now having asked Cary to show her the boat. She did not know what the parchment-skin man's anger looked like, but she knew she did not want Cary to have to face it because of her.

"*Doog,*" the man said at last. "*Ylrae. Doog.*"

Clo felt Cary exhale beneath her. For a moment, he waited as the man moved beyond them and up the stairs, the lantern sending shadows careening against the walls. Then Cary rushed down the remaining steps—*gasplurchshakestep*—practically falling, until they came to the end.

Bursting into the chamber, dropping Clo and the nets into a bundle on the floor, Cary collapsed in a gasping heap.

IN WHICH A STONE STANDS IN PLACE OF A FISH

U NDER THE VEIL OF NETS, CLO COULD SEE ONLY CARY'S cheeks ballooning and deflating with each heavy breath. The stone beneath her was damp and cold, and she squirmed in discomfort. Cary pressed his hand against her netted form.

"Shh. Ti–...wa-wait," he whispered. He stood, resting his hands on his knees, still breathing heavily, then rising tall. He looked around. "*Oollah!*" he called. His voice echoed *oollah, oollah, oollah*.

Silence.

"Er–...We-we're alone." He lifted some of the nets off Clo. "You don't need to hi-hide."

Clo, working to free herself, at first noticed nothing but the tangle of knots that had wrapped around her legs. But

when she at last looked up, she gasped, scrabbling back-ward. A wooden giantess, clutching two wretched wooden babes—naked angry boys—bobbed up and down over Cary's shoulder.

The boat! she realized after a moment's disorientation. It *was* the boat, the ship she had seen from her window. The woman hanging over her was its artful figurehead. She reached a hand toward the giantess but succeeded only in touching the dangling toe of one of the sour-faced babes.

The carving adorned an otherwise austere long, slim vessel with a single mast and a row of holes along its side. It was docked and resting...Clo glanced around. *Where were they?* Here, there was just a narrow path of water—hardly wider than the boat. Above them, the rock walls rose dark and straight and sheer; beyond, following the path of the water, Clo could just see gray light opening up. A cavern, a crack in the island. Yes, that was all it was.

Cary, bundling the nets onto his back again, nodded at Clo. "See...y-you see? Yl–...Only the fishing boat. Noth-ing else. No other boats."

As the boat bobbed there, gently, almost imperceptibly rising and falling, its sides showed the scuffs and scratches it had received tethered in its rocky port. Clo stared at these marks, listening to the pinched noise of wood rubbing against rock. *No boat, no boat,* it seemed to squeak, and Clo

knew this was true: no other boat could navigate here...or even likely find this narrow inlet.

Walking to the front of the cavern, she peered out, finding nothing but the same wide, empty expanse that greeted her on the other side of the island. Nothing but gray sky and gray water on and on and on. She leaned as far around the opening as she could and saw only the sheer walls of the cliff and deep water below. Her heart sank. *No other port. No other boat. Nowhere to go.*

Clo turned, pretending to examine the toe of one of the wailing wooden infants to hide her disappointment. "Where does this boat go?"

"I t–...don't know."

"Don't you sail on it? Don't you help the fishermen?"

"Never. Only here. With nets. I help repair them. And with the h–...c-catch–I help unload it. But I am gn–... tr-training to be a net boy. When I'm a net boy, then I'll go on the boat."

"Net boy?"

Cary smiled—perhaps the widest smile Clo had ever seen on the damp-haired boy. "Yes!" His head gave a happy wobble. "Yes! Em–...come see!" Nets still bundled in his arms, he hurried around the boat, walking quickly along the lip of rock that edged the water. Clo followed.

The rocks on the other side of the boat were crowded

with fishing paraphernalia: nets and baskets and oars and rods were stacked in neat piles by the vessel. Lowering his own armful, Cary searched through a stack of rods and removed one with a wide mesh basket on its end. He held it up triumphantly.

"This is mine." He twirled it through the air. "I'm g–... le-learning to use it. The ne–...fishermen say I am nearly ready to join them."

Cary *swoosh*ed the net above Clo's head. She watched his maneuvers skeptically.

"Is there very much to learn?" she asked at last. "Isn't it...really, I mean, as easy as"–she pointed to the water in front of the boat–"net in water, fish in net, net out of water?"

Cary halted his acrobatics, his smile fading. "No." He looked hurt. "No. Fish are heavy and hard to lift. And boats are hard to ec–...ba-balance on. And water...it st–...di-distorts things. Nothing is where you think it is. The others, they've always fished. But I haven't. They say I am the first they've ever taught. I must study if I want to n–...j-join them."

"What do you mean *always*? They must have learned, too," Clo said, but Cary, sorting through one of the piles, shook his head.

"*Always*," he said again. Turning, he handed Clo a pole and net. "Here." He knelt and lifted a large rock. Moving

to the front of the boat, he raised the rock above the water. "N–...c-can you catch this?"

Clo nodded. "I think so." Net raised, she took a spot beside Cary.

"Ready?"

At Clo's nod, Cary dropped the rock, its splash echoing through the cave. Swooping with the basket after the stone spinning through the dark water, Clo felt an unexpected drag as the mesh went under. Even so, pulling hard, she thought she had moved the net under its path. When she lifted her pole, though, she had caught nothing.

Cary took the net from her and handed her another large stone in return. "N-now you."

Clo tossed the rock. Cary stood a long moment, watching it pirouette through the darkness. Then, when it had fallen almost entirely out of sight, his net flashed, struck, returned with the dripping stone. He held it above the water, the pole curving under the weight, and expertly flicked the stone behind them. It clattered to the floor.

Clo nodded. "You *are* good." In truth, she wasn't sure how much skill he had demonstrated, but Cary blushed at her praise and looked pleased. She did not think she had ever seen his cheeks so bright and round: she liked seeing him this happy.

"I've de–...p-practiced a long time. A very long time. I

like to see how many I can catch at once—how heavy I can make the net. Or how deep I can let the stone fall before I catch it. I like to come here"—he tossed another rock in the water—"when I've f-finished my net repairs. When the fishermen aren't here...it's te−...qu-quiet."

The whole island is quiet, Clo thought, but she felt she understood. "My garden is quiet," she said. "When I've had a garden. At least, it seems that way. There's weeds and rocks and the soil is hard, but other voices, the townspeople, they don't seem so loud there."

"Garden...," Cary mused. "I don't...I don't kn−... th-think I remember gardens."

Clo watched Cary snap another rescued rock over his shoulder. "Did you ever fish"—she hesitated, not sure how to say the next word—"*before?*"

Cary's moons drooped so that Clo regretted asking. Still, he tried to answer.

"I remember, I *seem to* remember a little, *before*...I think I used to fish *before*...with my re−...fa-father. I think I remember...an ocean...and maybe sk−...h-hooks. I think I remember...lines and hooks and pulling up fish one at a time." Cary swooped to catch another rock from the deep. "The net is harder, I think."

"My father can catch fish with his bare hands," Clo offered.

"He can?"

"Yes. Sometimes, when we're traveling, if we pass a stream, he'll lie on his belly on the bank and hold his hands in the water until he feels a fish tickle his fingers. And then he'll grab it, like this"—Clo made a grabbing motion—"and bring it up, and we'll scale it and gut it and roast it on a spit over the fire."

"You traveled with your father?"

"All over." Clo nodded. "From village to village to village. We never stay long. My father...he cleans things. And sometimes"—Clo hesitated—"sometimes he steals things." Cheeks burning, she glanced at Cary, but if he was surprised or appalled, he did not show it. "Just food, usually. And sometimes...paintings. I think...I think he used to be an artist," she added after a moment. "But...something happened." She shook her head. "He's not an artist any longer."

"Traveling." Cary sighed and spun his net. "You must ev–...ha-have met so many people."

"Well..." Clo paused, realizing her answer would sound strange. "Not people, no. My father...he feels it is safer to keep a bit...*apart*. To not tempt fate. And he...he does not look well, so people...they keep apart from us, too..." Clo trailed off, surprised at her own last words. *This was true.* Had she known this? Had she ever admitted this to herself?

Cary's eyes widened. "Still, traveling, you must have seen so many things. You must have so many memories. I wish I had memories like these."

"Yes, memories." Clo heard her own voice beginning to tremble. "Traveling." Closing her eyes, she could see her father tramping beside her through dew-soaked fields and pine-dry forests. She could sense his swaying step beside her own. She could see him sitting next to her, warming their dinner over a fire as the sun sank behind the trees. She could hear his voice—*Once, Clo, there was a spider who longed to have wings like a moth*—telling stories as the stars came out one by one in the darkening sky and the nightjar churred and trilled in the shadows.

Her chest felt hot. The boat squeaked again against the rocks, *No boat, no boat.*

"You must miss him," Cary said, watching her.

"Mm." Looking away, Clo rubbed her palm over her eyes, then gestured to the net to change the subject. "Why don't you"—she cleared her throat—"why don't you practice with fish?"

"Dead fish?"

"Live fish."

"Da–...in-instead of rocks?"

Clo nodded. "Here, even. There must be fish in the water here, by the boat. Or at the shore by the tidesman. They don't just fall or hang like dead weight; they swim, they flop about."

"N-no fish." Cary returned his pole to its pile.

"They don't allow you to practice with fish?"

"There are no fish."

Clo laughed, a small surprised *ha!*, but Cary didn't laugh with her.

She gaped at him. "No fish? That's all there is here! That's the only thing there is here! There's fish enough for all the world here! Everywhere I look—baskets and barrows and cauldrons of fish!"

"No." Cary shook his head. "To—…n-not here. Think. In all the time ev—…y-you've sat on the shore, have you ever seen a fi-fish?"

"But…," Clo trailed off, considering. It was true. In all the hours she had spent staring at the water, never had she seen a fish.

She thought of how her father caught fish *barehanded*, how on their journeys, they would hear the fish in the water slapping their fins or see them leaping briefly out of their silver pools. How even she, Clo, infrequent and reluctant bather, sitting in the edge of a shallow pool, would find her toes nibbled by little minnows or her legs tickled by the brush of larger fins.

Fish were not usually so hard to see. She lay down on her stomach, staring into the watery pass. *There should be some movement. Some flash. Some life.*

The water was clear. She could see, far, far below, the rocks that shaped the bottom.

The water was dark and empty.

Beside her, the boat, with its wooden figurehead and mewling wooden babes, rose and fell, a gentle squeaking.

No boat, no boat, said the boat against the rocks that hemmed it in.

No fish, no fish, whispered the rocks that rubbed against the boat.

"Where are all the fish?" She turned to Cary. "They fill baskets and barrows and cauldrons full of fish—where are the fish?"

Cary's mouth opened and closed, an empty gulping that plainly said, *I don't know, I don't know.* "T—...N-not here," he said at last.

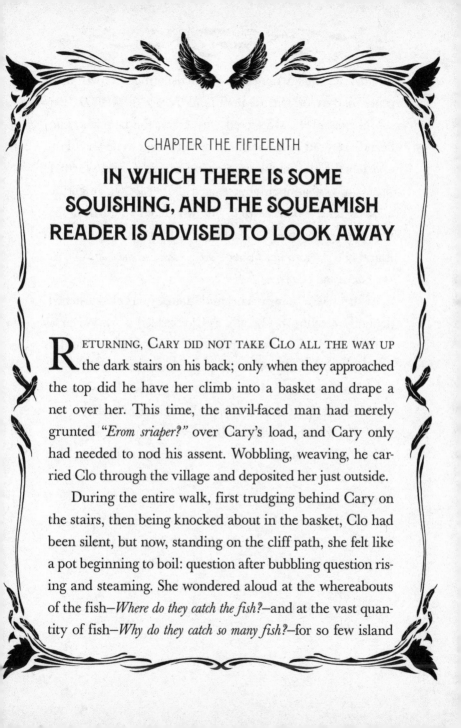

IN WHICH THERE IS SOME SQUISHING, AND THE SQUEAMISH READER IS ADVISED TO LOOK AWAY

RETURNING, CARY DID NOT TAKE CLO ALL THE WAY UP the dark stairs on his back; only when they approached the top did he have her climb into a basket and drape a net over her. This time, the anvil-faced man had merely grunted *"Erom sriaper?"* over Cary's load, and Cary only had needed to nod his assent. Wobbling, weaving, he carried Clo through the village and deposited her just outside.

During the entire walk, first trudging behind Cary on the stairs, then being knocked about in the basket, Clo had been silent, but now, standing on the cliff path, she felt like a pot beginning to boil: question after bubbling question rising and steaming. She wondered aloud at the whereabouts of the fish—*Where do they catch the fish?*—and at the vast quantity of fish—*Why do they catch so many fish?*—for so few island

inhabitants. She wondered if the fishermen traded with other islands or with a mainland—*Is there a port? Do they sell their catch?* She wondered why Cary, the boy who had been fished out of the sea, had been trained to be a net boy and whether he might soon go on the boat, and whether she, Clo, wall-jumper, cheese-eater, father-seeker, might be allowed on the boat as well. She wondered whether, if she was allowed on the boat, she might find her way off this island and back to her father—*Can we leave on the boat? Can we leave the island? Can we LEAVE?*

Cary, with damp hair and damper cheeks, listened patiently, catching his breath, as Clo burbled away. When at last she finished, he shook his head, seeing at once that, for Clo, there was really only one question that mattered.

"Clo, I'm sorry. I don't know…I don't know er—… wh-where the boat goes or where the fish are or if they ll—… sell fish somewhere else.…They don't tell me these things. They don't say much to me at all—that's not how they are. But I know they will re—…n-never, never allow you on the boat. You are not a fisherman."

Clo felt suddenly as though the sun that never shone through the island's perpetually gray skies must somehow be inside her, so inflamed was she at the notion that *she could not go on the boat*, though she had, in truth, no desire to ever, *ever* spend her days as a fisherman and only wanted

the opportunity to go on the boat and find her way off the island and to her father again.

"I can't go on the boat *because I'm not a fisherman*?"

Cary shrank under her gaze. "No. You t–…c-can't. They say you're not."

"They say I'm not? Who says I'm not?"

"The other fishermen."

"I can learn as well as you. I'm as strong as you. I can train just like you to go on the boat."

"No–"

"I've jumped over walls and walked over mountains and found my way through forests and swamps, but I can't go on the boat because I'm not a fisherman?"

"No, you–" Cary began, but Clo, her face hardening, had turned away from him and begun striding back toward the village.

"Clo!" Cary hurried after her, pulling the basket behind him. "Clo! *I* think you can. I kn–…th-think you're stronger and smarter than I am. You're better than a f-fisherman. But they say…Clo! Clo!"

Clo had reached the doorway to the old woman's house. At the far end of the street, Cary was still calling after her.

"Clo! The fish–*all the fish*–they're all for you! Everything, everything on the d–…i-island is for you! Is done for you! For you and the–"

Clo pulled the door shut on his echoing words. *She couldn't go on the boat? She couldn't leave the island? The fish—the mounds and baskets and buckets of fish—were for her?*

Inside, the apple-faced woman was, as usual, standing near the coals, stirring her always-simmering pot of soup. *Of course.* Of course the woman was stirring her fish. Fish, always, always fish.

Hearing Clo enter, the woman smiled, ladled a bowl, and held it out to her.

"No." Clo shook her head.

"Sey." Still smiling.

"No."

"Sey." The bowl again, but without a smile.

"No!" Clo nudged the woman's hand away.

"Sey!" The bowl in front of Clo's lips.

"No! I don't want it!" Clo knocked the bowl away, a violent push. It flew from the woman's hand, falling, clattering, the liquid rising in a silver arc across the room, the cat springing into action and crouching, growling, over the spill, licking up the puddles and sucking up the fishy pieces in quick greed.

"I don't want any fish. No fish!" Clo stared defiantly at the old woman, who had bent to retrieve the bowl.

But when the woman rose, the lines on her apple face twisted with anger, Clo knew she had gone too far.

144

"Uoy!" the woman bellowed. *"Tis!"* Taking Clo by the shoulders, she pushed her into a chair. *"Tis, lufetargnu dlihc!"*

Clo sat, expecting the bowl of fish stew to appear again in front of her, to perhaps be fed spoon by dreaded spoon as an unhappy baby is fed by its parent. But the woman tossed the bowl aside.

"Eht gnidrac." She yanked a large basket of fish next to Clo's chair. *"Ruoy krow."*

Clo stared at the glittering heap of silver fish, all still and staring at her with their black eyes. Glancing at the old woman, she knew refusal would invite greater fury.

"Should I scale them? Gut them?" This she knew how to do. Picking up a knife from the table and a fish from the basket, she ran the blade down the center of the fish, tail to head, opening it up to reveal its innards.

"On, on, on!" the woman cried, removing the knife from Clo's hand. *"Eht gnidrac."* She thrust two spike-riddled wooden paddles at Clo.

Clo looked from the fish to the paddles to the old woman in confusion. The flat wood paddles with tiny burrlike spikes, Clo knew, were meant for sheep's wool, for cleaning and combing fiber, for carding it, untangling it, readying it for spinning. Though she had never had a mother to teach her how to work with wool—never known the cloudlike woman her father had sketched *spinning for*

Clothilde, who could have taught her these things—she had seen countless villagers, settled in sunny doorways, wiping such paddles across each other, pulling pale tufts of fiber into finer and finer wisps.

She held the paddles up. "Carding combs?"

The woman clicked her tongue and took Clo's hands in her own. *"Ruoy krow."* Guiding the paddle in Clo's hand into the basket, she scooped and raised a clump of fish. The silver bodies rested lightly on the spikes.

"Oh—" Clo, motherless Clo, who had learned from her father to skin and debone and gut all manner of small game he captured on their journeys, who had herself never flinched when readying any part of an animal for eating— not tongue nor brain nor bowel—who was not delicate or squeamish or under any illusions about the innards of creatures, still found the thought of raking the fish through the combs entirely too much.

"Oh," she said again, and shut her eyes as the woman guided the paddles together. She felt the combs pull through the fish. A thick and squelchy tearing. The combs swiped again, again, the sound wet, squishy. Again.

"Ruoy krow," the woman repeated, still manipulating Clo's hands, the steady combing growing lighter, softer, drier. Then a pause, a swiping back. The woman took the paddles from Clo's hands.

Eyes still closed, Clo felt the woman place something

soft in her hands. "*Llor,*" she said, pinching Clo's fingers around the soft thing.

Clo opened her eyes. In her hands was a puff of wool–or something *wool-like*–airy, silvery, fine. Except for the color, the same gleam of fish scales, there was nothing fish-like about it.

"*Llor.*" Guiding Clo's hands, the woman showed her how to roll the fish-wool, and when it was curled into a cylinder, she placed it on the table. Lying there, an oval tube of wool, it looked again like fish, at least the shape of fish, eyeless, finless, gill-less.

The woman nodded approvingly at the cylinder. "*Ereht.*"

Though not damp, there was still an oiliness about the fish-wool. A stickiness. A smell. Not the lanolin smell of wool from sheep–the smell of earth and animal and light and green–nor even the humid smell of fish–the smell of pond and mud or salt and sea. This was a prickling smell, like darkness. Like sour milk. It felt cold and burning on her skin. Clo rubbed her palms back and forth across her tunic, trying to clean away the film.

The woman pointed at Clo, then at the basket. "*Lla fo ti.*" She pointed again more emphatically, and Clo understood her to mean she was to comb all these fish, the entire basket of fish, turn them all into airy cylinders of fish-wool.

"I don't want any fish," Clo said quietly, shaking her head. *Is this what Cary had meant when he had said all the fish were*

for her? She stood, still trying to rub her hands clean. "I don't want to do this."

Putting her hands on Clo's shoulders, the woman pushed Clo back into her seat. *"Ruoy krow, rethguaddnarg."* She pointed at the paddles, and then, reaching into her apron pocket, removed a long iron key. Lifting it for Clo to see, she crossed to the front door, locked it with a heavy *thunk*, and dropped the key deep into her apron pocket.

Clo stared in horror.

"Ruoy krow, rethguaddnarg." The words had become a refrain. The woman patted her pocket, pointed to the carding combs. *"Krow."*

Clo picked up the paddles. The woman smiled. It was not a smile at Clo. It was not a smile *for* Clo. The woman smiled to herself, the smile of long hours of work being suddenly lifted away. She chewed emptily.

"Sey, sey, rethguaddnarg." She watched Clo scoop up a clump of fish, a little smile of relief still floating in the folds of her cheeks. *"Sey, sey."*

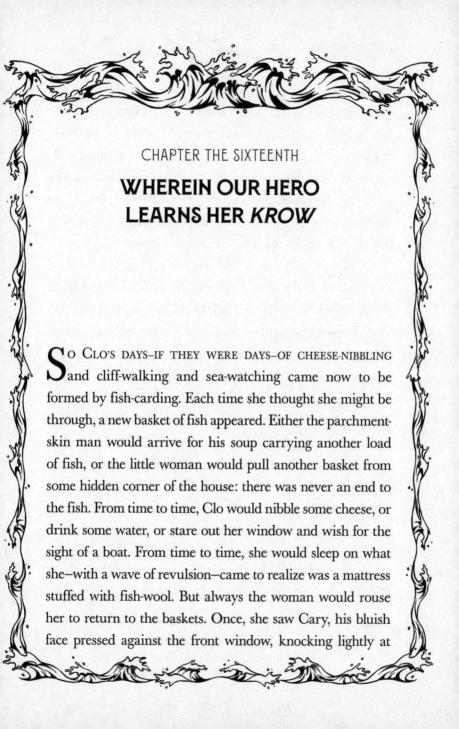

WHEREIN OUR HERO
LEARNS HER *KROW*

So Clo's days–if they were days–of cheese-nibbling and cliff-walking and sea-watching came now to be formed by fish-carding. Each time she thought she might be through, a new basket of fish appeared. Either the parchment-skin man would arrive for his soup carrying another load of fish, or the little woman would pull another basket from some hidden corner of the house: there was never an end to the fish. From time to time, Clo would nibble some cheese, or drink some water, or stare out her window and wish for the sight of a boat. From time to time, she would sleep on what she–with a wave of revulsion–came to realize was a mattress stuffed with fish-wool. But always the woman would rouse her to return to the baskets. Once, she saw Cary, his bluish face pressed against the front window, knocking lightly at

the glass and trying to catch her attention. But Clo turned away, pretending not to see. It was *he* who had said all the fish were for her. *He* who said she could not go on the boat. She felt he was to blame. At least, somewhat to blame. Partly to blame. *He should have warned me*, she thought. *He should have told me that I would be locked away with the never-ending fish.* When she thought of him, she scraped the paddles more fervently so that the fish ripped apart with ever greater squishing.

And so Clo combed and scraped and rolled, combed and scraped and rolled. Paddleful by paddleful, she lifted clumps of silver, black-eyed fish from the baskets; paddleful by paddleful, she combed the silver fish through the spikes, a grisly fleshy tearing that never ceased to turn her stomach; paddleful by paddleful, she saw the grisly, tattered flesh and spindly bones grow suddenly airy, light, woolly. She covered the table with clouds of silvery fish cylinders, while the fish oil seeped into her skin and coated her in a sour haze. She stared longingly at the locked door, which opened now only for the old man and his baskets of fish.

But as the hourless hours and dayless days passed and the fish-cylinder piles—stacked against the walls—grew higher and higher, the old woman looked more and more satisfied. And when Clo had at last lined all four walls of the front room floor to ceiling with rolled fish, the woman clapped her hands with childish delight. *"Doog!"* she cried before disappearing behind her own bedroom door.

She reappeared a moment later dragging a monstrous wheel behind her. Its feet squeaked across the stone as she pulled it toward Clo.

A spinning wheel.

Clo had seen such contraptions, of course, running under the hands of village women, but she had never used one herself.

The old woman, spreading her palms grandly before the machine, looked at Clo expectantly.

Clo stared back.

Sighing, the woman gestured to the fish-clouds. She lifted one of the cylinders and waved it over the wheel.

"Oh…" Clo understood. She was now meant to spin the carded fish into yarn. "No, I don't–"

"Sey, rethguaddnarg–"

"I don't know–"

"Won eht gninnips–"

"I don't know how!"

The old woman clucked her tongue. *"Uoy od."* Placing a fish-cylinder in Clo's hand, she tugged lightly on one end. It lengthened into a fluffy fishtail. She tucked the tail against a piece of string and, stepping on the treadle at the base, set the wheel spinning. The wool began to pull from Clo's hand, flying into yarn. The woman rocked her foot up and down, up and down, then gave Clo's ankle a small kick to join hers. When the motion fell under Clo's foot, the woman stepped away from the machine.

After the first few moments of stutter and stop and awkward pulling and bunching, Clo found a rhythm. Her foot tapped up and down, up and down: the wheel hummed, the spool spun around the spindle, the fish-wool flew into yarn, the yarn wound itself into ordered loops on the spool.

Clo marveled at the ease with which the wool slid through her fingers, felt it could have been sliding through her hands in this way for thousands of years. *Had she really never touched a spinning wheel before?* She watched it extend and slip, extend and slip, twist and wind, lengthening and transforming itself. It felt as though time itself were pulling through her fingers as the fish-cylinder coiled into yarn.

When at last all the wool in Clo's hands had been wound onto the machine, the woman reached over her shoulder. Removing the bobbin from the wheel, she unraveled an arm's length of the gray yarn to inspect—here, thick and ropy, there, thin and threadlike. She fingered the variations, tutting disapprovingly at them, but nodded anyway at Clo.

Her hand swept over the tower of fish-wool. *"Eht tser."* Dropping another carded roll into Clo's lap, she turned away.

Clo gazed with dismay at the piles. "Not all, surely."

"Lla," she said, opening the door to her own room. *"Lla eht tser,"* she said, closing it behind her.

And so Clo continued to spin. And her days (such as they were—or were not—in the time between sleep and sleep)

slipped through her fingers in the form of fish-wool. From time to time, the little woman would step from her room to fetch a newly spun bobbin, and she would cluck at the thickness of the yarn here, or the thinness of the yarn there, then shut herself away again. Sometimes, when all seemed still, when even the cat lay piggishly grunting by the coals, Clo would tiptoe to the front door to try the latch in vain. But no sooner would the latch rattle than the woman would bustle out in spluttering anger and push her back to her seat. *"Eht tser, eht tser!"*

Once she thought she heard a hesitant Cary-like knocking, and she sprang up, thinking she would see his moony face again in the glass—*but no:* the knocking was only the boarish cat batting a gem lethargically over the floor. Scowling, she sat again at her wheel. "Mutton-headed creature," she whispered, though she was not entirely sure whether she was berating herself or the cat. *She should not have turned away before.* She should have not pretended she had not seen him. Now he would not come again.

The yarn was all the same. All gray, colorless. Only sometimes, if Clo tilted her head *just so* and if the light from the coals fell upon it *just right*, could she see a bit of silver shimmer in the thread—the liveliness of a fish underwater. But mostly it was gray, the same flat gray as the sky and sea that surrounded the island. Only the thickness or thinness that Clo spun provided any variation.

Every spool Clo spun disappeared into the woman's apron pocket. Occasionally Clo wondered what the woman could possibly do with so much colorless thread in her chamber—a hushed shuffling, a constant soft *tap, tap, tap*-ping the only noise behind the door. But mostly, as the wool ran through her fingers, Clo wondered only how she might leave this room, this house, this island.

The fish-wool towers shrank slowly.

One day—or not-day—the woman emerged from her room and did not take Clo's newly spun bobbin. She watched Clo for a moment, nodded—"*Doog, retteb*"—and gestured at the remaining towers.

"*Eht tser,*" she said, removing the key from her pocket. She unlocked the front door.

Clo's heart leapt.

"*Lla fo ti.*" The woman pointed again at the towers, then to Clo. She stepped into the street.

Something about this motion unnerved Clo. She saw the woman framed in the light of the doorway, a small, shriveled figure, arranging a shawl over her head, settling a basket over one arm. The cat, lounging as close to the coals as the heat allowed, caught sight of its mistress leaving and streaked toward her skirts.

"*On, on, feihcsim.*" Pushing the cat away with her toe, she shut the door quickly behind her. The lock turned with a dreadful click. Through the window, Clo saw the woman

tie her shawl beneath her chin, and this gesture—the tightness of the knot, the firmness of the jaw—seemed full of satisfaction.

The cat yowled.

No, thought Clo. *She's never... she's never left before.*

The cat clawed the door, a pitiful guttural sound arising from its throat.

For a few moments, Clo sat in stunned silence, staring vaguely at the space the woman had left. Then, throwing her fish-wool aside, she raced to the door and pulled desperately at the handle. The latch rattled beneath her hands: the door was firmly bolted.

She looked at the front window. She could *break* it, break the panes and kick out the frames holding them. But when she looked through the glass, she could see that the street was filling with the hunched townspeople, pushing their barrels and carrying their baskets. She would be noticed.

Clo paced, crossing back and forth between her bedroom and the front room. By the door, the cat had worked itself into a snorting fit, and the wood was scored with its claw marks. Clo paused, watching it panic, recognizing her own desperation in its frenzy.

There was another door.

She looked over her shoulder. The woman's room.

Crossing to it, she put her hand on the latch and pushed: the door rocked against its lock. The noise startled the cat

out of its yowling, and it turned, bristling and hissing at Clo's attempt to open its mistress's door.

"Shh," she hissed back. "Stay away, piggy thing." She pushed again on the door, feeling the space around the lock. The movement felt loose, loose enough that it might give way.

Clo, lithe, boyish Clo, Clo of the cheese-nibbling and water-sipping, threw her insubstantial weight against it. The door rattled; the cat, hissing and snarling, crouched, ready to spring at her.

Clo swung her foot emptily toward the cat. "Get. Shoo." Rubbing her shoulder, she tried the door again. *Looser.*

She took a step back. "I'm going in," she told the cat, which was wriggling with its own anticipated attack. She eyed the door, then launched herself at it—leaping against its wood. She heard the *crack*, felt the pain in her shoulder as she fell backward from the impact, but standing, feeling her arm sore but functioning, she realized it was the door and not her bone that had given way.

She gave a small push. It swung open.

The cat, yowling, tore past her into the dark chamber.

Clo stepped inside.

At first, in the half-light, Clo saw nothing that would distinguish this room from her own. A low bed, a small table, a jug, a bowl, a shuttered window letting in thin lines of gray light. But as she crossed the room to open the shutters, she felt a movement on her left side. *A stirring. A soft swinging.*

Something moved when she moved, something responded to the changes she effected in the air.

She reached. Something soft moved under her hand. Gasping, she jumped forward, grabbing at the shutters, throwing them open.

Gray light filled the chamber. The soft thing she had touched was still moving, a gentle undulation. Clo blinked, trying to understand: it was as though the entire wall were moving. Rippling. The wall was rippling.

No. Clo's eyes adjusted. It was not the wall. Not the stones, though it was the same dull gray color as the stones.

The thing she had set in motion was suspended from a vast wooden frame that occupied the entire length of the room. Threads, hundreds upon hundreds, perhaps thousands upon thousands, of gray threads stretched up the frame, rising in taut lines nearly to the ceiling.

Clo stepped closer. Waist-height, the vertical threads were joined by gray yarn that had been woven into them; here and there, sharp bobbins dangled where the fabric was still being formed. Above them, another arc of gray thread looped toward the ceiling.

Clo picked up a bobbin. It was full of the yarn she had been spinning—the fish-wool yarn. The entire tapestry—for that was what it was—was nothing but gray fish-wool.

She felt the cat brush past her. Rising on its hind legs, it kneaded the tapestry, its claws catching and pulling at the

yarn. Clo could see where it had left its marks before: small runs or holes or pulls in the fabric were the only variation in the otherwise dull gray blanket.

Pulling aside the vertical threads, Clo looked behind the loom. Here, a mirror had been hung against the wall to reflect the front of the tapestry, the smooth side of the weaving, which should show some design. Some picture. Some *thing* the weaver would be trying to portray. But no—even from the front, nothing but the same flat gray.

Around the bottom beam of the loom, more masses of the tapestry had been rolled. Clo felt the rolls with her thumb. Layer after layer of woven gray fish-wool.

No color. No form. No decoration.

Next to her, the cat continued its kneading. *Pull—catch, pull—catch,* she could hear the ticks of its claws against the fabric.

Clo felt anger beginning to bubble in her, an uncomfortably hot feeling pushing against her chest.

The carding. The spinning. The endless stacks of fish-wool.

For this? For THIS?

Something inside Clo broke.

No.

She stared at the weaving, at the beastly cat pulling threads from the weaving, at the thousands upon thousands of flat gray strands that made up the weaving.

No.

She turned away.

Clo moved through the rooms slowly. The front window framed the sedate parade of barrow-pushers and basket-bearers. She could see the black-eyed silver fish spilling from their containers onto the cobblestones.

No.

She thought of the boat Cary had shown her, the boat that gathered all the fish, the boat that rested tucked into the innards of the island, the boat with its wooden woman and mewling babes, its piles of fishing nets and barrels, its fishing nets and barrels that could surely hide a spindle-shanked girl so used to staying in the shadows.

She had done this before.

She gathered her last crescent of cheese rind. Her father's notebook. The painting. His cloak. She tied the cloak over her shoulders and around her waist and tucked her few belongings into the folds at her back. She tugged at the knots of the cloak, pulling it even tighter.

Cheese-bearer. Wall-jumper.

From the fireplace, Clo took the long-handled poker the old woman used to stir the coals. She returned to her own room. She hesitated only a moment.

Window-breaker.

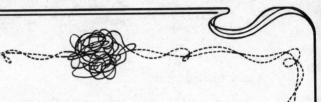

IN WHICH OUR HERO
REMEMBERS SHE CANNOT SWIM

H AVING KNOCKED AWAY THE REMAINING GLASS, THE shards falling with a bright crackle into the empty air, Clo leaned out her window as much as she dared. Far, far below, the water rocked against the cliff wall, and she felt herself grow faint with its motion, as though she were already falling into it. Breathing deeply, she forced herself to examine the cliff dropping away beneath her: it was steep, but not entirely smooth. Notches here and there, small fissures in the stone broke its expanse. Handholds. Footholds.

Could she?

Without giving herself a chance to reconsider, Clo lifted herself onto the ledge and swung out her body. Clinging to the window frame, tiny shards of glass pressing into her belly and

arms, she lowered herself out. She shivered against the coldness of the stone and the height of the drop below. Her arms burned against the weight they were being asked to hold. Trying to keep her eyes only on the stone around her and not on the water below, she scanned the wall for ledges, outcroppings, cracks. Any place to hold, to rest, any place for her fingers, toes.

There. And there.

Her feet found a fissure.

And there—a place to grab.

Another.

Another.

Slowly, slowly, slowly, Clo moved away from the window, down the cliff.

Step, grab. Step, grab.

She kept her eyes on the wall around her. A universe of rock.

Reach. Grab. Step. Hold.

Over and over.

Reach, grab, step, hold.

Over and over and over.

More than once, as she stepped into a small gap, the rock crumbled beneath her foot, and she felt herself begin to fall. She grabbed desperately; she clung to the rock, feet scrabbling for a hold. Then, rebalanced, she began again: reach, reach, reach.

Slowly, slowly, still not looking down, not looking up, aware only of the immensity of the cliff, Clo made her way. She felt her leggings, her tunic, her boots begin to fray and rip as they scraped against the rock. Far below, under her own ragged breaths, she could hear the gentle splash of the water. It grew steadily as she descended.

Reach.

Slosh.

Reach.

Slosh.

It was not a comforting sound. Clo had had no other thought but escaping the old woman and her fish-wool, no other thought but finding her way to the inlet, the cavern, the boat. She had not considered the water.

Cannot swim, splashed the water.

Cannot swim.

Cannot. Swim.

Body pressed against the rock, fingers hot against the stone, Clo thought of the morning this had all begun. How she had sat beneath the trees and waited for her father, how he had not come, how she had listened for the tower bells, how she had watched an emerald beetle climb into the leafy canopy overhead, how *leaf* and *green* and *father* now seemed so far away that a sob burst from her, echoed once against the cliff, and fell away.

Her fingers ached with holding. She ached with holding.

Reach.

Grab.

Step.

Hold.

Hold.

Hold.

Gray wall. Gray water.

Clo pressed her cheek against the stone.

There was nowhere to go.

She closed her eyes. Resting against the rock, she listened to her breath slowing. Her heart beat in time to the water that awaited her.

Little splashes, steady sloshings. *Cannot. Swim. Cannot. Swim.*

Then she heard it.

Something thrummed beneath the sibilant *slip* of water against rock. A cavernous sound, something vast and deep and rolling.

Clo craned her neck trying to see. Below, she could just begin to make out the faint ripples, gray wrinkles, that marked the soft movements of the water. The *slosh, slosh, slosh.* She looked back up at the face of the cliff, the monolith that towered over her, its height stark and silent. *No.* She listened again for the deeper sound.

Where was it?

It was gone.

As she leaned back into the cliff, the bass thrumming rose again to meet her. *There!* She pressed her ear against the rock. Yes, she could hear it, she could feel it; it was *in* the stones, *beneath* the stones. The cavern, she must be near it.

She cast about, looking for a way *into* the rock: there must be a way in.

She crept down, listening carefully for the heavier thrumming. She wondered if it was the echoing noise of the boat rubbing as it had before against the stones.

Reach.

Grab.

Step.

Hold.

Listen.

Reach.

Grab.

Step.

Hold.

Listen.

The sound grew louder. She was moving crablike now across the face of the cliff, sideways above the splashing lip of water. All at once, as she reached, looking for another place to hold, her hand touched empty air, air heavier and cooler than what surrounded her. She scuttled, scuttled again.

She had found the cavern opening.

IN WHICH OUR HERO DIES

CAREFULLY, CAREFULLY, CLO LOWERED HERSELF NEXT to the opening of the cavern. There, at the edge, she found a small lip of stone, just wide enough to stand on.

For a long while, she simply rested on this ledge gratefully, all the muscles in her arms and legs and hands shaking from the strain they had been asked to bear. Next to her, the deep thrumming sounded from the opening.

When she had at last caught her breath and felt she could again control her arms and legs, she pressed herself against the wall and began to edge herself into the opening.

Darkness. A colder, damper air.

The gray light over the ocean vanished as soon as it entered the gloom of the cave. She could see nothing, but she knew if she could maneuver deep enough into the

cavern, there would be room to walk. *And light, too*, she thought. *Before, there was light enough to see.* She thought of the boat rubbing against its stony mooring. She thought of how she would sneak onto the deck and hide herself away under a basket or barrel, how she would spring free the moment the boat made port somewhere. She thought of Cary, practicing with his net, tossing stones, catching stones.

Net boy.

She almost smiled.

In the darkness, beneath the gentle *slap-slap* of the water on the rocks, she heard the thrumming again. It did not sound like the boat scraping against the rocks.

It *felt* like music... was it music?

A deep and ancient humming.

Or something rolling. Spinning.

She made her way, shuffling into the deeper blackness, searching with her feet along the wet ledge. Where was the boat? Where were the baskets, the nets? Where was Cary, practicing with his rocks?

This was not, she began to realize, the cavern where the fishing boat was moored.

She clambered, groping in the dark, over a sharp tumble of stones. Hand on the wall, she felt her way farther into the darkness.

Where was she?

Just darkness. And cold. The slapping of waves against the walls.

And the music again. Droning.

And...

No, it could not be.

It was.

Blinding...suddenly...

beneath her.

Clo felt for the stones around her. *Was she standing? Falling?*

She could scarcely breathe. The droning. The turning.

It was...

light...

light and...

167

...Ah!

The universe had opened beneath her.

Stars, thousands upon thousands upon millions of stars, in the water below. Galaxies, their white arms open, spinning, burning. Lights sparking, gleaming, exploding, extinguishing, and clouds frothing and spilling out into the darkness, growing dim, glowing brighter, growing dim, glowing brighter, again and again and again. The whole brilliant cosmos, hemmed in by the rocks of the grotto now washed in milky light, groaned and hummed and turned, and the little waves lapped at the edges of the stones.

Clo pressed herself into the rocks behind her. She could not catch her breath.

It was beautiful. And terrible.

Beautiful.

How long she stood marveling, she could not say. Aeons were unfolding in the watery cosmos below. Above her, beside her, on the walls and ceiling of the cave, the stars flickered and cast their own shadows.

Mesmerized by the motion, the slow groaning revolution of the whole, the churning of its smaller forms, she knelt over the starry pool watching stars and galaxies flare into life, burn, and die away. She felt she herself might be

falling through this darkness and its unspooling threads of light. Pinpricks rose to the surface, glinted, sank again. A star burbled up right beneath her. Without thinking, she reached: her hand darted into the water—*Cold! Blistering cold!*—and she had it.

A star. A little orb of light.

It burned in her palm.

It was not a star.

Surprised, Clo grasped, but too late: it slipped through her fingers, flickered in the water, and was gone.

She grabbed again at the surface—*The cold! The cold!*—but now that she was trying, she could not catch one, and her motions roiled the water and the clouds of billowing light.

She sat back on her heels, forcing herself to wait. The stars rose, sparked, disappeared.

And there!

She had it.

Clo closed her palms around it, and the light glowed through her fingers.

It was wiggling, desperately flapping, trying to free itself.

It was a star.

It was not a star.

It was a fish.

Little silver black-eyed fish.

Fish!
Fish!
Fish!

Clo stared at the creature. Its black eyes stared back at her. It breathed erratically in her hand, its gills shivering open. Its scales shimmered with its own silver light and the light of the stars burning and flickering in the pool beneath it. Clo opened her palm.

The fish splashed into the water, a little orb of light once again, and sank, falling into the motion of the galaxies.

Cary's words came back to her. *The fish—all the fish—they're all for you!*

The cosmos turned and groaned in the grotto.

Fish-spinner?

Clo stood, dizzy.

Star-spinner?

With the noise of the universe spinning beneath her and the fearful roaring happening in her own mind, she almost did not hear the boat arriving. But over the din, she suddenly became aware of a regular splashing: sails down, oars out, the fishing boat was entering the grotto.

Half lit by stars, it rounded the corner into the chamber.

The vellum-skin man was standing in the prow. "*Sten tuo!*" he cried.

The boat was moving past her, almost close enough for her to touch. Clo pressed herself into the rocks, desperate not to be seen, but the fishermen on the deck were readying their long-poled nets. Eyes on the star-filled waters, they did not notice her in the shadows.

"*Ydaer sevlesruoy!*" the vellum-skin man called again.

The poles swung out over the edge of the boat.

"*Dna won!*" the man cried. The men swooped their nets into the grotto pool. The water roiled with the motion, and the cave echoed with splashing and the shouts of the fisher-men. Clo watched, mesmerized, as they lifted nets bulging and blazing with stars and tossed piles of silvery fish onto the deck of the ship. Over and over, the nets swooped and lifted light and flung and emptied fish.

"*Niaga!*" the vellum-skin man commanded from the prow, but Clo heard only "*Nia–*" before a net, sweeping down into the water, caught her and knocked her into the deep.

For a second, an instant underwater, Clo's hand grazed the rocks that marked the edge, and she grabbed frantically, thinking she could pull herself out. But she was dragged away…away and under…the water swept and closed over her.

She was sinking. Falling. Not breathing. *The cold, the cold!* The cold pressed into her bones, was as cold and white and hard as bones, and airless, airless, she was sinking,

falling...she flailed, still falling...stars, galaxies, gleaming clouds slipped past her...so far from her...she reached, flailed, still falling...airless...

Far, far above, stars flickered and spun and burned and dimmed. Far, far above, she saw the boat, its silhouette dark against the milky light. The nets and oars churned the surface, sweeping away the bright pinpoints.

She was still falling, now into darkness. Here it was dark and still and cold.

Perhaps her eyes were closed.

Perhaps she was sleeping.

So cold.

Quiet.

She breathed, gasping, without meaning to, and the cold–heavy and dark–rushed into her lungs.

She flailed, once, then grew still.

She was still falling.

Airless.

Heavy.

"Girly."

She heard it again.

"Girly."

Beneath her, somehow, was the bosun in his little dinghy. His oars stroked against the darkness. Coming up beside her, he leaned over the edge of the boat, his pebble mouth twisted in concern.

"Wellaway, girly, yer a half passage, you are. Half passage *only*. You shouldn't be here. Too far beyond. Get on wit' you." He prodded her with the oar, and she drifted away from him into the blackness.

The stars were very far away. Pinpricks. And so dim.

How tired she was.

Perhaps she should sleep.

Darkness. And nothingness.

Nothingness.

The body of Clo, turnip-picker, window-breaker, star-spinner, drifted in the void. She was a collection of limbs

and joints—skinny arms and legs and knees and elbows—floating at unnatural angles in the dark.

There was nothing left—nothing left that *was* Clo, Clo of the wall-jumping and forest-trekking and shadow-braving. She was full of the dark and the cold, full of the emptiness of the void.

The form of Clo drifted deeper into the darkness. In the distance, stars and galaxies spun quietly.

She was slipping into something like mist, something soft and indistinct, something like a smudge of chalk against the blackness. A pale cloud.

"Daughter."

Something was cradling Clo's form.

"Daughter."

The mist wreathed and swaddled Clo's form. She was a shadow held within the pale cloud.

"Clothilde."

Clo felt her lungs fill with air—*no, light—her lungs had filled with light, with fire*—and she gasped, her chest rising and burning.

"How have you come here, daughter?"

Clo opened her mouth to speak, but only flames curled against her tongue.

"You should not be here, daughter. You should not travel here." The voice was delicate, the words lilting between sorrow and joy.

Soft as fingertips, the mist pressed against Clo's cheeks, her palms, her forehead. It was cool against the blaze consuming her. "Yet how I have missed you."

The cloud breathed and closed around her, rocking her in its chalky form.

"How I long to keep you."

The mist encircled her like arms.

"Always…"

The pale cloud, soft light in the dark, swayed around her.

"Oh, daughter, do not let my mistakes become your own. Had I known what I could not change…"

Very far away, through the veils of mist, Clo could see the shape of the boat and the churning of the nets capturing the stars around it.

"Be brave enough to accept what I could not.…Light and life are fleeting.…"

The cloud billowed and stretched, eddying out and bearing Clo across the void. Galaxies pinwheeled past. Stars flashed, blazed, died away.

"Even here, daughter, stars give way to darkness.… Even here, *always* only flickers and is gone.…"

Above them, the water was turbulent with the commotion of light and oars and nets.

"Be brave enough to let go of *always*, my love."

Clo felt herself released, the cloud now ebbing away, a chalky smudge curling back into the darkness, and she

was again sinking, falling, drifting...airless among the stars...

Then a *something* struck her, heavy and hard and sharp, and she herself became heavy and hard and sharp...and the form of her, sagging, dripping, was lifted and borne and raised and tossed, expertly tossed, like a net full of stars, like a net full of fish, onto the deck of the boat, among the stars, among the piles and piles of fish.

"O-o...C-clo!"

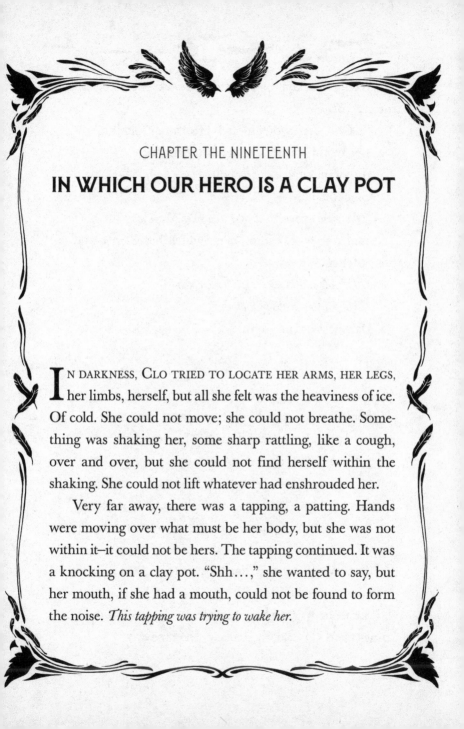

IN WHICH OUR HERO IS A CLAY POT

IN DARKNESS, CLO TRIED TO LOCATE HER ARMS, HER LEGS, her limbs, herself, but all she felt was the heaviness of ice. Of cold. She could not move; she could not breathe. Something was shaking her, some sharp rattling, like a cough, over and over, but she could not find herself within the shaking. She could not lift whatever had enshrouded her.

Very far away, there was a tapping, a patting. Hands were moving over what must be her body, but she was not within it—it could not be hers. The tapping continued. It was a knocking on a clay pot. "Shh...," she wanted to say, but her mouth, if she had a mouth, could not be found to form the noise. *This tapping was trying to wake her.*

Would the tapping not stop? Cracks were forming in the clay. *Shhh....*

"C-Clo...Are you gn−...b-breathing? Clo?"

The world was wet. And dark. And cold.

Full of murmuring. Stomping.

Cracking clay.

"Ohw deucser reh? Eht yob? Ten yob? Ni sih ten?"

Someone was holding her. She felt breath rise and fall beneath her.

"Eht rethguaddnarg...gnirb reh emoh..."

"Yob, ten yob, si ehs gnihtaerb?"

Darkness again. A pot.

"Clo, can you r-ra−...h-hear me?"

Someone was touching the walls of the pot. It had the same shape as her cheeks, her hair, her forehead.

Someone was whispering over it.

"Clo, n-ne−...wh-when they fished me out of the sea... I remember how cold I was. For so long. O−...s-so cold."

Someone was wrapping something over the clay. Something dry. Scratchy.

"I remember...how hard it was to wake. How much I de−...w-wanted to sleep."

Someone was rubbing her hands. Not her hands. These things were too cold, too lifeless. Too far away.

"I remember gn−…wo-wondering why they fished me from the sea. Why they saved me…"

Warmth. So very distant, but warmth. A pinpoint. A fingertip. The shape of her hand.

Crumbling clay.

"I remember…how ss−…h-hopeless I felt. I was so alone. So very alone. I ts−…l-lost my father."

Breath crossed her skin.

"I know you le−…f-feel alone. I know you miss your re−…f-father, know you worry you will not see him again. But I am da−…gl-glad you are here. Don't go. Please."

She could feel herself within her body, feel the sensation of her skin returning, the prickling of the cold, the air scraping her lungs. Exhaustion had settled deep into her bones.

She slept.

From time to time, Clo was aware of someone tending to her body. Water was raised to her lips. A blanket was tucked under her arms.

Soft footsteps came and went.

Someone sat near her. Someone went away.

She tried to open her eyes.

If her eyes were open, there was only darkness.

"Rethguaddnarg. Uoy tsum ekaw."

Darkness.

"Rethguaddnarg." A shaking.

Someone lifted something to her lips. It smelled of cold. And ice. And bitterness. She tried to turn her head away, but someone held her firmly and pushed a thing in between her teeth.

Clo gagged and spat. The taste was of old metal. Another spoonful was pushed into her mouth.

"Granddaughter! Eat this!"

Still in darkness, Clo gagged and spat again.

"Oh, granddaughter. You must!" Sighing, someone wiped at Clo's lips and face. "There is too much of your father in you..."

The footsteps padded away.

"...and too much of your stubborn mother."

Darkness.

When Clo next woke, someone was patting her hand—off and on, a gentle, aimless patting that came slowly through her sleep. It roused her, and the taste of old metal, still heavy in her mouth, woke her further.

She blinked. The world was shadowy and wet. Smudged paint. She blinked again.

Above her, Cary's moonish cheeks were huffed in concern. He was staring at her without really seeing her, and when he at last saw Clo's eyes open and gazing at him, he jumped.

"Y-yo... *U-uoy era ekawa. Olc. Uoy era ekawa.*" Startled, he dropped her hand. "She is awake!" he called over his shoulder.

Clo's throat was sore. "What are you saying?" she tried to ask, but only a faint raspy *wha* came out. She struggled to push herself into a sitting position. She was in her bed in the old woman's hut; the room had taken on a strange spinning quality.

The apple-faced woman hurried into the room. "Granddaughter!"

"Granddaughter?" Again, no sound at all came from Clo. She looked desperately from Cary to the old woman.

Face crinkling, the little woman stood over Clo and stroked her cheek. "Granddaughter. How good to see your eyes."

Clo scrabbled away from the woman's touch, and the woman frowned. The room spun wildly.

"She is awake. Wonderful. Boy, wait here with her. Watch that she does not attempt to rise." The woman shuffled out of the chamber.

Clo grabbed Cary's hand.

"Granddaughter?" she tried to ask, but only "Gra–" came out.

"C–... *Olc, Olc, uoy sh-sh...d-dluohs eil nwod–*"

"Cary, I don't understand." Clo's voice failed her again. She could make no sound. Still holding Cary's hand, Clo pulled him close. *This woman is not my grandmother,* she wanted to say. *She locked me in here,* she wanted to say. *She forced me to card fish! She forced me to spin fish! Thousands of fish! Stars!* she also wanted to say, but instead she just looked hopelessly at the blue-cheeked boy. "Help me," she finally managed to whisper.

"Y–... *Uoy kaeps*...You speak, learned to speak...I don't need to reverse–I mean, you can understand me? This way?"

Clo nodded.

"This way? And you can speak..." He turned to the apple-cheeked woman, who had reentered the room with a mug and bowl. "She speaks...."

Fastening her eyes on Clo, the little woman waved a dismissive hand at Cary. "She has had the stew."

"Clo?" Cary said. "You understand?" He reached a hand to Clo, who was now struggling to free herself from the bedclothes. "You should lie down...."

"Boy, you should leave now. My granddaughter needs her rest."

Heaving herself out of bed, Clo braced her body against the wall. The room wheeled around her. "No," Clo rasped. "No. I am not your granddaughter."

"You are, you are," the woman crooned, her face folding first in delight and then aggravation. "The daughter of my daughter. And you need to eat. And rest. Boy, you need to leave."

"Don't–" Clo tried to say, but what little voice she had managed to find had gone again. And the room would not stay still.

The woman held a spoonful of the shimmering liquid out.

"Take this," she said, pushing it toward Clo's lips.

Clo batted the hand away.

"Granddaughter. You must." The spoon had reached Clo's mouth. The smell of cold. *No. She would not eat the soup. The fish. The stars.* She gritted her teeth and turned her head away. The room was turning upside down.

"Boy! Catch her!"

Darkness.

It was the piggish cat that woke her next. She felt it kneading her, pushing at her through the blanket, its long claws catching her skin. It was making a rumbling noise, a throaty and phlegm-like growling.

"Off, off." She heard Cary's voice. "Go on, you."

She opened her eyes. At the end of her bed, Cary was attempting to lift the snarling, scratching cat.

"Cary," Clo whispered.

He dropped the cat, and it scuttled out of the room. "You're awake!"

Clo put her finger over her lips. Cary walked to the head of the bed and knelt beside her, his brow rumpling with concern.

"Are you feeling better, Clo?"

For a moment, relieved just to have him beside her, not wanting the old woman to send him away again, Clo did not say anything. She grasped his fingers, soft and damp, and squeezed.

"Yes." Clo shook her head. "I mean, no. No, I'm not." She paused for a long moment, staring down at the blanket that had been wrapped over her form. "Cary," she said at last, "I don't understand...how...*how did I come here?*"

"You were drowning," Cary said slowly, his expression pained. "You were in the cave. I saw you just before you fell, saw you splash into the water. It was my...first time on the boat. I swung my net in after you...again and again...I couldn't reach you. I saw you falling...I thought you were gone. And then, just barely...I caught you, I scooped you up out of the water. Somehow. I don't know how. You nearly drowned. Nearly..."

Clo felt again the emptiness she had sunk through. She saw herself as one of his stones tumbling through darkness; she saw his net flashing to save her. She could not find the words for what she wanted to say. *Thank you* seemed too

small for what he had done; still, she said it anyway, regretting the paltriness of the sounds in her mouth. "Thank you."

Cary nodded, his face still full of the memory of Clo sinking.

"Cary..." Glancing away, Clo hesitated. "How did *you* come here...*before*?" she finally asked. "How did you come to be in the sea?"

Cary's hair looked damper than ever. Dark tendrils clung to his cheeks and brow. "My father...he...he tied... but the sun...and I..." He twisted a corner of Clo's blanket. He could not say the words.

Clo nodded, her throat tight. Even without knowing the words Cary could not say, she understood the fear and sadness behind them. From the next room, the old woman could be heard sighing to the cat, "Oh, do you want some fish, my sweet?" Cary kept his eyes fixed on the corner of twisted blanket.

Something sharp, needle-like, seemed to be piercing Clo's heart. "My father sent me here," she managed after a long silence. "My father sent me....He's abandoned me here. Cary...I don't understand why he'd do this to me."

Cary untwisted the square of blanket and smoothed it around Clo's shoulder. "I know," he said softly. His moons drooped sympathetically. "I know."

WHEREIN SOMETHING GIGGLES AND SOMETHING *GMMMS*

C LO, ONCE WALL-JUMPER, FOREST-WALKER, AND WINDOW-breaker, became now a bed-lier. She recovered slowly, drifting in and out of sleep.

She had been changed, she noticed, her short tunic and leggings replaced with a long, pale smock. Sometimes she would lie staring down at this unfamiliar vision of her body, long and pale and flat and paperlike, and wonder what had become of her own self.

Though she could now understand the old woman, she found no solace in her prattle, and she did not care enough to ask her questions. *Granddaughter.* The word held no comfort. The woman was a stranger.

Clo thought of the airless falling, the stars and water and quiet. She thought of the cloud that had cradled and

comforted her in the darkness. She wanted only that comforting; because no comfort was coming, she wanted only to sleep. What was the purpose in waking? She had tried to escape; she had failed. She had before her only endless gray days and baskets of fish. When she thought of her father now, she felt only anger. She imagined him standing under the tallest pine as he should have done that morning long ago. *How could you do this to me?* she would hiss to her empty room, to the imagined image of her father waiting at the edge of the dew-soaked field. She would curl into her mattress, press her fingers against her eyes. *How could you abandon me here? Why would you leave me like this?* She would never find her way to him now.

She thought of the cradling cloud, the words that had echoed around her. *Be brave enough to let go of always.*

Let go, she thought.

She closed her eyes again.

The next time the little woman entered her room, Clo pretended to be asleep.

"Granddaughter. You must wake. You must rise."

Clo turned away, pulling the blanket higher.

She heard the woman's footsteps leave and then return, accompanied by a dragging sound. "Your work, granddaughter."

Clo felt herself tugged into a sitting position. She opened her eyes. The woman had pulled in a basket of fish. Clo stared at the black-eyed silvery creatures sliding over one another and onto the floor. She felt a wave of revulsion. *Endless fish. Endless fleshy tearing. Endless oily prickling.* "No," she said.

"Yes. The carding, the spinning." The woman pushed the carding combs into Clo's hands. She wrapped Clo's fingers around the handles.

"No." Clo pushed the loathsome combs away. Her voice rose, trembling. "This is not my work." She lay down again and rolled away from the old woman.

The woman sighed a long exasperated sigh, but she did not try to make Clo rise again. "So much like your stubborn mother you are," she murmured as she settled into the chair beside the bed. "Once she fixed on an idea, how she clung to it...no matter how misguided. Headstrong child." She clucked her tongue lightly. "But she, at least, never shirked her tasks. And this, this is your work, granddaughter. You must see it. You will see it now."

Closing her eyes, Clo curled into herself. *Her mother was headstrong?* She thought of the chalky figure her father had drawn, the woman whose gaze hovered between joy and sorrow. *Had this soft-cloud woman been stubborn?* She thought of the pale light that had cradled her in the darkness, warning, *Be brave enough to accept what I could not.*

Was she meant to accept these interminable days of gray? The never-ending fish-carding, the ceaseless fish-spinning?

Teeth clenched, Clo lay wishing the old woman would go away—*Would she not leave her alone?*—but the woman just sat, indefatigably carding and carding. Clo pulled the blanket over her ears to muffle the endless *sh-sh-sh* of the paddles pulling through the fish-wool.

Later, much later, it was the woman's snoring that woke her.

Sitting up, Clo stared at the woman. She had never seen her sleep before. She had never even thought of the old woman sleeping before, though she realized now she must. She obviously did. Still, it was strange to see the little black hole of a mouth open in the center of her apple face and the long shuddering breaths she took.

Clo thought of how sometimes in the afternoons in the villages she would see children napping on the laps of their mothers and grandmothers, the women's cheeks resting on their babes' soft crowns. *She and the old woman were not like this.* She did not like to see the woman this way—did not like that the woman felt comfortable falling asleep, vulnerable and open, near Clo. She did not want to go back to sleep next to her.

Slowly, carefully, Clo began to make her way out of the bed. The woman had dropped the carding paddles on the mattress when she had fallen asleep, and Clo reached to move them.

She froze.

The fish-wool...

She pulled a tuft from the comb and held it between her fingers.

It was not gray...

It was full of light and color, vibrant shimmering waves of light and color.

Not fish-wool...

So much light and color, so many changing hues and shades—Clo brought the wool closer to her eyes—it seemed like it was almost...

singing...

She rushed, as quickly as her weakened legs would allow, to the front room.

There the walls were still lined with the fish-cylinders she had carded. But now the towers of gray had become towers of rippling color and light, as though the walls were blooming with flowers. The colors opened and dimmed, and opened and changed—the whole room was awash in their light.

Wonderingly, Clo picked up one of a handful of bobbins that had been left on the table. The color and light were now a single bright strand, twisted and focused and wound around the spool. It, too, shimmered and pulsed and changed. Clo unraveled a bit of the thread.

Something giggled.

Clo gasped and dropped the bobbin.

Its thread unraveled and floated wide around her, a filament of light. Unspooling in the air, its bright coils drifted and settled gently about her. Mesmerized, Clo stared for a moment at the shimmering fiber before she shook herself, bent down, and rewound the thread. Again, *a giggle*.

Clo held the bobbin to her ear–nothing–but pulling out the thread again...a giggle. A giggle like a hiccup.

She squinted at the thread. There was nothing to see in the fibers, nothing but the shifting wash of reds and blues and lights and shades that had been twisted and shaped into a long, strong line.

She lifted another bobbin from the table, unspooled a little of its bright line. There was no giggle, but a sigh, faint and indistinct, rose from the fibers.

A third bobbin let out a pensive *gmmm* when she unwound it. *Gmmm. Hmmm,* it murmured as she spooled and unspooled it, growing ever more anxious at the noises wrapped in the threads.

She cast about for another bobbin, but there were none. The bobbins were usually kept by the woman. In her apron. Or in...

Oh.

The thought of the tapestry, that vast gray cloth hanging in the old woman's room, woven with thousands upon thousands of these bobbins, bobbins with light, bobbins

with noises that unspooled with the unspooling of the thread, filled Clo with anticipation... then uneasiness. More than uneasiness. Dread.

This is your work, granddaughter.

Thousands of *gmmm*ing threads. Thousands of giggling fibers. Thousands of sighing strands.

What had been woven?

She was not sure she wanted to look.

She stared at the closed door.

The quiet was punctuated by the rhythm of the old woman's snores.

She felt she must look.

Nervously, Clo wound and unwound the bobbin she still held in her hands. *Gmmm. Hmmmm. Gmmm. Hmmm.*

This is your work, granddaughter. You must see it.

Quietly, quietly, Clo lifted the latch of the door to the woman's room. The lock she had broken had not been fixed, and the door swung open.

This is your work, granddaughter. You must see it. You will see it now.

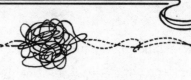

IN WHICH A MAN LEADS A SWEATY OX TO MARKET

C LO SAW.

As before, the window was shuttered. But now the whole room was aglow with the light from the tapestry. Its colors did not shift and bloom like the unspun towers of fish-wool in the front room did; instead, the cloth held fast its thousands of bright patterns.

It depicted nothing—nothing distinct, anyway. Clo could see no scene, but as she turned her head from side to side, she had the sense of bright fields. Dark forests. Glimmering mountain heights. Sleepy hamlets and bustling cities. But each time she thought she had spotted an image in the design and tried to focus on it, it became abstract once again—a wash of light and color.

Remembering the mirror she had seen hanging behind the tapestry, she realized she was perhaps only seeing the reverse, the wrong side of the fabric without a clear image. Still, her throat tightened with the beauty of it.

As she stood marveling, the piggish cat darted through the open door into the chamber and took up a spot by the tapestry. Standing on its hind legs, it stuck its thick claws again and again into the fabric, tearing gashes into the cloth. Clo moved to shoo the creature away, to stop its destructive kneading, but just as she stepped forward, she paused. She watched mesmerized as the dark holes the beast opened in the cloth took on brighter and brighter edges. Everywhere the cat ran its claws, the ragged edges gleamed—little in the tapestry glowed as brightly as its torn patches. Even the shadowy gaps the cat made seemed part of the larger design.

"So much color...and light...," she whispered, touching her fingers to her eyelids. After so many many days of gray, her eyes ached with the radiance of the fabric. She shook her head, overwhelmed.

She thought of the little apple-faced woman, chewing emptily, sitting alone on the low chair and drawing through the bobbins one by one, weaving thread by thread, hour after hour, to create this vast work. She was surprised to feel a sudden rush of sympathy for the woman, her quiet weaving alone in this dark room.

This is your work, granddaughter. You must see it.

Clo walked slowly toward the tapestry, fingertips buzzing with the memory of the wool sliding through her hands. *This was the fiber she had spun?*

She wondered if the threads would sigh or make noise as she drew close. But no, the room was silent but for the *tick tick* of the cat clawing at the fabric and the faint sound, now and again, of snoring in the next room.

She sat on the little stool placed before the tapestry and watched the cat pull a long thread away. Up close, the glowing tear it made looked more like a hole and less a part of the design, but Clo smiled at the beast all the same. "Good kitty." She reached out a hand and stroked its bristly head.

Hissing, the cat moved away and took up another spot to knead and pull.

Clo turned her attention to the fabric. Parting the vertical threads, she looked into the mirror placed behind the weaving. There was no clear design as she tried to take in the whole image, but again, she had the sense of vast spaces—deserts and moors, farmland and cityscape. When she tried to focus, all was still undefined. Vast undefined beauty.

A collection of bobbins dangled in front of a stool where the old woman had last been working. Clo lifted one: the thread spooled around the bobbin still shifted, a little, in light and color, but where it had been woven into the tapestry, the color had set.

She leaned closer, peering into the mirror at the woven line of thread from the bobbin she held. She followed its path, in and out, its entanglement with other bright lines, the warp and weft, and suddenly, she saw a clear image.

There was a man. There was a man woven in the thread.

Her breath caught.

He was leading an ox to market.

In the mirror, as though he were there before her, Clo watched him walking the path to town, saw the rough rope he had swung loosely around the ox's neck, saw the sweat damp on the beast's white hide.

Clo traced the thread back.

Earlier, in the dark of night, the man had risen and comforted a crying babe, had rocked him by the window and shown him the moon through the branches of the trees.

Clo's gaze raced backward along the thread, following the man's woven story. She saw him as a young man, dancing at a village fair, with a young woman laughing at his clumsy steps. Farther back, she saw him as a boy, following his own father into the barn, leaning his cheek against the warm flank of the family goat, learning how to milk. And then as an infant, held in his own mother's arm, rocked by the fire while snow fell in heavy drifts outside their door.

There were other threads entwined with his—the babe, the girl, the father, the mother, they each had their own strands. They twisted in and out with his, over and around

his, and Clo marveled at the artistry of the old woman who had woven them. Story after story after story. Clo could follow these other threads, too—the girl he had danced with, how she later married another boy, dark and freckled and even more clumsy-footed, and how this boy—*he* had been apprenticed to a cooper who had once sold his barrels to a scowling merchant. And the merchant had a family. A wife. A son. A daughter. Clo saw them all around a table lit by candles; the little boy had been set upon a wooden box so he could reach his plate.

Something was familiar about this family. Clo looked at their strands with growing interest. They lived in a city, a finer city than Clo had ever seen. The little boy and little girl had a whole room of their own in a great house, and they had a servant, a tall, angular man, who placed a book before them each morning and showed them how to write the alphabet.

Clo ran her fingers along their threads. She saw how the little boy had once snuck into the kitchen at night and eaten three rounded spoonfuls of bilberry jam. How his sister had skinned her knees and torn her skirts jumping from the bench of her father's cart on a whim. How their mother sang them the same lullaby every night—every night, every night, even when she herself was drowsy-eyed and yawning—a song her own mother had once sung to her, about a peahen and a grazing sheep. How their father

kept a small coin in his pocket—the first he'd ever earned—and pinched it between his thick fingers whenever he felt uncertain of a sale. How the boy chewed on his sleeve when he was concentrating. How a tiny mole on his left earlobe looked like an earring.

Clo drew closer to the mirror, squinting. The family's threads had become difficult to follow. Here the cat had run its claws, and the weaving had become distorted with holes.

When Clo found their lines again, she saw first the boy, then his sister fall ill. *Spots. A fever. Coughing.* She saw the mother tending to them, their little bodies barely visible in their vast white beds. The mother stayed with them all night, all day, and where she cared for them, the threads seemed brighter. And then the mother, too, began to cough. And then the merchant, who had not stopped his work to care for his family, became ill himself.

But then their threads disappeared.

Startled, Clo studied the place where their lines suddenly left the fabric.

Nothing. The family had gone to sleep in their beds, the rain pattering outside their windows. The little boy had woken once, coughing an empty *hee*, and the mother had been too feverish to rise. And then they had all slept.

Their woven story had simply ended. Their threads simply ended.

Clo looked at the little boy and his midnight cough.

Hee.

His delicate white nightgown.

Hee.

Trimmed with lace.

Hee.

No.

With rising panic and rising certainty, Clo pulled at the warp threads. She followed the other threads that linked to the family's—the other merchants and maids and sailors and servants—their lines distorted and torn by the cat as well. One by one, the rash and fever came to each. One by one, the threads disappeared.

And here and there, the fabric, run with holes, was lit more brightly at the edges of these tears, where Clo found *someone*—a mother or father or minister or shopkeep or trades-man or streetsweep—tending a fever or taking in a child or preparing medicine or even slicing onions into a soup.

But the boy... She returned to the little boy asleep in his bed in the delicate nightgown. His lace-trimmed cuffs. His empty coughing *hee.*

The boy from the boat. The full passage.

His family. Mother. Father. Sister.

Their heavy trunk.

Hee.

Full passage.

Hee.

She brushed the little boy's thread—followed its short path, felt where it ended—with quivering fingertips.

This is your work, granddaughter.

You must see it.

She could not catch her breath.

CHAPTER THE TWENTY-SECOND

WHEREIN THREE ROUNDED SPOONFULS OF BILBERRY JAM ARE SOFT AND TREMBLY

IT WAS THE KNOCKING THAT FINALLY PULLED HER AWAY.

Clo looked up, bewildered. The weaving swayed under her hands.

The snoring in the next room—breath, *snargle*, breath, *snargle*—had grown more ragged. But at the front door, someone was knocking—hesitant yet persistent tapping.

Feeling she might be dreaming, Clo walked to the front door and opened it.

"Clo. You're here. You're…Have you recovered?" Cary, who had broken into a wide grin on seeing Clo open the door, now peered at her with puckered brows. His smile faded. "Clo…what is it? What's happened? You look…"

"Cary." Clo stared at the blue-cheeked boy, the curls that clung to his skin. She thought of the little boy and his

mole and his empty cough. The father and his coin and the trunk. The full passage. She shuddered.

"Cary." Clo grabbed him by his hand. "You must…" She faltered, overcome. *How could she explain this horrifying thing?* "You have to see this."

"Clo, are you all right? You've been sleeping for so long.…Where is the old woman?"

Without answering, Clo pulled Cary through the house and into the woman's chamber. The tapestry was still trembling where she had touched it.

"Oh…Clo…Is this the old woman's room? I'm sure I'm not meant to be here.…" As Cary tried to back away, Clo gripped his hand more tightly.

"Look at this!" she hissed. She pulled him to the fabric and parted the threads. "Look in the mirror. Do you see it?"

"The gray?"

"No, don't you see it? The colors…and light. And here…" She pointed. "The boy. Do you see the boy?"

Cary shook his head, puzzled. "It's all just gray."

"Oh, Cary, you have to see. There's a boy. With a mole. And he tiptoed out of his room at night to sneak bilberry jam. Three spoonfuls in his little white nightgown. And he has a father who keeps a coin in his pocket. And a sister who jumped from a carriage and tore her dress. And a mother who sang a lullaby about a peahen. And they had a cough. And, Cary, I *saw* them. I saw them coming here. They had a

full passage. They're real. Real people...or"—she hesitated—
"*were*. They were real."

"You're not making sense, Clo." Cary tried to place
his hand on Clo's forehead, but exasperated, she pushed it
away.

"The soup," she declared. "It must be the soup. It was all
gray for me once too, but after the soup, I could understand
the old woman, I could see the colors in the wool....It's the
soup. Just wait, you'll see...."

Clo hurried out of the room and returned with a bowl
of the silvery broth. "Drink this." She pushed the bowl into
Cary's hands.

"I don't think—"

"Drink this." She pushed again, nearly raising the bowl
to Cary's lips for him.

Hesitantly, he swallowed.

"The whole thing."

Cary drank down the bowl and showed her when he
had emptied it.

"Now look."

Cary stood staring at the fabric. Clo watched him
expectantly.

Next to them, the cat was still running its claws across
the weaving. Its *tick-tick-tick* reshaped the silence.

Finally, Clo asked, "Do you see it?"

Cary squinted and huffed, huffed and squinted.

Stepping toward him, peering at his eyes, Clo suddenly felt the hard edge of a bobbin beneath her foot. She tried to pick it up; it would not come. She yanked again, and the finished fabric near the floor puckered; she realized the bobbin was still attached—but to cloth that had long been finished, far from the working edge. "What's this doing here?" she murmured, rewrapping and lowering the stray spool. She smoothed the tapestry and glanced again at Cary. "Can you see yet?"

Cary had his hand on his brow; small beads of sweat stood out on his skin. "I'm...I'm sorry, Clo. There's just gray. I think the soup has made me..." He shuddered. "I had a bit of a...sharp. Something sharp. For a moment, and now it's gone. Where is...where is the old woman?"

"Something hurt? Perhaps it was the soup changing your eyes?" Running her fingers over the threads, Clo tried again. "Look, Cary, there's people. Thousands. They're here...they're woven in the threads. They *are* threads. And Cary, I think they are real. Alive. *Here...*," she said, parting the warp, "here's a woman...skinning a rabbit. She's kneeling in the middle of the woods, all alone, and there's frost on the leaves, and her knife is more...like stone. And here"—she jumped to another part of the cloth—"here's a boy whistling. With a blade of grass. Or trying to whistle. He's blowing and blowing, and there's no sound, and he's red-cheeked and barefoot, and he has his feet sunk deep in the

soil. And here"–kneeling over the cat, she peered around a dark hole it had just opened in the cloth–"here's a man–"

In horror, Clo drew away.

She looked at Cary wide-eyed, then leaned in again. Her fingers traced the tear in the fabric. In the mirror, she followed all the threads that had been pulled and frayed and torn around the hole.

"Here...it's..." She could not bring herself to say. *Here was a figure more blood and mud than man. Wounded, gasping, he had become a part of the soil of the ditch where he lay. A chaos of legs and arms and sludge churned above him, as men–more blood and mud than men–rammed their spears and swung their axes and grappled desperately at one another.*

"Clo?"

Shaking her head, Clo stepped back, trying to take in the whole weaving at once.

So many holes. Frayed threads...

Trembling, she pushed aside the warp threads. Here. And here. Here. Wherever the cat had left a tear or a run or a gaping hole. War. Famine. Disease.

"Clo?"

By her feet, she heard again the *tick-tick-tick* of the cat. Perched on its hind legs, it kneaded the fabric, again and again and again. *Tick-tick-tick.*

She stared at it. Its hoofish paws. Its bristly face.

"Get!" she shrieked. "Get, you miserable beast!" She

tried to grab the creature, but growling and hissing, it darted away from her. "Get, you horrible creature!"

"Clo—" Cary's hand was on her shoulder.

"Oh, get it out of here! Catch it, catch it! Shut it out! You don't know what it's done! Keep it away!" She lurched after the cat.

"Granddaughter," said a cold voice at the door. "You are not meant to be here. And, boy, you are not permitted. This is not your place."

Clo spun around to see the woman who called herself her grandmother standing in the doorway. All the wrinkles on her face seemed to be frowning at once, but Clo cared nothing for her anger.

"How could you? How could you let it?" Her voice shook.

Kneeling, the woman scooped up the cat in her arms. "There, there, Mischief." She rubbed behind the beast's ears. "There, there." From beneath her apple-skin eyelids, the woman looked stonily at Clo. "There is always Mischief," she said. *"Always."*

"That beast? Mischief? You call it—what it does—mischief? And you let it? Can't you see what it destroys?"

Lifting a hand from the cat, the little woman waved at the tapestry. Her cheeks grew ruddy and round, almost beaming. "And can you not see the beauty he adds? Look

how the fabric almost glows where he has placed his claws. How he adds depth to the design." She stroked the beast's fur, and he rumbled under her fingers. "Certainly, you must see now, granddaughter. I believe you hear and see very well now."

"But up close...it's horrible! There's so much...so much sadness! So much suffering! You know what he's done! There is no beauty up close!"

"Granddaughter. You disappoint me." She tutted disapprovingly. "You should be able to see the necessity of Mischief. Even your mother never doubted his artistry. But perhaps you have not yet fully recovered. Perhaps your eyes...well. We shall see. And boy"—she turned now to Cary, who had edged into the corner—"I do not think one who has waited so long to be a net boy would risk such disobedience."

Eyes on his feet, Cary nodded. "I'm sorry."

"And do not think the stew is for you. It will do nothing for you. It is not permitted."

"Yes."

"The tapestry is not for you. It is not permitted."

"Yes."

"You should leave."

"Clo—" Cary hesitated.

"Leave *now*."

"Yes." Casting one last quick glance at Clo, Cary shuffled hurriedly out of the room. Clo heard the front door shut behind him.

For a long moment, the only sound was the grumbling of the piggish cat lolling in the woman's arms. Clo stared with revulsion at the woman's fingers as they caressed the creature's bristly fur. *How could she touch such a beast? How could she keep such a creature?*

"Well, granddaughter," the old woman said at last. "I am pleased, at least, that you are awake. Out of bed. On your feet. You may return to your work."

Clo thought of the towers of wool that she had carded out of fish, blooming in the next room. Of the thousands of spools that had been tucked into the old woman's pockets. Of the noises—the giggle, the sigh, the *gmmm*—that came from their unraveling threads. Of the threads woven into the tapestry…the woman with the knife, the man and the ox, the merchant and his coin…and the boy, the boy with the cough, *hee*, the full passage, *hee*. Of the beastly cat, and the nightmarish holes—*war, famine, disease…Mischief*—torn by the cat. And though Clo would not have resumed her work, had on her tongue a ready "No! This is not my work!" she realized at once that she *could not* take up this work, that she was physically incapable of this work, that she could no longer stand, really, her legs having turned to

something soft and trembly, to something like jam—*bilberry jam, three rounded spoonfuls of bilberry jam*—beneath her.

"I..."

"Granddaughter?"

"I...cannot...I cannot..."

Bilberry jam.

"I will not."

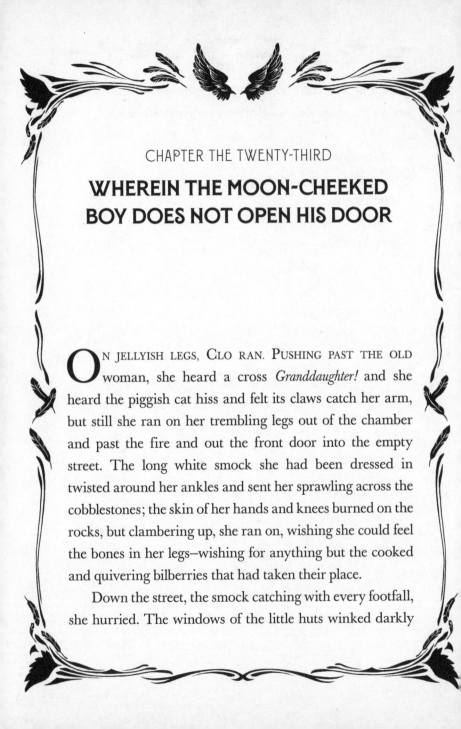

WHEREIN THE MOON-CHEEKED BOY DOES NOT OPEN HIS DOOR

On jellyish legs, Clo ran. Pushing past the old woman, she heard a cross *Granddaughter!* and she heard the piggish cat hiss and felt its claws catch her arm, but still she ran on her trembling legs out of the chamber and past the fire and out the front door into the empty street. The long white smock she had been dressed in twisted around her ankles and sent her sprawling across the cobblestones; the skin of her hands and knees burned on the rocks, but clambering up, she ran on, wishing she could feel the bones in her legs—wishing for anything but the cooked and quivering bilberries that had taken their place.

Down the street, the smock catching with every footfall, she hurried. The windows of the little huts winked darkly

at her and echoed back to her the slap of her bare feet on the stones. *Hee*, they coughed at her. *Hee*.

As she neared the last of the huts before the cliff stairs, suddenly a man—*the parchment-skin man*—stepped out of a door and into her path. Clo tried to weave around him, but on her jam-filled legs, she could not keep her balance.

"Girl." He put down the basket he was carrying.

Clo glanced behind her—the old woman was not following—then looked up. In the gray light, the man's skin seemed all the more translucent, so that even the cliffs above formed shadows in the flaps of his nostrils and ears.

"You have recovered." Placing a finger under her chin, he turned her head first one way, then the other. "Good. Your grandmother was filled with worry."

Clo tried to pull herself from his grasp, but the man continued. "Yes. Your work—how important it is for you to take this up. And drowning…you are fortunate, child. The net boy, you must know, saved you. You might have been lost in the grotto."

Clo thought of how the cold and dark had rushed into her lungs, how she had sunk airless and heavy into the void. How the stars had been swept and scattered by the nets and the oars above her. How the bosun had knocked her away. How she had once sat in his dinghy with the little boy in the delicate gown. How she had felt where the little boy's thread in the tapestry simply ended.

His thread.

The realization came to her all at once.

Her thread. How had she not thought of this? Thought to look for it? Her thread under the hands of the old woman.

The bitterness of it nearly took her breath away. *Had it been the cat's claws that had raked her into the grotto? Had the old woman stroked its fur while Clo sank beneath the water? Tossed it another fish while she struggled to breathe? Or had the old woman herself placed the thread that caused her drowning?*

"I expect the old woman could have saved me herself, if she was all that worried," Clo responded sharply.

The man's skin rattled with surprise. "N-no…" He seemed taken aback.

"No?" She crossed her arms. The bilberry jam did not feel so jammish now. Boniness was returning to her legs.

"No, she could–"

"Where's Cary?"

The parchment brow crumpled in confusion.

"The net boy. Where's the *net boy*? I'd like to…" Clo paused. She tried to make her voice sweeter. "…to thank him. For saving me. As you said." She forced a small smile.

The old man nodded, mollified. "Yes. Certainly."

"Where?"

Again the parchment folded in bewilderment.

"Where is he?"

"I do not know. He has completed his net repairs."

"Well…" Clo felt at once her own shortcomings. Why had she never thought to ask this? To ask Cary himself? Wasn't he her friend? Her cheeks grew hot with shame. "Where does he live?"

The man shrugged, and his shoulders made a brittle crinkling sound.

"You fished him out of the sea," Clo said, all the sham sweetness now gone from her voice. "One of you, one of the fishermen. So when you rescued him, when he came here, where did he live? Which of these houses"—she gestured sharply up the street–"is his?"

"The houses are for the fishermen. And the weaver."

"But he's a net boy. He's a fisherman."

"But he *was not* when he came here."

"But he is *now*. And he is only a boy. Who cares for him? Who lives with him?"

"Care?" The man picked up his basket. "No one has to care for him."

Clo gaped at the man, the bilberry jam suddenly overtopping her in a sickening wave. She thought of Cary fished out of the sea, fished out of the sea and left alone among the fishermen and sea-coal-pickers and barrow-fixers going about their chores, their *tasks*, as though he did not exist. She thought of the nightgowned boy who had coughed–*hee*–alone in his room, about his mother, who would have risen to comfort him had she been able. She thought of how

Cary himself had guided her through the village when she was too weak to walk alone. How he had carried her hidden in his nets past the guard and the vellum-skin man to the boat because she had asked for his help. How he had fished her out of the sea of stars and fish and lifted her onto the boat and brought her to life and sat by her side all through-out her long recovery. "Of course someone has to care—" she began hotly, but the man was already moving away from her. "Someone has to care!" she shouted at his back. "Someone must care!"

Partway up the street, he paused, considering. "Try that door." He nodded at the smallest of the structures that lined the street. Squat and crooked and windowless, it was little more than a door between two contorted huts. "That is where the fishermen brought him to recover. But it is not a house."

The man was right, it was not a house. Standing before the door, knocking, Clo could see it was not a house, nor a hut, nor a shack, even, of any real sort. It was a crooked door and a bit of wall.

No one answered.

She made her fist heavier.

In the windows of the neighboring houses, faces appeared and disappeared.

"Cary!" she called into the wood. "Cary!"

No answer.

Clo pressed her ear against the door. *Silence.* She placed her hand on the latch and pushed. The door swung open.

Was this where Cary lived?

It was a long corridor of darkness, nothing more. On the far end, a tiny window let in a pale square of light, just enough for Clo to see a white shape, a misshapen heap, on the floor occupying the center of the hallway. Fishbones were scattered here and there along the walls. The air was stale—dusty and damp in her lungs all at once.

She shut the door behind her.

The white thing in the middle of the corridor—she could see at once it was meant to be a bed. Someone slept here.

"Cary?" Her voice bounced along the narrow walls.

She walked toward the heap. It stirred, somehow, shifting at her approach, and when she reached it, kneeling beside it, she realized why.

Feathers. Thousands upon thousands of feathers piled on the floor. Nothing contained them—they were simply loose, and though Clo could see the imprint of a body in the center of the pile where someone had slept, she could also see how the feathers must spread and disperse, how they could not possibly cushion the cold stones below.

"Oh, Cary..." Her hands hovered over the pile. *How could he have been left to live like this?* A few feathers rose at her agitation.

Farther down the hall, she found a bucket tucked against the wall, half filled with water, silver fish scales floating on the surface, and then, farther still, another bucket stashed in a dark gap in the stones.

As she reached the window at the end of the corridor, Clo was surprised to find that the passage continued, cutting sharply around a corner so tight she had to turn sideways to pass. The floor here rose rapidly—a tunnel that disappeared up into the darkness.

"Cary?"

Only the echo of her voice answered.

Half crouching, half tripping on the wide fabric of her hem, Clo climbed into the blackness, groping along the floor and walls with her hands. Breathing heavily, she felt the jammishness returning to her legs: she had lain too long in bed, her lungs had held too much water, the path was steep. The passage narrowed further: she knocked her head against the ceiling once, twice, and she nearly stopped in frustration. She did not feel like Clo, wall-jumper, forest-trekker, window-breaker. She felt like Clo, smock-wearer, air-gasper, jelly-leg-walker. Insubstantial as thread. Frayed thread.

Gritting her teeth, she tore at the hem of her smock, ripping away the wide circle of fabric below her knees. She sighed—*her legs were free*—and climbed on.

Slowly, the darkness became grayer. She could see an

end to the passage—a blot of light. And then, under the *tpp-tpp* of her footsteps, she heard, faintly, piping. Cary-like piping.

Crouched so low she was nearly crawling, she rushed toward the blot of light.

The tunnel ended, and she found herself, abruptly, in open air—gray sky all around her. She had reached the very top of the cliff. She stood, shakily. A few steps forward would land her in the crevasse where the village was tucked—she could see the roofs of the houses far below. A few steps to the side would send her tumbling into the sea. The wind tugged at her smock.

"Clo?"

She turned. Behind her, sitting in the middle of a pile of nets and tucked under a white, sail-like thing, as far as possible from the edges of cliff and crevasse, was Cary. Moons bright with surprise, he put down his flute.

"Be careful..." He held out a steadying hand as she approached. Lifting the white thing, he made room for her beside him.

Clo sat beside him in the pile of nets. He lowered the white thing over their laps like a blanket.

"Cary," Clo said. She had not caught her breath.

The two sat in silence. In the distance, Clo could see the line of waves the bosun had rowed her through. She watched the line shimmer against the otherwise monochrome expanse.

"I'm sorry I couldn't see anything but the gray," Cary said at last. "But I believe you."

Clo nodded. "Do you..." She hesitated, lifting a handful of the nets on which they were sitting. They were old and salt-encrusted, full of holes. "Do you sleep here?"

"Sometimes here," Cary murmured. "Sometimes..." He jutted his chin in the direction of the tunnel. "Down there...but I don't like the dark."

Clo watched Cary. Seemingly embarrassed, he was running his hands over and smoothing the white blanket-thing covering them. It was warm, Clo realized, but not really a blanket. It was too solid, too stiff. Though it flexed, it kept its dome shape over their laps.

She looked more closely and ran her own fingers over its edge.

When she realized what it was made of, what it *was*, she nearly gasped. She wanted to lift the thing, to see its shape all at once to be sure, but she knew. She knew from the pale feathers in the middle of the dark corridor below. She knew from the way this blanket-thing flexed but held its shape. She knew from the self-conscious way Cary smoothed its surface over and over. And she thought at last she understood what he had never been able to tell her.

"Cary, how did you come to be in the sea?"

His hands grew still.

"Before they fished you out...how did you come to

be in the sea?" Clo pressed gently. "You told me you fell. Where did you fall from?"

Cary's lip trembled. He could not look at her.

"I fell from the sky," he said at last.

"And how did you come to be in the sky?"

His hands fluttered nervously over the blanket-thing.

Clo looked again into the gray expanse. She imagined the terror of tumbling through the air and into the sea, the water rushing up to meet the falling boy, the slap of the wet surface turned solid by distance and speed.

"My father..."

Clo waited. Cary dug his fingers into the whiteness of the blanket-thing.

His voice shook.

"My father...he tied..."

He tore away a handful of feathers. They slipped out of his palm and into the wind, carried off the cliff and into the air, delicate white specks vanishing into the gray sky and gray water.

"...he tied wings to me."

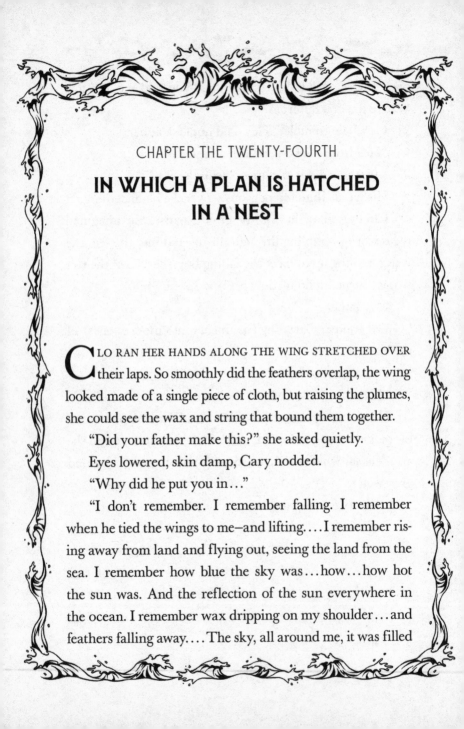

IN WHICH A PLAN IS HATCHED IN A NEST

CLO RAN HER HANDS ALONG THE WING STRETCHED OVER their laps. So smoothly did the feathers overlap, the wing looked made of a single piece of cloth, but raising the plumes, she could see the wax and string that bound them together.

"Did your father make this?" she asked quietly.

Eyes lowered, skin damp, Cary nodded.

"Why did he put you in…"

"I don't remember. I remember falling. I remember when he tied the wings to me—and lifting. . . . I remember rising away from land and flying out, seeing the land from the sea. I remember how blue the sky was…how…how hot the sun was. And the reflection of the sun everywhere in the ocean. I remember wax dripping on my shoulder…and feathers falling away. . . . The sky, all around me, it was filled

with feathers.... I remember, as I was falling, my father was flying overhead. And he saw me fall. And he did not come for me.... I remember... I remember the darkness of the water. The weight of the wings pulling me down. For a long time—just darkness. And then the nets. And the fishermen. And then I was here on the island."

Cary plucked a feather from the wing and held it in his fingers. They watched the wind tug at its edges before he let it go and it drifted out across the cliff.

"I missed him. I *remember* missing him. I remember waiting for him, hoping he would come for me for... ages. Ages and ages. But I don't remember *him*. Not really."

Clo thought again of Cary falling, wings disintegrating around him, desperately flapping, then falling through open space, the bright water rushing up, his father a speck with wings above. She winced. "Cary, all the time you've been here, the old woman... what did they tell you about her?"

"Nothing. They tell me hardly anything. I knew the fish were for her. I knew there used to be another woman with her, a younger woman, but I never really saw her. Just once, in the window. Only the old woman, sometimes, came out to the street. And I never saw the weaving... until you showed me."

"When you've fished—"

"Only once. My first time was when you... when I saw you in the water. And I haven't been again."

"What did the fish look like to you?"

"I don't know what I saw. It was so dark, and there were so many nets moving, and then I saw you fall, and I was trying so hard to catch you. But...around you..." Cary raised his hands helplessly. "It looked like the reflection of the sun in the water. Small. Everywhere. Not like fish. Not like what came up in the nets. Not what they bring in baskets into town." From under his damp curls, the boy cast a quick glance at Clo.

"Do you know what the woman does with the fish? Why they give her all the fish?"

"Not *all*. Some the fishermen keep to eat. Me too. They give me some, too."

"And the cat, it gets some as well. But, Cary—the woman, she *spins* them. The fish...they're the wool for her tapestry."

Cary made a noise of understanding—*Ah*—but it was clear from the way his brow furrowed that he had no sense of how fish could become wool.

"That's not...it's not really what's important. The tapestry..." Clo spoke slowly, trying to piece together for Cary what she had seen. "I told you, I think the people in the tapestry are *real*. The boy I saw, the boy with the cough, his family...I think they were real, and their lives...*ended*. Their threads in the fabric ended where the awful cat had scratched. And I saw them *after* the end of their lives, traveling on the boat...traveling somewhere *beyond* here. They

were full passage. My ticket was half passage. We...you and I, we must be somewhere... *in between.*"

"In between?" Cary looked stunned. "So the old woman..."

"Yes, she weaves them. Weaves people. *Lives.* And she's made me...she had me carding. And spinning. Thousands and thousands of threads she has yet to weave. And I didn't know, but I do now—the threads sigh, and giggle, and *gmmm*, and I might have taken more care with them if I had known...I would have been more careful. But, Cary...*we* must have threads, too. We must be in the tapestry, too. You when your father tied wings to you and you fell from the sky, and I when my father sent the swineherd to me with a wheel of cheese and a slip of *half paffage.* Our threads must be there."

For a long moment, Cary stared at Clo, saying nothing. Clo watched his shoulders rise and fall with increasing agitation. "Di—did my father tie wings to me? Did my father do this?" he finally stammered. "Or did the old woman? Or the cat? Who made me fall? Who made the wax melt?"

"I don't know," Clo admitted. "I don't know how much the woman...how much she decides. Or how much the cat destroys. But we need to find our threads. Maybe there's something"—she waved her arm across the expanse of gray water—"to help us out of this. Something to help us home."

"Help us home?"

"Yes, home."

"But, Clo..." Cary shook his head. "There is no other home for me."

"What do you mean?"

"You've only been here a little while...not so long, really...but this island is all I know. What do I have? A memory of falling...and a memory of missing a man I called Father, but I do not actually remember him! Clo, I hardly remember my own name! And even if I did...what could be waiting for me now?"

Clo watched Cary smooth a line of feathers on the wing. His knuckles were soft, almost dimpled; his hands were still the hands of a boy.

"You must want more than this," she said quietly. "More than...fish. And gray sky."

"No, Clo." He pulled another feather from the wing. "I will help you...if you want to leave. If you can leave. I know you miss your father; I know you want to be with him. But for me...I will stay."

"But, Cary...no one here, no one..." Clo gestured widely, her words growing heated. *How could she leave him here alone?* "They've left you here with a pile of feathers and a bucket. They don't care—"

"I know what my life is here. I am used to it; it's comfortable. And they've let me become a net boy. That is enough for me."

"You don't belong here!" Clo cried. "All the ways you've been kind to me—no one else would do the same! Please—"

"No," Cary repeated. "Tell me how I can help you, and I will. But I will not go."

His face was set, was full of the gray sky. Clo wanted to argue, to convince him to go with her; instead she dipped her head, a reluctant assent. "I'm not sure how you can help yet. I know I'll need to look at the tapestry again, but I don't know if the old woman will allow me near it. And even if she does, she's not likely to leave me alone with it."

"If you can find a way, how long will you need with it?"

"I don't know....I have to find our threads...or my thread. And my father's. There are so many, I don't know how long it will take. And then I'll need to see if there's anything that will help us leave...if there's anything I can do with the threads or even...weave in the tapestry." Clo, frowning, rubbed her brow. "I think," she said after a moment's reflection, "I think the best way may be for me to return to the old woman now, return to my work." She shuddered, thinking of the giggling and *gmmm*ing bobbins; she did not want to hold these, spin these...spin these *lives*. "I'll do what she expects me to, and whenever I can, I'll search for our threads. I'll need you later, I think, after I've found them. When I try to find a way to help us home..."

"No." Cary was shaking his head. "Not *our* threads. It's *your* thread you need to find, *you* who needs to find a way home."

225

"Yes. Me. Only me. I know." Clo pretended to agree. Still thinking of how they both might leave, she stood and looked out over the water. From here, she could see in all directions around the island. "When I arrived, were you here, watching?"

Cary pointed. "I saw your boat breaking over the waves. I saw when you walked in the water to the shore."

Clo pursed her lip, considering. "Has anything else ever crossed the waves? The fishing boat?"

"No. Or, at least, I've never seen anything."

Clo watched the distant crashing line for a minute before turning to head back into the passage. As she started to descend into the tunnel, Cary called after her.

"Clo...you should know...they were waiting for you."

"Waiting?"

She looked back at the boy. He was standing, holding the wing in front of him like a shield.

"They were expecting you. The fishermen. The woman. Even before you came...a long time before, I heard them say that the old woman's granddaughter would come one day. They knew you would come. They were waiting for you."

"And?"

Cary's face had taken on an ashy hue. "Clo, it might be...it might be you're supposed to be here. That you aren't meant to leave either."

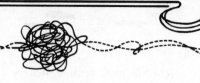

CHAPTER THE TWENTY-FIFTH

IN WHICH THE SWINEHERD RETURNS

WHEN CLO RETURNED TO THE OLD WOMAN'S HUT, Cary's *you aren't meant to leave* flapping in her head, the old woman merely nodded as she opened the front door and waved her hand toward the spinning wheel.

"Your work, granddaughter."

And so Clo, filled with disquiet, returned to her spinning. Under her fingers, the fish-wool slipped and twisted itself into long strands—the colors bright, sparkling, shifting—but now she fretted over the variations, the places where it grew lumpy or too dangerously thin because her foot did not keep pace or because her hands held the wool too tightly. It seemed to her, as she filled each bobbin, that the voice she would hear as she checked the finished strand depended

entirely on how evenly she had spun: a particularly thick yarn might unravel with a hearty guffaw; a fine, wispy thread might whimper as it unspooled. Uneven strands that bounced between fat lumps and flyaway fiber expressed uncertain *Uhh*s when finished. Her finest bobbins, bobbins where the thread was perfect and even throughout, let out smug *Yes*es as she unwound them, but their conceited sniffs unnerved Clo as well.

As before, the old woman would collect the finished bobbins from Clo. "Good," she would say, and return with them to her room to weave. Only now, the woman left the door open, and from her spot near the fire, Clo watched as the tapestry—strand by strand by strand—shifted with the woman's work. And the cat's. Whenever Clo saw the creature at the weaving, slicing its claws into the fabric, it was all she could do not to throw the beast out the front door. But to give the appearance of acceptance, she kept herself still. Later, she learned to hide a fish or two in the pocket of her smock and toss them to distract the cat. And eventually, the cat learned to sit by her feet, waiting for the smock-pocket fish.

In this way, time—whatever it was—passed. Now Clo joined the old woman at the table (and sometimes the parchment-skin man); now she ate the cold-smelling stew. Now the woman did not try to lock Clo in: Clo stayed and ran the wheel. Sometimes Cary would come—a hesitant knock on the door—but as there was nothing they could

say to each other under the eye of the old woman beyond *Hello, hello* and *How are you?* Cary would more often simply peer in the front window and Clo would shake her head: *No, no, she had not seen the weaving.* Once, when the street was empty and quiet, Clo heard him piping his flute, and she knew he must be standing nearby, tucked in some village doorway, playing just so she could hear. Under his skipping tune, the wool slipped more easily through her fingers, and her foot bounced happily along on the treadle, following his sunny notes, until a villager intoned, "That's not needed here, boy," and the playing abruptly ceased. Though Clo bounded from her chair to wave through the window, to show Cary that whatever the villager had said, *she* had liked his music, and though his moons grew bright as he caught sight of her gesturing hand, he still put his flute away. Nevertheless, as Clo returned to the wheel, she smiled to herself, grateful that the endless, lonely spinning had seemed for a moment less endless.

Sometimes Clo slept; more often she waited, hoping the old woman would nap—but to her dismay, Clo discovered that the old woman rarely left off her weaving. She would sit on her little stool for what seemed like days—if they were days—following the same ceaseless motions: she would grasp the loops of the heddle to open a gap in the warp threads, run a bobbin of thread through the opened spaces, tap the new line of thread down with the tip of the bobbin. Weave

a thread, tap it down–*thread, tap, thread, tap*–over and over and over. Eyes heavy, yawning, determined to stay awake, Clo would watch the old woman's gestures from the corner of her eye as she spun, trying to learn how she shaped her fabric, trying to catch the moment she drifted into sleep.

But finally, one day (if it was a day), Clo noticed through the *hush*ing sound of her own spinning that the woman's tapping had fallen silent. Clo glanced up: the old woman's head had fallen forward on her chest. Her hands, though resting on the tapestry, were still. Her back, curved into a gentle *n* shape, rose and fell with steady breathing.

Carefully, Clo stood. At her feet, flopped on its side, the cat tried to roll itself onto its paws, but Clo dropped a handful of fish by its bristly maw, and it lay happily down again, taking messy bites from the side of its mouth.

Approaching the tapestry as quietly as she could, Clo was again struck by the beauty of the design–the impressions of humid forests and gleaming deserts, rimy fields and green valleys. As before, the edges of holes torn by the cat glowed brightest of all, but Clo, stomach turning, kept her gaze away from these.

Where to begin?

The enormity of the design–*how would she ever find her own thread? Her father's?*

They would have to be near the working edge of the fabric–the threads still being woven.

Starting at the far side, as far from the old woman as possible, Clo parted the warp and began examining the threads. Lives opened up for her. A well-to-do hunter who kept a prized pack of glossy, long-nosed hounds. The hunter's dog-keeper, who, mortified by his own rough voice, never spoke. The dog-keeper's mother, who had a little herb garden and offered advice to any villager who asked on any medical question. The villagers, who sought out the dog-keeper's mother—for advice on a swollen toe or a painful tooth or a raspy cough that kept them up at night—all with their own openhearted or petty, refined or paltry, vain or modest, grand or mediocre whims, desires, dreams, loves, accomplishments, regrets. Stick-thin or plump, frail or muscle-bound, withered or new, lovely or ugly, lame or lightning-fast...Clo followed the threads of men and women and children out and over the tapestry, searching for something, anything familiar.

In some places, around *some* people, the fabric...Clo wasn't sure, but it seemed to... *bubble*. It wasn't a hole left by the cat. There was nothing violent or strange—no battle or plague, no suffering, no lives cut short—but there was still a change in the weaving. A distortion. The fabric gaped a little, or formed small pockets...and, around some gaps, a few bright threads spun out. Here, around a man who carved dolls for his children out of wood from an apple tree that had fallen in a storm. Here, around a king—*no*.

Clo looked more closely. *Not around a king.* Around a young man who traveled with the king, announcing his exits and entrances with bright fanfares on his horn. Here, around a long-limbed girl who told stories to her young siblings while they carried pots of water on their heads on the long walk home from the river each day.

The more Clo looked, the more bubbles she saw. Some small, barely a wrinkle in the fabric. But others, others... they reshaped the fabric entirely, so it was no longer smooth and flat, but three-dimensional—with hills and hollows and ripplings... and light gossamer threads all around.

Here were a string of bubbles—some of the largest in the whole weaving—with shimmering filaments spinning out in all directions from them and crossing to other threads, other lives. But then, right beside them—*Oh! The smell, the smell.*

Clo drew back, holding her breath. *Fish guts.* Here the thread was no longer fine wool but a fat stinking line of fish guts—pink and gray, slippery, decaying. The fabric around them was wet, beginning to molder. The smell of rot hung over the weaving here.

Ugh. Pinching her nose, closing her mouth, Clo examined where the fish-gut thread first entered the fabric, where the cloth around it first began to fester. In the mirror, the line of gut was reflected cloudily—a smear on the glass. But still, Clo could see that it belonged to a young woman standing in a field. Her head was covered, her hands empty. Clo tried

to trace the rotting thread back to wherever the woman had come from, but no, it did not go back. She could not find the woman's childhood. She was not there—and then suddenly she was, a lone figure in a midsummer sweep of hay. Her thread—stinking fish gut—had simply been jabbed into the fabric, into one of its bubbling distortions.

Clo felt she ought to look away—she had to find her own thread, after all. But something about the woman, the disintegration of her line...She could not tear her gaze away.

She followed the smeary reflection of fish gut forward. The woman had walked from the field into a city. She had wandered up and down cobbled streets. She had gasped, gaping at the simplest things—the muddy river churning beneath the bridge, a cart horse flicking its tail, a woman selling strawberries. She had even stopped and, wide-eyed, tried to hold the bright red berries, tried to stroke the horse's velvety nose, but had been shooed away by the merchant and the driver. "Are y' mad?" the driver had shouted when she would not step away from the cart. "Buy or begone!" the strawberry lady had cried when the woman had tried to fondle the fruit.

So the woman had wandered through the lanes until she at last caught sight of a great house perched on the hill high above the town. Smiling, hurrying, she had climbed the road that snaked up the slope to the estate wall. She had touched, lightly, the blooms and vines that clambered over

the wall—had leaned in, sniffing deeply, burying her nose in the sunny yellow petals. Turning then, she had knocked and knocked at the gate, until finally a young man opened it for her. "Yes?" She had held out her palms—wide, empty. A beggar.

Skin prickling, Clo stared at this moment—its milky reflection—in the mirror. Just before, the young man had been so lost in thought, strolling under the cypresses on the other side of the wall, that he had nearly failed to hear the knocking. But when he opened the gate, the woman—her empty hands, her covered head, the way her expression hovered between joy and sorrow—had captured his full attention.

The young man's skin was plummy and rich and full of life; he moved with ease and grace. With youth and health.

He was not gray and wizened, stooped and shuffling. He did not have a leg and an arm and a foot in the grave.

But Clo recognized him all the same.

"Father," she whispered.

She looked at the woman, head covered, hands empty, standing before a wall of flowers.

"Mother?"

And it was. They were. *Mother. Father.*

Her gaze tore forward along the hazy reflection. She saw the moments her father had drawn in his notebook: she saw him sketch the apple-pickers, the wedding feast,

the washerwoman. She saw him painting a portrait of the young lord of the estate, the trouble he had convincing the young man to hold his pose. The fabric bubbled and rippled, but Clo paid no attention to these changes; instead, she watched the pink, stinking line of fish guts—the rotting line that she now realized belonged to her mother—become ever more entangled with her father's thread. It crossed and crossed and crossed again. The woman brought her father a pot of herbs and honey when he was ill in bed. He showed her one of his canvases hanging in the house's great hall. Arm in arm, they walked through sun-dappled woods and flowering gardens and bustling city streets. Finally Clo saw her father and mother standing, hands clasped together, in front of a dark-robed cleric who blessed their marriage.

And now the smeary line of fish gut was fully twined with his, and Clo saw the joy that filled her father's days. The woman joined her father in his cottage on the estate grounds. And then her mother's rounded dress—the anticipation of a child. She saw their happy expectancy, the way her father brought something home every day—a flower from the garden, a little cake from the kitchens. She saw her father—the fabric bubbling all around him—sketching her mother, painting her, painting small moments of their life together, canvases just for himself, and she saw the sorrow that seemed to creep into her mother's face, sometimes, even when they laughed together.

And then her birth... "Oh!" Clo exclaimed. Clapping her hand over her mouth, she glanced over at the old woman, whose body shook with a startled *snargle*. But the old woman did not rise: her head drooped forward; her breaths grew slow once again. *Still asleep.*

Sighing in relief, Clo stared in awe at her own thread arising in the fabric. *There it was.* She touched a quivering fingertip to the line of her life. *This thread was her own.* She looked wonderingly where its shining curve entered the weaving. She saw her earliest hours, her little body bony and red and wailing; she saw her earliest days, her father and mother taking turns cradling, rocking, cooing, and she saw both the sorrow and the joy grow deeper in her mother's eyes. And afterward, not long afterward, the death of her mother... she saw her lie down to sleep and then not rise.... She saw her father's grief, his howling as he discovered and cradled the lifeless body....

Clo backed away from the fabric. She could not bear it. Pressing her fingers to her eyes, she found her cheeks already wet with tears. *How could you, how could you*, she raged silently at the woman's sleeping form. She wanted nothing more than to run from the room, but she forced herself to stay.

When she had calmed enough to return to the tapestry, she steeled herself to look again at the rotting line of fish gut and her mother's death. *There. The end of the rotting thread.*

But the fish-gut line... it didn't end. Confused, Clo

pulled at the fabric. *No, it did end.* There, at her death, her mother's rotting line ended as her life ended. But then there was more decay…another thread of sludgy guts continued on from the same place, all pink and slick and foul.

Clo's breath caught. It was her *father's* thread now, rotting and moldering. No, not entirely: Clo could still see a wisp of yarn, a single overstretched fiber, deep in the jelly of the guts. But mostly—it was her father, his decaying line twined now with Clo's own.

Clo followed her life with her father—its smudgy reflection in the glass. He grew old, seemingly overnight. His skin grew waxy, his step unsure. He became, quickly, the man she knew—the man with a leg and an arm and a foot in the grave. He tried to paint: he could not. He tried to draw: he could not. She saw his despair. He lost his position; he was cast out of his home. She saw him rocking her infant form, despairing.

She traced their travels from town to town. Their journeys under the thick shadows of trees and at the edges of windswept moors and in the gloom of dank and terrible swamps. She saw herself as a small child, toddling, skipping, picking wildflowers and weeds along the paths, weaving crowns of blossoms and greens that her father, graciously, indulgently, wore for mile upon mile until the blooms wilted and dropped away. She saw herself listening rapt—her face shining with concentration—while her father told her tales

of frogs and foxes and spiders and moths as they strode through fields or rested by fires. She saw him search out small things to make her happy—a sweet roll he snuck from the kitchens, a disused primer he found on a shelf, a pair of boy's leather boots he bought with his last coin, for he knew they would keep her feet dry—and she saw how much he delighted at seeing her delight. She saw herself at their table ladling out the watery soup she had cooked, and her father beaming as though he sat at a feast.

She saw, too, what her father had endeavored so long to hide: the pain in each step, his exhaustion, his grief. She saw him struggling to regain his talent—his ability to paint. How at night, working by candlelight as a cleaner to remove the grease and grime from a ceiling fresco, he would practice, following brushstroke by brushstroke the work of another painter. How he would steal paintings to study the lines and work of another in the desperate hope of regaining his own craft. How—as Clo slept in the moss by a riverbank or in a hayrick under the stars—he would try again and again to copy the forms and lines of the stolen canvas...and how he'd burn every failed attempt in the fire. How finally, giving up, he would trade the stolen canvas for a few coins or a sack of flour.

She saw herself—dark hair shorn as tight as a lamb's in spring and in a boy's dirty tunic and leggings and boots—alone and skulking in the shadows of buildings and poking

in the dirt around a miserable patch of turnips and weeds. She saw the villagers peering at her and her father, gossiping about the man with *a leg and an arm and a foot in the grave* and the *perhaps-a-girl who poked at the weeds*. But from here, she could see the concern lurking beneath their gossip: in their own rough way, they worried about her, about her ailing father, these strangers who had arrived in their village. She could feel the shyness and fear of the children who stared at her and refused to take their wayward ball off her palm. She saw how all the villagers had their own troubles and joys—warm fires and empty larders, wedding celebrations and quiet burials, winters of hunger and summers of plenty... How had she never noticed, Clo wondered, fingers hovering regretfully and helplessly now over the fabric, the neighbor whose cupboard was always bare?

She saw her own life lived in the shadows. She saw how her thread and her father's rarely touched another's—how they kept to themselves in forgotten corners. She saw the gaps left in the tapestry all around them.

How lonely their lives seemed from here.

Hurrying forward, she followed her own thread until she found herself at the edge of the field waiting for her father, and the swineherd arriving instead. She saw her midnight rush through the forest, saw herself arriving at the shore.

There she was at the edge of the sea. There she was uncloaking the cheese. There she was no more.

There she was. There she was no more.

But dangling right there in the tapestry, at the very moment of the uncloaking of the stinky cheese and the unwrapping of her father's notebook and the ticket of *half paffage*, was a bobbin of thread.

Clo lifted it gently. Her bobbin. Her own.

It was still attached.

Still wound with thread.

Relief flooded over her—the knowledge of *not dead not dead not dead*—rushing through the very marrow of her bones, a terror that she had not realized she had been carrying. The wound thread shimmered with shifting light and color. Touching it, she felt a brief spark against her fingertips.

But…what of her father? What had kept him from traveling with her? Clo traced her line back to the moment when she had waited for her father under the pine.

There was the swineherd, angry skin and cauliflower nose and muck-covered boots. His lip was curling. An unsure smile…*not* a sneer, Clo could see that now. She shook her head. He was nervous. He was looking at her pityingly.

She followed his thread as he left her by the woods, carrying the woad and madder she had given him back toward the town.

He clambered over the wall, dropped to the other side.

In twilight, he made his way through the streets, past Clo's own crumbling house with its freshly swept stoop. He nodded a greeting to a man raising a bucket from the village well. He climbed the path that led to the manor house; he looped around the gardens to the stables, entered, and walked down a dim corridor to the very end—the pigsty.

He opened the door. In the half-dark, grunting softly, the pigs moved as oblong shadows through the straw.

"*Shh-shhh*, girls. 'S all right, then," he murmured to the shadows. Then more loudly, "Are ye here?"

. . .

"Are ye here? I've seen yer lass."

. . .

"And I've delivered yer parcel. And yer letter. She gave me th' wood'n matter." He waved the wilted plants. "And y' promised another coin if I brought it."

. . .

"And I didna tell yer daughter y'are still here in th' stalls."

. . .

"She's on her way to the harbor . . . like ye wanted."

. . .

"Y' might come out now. No one's in th' stalls but me."

The boy tripped over something in the straw and knelt to look for what had caused him to stumble. There, half buried beneath the straw and muck, was Clo's father.

241

"Wake yerself up, old man. Time t' wake." The boy shook him, but Clo's father could not be roused.

In the weaving, Clo watched with horror as the boy looked about, then tenderly lifted her father's bony, aged body into a barrow and covered him with straw. He trundled him through the dark streets until he reached his own crumbling home. He carried her father through his own doorway, placed him on his own floor. He called out, "This 'un's in a bad way, Ma," and a woman, wiping her hands on an apron, knelt to help the stranger her son had carried in. Their threads shimmered with light.

For a long while, Clo could not tear her eyes from the image of her father in the barn. Over and over, she watched him struggling to lead an ass from a stall, struggling to hold a wheel of cheese, struggling to fill a skin of water. *He had wanted to leave with her.* He had not had the strength. The breath. Finally, in the dark, in the muck with the pigs, he had wrapped up the cheese, the stolen painting, the notebook. He had waited in the shadows. He had grabbed the swineherd. Voice cracking, he had begged for the boy's help. Had handed him the cloak. *Bring this to my daughter. A coin now, a coin when you return. Bring the woad and madder so I know she's received my words.* He had scribbled his message to her, the ink dripping and smudging under his hand in the dark.

In the mirror, backward and smeary, Clo could just make out the letter now:

> *My dearest Clo,*
>
> *Forgive me. Forgive me–this time you must travel alone. I wish it were not so. You must be brave. The ticket is a promise I made long ago to your mother. It will give you safe passage, and will, I hope, bring you to her, wherever she has gone. Follow the path through the woods to the harbor to Haros; I believe he will find you. We will, I am certain, be voyaging together on his craft.*
>
> *The canvas is for you. It is the last I painted. How much your mother loved you. You will see, and perhaps even Fate will forgive me and save me.*
>
> *I hope you will come to understand.*
>
> *Clo, know I love you. So much my daughter.*
>
> *You are the beauty of all the stars.*
>
> > *Always, always, always,*
> > *your loving father*

IN WHICH A BOY EXAMINES
THE SILVER ON A PLUM

CLO READ AND REREAD THE BITTER WORD. ALWAYS. Always. *Always.*

She read and reread the bitter line. *Perhaps even Fate will forgive me and save me.*

She stared at the tapestry, at the line of rotting thread, at the bobbins dangling at the working edge. She stared at the old woman's hands resting in her lap. At her head nodding with each deep breath.

At last, eyes hot with tears, Clo put her finger on the old woman's shoulder.

She poked her.

Again.

Again.

Caught midbreath, surprised awake by the sharpness of the poke, the woman gargled, coughed, blinked.

She blinked several times before her eyes focused on Clo.

"Granddaughter," she said slowly.

"How could you?" Clo's voice shook.

"How could I?" The woman's gaze followed the length of Clo's arm to her fingertips, still resting on the line of fish-gut thread. "Ah." Her jaw worked furiously, an empty chewing, chewing, chewing.

"How could you do this to my father? Did you want to punish him? For what? What did he ever do to deserve this? In his letter, he said *Fate* could forgive him. *Save him.* Is that you? Did you mean you? He must mean you. But you do nothing. Look how he has suffered!" Clo tried to pull her father's section of the tapestry closer. "How could you be so cruel?"

The woman's apple face crumpled. "You should not have looked at this," she said quietly.

Clo started: she had expected anger, not gentleness, or perhaps even remorse, but still she continued. "You've taken my father's life. You've made him ill and old and… and *alone.* You gave him a rotting thread, and gave the same to my mother! And she is supposed to be your daughter? I never had the chance to know her. Why did you want to punish them…punish me?"

245

"Granddaughter." The old woman shook her head. "I did not want this. I did not do this." She slumped mushroom-like into her stool. "And you should not have seen it. It is too painful."

Clo watched the old woman, surprised but unmoved by her apparent regret. "I've seen you weaving. I've seen you place the threads, tamp them down. I've seen you creating this...this thing!" Clo slapped the cloth again, and it billowed under her hand. "Who did this if not you?"

"Granddaughter..." The woman put her face in her hands. She was silent for a long moment. At last she raised her head. "How much...how much of your father's thread did you see?"

"I saw where he met my mother. I saw where I was born and my mother died. I see where he is now."

"Look at the rest." The woman jutted her chin. "Maybe then you will understand."

Hesitating, Clo glanced at the old woman, who nodded and led Clo to a spot in front of the tapestry. She poked a finger at the fabric. "Look, granddaughter."

Parting the warp threads, Clo looked into the mirror at the design. For a moment, she thought she was looking at herself.

There was a boy—a boy with hair shorn tight as a lamb's in spring. Gangly in his dirty leggings and boots, he was standing on a pickle barrel outside a building on a crowded

street. Behind, street vendors were hawking their wares in shrill, cracking tones, but the boy was rapt—his eyes wide and dark as walnuts—staring in the window at a man painting a bowl of fruit. He watched with a kind of reverence and wonder, not even noticing when the painter became aware of him and his shadow falling across the fruit.

"Father?" Clo was not really asking a question; she knew this dark-eyed, wonder-struck boy was her father, but she sensed the woman nodding beside her.

"Look," the woman repeated, though Clo could not now look away.

Hauled off the pickle barrel and dragged by his collar inside the house by a servant, the boy was confronted by the painter. Clo watched the boy standing, knees shaking, in the middle of the studio as the man wiped his brushes.

"You like my painting?" the man asked the boy.

The boy, terrified, nodded.

"I've seen you at the window before."

The boy nodded again. Swallowing, he found his voice. "It's like magic," he said, pointing at the man's canvas.

The man's eyebrows rose in surprise. "It is," he said. "But see here—it's like magic *if* I can capture the light. But when there's an…urchin in the window blocking the light, I cannot paint the object as it is."

The boy's gaze shifted between the window and the bowl of fruit. Comprehension settled over his features. "I

understand," he said sorrowfully. "I won't stand on the barrel again."

"Ah. Good." The painter motioned to his servant to take the boy out of the room and turned his attention to his palette.

"If I was standing there," the boy went on, "then the apple wouldn't be quite that shade of red now, would it? It would lose all its white, glossy bits, and it'd be more purple-like."

The painter looked up in surprise and held up his hand to stop the servant.

"What's that, then?"

"The colors—they'd all change, wouldn't they, if I was standing in the window? So you'd need..." Tentatively, the boy crossed to the painter's side and leaned over his palette. "Well, you'd need almost that color"—he pointed to a mustardy blob—"but with a bit more gray in it to get the pear just right."

The painter's eyes traveled over the boy. He looked at the pear and the mustardy blob and pursed his lips.

"Would you like to watch, then? The painting?"

"But...the light..."

"No, no," the painter said. "Not from out there. In here. I need an assistant. My man, here"—he gestured at the servant—"is excellent with affairs of the house. But not with paint. And you seem...inexplicably...to have a good eye.

So if you'll return at this time tomorrow, and you prove yourself dependable, you might be my assistant. And you might watch me paint. Quietly."

The boy's whoop of joy, the painter's startled jump made Clo laugh out loud.

The old woman tapped the tapestry again. "Keep looking, granddaughter."

Following the thread, Clo saw how the boy served the painter faithfully, and how, as he did so, he became more and more skilled himself. The painter first trusted the boy to set up his easel, then to buy his paints, then to mix his paints, and then later, much later, to paint parts of the work himself—small details here and there—and then at last to fulfill whole commissions.

Clo saw how as he grew more and more skilled, the boy's work began to diverge from the painter's, until finally, sadly, the painter asked him to depart—the two could no longer work together, as the boy was clearly no longer an assistant but a master himself. And how the boy—now a young man, a young man she definitively recognized as her father—at once secured a position as a court painter in the city.

Clo watched the young man take up his position, be given his cottage on the grounds, and receive the first orders of his employer. In the beginning, only decorative objects occupied his time: floral vines and patterns on the

edges of mirrors, mantels, trays, doors. But soon he was asked to paint his first portraits—a new baby, her mother. The young chancellor and his son. The aged treasurer and his wife. Various court ladies and gentlemen in luminous court dress. He painted all with the same rapt attention, the same wonder he had shown as a boy standing on the pickle barrel. He worked for hours to make a stroke, a line, a shade just right. And his paintings...when finished...

Clo leaned closer to the mirror. She could see his paintings almost as if she were there in front of them. The silver thread of drool where the baby had been sucking on its own plump arm. The crease in the leather of the chancellor's shoe. The bloom on the plums beside the treasurer's wife. The shred of yellow light that edged the clouds scudding past the open window. Clo felt she was there—not just beside the artworks, but there—*with* the drooling babe and the vain chancellor and the plums beside the treasurer's wife.

Around each of her father's paintings, Clo saw, the fabric was full of distortions: waves and pockets and hollows. *It nearly bubbled.* And fine golden threads spread like cobwebs. *What were these threads?* They were not like the fish-wool, not like the thread she herself had learned to spin.

Clo lifted one with a fingernail. *So light, thin...* She narrowed her eyes to see the reflection of the golden filament in the mirror. *It was there, but sheer...gauzy...*

She followed the gossamer strand across a section of

tapestry to its end. Here, it wrapped with a thicker thread belonging to a pillowy nursemaid who was standing, arms crossed, in a great chamber in front of her father's painting of the mother and child. "So that's the young master when he was just a wee bit of a babe, then?" she was saying. "An' how young his mother does look, too!"

Clo returned to the bubbles around her father's thread. Again she lifted a golden filament and followed it across the tapestry to where it wound with a fatter yarn: here was a little boy standing on a chair, holding up a plum beside the painting of the treasurer and his wife.

"Look, Mama," he was saying as his mother lifted him off the chair and scolded him. "Look how this plum is like the ones in the painting! Even this silvery bit here—do you see? This silver? On the skin?"

Clo took a step back from the tapestry. She looked at the old woman whose jaw was moving up and down, up and down emptily.

"Do you see, granddaughter?"

"No." Clo's cheeks were hot. She tried to keep her voice steady. "I see my father was a talented painter. Once. You...you stopped him from being so. You took this away from him. I think this must cause him even more suffering—even more than his...infirmity. There"—Clo thumped the weaving—"where he was watching the painter, when he began to study...how happy he was! And his

paintings—well, they almost live themselves, don't they? They're so...so beautiful. And others see them, and for a moment, they see what my father saw. Just at that moment. They see the baby. Or the bowl of fruit. Or the sky—just at that moment, how it seemed to him. And maybe they see their own lives, the things in their own lives, a little differently, too; they see them again, *know* them in a different way, when they look at the painting. But I *don't* see"—Clo could not stop her voice from shaking now—"I don't see how the rot—the rot that has surrounded his thread and is torturing him—is not your doing. Part of your own weaving."

"You do." The old woman's apple face had settled into a firm, satisfied expression. "You see your father's work—you understand."

"No, I do not!" Clo exploded. "And I don't see how what has happened to him is not your punishment!"

The old woman pushed Clo in front of a patch of tapestry distorted with bubbles.

"See what your father did here," she said. "See how his painting transformed the fabric."

"So you are puni—"

"*Shh.* Listen, child. There is no punishment." Her hand traced the bubbles and hollows that rose around Clo's father's paintings, the ripples in the weaving and the gossamer threads that spun out all around them. "You saw your mother, yes? In the tapestry? At the gate?"

Clo nodded.

"Imagine your mother, here. In this room. Imagine her weaving. Here. Beside me." The woman's voice wavered, just slightly, as she spoke. "Imagine her weaving here, and seeing her weaving reshape itself. Seeing it ripple, seeing these golden filaments rise out of the fabric. Imagine her watching your father's paintings come to life—seeing them, as you saw them, and feeling the fabric *change* under her hands." The woman's arm, sweeping over the tapestry, lingered over other waves and hollows. "There are others, of course. Always others like your father, whose work re-forms this fabric. Who reshape time with their paintings or stories or sculptures or dances or songs. Whose work gives their subjects a kind of life beyond their own. But your mother..."

Lapsing into silence, the woman pinched the line of fish gut where it first entered the fabric. Gently, she twisted it into shimmering wool, let it spring back into rotting innards. Twist, relax. Twist, relax.

Clo sat quietly waiting for the woman to continue. For the first time, she saw—*she had a sense of*—her mother, her *never-known* mother, here, in this room, in this house...on this island. And for the first time, Clo began to feel her own self as a part of this place. She touched one of the tapestry's rippling patches and tried to imagine her mother doing the same. "These bubbles are my father's paintings...*reshaping time?*" she asked, trying to understand. "They're my father's

paintings capturing...moments so they last longer than they were meant to?" She glanced at the old woman, who was nodding.

"Yes. Your father's paintings. But any artist, any art may do this. Songs. Dances. Stories. Sculptures. If the art is...*true*, the fabric will change, even as it's being woven. And when people see your father's works—or any artist's work—they see that moment as he did and live it for themselves. And their own lives change in seeing that moment as he did."

The old woman sighed, her cheeks crumpling into softer folds. A line of salt seemed to glimmer in the deepest crease. "Your mother was young," she said at last. "She was not as used to weaving as I. She did not have the proper... *distance*. There must always be some distance. The individual threads..." She shook her head. "No. One must stand far back. The design, the whole. Or"—she brushed her eyelids with her fingertips—"one's sight must not be so clear. I should not have let her begin so young. The carding, the spinning—these are easier. Potential only. But weaving... there is permanence. And she saw your father painting. She watched him the way your father watched the painter.... You saw him? Standing on the pickle barrel at the window?"

Clo nodded.

"Yes? Just as he was—she was entranced. And she was weaving and watching—these beautiful paintings. His beautiful

paintings. She wanted to see for herself....She wanted to see more than shadows in the mirror. And she did what she should not have done."

The old woman removed a spool from her pocket. Unraveling it a little, she held it so the fibers caught the light, and the thread made a quiet *slurp-slurpp*ing noise. Respooling it, she tucked it again in her pocket.

"She gave herself a thread. She should not have done so. This is not for us—the world is not for us. She jabbed it here, at the edge, where your father's painting had already opened the fabric. She meant only to see...to watch your father painting, once, and then return. The thread on the bobbin was dwindling, and she wanted to see him work before—"

"What bobbin? Whose?"

The old woman looked up in surprise. "Why, your father's."

"My father's thread was ending?"

"Yes."

Clo felt suddenly cold. "But that—that is your doing. *You* decide the thread. You can make it longer."

"The thread is the thread on the spool. No more, no less. Well, no less if Mischief, with his claws, does not cut it short. But no. The length is the length. It is spun on the wheel. *You*, granddaughter, *you* have spun it on the wheel. *You* have decided lengths. And your mother saw your

father's bobbin nearly empty, and she wanted to see his painting before his thread had all unspooled. She wanted to see the artist who could reshape the fabric, reshape her own weaving, under her hands. She did not keep the distance she needed to keep."

"Distance?" Clo said slowly. She could not hold any thought but that her father's thread had been meant to end and yet had not.

"Granddaughter. Understand. Your mother, my daughter, went to see your father's artistry. And the world kept her. How could it not? This mirror"—she tapped the glass behind the fabric—"this reflection...could not compare. She came to love the world. She came to love your father."

Clo could not catch her breath. Deep in the guts of her father's strand, she could see the wisp of real wool—stretched so thin, so far...no more than a whisker, really.

"But...he has been with me, all this time...." She thought of her father as she had known him, as others had seen him. The gray and wizened, stooped and shuffling man with a leg and an arm and a foot in the grave. She saw him now and saw the thin hold he had kept on life for so many years. Just a whisker.

She thought of the cloud that had wrapped around her in the grotto and borne her back to the stars. She thought of the voice echoing in the darkness: *Do not let my mistakes become your own...be brave enough to accept what I could not...*

She turned to the old woman. "My mother...she gave him her thread, didn't she?"

"Yes."

"And that is why she died."

"Yes..." The apple wrinkles were deep and pained. "Yes. She took herself out of the world. She gave him her thread, so that he might continue to live. So that you might know your father."

"And her thread...it was never meant to be here." Clo's hand fluttered over the fabric.

"No."

"And that is why it began to rot—even here, even where she first placed it."

"Yes."

"His thread..." Clo swallowed. "Only a wisp of his own thread is still here. All stretched inside the rot." She tapped the weaving. "His thread was...meant to end. A long time ago."

"Yes."

Clo stepped away from the woman's hand, now reaching toward her shoulder. The gesture fell emptily and marked the space between them.

"He has been suffering."

The woman hesitated. "He has had joy as well."

"Why have you not stopped his suffering? Even if you did not cause it, why have you not helped him?" As she motioned toward the fabric, Clo's voice rose. "Even now,

he's lying on the floor of the swineherd's hut. Why do you not help him?"

"Granddaughter, I place the threads. I do not change decisions made in the world. Once the thread is woven, I cannot unweave it. Too many other threads will unravel. One must keep a distance—even here."

"But there must be something—"

"No."

"There must be—"

"No."

"But—"

"Your mother wished for you to have a life with your father. To know your father. To know the world. She gave her own thread for this. What can be done? What would you change?"

With rising desperation, Clo pulled at the fish gut that marked her father's life. "Can't this be removed? Or turned again into thread?"

"No."

"Can thread be added?"

"Only with more rot."

"But... new thread from a new spool..."

"Granddaughter. That was your mother's mistake. New thread must be for a new life."

"If my mother's thread were removed, would the rot disappear?"

"If your mother's thread were removed, see what would happen, granddaughter. Here." She pulled the strand for Clo to hold. "Pull it a little, granddaughter. Only a little. See for yourself."

Seizing the slippery pink line, Clo pulled, trying to tear it away. It arched over the weaving, and as it came up, the threads entangled with it began to twist and rumple. Her father's thread twisted. Her own thread twisted. As it warped, Clo felt a shivering wave cross over her—a shock of light and blackness. Gasping, she dropped the thread. The weaving grew smooth again.

"You see?"

Clo touched her lips; she had felt the impact through her skull, across her tongue. Still, she shook her head. "There must be a way."

"No. And it is not for us to find a way. One must keep one's distance. We place the threads only."

"But don't you miss her?" Clo asked, her voice rising, almost pleading. "Don't you miss your daughter at all?"

The woman's dried-apple face seemed suddenly more shriveled and dry. She glanced away. "Absence," she began. "Of course one feels an absence, granddaughter." She ran a fingertip along her daughter's thread. "But not as you do. Not as you feel your father's absence. Not as you grieve for him." Her hand moved as though she meant to touch Clo's cheek, but she let it drop and turned away. "The tapestry

has its own beauty, granddaughter. It is the whole that is beautiful. You will learn this," she said from the doorway. "You must learn this."

For a long time, Clo stood staring at the rotting line that marked her own family. In the next room, she could hear the woman clanking at the pot of stew and murmuring to the cat. "Yes, Mischief, of course. But what can one do? She will come to see this is the only way. One must keep one's distance."

Clo looked reluctantly where the old woman had last tapped the fabric, the decision her mother had made. In the glass, she could see her mother's cloudy image moving late at night through the shadows of the house. While her father slept, her mother was piling provisions—a loaf of bread, a skin of water, a few plums—and a collection of things— a shawl, a skein of yarn, a small canvas, a slip of paper—into a basket hooked over her arm. Even in the smeary reflection, Clo could see that all joy had fled from her mother's face: she was stricken.

When her mother had finished loading her basket, she stood silently by the bed. Palm on her rounded belly, she lingered, watching Clo's father sleep, before abruptly turning and, head down, walking quickly to the front door. She opened it and stepped outside but did not shut the door behind her. Instead, she stood in the darkness, her hand

trembling on the latch, her figure only half lit by stars. For a long moment, she did not move, but then at last, she turned and went back inside the little house. She unpacked her basket, hesitating only once as she came to the slip of paper. She held it up to the light of the fire, then folded it and tucked it in the pocket of her dress. She returned to her bed and lay down beside Clo's father. Though she did not sleep, she no longer seemed troubled; she rested peacefully, arms cradled about her middle, her face calm, composed, decided.

Heart dropping, Clo stared at this moment. Her father's deep sleep, the woman's tranquil expression—these might have been gratifying to see if she had not recognized what the woman had folded and tucked deep in her pocket. The slip of paper. *The slip of half paffage.*

Her mother's decision.

She could have left. She could have returned to the island.

She could have let her father's thread end as it was meant to.

Your mother wished for you to have a life with your father. To know your father. To know the world. She gave her own thread for this. What can be done? What would you change?

Clo, defiant, disbelieving, tried again to lift the rotting thread, to shift the rotting thread—she pulled it *this way, that way.* She felt the same glittering blackness burst across her teeth and spine.

Again.

The shock carved emptiness through her limbs. Her toes. Her fingertips.

Again.

Again.

Within the carved-out emptiness, rising to fill it, Clo felt despair flooding in.

Again.

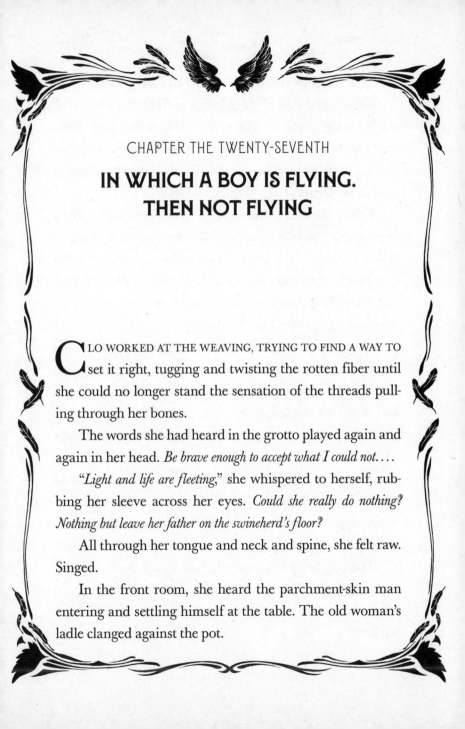

IN WHICH A BOY IS FLYING.
THEN NOT FLYING

CLO WORKED AT THE WEAVING, TRYING TO FIND A WAY TO set it right, tugging and twisting the rotten fiber until she could no longer stand the sensation of the threads pulling through her bones.

The words she had heard in the grotto played again and again in her head. *Be brave enough to accept what I could not. . . .*

"*Light and life are fleeting,*" she whispered to herself, rubbing her sleeve across her eyes. *Could she really do nothing? Nothing but leave her father on the swineherd's floor?*

All through her tongue and neck and spine, she felt raw. Singed.

In the front room, she heard the parchment-skin man entering and settling himself at the table. The old woman's ladle clanged against the pot.

"Join us, granddaughter," the old woman called.

Clo ignored this. She was sitting in front of the tapestry, staring at the fabric without really seeing it. She kept thinking of her father lying in the pigsty. The swineherd who had carried him home. The swineherd's mother who knelt to tend to her father. Their shining threads.

Sitting like this, she gradually became aware of a sharp edge pushing into her leg. "*Oh,*" she murmured, looking. *A bobbin.* Lifting it, she found its thread attached to the finished folds of tapestry near the floor. *Oh, yes,* thought Clo. She remembered how she had tripped on this stray spool when trying to show Cary the fabric.

Absentmindedly, half wondering again why a bobbin would still be attached so far from the unfinished edge, half wishing Cary had been able to see what she saw, she lifted a fold of fabric to tuck it away.

Poor Cary, she thought. Even after drinking the soup, he had seen nothing, and the soup had made him ill. She thought of how clammy and unsettled he had looked. *I had a bit of a ... sharp. Something sharp. For a moment, and now it's gone.*

And just as she nudged the bobbin out of sight, she understood.

The way he had shuddered, the way the beads of sweat had stood out on his brow ... He had looked as she felt now, after pulling and twisting her own thread. Raw. Singed. Shaken.

Pushing the stool out of the way, Clo lay on her stomach on the floor. She felt with her fingers for the bobbin, found it, and gently—*oh, so gently, she did not want to cause any pain*—pulled it out.

Heart pounding, she unraveled an arm's length of thread and moved the bobbin out of the way. Then she shifted and turned and prodded at the tapestry—*There, where the thread left the fabric, could she see?*

She saw some bubbles and distortions in the fabric, like the ones around her father's paintings. Nearby, she saw some bright holes like the ones the cat had torn. But the mirror was too far above this section of tapestry, and no matter how much she strained, she could not see the images of the thread, *this thread*, without the mirror. All was vague landscape—and from here, so close, only a wash of color.

She had to find a way to see its reflection. *Could the mirror be moved?* Clo looked behind the tapestry. *No.* A frame held it against the wall.

Clo tugged on the rolled tapestry in exasperation. Could she loosen it? Was there any way to see its underside? She had to know if it was...

"Granddaughter, join us," the woman called again, brisker this time.

Clo rose reluctantly.

In the front room, the woman was just sitting down across from the parchment-skin man. Seeing Clo enter, the

man paused his eating, his lips crinkled in a dry O at the tip of his spoon. He patted the seat beside him. "Yes. Join us."

Clo looked at the two figures, at the walls lined with cylinders of fish-wool, at the woman's pockets bulging with thread, at the cat crouched over a puddle of stew. She felt ill. "I am not hungry."

"You will lose your sight, granddaughter."

"Why should I want it? What good is it? You sat here, eating soup, tossing fish to the cat—while your own daughter disappeared. And my father—you sit here doing nothing, *nothing* to help, while he suffers. What good is your sight if you refuse to help? If you let this beast"—Clo nudged the cat, which had sidled up to her—"tear holes in lives? Why should I want to hear the spools of thread giggle or sob if I can do nothing to make them more serious or less miserable? It was better when all was gray. When nothing made noise."

The old man's lips quivered at his spoon. He *slurrup*ed loudly and rubbed his fingers across his mouth to mop the wet. "She has been too long in the world."

"*Tsss.*" The woman flapped her hand at the man. "Even in the world, she kept herself apart from others. She will come to see. You will"—she pointed a dripping spoon at Clo—"you will come to see. It is the whole we create. The whole that is beautiful."

As Clo watched the woman run her tongue over

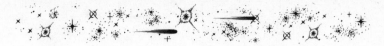

the bottom of her spoon, an idea began to form. *Yes*, she thought. *Yes, that could work.*

"You know," she said slowly, "I think I am hungry."

"Hungry?" said the man.

"She will eat," said the old woman. "Good." She set a bowl and spoon in front of Clo and gave Clo's head a light pat. Clo tried not to flinch. "Eat, granddaughter."

Though Clo had never come to like the soup that smelled of ice and cold, she ate quickly, scraping her bowl clean before her tablemates had even half finished.

"There is not much for Mischief to clean," the old woman said approvingly. She bobbed her head in a round and satisfied way.

"Not much."

"Well, give it to him all the same."

Bending beneath the table, Clo put her bowl on the floor. The spoon she lifted into her sleeve. "I will return to my spinning," she said, rising. Preparing to sit at the wheel, she glanced out of the corner of her eye. The old woman was nodding, her soft fruit face round and, Clo thought, almost proud.

"Before you begin your work, granddaughter, look again at the tapestry. Your eyes are fresh. See the whole, the entirety of the fabric."

Clo shrugged. "If you wish."

"The whole has beauty," she heard behind her as she

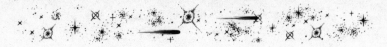

entered the woman's chamber. "We place threads to form the fabric. But the small details, the decisions that determine the color of a thread, are not ours."

"She will only ever see the threads," came a lower murmur.

"*Ffft.* You misjudge my granddaughter. She will come to see the whole. She has no—"

Clo closed the door partway—not enough to arouse suspicion—and hurried to the tapestry. She knew she would not have much time.

As before, she lay flat on the floor next to the errant bobbin. She let the spoon drop from her sleeve.

Carefully, with her fingertips, she worked the threads in the weaving apart as much as she dared: she stretched but did not tear a small opening in the fabric where it already bubbled.

"*Please,*" she murmured. Holding tight to the handle, she pushed the bowl of the spoon through the gap.

It was so dim. The rolls of fabric below, the expanse of weaving above made it hard to see. "*Please,*" Clo said again. She put her eye to the opening she had made; she twisted the spoon this way and that, trying to get it to reflect what she needed to see.

There. There was the thread still wound on its bobbin, still dangling from the fabric. The image was silvery and dim, curved in the shape of the spoon, but Clo could see it all the same.

A boy.

Portly. Pale. Moony-cheeked.

Strapped to giant wings.

He was flying.

Then he was not flying.

He was falling.

There was the ocean rushing up to meet him.

There he was. There he was no more.

Clo lay on the floor, angling her spoon this way and that way, following the thread back. She saw the father and son walking an island that was full of blue light and bright cliffs. She saw the father—like her own—an artist, a sculptor, making things with his hands, and Cary as a toddling child watching in fascination beside him. She saw Cary taking his flute into the green hills, trilling happy tunes at the herds of grazing sheep and goats. She marveled at how Cary's cheeks glowed in the sunshine, how his curls were tousled by the wind.

She twisted the spoon to see the father's fateful choice and stared for as long as she could, trying to understand. She saw Cary standing on a precipice, arms outstretched, while his father with trembling hands tied the straps to fasten the crafted wings. She saw him warn his son, voice shaking, not to fly too close to water, or the feathers would become too wet, not to fly too close to the sun, or the wax would melt. She saw how tears had sprung from his eyes as

he watched his boy beat his wings and lift up from the cliff. She looked for as long as she dared at Cary's thread, piecing his story together in as much detail as the small spoon would show her, feeling her own heart break a little for the boy who had fallen and for the father who had lost his son.

In the next room, she heard the scraping of bowls, the scraping of chairs. She heard the front door open and close. She pulled the spoon from the fabric, rewound the spool, and tucked it *oh-so-carefully* under the roll of fabric.

When the old woman entered, Clo was standing complacently against the far wall.

"Well, granddaughter?"

Clo nodded.

"Do you see the beauty of the whole? The larger design?"

"I do." This was true. Clo did see the beauty of the larger design. But she could not forget the nightgowned boy coughing—*hee*—alone *there*, at the edge of that gap the cat had made, or the soldiers *there*, at that claw-shredded place, bleeding into the mud. Or Cary, flying, then not flying, but falling and tumbling through the air into the sea. Or her father, still lying on the floor of the swineherd's hut.

"Good, granddaughter." Something like a smile folded her cheeks. "Perhaps in due time you will yourself be ready to weave. Later, of course," she added. "Much later. Distance and"—she tapped her eyes—"young eyes. You would not want, like your mother, to be swept away by details."

At this, Clo said nothing, but she set her lips and nodded.

The old woman began to turn away but paused, reconsidering. "Granddaughter..." Her mouth opened and closed in empty chewing. "It is good you are here, good that you are here to take up your work." She looked at Clo as though she expected a response, but when none came, she pointed her chin at the door. "You should return to your spinning. There is more to be done."

"Yes. The spinning." Clo nodded again, though she had no intention of returning to this. "At once." She turned to go back to her wheel. "But first..."

"First?"

"First I might like to sleep. A little."

"Sleep?"

"Yes. Just a little. I have not slept in a long time. And this—seeing my father's thread and my mother's thread—has been tiring. And when I begin spinning again, I would like to be fresh." Clo stretched and mouthed a vast yawn.

The old woman looked over Clo with a critical eye. "Very well, granddaughter," she said finally. "Sleep. And then return to your work refreshed."

"Yes." Clo yawned again. "I will return to my work after...just a nap, really." Backing out of the room, she closed the woman's door after her. "A little nap," she said as it clicked shut.

Clo opened the door to her own room but did not go

in. Instead, still standing in front of it, she pushed it so it closed with an audible *thunk* and then tiptoed to the front door. "Shoo." She nudged the cat away.

She eased open the latch, slipped outside, and pulled the door *nearly* closed—leaving it just enough ajar that it would not make its obvious *click*—behind her.

Cary. She had to find him.

As she tore along the cobblestones, she debated where she would be likeliest to find the moon-cheeked boy. If he was at the boat, repairing nets, how would she reach him? She did not know how to find the passageway—or how she might get past the guard if she did. She looked up, beyond the roofs of the huts to the edges of the cliff high above—was Cary there under his wing? If he was, surely he would see her and come after her. She would try the beach first.

Clo hurried to the cliff path. Half climbing, half sliding down the stones, she listened for Cary's steps or voice behind her, but she did not hear him until she had nearly reached the bottom.

Not his voice—the fragile trill of his flute.

As she came onto the shore, she saw Cary sitting at the water's edge. His back to her, he did not notice her arrival.

She approached quietly, listening to his melody. It was just a few notes, low and sweet and almost mournful. As though the water itself were singing, the surface appeared to ripple at his notes. To Clo, the melody felt full of the sea—not

of the water that was full of salt and without an edge, but of the starry darkness she sank through.

She listened, entranced, watching the delicate little waves spread in the water, until pebbles crunched under her shifting feet and Cary started, breaking off his song. Seeing her, he smiled.

"Clo."

"I'm sorry." She sat down beside him.

"For what?"

"For...for interrupting." She gestured at his flute. "It was beautiful. Your song—"

"No." He tucked his pipe in his pocket, embarrassed. "That was nothing. I was just thinking of when you will be leaving. I was wondering...have you found a way? Did you find your thread?"

Clo nodded. Sitting down beside Cary, she hesitated, considering how she might tell him. "I did. I found my thread, that is, and my father's. My mother's. I'm not sure yet what to do with it—with *them*—but that's not why I came to find you."

Cary looked at her expectantly, his moon cheeks placid and round.

"It's just...Cary, I found *your* thread."

A shadow passed over the moons. "I told you not to."

"I know. I'm sorry. But I thought you would want to know."

"Clo, I told you. I don't remember. There is nothing—"

"*Listen*. This isn't about what you do or do not remember. But you need to know. Your thread—it hasn't ended."

"What do you mean?"

"I mean...you saw the tapestry, right? I know you didn't see the designs or the images, but you saw the finished fabric, even if it was gray, and you saw the working edge? The edge with all the dangling bobbins—the edge still being woven?"

Cary nodded.

"Well, you were right. You have been here a very long time." She bit her lip. "I'm sorry...I didn't realize...I didn't realize how long. I'm surprised you can remember anything. Your part of the fabric—it's so long ago, it's been finished for so long, it's about to be rolled up. And all the threads— all the *lives*—in the finished part of the fabric, where your thread is, are...done."

"Done? All those lives are *done*?" A shadow overspread Cary's moons. "Clo, why would you tell me this? What good is it for me to know?"

"Because, Cary, lives that have been lived have no bobbins. The thread on those bobbins has all been woven into the tapestry. But where you fell into the sea, your thread is *still attached*. You still have almost a whole spool of thread. Your life wasn't finished then. It *isn't finished* now."

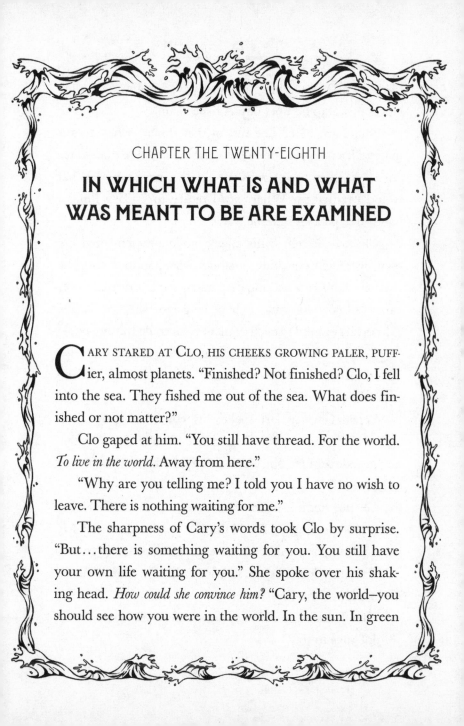

IN WHICH WHAT IS AND WHAT WAS MEANT TO BE ARE EXAMINED

CARY STARED AT CLO, HIS CHEEKS GROWING PALER, PUFF-ier, almost planets. "Finished? Not finished? Clo, I fell into the sea. They fished me out of the sea. What does finished or not matter?"

Clo gaped at him. "You still have thread. For the world. *To live in the world.* Away from here."

"Why are you telling me? I told you I have no wish to leave. There is nothing waiting for me."

The sharpness of Cary's words took Clo by surprise. "But...there is something waiting for you. You still have your own life waiting for you." She spoke over his shaking head. *How could she convince him?* "Cary, the world–you should see how you were in the world. In the sun. In green

fields. With your father. You were never meant to be here. Never meant to be a net boy. A fisherman."

"But I am here. The rest of that thread—what does it matter? It's part of a life I don't remember. A life that—*as you just told me*—is empty of everyone else I've ever known. What would I return to? What *could* I return to?" Cary flung a handful of pebbles into the water.

Clo saw herself in his angry motion—remembered her own distraught chucking of stones when, so long ago, she first sat with Cary waiting desperately for a boat that never came. "I know you gave up hope long ago," she said quietly. "I know it's painful to even think of what could be now, but—"

Cary shook his head. He did not want to hear more.

In silence, the two watched the watery rings spread and overtake one another.

When Cary at last spoke, his voice had grown soft again. "What about you?" he asked. "You're the old woman's granddaughter. She was waiting for you. Are you meant to be here?"

Clo dug her fingers into the stones. "Y-yes," she said, her own answer surprising her. "I think…yes. I had a ticket. My mother left it for my father to give me. I was meant to come."

Cary nodded. Though he tried to hide it, a smile curled at the edges of his lips.

"But I don't think I'm meant to stay. At least, I don't think I have to stay."

Cary, moons falling, turned his gaze toward the water. "Why not?"

"I have a bobbin, too. Almost full. It's dangling there right when I found the ticket for the boat. And I think, I mean, I'm *almost* sure...the old woman, the fishermen, the people meant to stay here—no one *here* has a thread. My mother had to give herself one when she wanted to leave this island. And her line is...rotting. It was never meant to be placed in the tapestry. But my thread, your thread...they're still there. We were born in the world. We are not of this island. Our threads are waiting for us. They're bright, shining—"

"So why *are* you here, then?" Cary asked bitterly. "Why did you come if you're just going to leave? Why were they waiting for you?"

"I..."

"Yes?"

"I didn't know...when I got on the boat...I came because my father's note...I thought he would meet me. The words *save me* were in his letter...I thought he needed me, but the ink had splattered, and I couldn't see what he meant, and I didn't know how ill he really was...."

"And can you save him? You've seen his thread, I imagine. Are you meant to save him?"

Clo closed her eyes. She thought of the ink-splattered note; she thought of the wisp of thread in the fat line of fish gut. She thought of the glittering pain that shot through her body when

she pulled at the yarn. She thought of how long her father had been suffering, how long he had hidden his pain from her.

"Can you?"

Clo's chin began to wobble. *Be brave enough to let go of always.* Clenching her teeth, she turned away from Cary, but a sob broke from her all the same.

"Oh, Clo. Clo. I'm sorry. I didn't mean…"

"I don't know!" Clo wiped furiously at her eyes. "The truth is, he was meant to die years ago. Years ago. My mother gave him her thread to save him, and she didn't know her own thread was rotting when she gave it to him…she didn't know he'd be changed, that he'd lose his talent.… Cary, his paintings—they were so beautiful, I wish you could see how beautiful…but when his thread began to rot, he could no longer paint. He tried, but he couldn't. His thread was meant to end so long ago, and he has been suffering for so long. And I shouldn't have even known him. I am lucky to have had him for a father at all.…" Taking a long shuddering breath, Clo looked up, eyes wide, at Cary.

"Clo?"

"I shouldn't have known him. *I* shouldn't ever have known him," Clo repeated, her words wondering at first, then certain. "Cary, I never should have known him."

Cary nodded, not fully understanding. "You are lucky to have memories of him."

"Yes…" Clo drew out the word. "Yes. Memories." She

sat, staring at the ocean, but she was not seeing the ocean. Instead, she was thinking of how her expectant mother had stood on the threshold with her slip of *half paffage* and her little basket packed full of provisions and her hand trembling on the door. She was thinking of how her father had sketched her mother spinning in the pages of his notebook, drawing her cloudlike and beautiful and joyful and sad waiting for the birth of her child. *Spinning for Clothilde.*

She stood, brushing the pebbles that clung to her smock. "Cary...I have to go back. I think...I have to see. Something my father sketched...it's made me think about my mother, how there might be something else she intended before she decided to give him her thread....If I look in the tapestry, maybe I can see it there...."

As she hurried away, Cary called after her, "Wait!"

She paused, turning.

"Did you see my family? In the tapestry?"

Clo nodded, taking a few steps back toward Cary. "A little," she said apologetically. "It was hard to see."

Cary hesitated, tossing another pebble at the water. When he looked up, his eyes were full of pleading. "I don't remember them."

"I only saw your father," Clo said carefully, measuring her words. "He was a sculptor, a very good one. The tapestry, well, this won't really make sense to you, but it *bubbles* around his sculptures. That happens around my father's

paintings, too." She shook her head. "But your father, he wasn't just an artist, he was an...inventor, I think. He made things—just as he made your wings. But something he made, I'm not sure, it was hard to see...something he invented had angered a king, and the king had trapped him on an island. You were trapped with him."

Cary squinted as though trying to see the distant island. "I don't remember."

"He loved you," Clo said softly. She thought of how she had seen the inventor's hands tremble as he had strapped the wings to his son's arms. "Your father loved you. He made the wings so you could escape. He was trying to save you, to set you free."

"I don't remember," he repeated, but his moonish cheeks deflated just a little with a sigh.

"He did. He wanted to give you freedom. He wanted you to have a different life." She paused, considering. She thought of her own father hiding his suffering, her own mother sacrificing her thread—how much they gave up for her. "I'm not sure he would have tried so hard to escape if you had not been with him," she added gently.

Cary took this in silently. His cheeks deflated a little more.

"Did he look for me?" he asked after a long moment. "When I fell, did he look for me?"

"For ages."

"Ages," Cary repeated. Though he was not smiling, his face flushed with comfort. "I wish I could remember."

Clo watched Cary shuffling pebbles from hand to hand. She opened her mouth to speak, shut it, opened it again, and finally said, "You know, he did not call you Cary."

"No?"

"No. Icarus. He called you Icarus."

"Icarus." Cary rolled the word through his mouth.

Clo nodded curtly. She turned to go up the beach but stopped at the entrance to the path. "Do you want me to call you that?" Her voice echoed across the shore.

A long moment of silence followed.

"No," Cary's answer finally came bouncing back. Even from the base of the cliff, Clo could see his smile. "I like the name you call me. That feels like my name. Icarus…that feels like another boy."

Lifting her hand in farewell, Clo hurried up the shore path. She was smiling, just a little, pleased Cary wanted to keep the name she called him, but as she climbed, she felt a growing sense of urgency. *I never should have known my father.* The words felt as solid and sharp as the rocks under her hands and feet. *I never should have known him.*

Her father's sketch. She had to see the moment her father sketched to be sure.

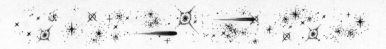

The faster she climbed, the more the words echoed in her head, *never should have known, never should have known,* until finally each step thudded with a *never never never never.*

Nearing the top of the path, she heard a murmuring that grew steadily more ruckuslike. Two distraught syllables— *Msss! Ef! Msss! Ef!*—echoed off the stones. *Msss! Ef!*

As Clo entered the town, she saw all the townspeople— not with their baskets and barrows as they sometimes were—but frantic, rushing, chaotically clambering up and down the street, calling into nooks and corners and holes.

In the center of them all, nearly howling, was the old woman, her apple face red and hot.

"*Mischief!*" she cried. "Mischief!"

The cat. The door. The latch she had not closed.

Clo felt a flash of guilt, then a sense of satisfaction. *Good.* It was better the cat should be gone. Better it should not tear into the fabric. Better it should not destroy lives.

In the commotion, no one noticed Clo. She padded through the crowd, past the wailing old woman, and into the house. She shut the door behind her and listened.

Mmm! fff! The clamor outside was muffled. The rooms were quiet.

The idea she had—she wasn't certain. But her father's sketch . . . the little basket her mother had packed . . .

In the old woman's room, Clo shifted the few items

around. A basket of bobbins. A chamber pot. The stool.
The folds of the tapestry.

Tucked deep in the pocket of a spare apron, she found it.
The final drawing in her father's notebook, the one the old
woman had taken, the one of her mother spinning, there, in
the firelight.

Spinning.

For Clothilde.

Clo looked at the hazy portrait of her mother—at her
gaze fixed on some distant point, at her dress stretched over
her middle, at her hands holding a spindle and thread. The
sketch alone wasn't enough to know for sure. Could she find
this moment in the tapestry? Would it show what she thought
it might? Clutching the paper, Clo crossed to the weaving,
following again the fish-gut thread in the mirror.

She skimmed again through the lines of her father
and mother, their marriage, their housekeeping, their time
waiting for Clo to arrive. She looked at the evenings they
spent together, the shortening days of autumn, the fires lit
on chilly afternoons. And then, not long before her mother
hesitated on the threshold and decided not to leave, not long
before her own birth and her mother's own passing, Clo saw
her mother spinning, just as she was in her father's sketch.
The spindle turned in the light of the fire. Nearby, her father
hunched over his notebook, chalk in hand.

Half holding her breath, Clo drew closer, wishing she could make the reflection clear; the details—colors, lines, form—were lost in the smeariness of the rot and the dim light of the room. Everything seemed washed in gray. Even her parents' voices were soft and indistinct. Almost smudged.

"Such a vibrant color," her father was saying. "The thread you spin—such a rich shade."

"Yes, it is," her mother said. "I haven't spun thread quite like this before."

"What will you make with it?" her father was asking.

"Oh…" Her mother spoke hesitantly. "I think I spin this for our daughter." She watched the spindle turning. "I would like to give this to her one day…so she might make something beautiful in the world…something that's all her own."

Still sketching, her father smiled. "Daughter?" He glanced at his wife.

"I think, yes," she said. "I think a girl."

Her father was quiet. Beaming. "How I look forward to seeing that day," he said at last. "Seeing our child create something beautiful and all her own."

"Yes." Her mother's voice was soft as wool. "How I would like to see that, too. Would like you to see that, too."

They were quiet after that. Her mother continued spinning; her father began readying his brushes for painting. But Clo could not tear her eyes away from the spindle.

This thread had been meant for her.

She glanced ahead in the tapestry—*yes*, there was the moment when her mother had almost left. She had placed her spinning—the skein of yarn—in her basket; she had nearly returned with it to the island.

Would her mother have given the thread to Clo here on the island? Given it to her so she might visit the world one day?

But her mother hadn't returned to the island. She had made the choice for Clo to be born in the world. To know her father. *So what had she done with this thread she had spun?*

Trembling, Clo scanned the smeary fish-gut thread, rushing over her mother's days, but she couldn't find an answer. There was her mother working with her hands—but she was embroidering a tiny nightgown. Or there, mending her father's shirt. Or there, shelling peas. Clo could not find her with the thread again.

Clo returned to the fireside spinning, cursing all the hazy reflected details. She tried to see what else her mother had done that evening, but she had simply sat, spinning quietly, until she had taken herself off to bed. And her father, while her mother spun, had turned to painting. He had rummaged through his pots and jars and papers, had searched in vain for a clean canvas on which to paint. Finally he had given up and, with a shake of his head, taken a finished painting from a stack on the table and flipped the canvas to its unpainted side on his easel.

Clo's eyes widened. Her breath slowed.

She brought her face as close as she could to the mirror, staring at the image of her father as he took the used canvas and flipped it over. It was just a moment, and the canvas was so small, and the images were so cloudy, but still...she could just see...*yes*.

"Grapes!" she exclaimed, standing so abruptly that she sent the stool tumbling and the weaving swaying against the wall. She rushed from the old woman's room and into her own.

Grapes.

The last painting her father had stolen still hung on the wall where the woman had fixed it. The frame was now nearly empty of its decorations—most of the gems had been plucked and rolled to the cat—but the painting...the cluster of dark-skinned grapes, *yes*, this was the same small canvas she had seen him overturn on the easel.

Wrenching it from its hook, Clo rapped it soundly against the stone floor a few times until she heard a *crack* and the joints loosened. Working the frame open, she pulled away the backing board to reveal the underside of the canvas.

There was the painting her father had worked on that night. Still unfinished, it was only a wash of color patches— no details—just soft amorphous forms. Even so, Clo could see—the image was of her mother spinning. It was the same image he had sketched in his notebook.

In the painting, the colors suggested the glow of firelight.

The shadows on the floor. The rosy hue of her cheek. The dark whorl of her spindle turning on a long blue thread.

Her spindle turning on a long blue thread.

Clo, her knees suddenly weak, sat on the bed.

A long blue thread.

Clo looked at the chair beside her bed. Her father's cloak lay draped over it. Reaching, she pulled the cloak onto her lap.

She held the paper ripped from her father's book next to the cloak.

The title: *Spinning.*

The words beneath. Hasty, inked, almost a smudge: *for Clothilde.*

Clo brought a corner of the cloak onto the canvas. She held it next to the image—next to the shape of her mother spinning, soft and indistinct, next to the spindle turning on a long blue thread.

The blue of the thread—the blue of the cloak.

Spinning.

Blue—the same blue.

For Clothilde.

◈

Spinning for Clothilde.

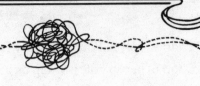

PERTAINING TO THE RECOGNITION OF NIGHT AND DAY

SPINNING FOR CLOTHILDE.

Clo stood and spread the salt-stained cloak over the bed. Her father had worn this her entire life. It was part of all her earliest memories. She had never wondered who might have made it or how it might have been made, whether it was knit or woven or even cut from heavy cloth... but now, peering closely, she could see the threads that overlapped, see the knitted loops and legs of yarn that formed the heavy material.

Clo traced her fingers all along its bottom edge but could find no seam, no stray thread to pull. Even at the corner she had cut so long ago to get to the wheel of cheese, the fabric was tight; the wool hem had felted and the cut stitches

had sealed after being dragged, still damp with seawater, across the rocks.

Along the top edge, there were a leather strap for a button and the button itself, worn at the neck. Clo pulled at the strap—it was nothing remarkable. Just a piece of leather pushed through the fabric and tied into a knot.

She looked at the button, a flat stone disc, black, with a single hole through its center. She had looked at it countless times, seen her father fasten it countless times, but now it seemed to have a different familiarity—*its color, its shape, its size...*

Sea coal, Clo realized, shaking her head, amazed she had not noticed before. The stone was the same sea coal spread over the beach here. It was sewn onto the cloak with the same blue thread.

Carefully, Clo pulled back the fabric to see the underside of the button, to see if she could unknot the thread that held it. *Yes...the thread...* There was a little extra....She could just catch it with her fingernail....

As she caught the thread, pinching it more firmly between her thumb and forefinger, she felt a loosening: the button came undone, rolling into her palm on its long line of blue.

It landed upside down. Its underside, the side she had never seen, was not plain, matte black.

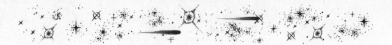

Its surface was carved. With fish. With stars. With a single scratched word: *Clothilde*.

As she raised the button to look wonderingly at its design, the thread that had fastened it unraveled...unraveled and unraveled and unraveled...the cloak was unwinding itself, turning itself into a long line of unbroken thread... unbroken blue thread her mother had spun for her.

Clo pulled and pulled and pulled. The yarn piled, a kinked and crooked web; the cloak grew smaller and smaller until only the very edge of the hem, felted from the rocks and the damp, remained. Clo tugged, and the salt-crusted edge broke away, leaving her with a sea of crinkled thread spread all around.

So much thread. She stared at the waves of rumpled yarn. So much more than Clo had ever wound onto a single bobbin, it cascaded over the mattress and onto the floor. Unwound, it no longer appeared uniformly blue; instead, it held a darker shimmer, the unsteady color of starlight in water.

She understood—faintly—in the way that the piles of yarn still faintly resembled the cloak they had unraveled from—that this was *her thread*. Thread her mother might have given her had she decided to return to the island.

With more certitude, Clo understood that *she was never supposed to have known her father.* That the tapestry thread that held her life—her wall-jumping and corner-skulking and

forest-trekking—should never have been placed for her. But how she could link these two pieces of knowledge...she was not entirely sure....The idea she had, how she envisioned the way forward—it was not pleasant. It set her teeth on edge. She felt again that spark of blackness across her tongue.

Still thinking, she began winding the blue thread, wrapping it around itself, over and over and over. A ball of yarn grew in her palms; the crooked web around her shrank gradually, and when she had finished, she stared with surprise at a gleaming sphere. Though it had shaped an entire cloak, wound, the ball of yarn fit easily into her hands. As she turned it over wonderingly, feeling it warm, almost prickling in her fingers, she heard a surge of sound. *Mmm! Ef! Mischief! MIS-chief! Mis-CHIEF!* Someone had opened the front door: the clamor outside came rushing in.

"Mischief! Mischief!" It was the old woman, wailing the cat's name. She hastened through the house. Clo heard first one chair, then another knocked to the floor in the front room.

"Mischief!" The old woman was searching the room with the tapestry. Another thud.

Clo, dropping the ball of yarn into her pocket, stood facing the door.

"Mischief!"

The door flew open. The old woman, red-faced,

damp-skinned, stood at the threshold. "Granddaughter! Mischief! Have you seen him?"

Had the missing creature been anything other than the savage, piggish cat, the helplessness wrung through the woman's cries would have moved Clo to sympathy. As it was, she answered with as kind a tone as she could muster. "No, I'm sorry."

"Mischief!" On her hands and knees, the old woman crawled, searching under the bed.

The sight of the old woman so distressed made Clo uncomfortable. "Perhaps...it's better?" she suggested. "Because Mischief destroys so much of what you weave, perhaps...it's better?"

The old woman stood and drew herself up. Though she was smaller than Clo, her gaze, imperious and severe, seemed to come from some great height.

"Mischief is necessary." Her voice now carried no distress or trembling. "He creates as much of the tapestry as I do."

"But–"

"No. You fail to understand. You fail to understand the purpose of Mischief. *Think*, granddaughter. How do you know joy?"

"I...don't understand what you are asking."

"You do. It is a simple question. How do you know joy?"

Clo tried to think of the feeling of joy. She thought of her father smiling as he offered her a pastry he had pilfered

from the kitchens. She thought of tramping with him through sunlit valleys and shadowed forests. She thought of their evening fires, the sparks rising into the dark. She thought of the nightjar churring her to sleep, the blackbird whistling her awake in the dawn.

"I feel..."

"No. Think more. It is not just about feeling. Or–another question. When you were in the world, how did you know it was day?"

Clo looked out the half-shuttered window at the endless gray sky.

"It was not dark. The sun rose, the sky was blue."

"And how did you know it was night?"

"The sun went down. There was no light."

"Then you understand the necessity of Mischief, granddaughter."

"No, I..." Clo hesitated. She understood the answer the woman wanted, but she could not bring herself to say it. Surely Mischief was not truly *necessary.*

Her gaze fell on the canvas she had wrenched from the frame: the little bowl of grapes her father had painted. *This painting is beautiful*, she thought. *Mischief had nothing to do with this.*

But–Clo frowned–*did he?* She looked again at the plump painted grapes. Why had her father painted this bowl of fruit? *Why* was it beautiful? Why did she, Clo, feel its beauty?

Clo understood.... But she wished she did not.

It was beautiful because it would not stay. It was beautiful because the fruit—which just then, just at that moment he painted, was so ripe and lush and full—would rot. Would shrivel and sink and grow foul and rank and pale with mold. Peering closer, she could see, even, how her father hinted at this, hinted that the decay was already beginning: just there he had touched a single orb with wrinkle and mold.

If that ripeness never changed, if the fruit stayed always plump and round with dark and burnished skin...Clo glanced toward the window...then it would be no different than the island's ever-gray sky.

"I think you see now," said the old woman, watching her. "Tell me, granddaughter, how do you know joy in the world?"

Clo stared at the woman, whose blousy cheeks had swelled like full sails. She still could not bring herself to give the answer the woman wanted. Instead, she said, "There is no night or day here."

"There is neither." The old woman nodded.

"Is there joy?"

"Not as you know it."

"Sadness?"

"Not as you know it."

"But I feel sadness."

"You are not of this island."

Clo considered this. She thought of how the yarn,

unraveled from the cloak, had buzzed warmly in her fingers. "Am I meant to be?"

"I had hoped you were."

For a long moment, Clo turned the words *had hoped* over in her mind. She thought of asking if the old woman still felt she belonged here, but instead she returned to the cat.

"I understand that beauty and joy in the world...I understand, well, that everything must end. There must be pain. And sorrow. There must be"—Clo hesitated—"death.... Joy would not be joy if it were *always*. But Mischief—the world cannot possibly need what he does. Where he claws, he destroys so much. It's beyond sadness. So many..." She thought of the little boy alone in his bed, *hee*, calling for his mother. "So many suffer for his actions."

"And there, where he claws, where the threads glow brightest, do you not see the opportunity he provides? Mischief enables the noblest actions. The healer who tends the plague victim though she knows she risks herself. The man who shares his bread though he himself is starving. You must take the wider view, granddaughter. The tapestry is most beautiful at the edges of its darkest tears."

"But"—Clo's voice trembled—"surely you must care... must want to help—"

"For someone who spent her time in the world in the shadows, you are unusually concerned with care and help now. I cannot help. *Help* and *care* are for the world. You see

what happens when one cares here—what happened to your mother. I care about the tapestry. The *entirety* of the tapestry. That is all."

"You have *never*—like my mother—worried about the ending of a thread? About a person in pain? Even when you first began the tapestry?"

"Granddaughter, *I* began with the tapestry. The island began with the tapestry. The boat, the fishermen...We were called out of darkness, formed out of darkness. For us, there is only the *always* of the tapestry. It has been my only task, our only concern."

"But my mother cared...."

"She arrived in the moments after. She was always younger. With younger eyes. Because of that"—the old woman shrugged—"she allowed herself to be swept away by the details of the world...forgetting that the whole is also a fragile thing worthy of care."

Clo glanced down at her father's painted grapes, the sphere just touched with mold. *Yes,* she could admit that the brilliant edges of Mischief's tears were beautiful. *Yes,* the tapestry as a whole was beautiful. She could admit that—for the world to have joy—the woman needed to weave both dark and light. But she did not think she could sit in front of the weaving and close her eyes to the people suffering.

She thought of herself *before,* before when she skulked in the shadows and forgotten corners of the villages. She

thought of everything she had failed to see then, the shy children, the watchful adults. *She hadn't known.* Her eyes had changed here, but not, she thought, in the way the old woman had wanted.

The woman, having turned away, was now peering behind the door. "Mischief!" she called. She shuffled out of the room.

"Won't he come back whether you look for him or not?" Clo asked, following. "This is an island. Where can he go?"

"He is helpless," the old woman said, crouching by the table. "A helpless kitten. We cannot have him loose. . . . What does he know of stones and cliffs and seawater? Should he be lost . . . Oh, the tapestry—what should happen to it then!"

Though Clo did not believe that either cliffs or sea could damage that beastly creature, she still nodded. "Yes, the cliffs. The sea," she repeated solemnly, hoping to convince the woman to search elsewhere. "Let's look for him outside, then. Find him before any harm comes to him." She opened the door for the old woman.

"Yes, yes." The old woman scurried past her. "Mischief!"

Outside, they joined the villagers swarming over the street calling for the cat. *Mischief! Mischief!* Clo followed the crowd, halfheartedly calling the cat's name. But when at last she was sure no one was watching, she scurried back to the woman's house and shut the door tight behind her.

The noise of the villagers quieted with the closing of the

door. Clo brought the ball of yarn from her pocket. Though she liked its shimmering, all the possibility it carried, she felt a growing sense of dread about what she thought she must do.

In the tapestry, she found her father's fish-gut thread. There he was, his smeary reflection, lying on the floor of the swineherd's hut.

"Father," she whispered.

He was dreaming. In his present, he was dreaming. Pale, waxy, feverish, he had been moved next to the fire and wrapped in blankets, but still he shivered in his sleep. A bowl of broth sat untouched on the table near him.

Deep in the center of the pink-and-gray viscera was his own wisp of thread. How far it had been stretched.

Never should have known him.

She followed the threads back and back and back, past their travels across silty bogs and wind-scrubbed fields, past her earliest toddling steps, to when he was a new father, all alone, swaddling her and rocking her through the night when she would not stop wailing.

She saw her mother at the moment she let go. In the middle of the night, she stroked her baby's cheek, touched her husband's hair. She lay down beside him, then did not rise again.

How had she given him her thread? The old woman said she *took herself out of the world,* but she only seemed to sleep. Clo stared, trying to understand.

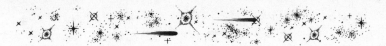

It was her father who had taken to his bed earlier in the day. He had held his head, complained of pain. Of numbness. Her mother's face had twisted strangely, but she had soothed, *It's all right. Rest, my love.* She had sat beside him all day, infant Clo bundled in her arms. When night came, she had swaddled her child and set her to sleep in a cradle. She left a folded square of paper on the table beside the sleeping babe. She stroked Clo's cheek. She ran her fingers over her husband's hair.

He did not stir. His sleep was stiller than sleep. Quieter than sleep.

Her mother lay beside him. Her hands fluttered over her own brow, a quick plucking-like fluttering; then she, too, grew quiet and still.

The room was dark. The infant slept. At last, Clo's father turned in his sleep. He placed his hand over his wife's. "All right, my love," he murmured, then all was silent and dark until morning, when her mother did not rise, and her father found the quiet body.

Clo, leaning away from the tapestry, placed her hands over her face.

She could see that her mother had saved him. She could see that the stillness of her father's sleep was—her chin quivered—where his thread had been meant to end.

But—she shook her head in frustration—she could not see what her mother had done. However she had given him her thread, it was outside the tapestry. Beyond it.

Experimentally, Clo touched her own brow as she had seen her mother do, her fingers flickering at the crown of her head, but she felt nothing. Her mother understood something she did not.

Clo again took the shimmering blue sphere of thread her mother had spun from her pocket. *Well,* she thought. She looked from the sphere of thread to her thread in the tapestry.

Never should have known him.

Hesitatingly, Clo picked up her own bobbin hanging at the fabric's working edge. *It would not hurt just to see,* she thought. *Just to see what happens.* Tugging lightly, she braced for the same shock of blackness across her mouth and spine that had come when she pulled her mother's line.

An iciness curled along the edges of her skull. The top of her spine. The bones of her body. She paused, shuddering.

The pain was different this time. Colder. Emptier. More of a hollowing.

Gritting her teeth, trying to see, for she had to see if she could remove the line that *should not have been* hers, she pulled it a little more. The thread slid out of the fabric. *There and there and there,* the shore and the woods and the swineherd under the pine...she pulled the thread away from these places.

Her memories—under the coldness, she felt her memories growing fuzzy. *Had she come through the woods? What had the*

boy, the one, the one who had—something about his...She could not recall.

Something was giving way inside her.

Horrified, Clo pushed the thread back into place in the tapestry, frantically smoothing the weaving, and she knew again how the boy, the swineherd, had helped her. He had red hair and a cauliflower nose and muck-covered boots and he had spoken with a garbling accent.

Clo, breath as dry as wool, sat for a long while trying to steady herself. The tapestry's patterns wavered before her. She felt a buzzing in her head, a trembling in her heart. In her hands, over and over, she turned the ball of yarn.

She knew what she would need to give up to save her father.

IN WHICH A STORY IS TOLD
AND RETOLD

S HE ALMOST DID NOT HEAR THE KNOCKING.

Between the buzzing in her head and the warm buzzing of the yarn in her hands, the knocking rattled for a long time before she became conscious of it. Even then, she rose slowly and opened the door slowly, still confused, until she saw Cary, claw-marked and bloody, gripping the snarling Mischief in his arms.

"I found him," Cary huffed, setting the cat down in the doorway. Immediately, the animal bounded under the table and bristled at them, hissing.

Clo scowled at the cat before looking down the narrow street: empty. "Where is everyone?"

"I saw them on the beach, looking. They came down the path, calling and calling, and now they're on the shore.

Even the tidesman is searching for him. The little old woman is splashing in the water. But I found him when I returned to... where I sleep. He was..." Cary's gaze shifted to the cliffs above the town. "He was under the wing. He did not want me to pick him up."

Clo made room for Cary to enter. "It'd be better if he disappeared."

"Would it?" Cary looked surprised.

Clo hesitated. "No, but"—she frowned—"you don't know... what he does."

"Hm."

Cary paced the small chamber. He peered into the soup pot, the fire under it having now gone out, and he peered into the old woman's room—only a little, only out of the corner of his eye, not enough to look as though he were actually *looking*, but Clo saw all the same.

"Cary?"

"I..." Cary shook his head. He crossed the room again, agitated.

"Do you want to wash..." She touched her cheek to indicate the scratches on his.

"What?" Cary ran his fingers along his face. "Oh. No. I'm all right." Stopping in front of the old woman's room, he leaned in the doorway, no longer trying to hide his interest.

"Cary?"

He spun abruptly. "Will you show me?" His voice

cracked. "Will you show me my thread? I know I can't see it, not like you can, but will you show me all the same?"

"Yes." Clo took a spoon off the table. "I can describe what I see... if you like."

"Just... show me. Please."

Nodding, Clo led the way to the tapestry. "It's still gray for you," she said, more a statement than a question.

"Yes."

Clo lay down in front of the rolled weaving. She ran her hand under it until she found the bobbin. Carefully, so as not to tug the fabric, she pulled it out, unraveling it a little, and held it up for Cary.

Kneeling beside her, Cary cupped his hands gingerly around the bobbin. "This is mine?"

"Yours."

He squinted. "What's on it?"

"What do you mean?"

"What's meant to happen to me?"

"It's not like that. There's nothing set." Clo lifted the bobbin from his palms. She held the thread up to the light. "If you could see, it's all shifting color. Everything is left for you to decide."

"For the old woman to decide."

Clo shook her head. She put the bobbin back in Cary's hands. "She *gives* you a thread. And weaving, she *places* the

thread. She shapes your"—Clo cast about for the word she wanted—"*circumstances*, I think. But your decisions shade your thread."

Cary pulled at the thread to see where it entered the tapestry. As the fabric puckered, Clo saw him shiver.

"It's there—" He pointed where the thread left the fabric. "That's where I fell?"

"Yes."

"And my father searched for me?"

"Yes." Lying on her stomach, Clo slipped the spoon through the weaving. She saw Cary's father flying, circling, calling. "He was desperate to find you. He was...heartbroken when he could not." She paused, glancing at the boy, who had now shut his eyes. His cheeks were bright with the effort of remembering. "He loved you," Clo said sorrowfully. "So much."

Cary nodded, his lashes dark and damp. Clearing his throat, he looked again at the tapestry, running his hand over his own thread. "What is this?" he asked.

"This?" Clo looked where Cary touched the fabric— a bubble in the weaving. "It must be one of your father's sculptures." She moved the spoon to look and squinted at the reflected image. "It happens around art. Paintings, sculptures, even dance and song. It's almost as if the art...changes time. Slows time. And your father's sculptures...they were

so lifelike, people mistook them. They thought they were real. Alive. But..." She squirmed, trying to angle the spoon for a clearer view. "I don't see your father here."

"What do you mean?"

"At this pocket. I don't see your father. There's no sculpture. It's only"—she shifted again—"you."

"Me?"

"You're sitting alone. Your father..." She twisted the spoon. "He's way over there. He's building something... but the fabric isn't bubbling around that. It's..." She looked again. "It's *you*. You're reshaping the fabric. You're sitting on some rocks, by the sea. You're on an island, like this one, but the water is blue and green, and the hills are covered with trees, and the sky is an even paler blue, and you...you're a little younger than you are now. You have your flute, only it's not cracked, and you're playing..." Clo leaned into the tapestry. "Oh, Cary, the song is so...it's full of the warmth of the hills and the tide...the colors of the sea and sky and the bright air...it's happy.... *You're* happy."

Cary closed his eyes. His chin quavered. "I don't remember."

"You were. You *were* happy. And your song..." She traced the bubble in the fabric. "You can see you had something true. You held it in your song."

Clo rocked back onto her heels. Cary took a long, shivering breath.

Opening his eyes, he looked searchingly at Clo. "If I leave here...what will I return to?" He touched the tapestry at the moment of his fall. "Will I return to this? To the island you describe? To my father?"

"I–" Clo hesitated, looking over the fabric. She thought of how her mother had jabbed herself into the weaving, right where her father's thread was. "I'm not sure," she admitted. "But I think wherever your thread is...I think that is where you will return. Or at least, near where you will return."

"I don't want to. I don't want to go alone."

Clo took the bobbin from Cary's hand and let the thread spin out. *No*, she thought, remembering the icy uncoiling that had come when she pulled her line. *No one wants to be alone.*

She looked at Cary's dimpled hands. She thought of how he had sat with her on the shore. How he had played his flute to cheer her. How he had fished her from the starry darkness. How he had been left to sink beneath the waves. She was not sure what she could do, but she knew she could not leave him alone—here or in the world.

She looked up and across the weaving at the unfinished edge, where her own bobbin still hung. "If I can find a way to bring your thread near mine...or near where mine is now, at least, near the working edge of the tapestry, the present..." She eyed the distance Cary's thread would need to cross. "Will you go with me? Would you travel with me?"

Cary's moons were pale, but he nodded. "Y-yes." His

gaze settled on the thread she held in her hands. "Yes," he said again more firmly.

Even from here, Clo could see the slick line of fish gut. "But you should know..." She turned away, trying to steady her voice. "I know you don't remember the world, but... there is so much. *So much more*, and I want you to see it all again. I want you to come with me. But you need to know... I'm not certain what I will have to return to. The *way* I need to return... I don't know if I will know anything. *Remember* anything. Or anyone."

Cary's brow furrowed, questioning, but when Clo did not elaborate, he did not press further. "Whatever we return to, I will be happy if we are together." He smiled just enough to lift the curve of his moons. "I would like to see the world again—how you describe it. Hills covered with trees... and bright air... water that's blue and green... and sunlight... and starlight... I don't remember, but sometimes I dream, and I see things that are not here...."

Clo tried to return the smile, tried to say *I will be happier if we are together, too*, but neither smile nor words came. "I will need your help," she managed at last.

"Help?" Cary paused, confused. "Are we... now?"

Clo shook her head. "No. I mean that I will need your help later. Afterward. But now we have to ready everything we'll need. We'll need to be quick once I"—she looked again at the slick line of fish gut—"once I start."

"What can I do?"

Still staring at the rotting line, Clo rubbed her temple. She could not repeat her mother's mistakes. "We need... *a boat*. With a boat, I know we can find the world again beyond the waves."

"No. It's impossible. I cannot sail the boat. You cannot sail it. They would never... they would notice... and then, the fish, how would they fish—"

"Not the fishing boat. I know we can't take that. Can you find a barrow? The best. The—the one that's least dented. Not rusted. And a bucket."

"A barrow?" Cary's face twisted in puzzlement.

"And," Clo added, "oars. Do you think you can filch two oars? Will they notice?"

"Not... immediately." He gazed blankly at her, still not comprehending. "Where should I bring them?"

"To the shore. But not all the way, not so the tidesman can see. I'll stay here and try to bring your thread closer to the present. When you've collected everything, come back. I'll need... I'll need you."

"Won't the old woman come back? And won't she not like you... doing whatever you will do at the tapestry?"

"She's already looked here for the cat. I'm hoping she won't return until she finds him."

Nodding, Cary turned to go.

"Cary?"

He paused in the doorway.

"Your wing. Bring your wing as well."

Cary blanched. His lips opened once, twice, before he managed to speak. "My wing. Yes."

When Clo heard the door shut, she sat at the tapestry holding her ball of yarn and Cary's unfinished bobbin. *How would she bring Cary's thread to the fabric's working edge? How could it cross so much time?* Tentatively, she raised it, unraveling as she went, and lifted it so it reached her own, but when she tried to secure it, the thread drooped and slipped—it would not stay.

She tried sliding it beneath other fibers, tried knotting it to the warp threads, tried looping it around two, three, four, five other lines...stomach turning, she even tried lacing it up through Mischief's claw-rent patches....No matter how tightly she twisted or tied, each time she took her hands away, the thread would fall again. She bit her lip in frustration. "Stay," she commanded as, fingers shaking, she tied another knot. No. *Another.* She pleaded. The thread dropped again. "Why won't you stay?"

She cast about despairingly, her gaze landing on a stray bobbin. *Could she take a bit of extra thread? Cut a few small pieces to tie Cary's line and anchor it to the weaving?* Still thinking, she picked up the spool and unraveled a little.

A delicate *coo* rose from the fiber.

"Oh!" In her horror, Clo nearly dropped the spool. *What was she thinking?* There was no *extra* thread. Nothing she could cut without harm, nothing she could insert without rot.

Had she made a promise she could not keep? She put her hand to her mouth. She felt ill.

Lying on the floor, she looked again at the moment of Cary's fall—the way the feathers drifted away, the way he tumbled into the sea, the way his father, anguished, heart-broken, searched and searched for him. She thought she must feel now a little like his father did then—desperate to help but able to do nothing but leave the boy lost in the waves.

Did his father ever forgive himself for leaving his son? She followed his thread forward as far as she could: she saw the man years later, still thinking of his lost child. He told his son's story over and over and over. And others repeated the story—how could they not? The story of a father who had tried to save himself, tried to save his son by creating wings? The beauty of the flight, the terror of the fall into the sea...

He flew too close to the sun, said a thick-knuckled goatherd as he shielded his own eyes in the late-afternoon light.

He did not heed his father's warning, said a young mother nursing her child. *He did not take the middle way.*

Almost serves his father right, said a man in heavy gray

robes, chiseling a wing out of marble, *for going against nature. Man was not meant to fly.*

Again and again, following the threads across the tapestry, from one person to another, Clo saw the story repeated. Or painted. Or sculpted. Or sung about. And each time it was repeated with a detail about the feathers—*Goose feathers, they were*—or a detail about the sea—*There was a ship that saw 'im fall—a tradin' ship filled wit' silk, an' all t' men on deck seein' a boy fallin' through t' sky*—or a detail about Cary, even if it was wrong—*A golden-haired lad, eighteen and old enough to know better*—the fabric bubbled. Just a little. And one or two fine gold threads, light as gossamer, almost invisible, appeared near the bubble.

Clo's gaze shifted between Cary's bobbin and the first gossamer threads. *They were not far.* The loops almost touched.

Hesitantly, Clo raised Cary's thread to the first hint of gossamer. She thought she might try to tuck it, slip it beneath the gossamer, but just where it touched the golden line, without any tucking or looping or knotting, it held.

It held fast.

Clo pulled, gently at first, then more roughly, but where Cary's thread had caught, it stayed.

She looked over the expanse. *For how long had his story been told? Could she find enough to reach her own?*

For what might have been hours, if there were hours to count, Clo traced the repetitions, the storytellings, of Cary's descent into the sea. Fathers who told it to their children to warn about the dangers of disobedience. Healers who told it to explain hope and grief and suffering. Children who repeated it for the adventure in the air and in the splash of the waves.

Inch by inch, Clo raised Cary's thread up and across the tapestry until it dangled only a hand's length away from the working edge.

But how to cross the final stretch?

No matter how she tried—*such a short distance*—she could not tie it near her own. She raised it; it fell. She looped it; it slipped away.

There, where it was last attached, a mother was telling stories to her daughter as they toiled in the fields, breaking up the earth and picking stones to ready the land for planting.

It was one of a half dozen tales the mother told—the others all about animals, foxes and weasels and cranes and frogs wishing for a king. She told the story about Cary last— as the sun was setting and the daughter was most fatigued.

It was not the worst place for Cary to return. The

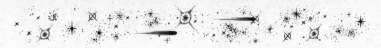

mother was kind; the daughter wore a friendly gap-toothed smile.

Still. They were strangers. And Cary did not want to be alone.

More—Clo did not want to be alone.

"What did the boy with wings look like?" the daughter was asking.

"Oh, well," the mother was answering. "You know Adalwin, the blacksmith's apprentice? I imagine he looked something like that."

"Could he not look like Master Balbus's boy instead?"

"The pigman's lad?"

The girl blushed.

"Well, yes, I think that's right. I remember now. The boy with wings *did* have red hair and ... ruddy skin and a ... *prominent* nose. But he didn't tend the pigs, for there were no pigs on his island. He walked on the rocks and collected feathers that had fallen from the birds for his father."

Clo started. *The pigman's lad.* With red hair. And a prominent nose.

She scanned the threads of the mother and daughter, looking back over their lives. No, they did not live in the village whose wall Clo had last jumped. But ...

But the pigman's lad—her heart gave an extra *thump*—he was *the swineherd*! The one who had grinned at her with a curling lip. The one who had carried her father from the

314

barn. Here, where his thread twisted with the daughter's, he was smaller, younger. With his father, selling piglets at the summer market. The girl's mother had traded a half sack of potatoes for the runt of the litter, and the swineherd had shown the girl—years younger here—how to settle the piglet in her arms and get it to drink a bit of milk from a spoon.

"My mother told me a story about a boy who looked like you," the girl had said.

"An' wot's that, then?" The boy was not really listening. He was dipping the spoon into the pan of milk.

"It was a boy whose father made him fly because he was trapped on an island and then he fell in the ocean and the father was sad."

"Oh." Another spoonful against the piglet's snout.

"And he looked like you."

"Oh."

The story—there was no bubble around the girl's story, though she had told it with her gaping smile and though the pig, slurping milk with its little pig tongue from the spoon, had seemed to listen intently. No gold gossamer spun out around it to catch Cary's thread.

But the pigman, the swineherd—he had heard it. Might he still remember it all these years later?

Could she bring Cary's story forward? Bring it all the way to the present? Bring it even to her father in the present?

Staring into the mirror, Clo looked for the swineherd at

the tapestry's working edge. There he was, just now, sitting at his table, picking at a blister on his palm. Clo's father lay on the pallet before the fire, his breathing still unsteady. The boy's mother stood nearby cutting vegetables for a soup.

Clo could not change the threads or reweave them. She could not make the girl retell the story at the market, could not make her telling more vibrant or memorable. *But could she, like Mischief, change... something?* She touched a fingernail to the weaving. No, she did not want to tear any threads or damage the fabric as Mischief did. But could she *nudge* a thread? Just a little? Just enough to change *something* in the swineherd's present, something that might make him remember now, in this moment, the piglet, the milk, the grinning girl, the half sack of potatoes? And if he remembered, now, sitting by Clo's father, might he not tell the story he had heard?

Clo stared at the scene around her sleeping father. *Not the pallet*, she thought. *Not the boy's blister, not the fire.* But the vegetables his mother was cutting... the runty array of carrots, turnips, potatoes... *Yes*, she thought.

The potatoes. Could the potatoes be enough?

As poor as the gap-toothed girl's telling was, just the bare bones, really, it was the best Clo could do.

Holding her breath, she set her pinky as lightly as she could on the thread.

"Not like Mischief's claws," she whispered. *"Not so much..."*

If she pulled, just a little, and this potato rolled…

She nudged the thread a little, the barest nudge, to set a potato rolling across the floor. The swineherd would have to pick it up, wipe off the dirt, hand it to his mother.

Clo would have to hope it was enough to make him remember.

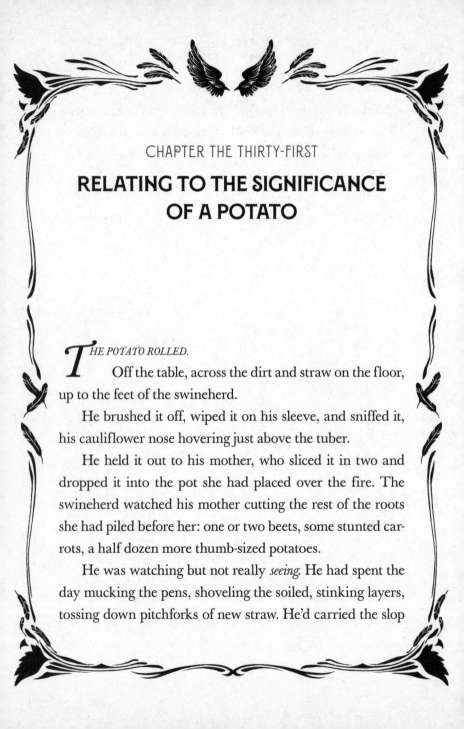

RELATING TO THE SIGNIFICANCE OF A POTATO

*T*HE POTATO ROLLED.

Off the table, across the dirt and straw on the floor, up to the feet of the swineherd.

He brushed it off, wiped it on his sleeve, and sniffed it, his cauliflower nose hovering just above the tuber.

He held it out to his mother, who sliced it in two and dropped it into the pot she had placed over the fire. The swineherd watched his mother cutting the rest of the roots she had piled before her: one or two beets, some stunted carrots, a half dozen more thumb-sized potatoes.

He was watching but not really *seeing*. He had spent the day mucking the pens, shoveling the soiled, stinking layers, tossing down pitchforks of new straw. He'd carried the slop

from the kitchens, the water from the well; he'd pushed a
five-hundred-pound sow off the piglets she'd rolled under
her. He'd saved all but one, the littlest, with the black snout
and black ear. That one had been crushed. He grimaced,
remembering.

He had the reek of the barn all around him, the weight
of everything he'd carried still heavy in his arms. Idly, still
half watching his mother, he picked at a blister that had
opened in his palm.

"Th' potatoes are small, Mother."

"It is what I could get."

The swineherd looked at the man sleeping on the floor.
He'd need to be fed, too, spoonful after spoonful, the way
a runt might be nursed back to health. Only the broth for
him, he'd not chew, but still. That'd be three for the pot to
feed.

"Before Da died, we'd trade a pig for potatoes. Just a
runt'd bring a half bushel."

"Would it now?"

"Mm." The swineherd peeled away the skin that had
ballooned over his blister. "One little potato-picker, one
time, she tol' me I looked like a boy she knew with wings."

"Wings? And wot wouldst tha do with wings?"

"The boy she knew, he flew with 'em. Across th' sea."

"And wouldst tha fly away, too? Leave me here, slicing

potatoes?" The swineherd's mother glanced up, *poof*ing with a quick breath the hair that had fallen over her eyes.

"That'd be something, now, wouldna it? Think of it—liftin' over the village, seein' the rooftops an' the streets? Then o'er the fields and then th' pines...imagine, seein' all th' birds' nests from above and coverin' the length of the forest with just a few flaps..." The swineherd tried to imagine what it would be like to fly, what wings would feel like on his arms. Without meaning to, he flexed, lifting his elbows as though he had wings attached. He dropped them abruptly when he saw his mother still watching him. "Of course *I* wouldna use wings if'n I had 'em," he said, laughing. "Where would I want to go? Besides, th' boy drowned. He fell into th' sea."

"Fell? Drowned?"

"Th' wax that held his feathers melted."

"Ah. So they wasn't real wings. Like birds."

"No. Made."

"And who made 'em? What kind o' cleverness made 'em?"

The swineherd shrugged. "I don't know. Maybe th' boy did."

The swineherd's mother tossed the last of the vegetables into the pot and stirred the coals beneath it. On the pallet by her feet, the sleeping man groaned and shifted.

"Well, see if thy cleverness'll mend that stool, so th' man'll have a spot to sit if'n he ever wakes."

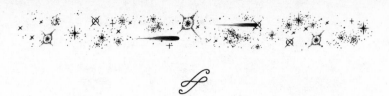

The gossamer line that formed at the swineherd's telling was so airy, so insubstantial, spider silk seemed ropelike in comparison. Clo hardly dared breathe for fear it might break. *Still.* It was enough to *hope*.

Raising Cary's thread, she touched it to the golden filament.

It slipped away.

She tried again; it would not hold.

She did not want to have to tuck it, to slip it beneath the swineherd's gossamer line, but she could see no other way.

Holding her breath, she lifted Cary's thread and pushed it gingerly, timidly beneath the gold line.

It stayed.

In her hand, Clo still held Cary's spool. She knew the filament could barely hold the yarn; it would not take the weight of a full, dangling bobbin. Unraveling and unraveling, she let out enough thread to rest the bobbin on the floor.

She would have to hope that the swineherd would retell his story. That someone might repeat it. That her sleeping father had somehow heard it. Or that she and Cary would return to the present before the old woman picked up or pulled away or knocked over his bobbin and ripped him from the swineherd's telling, and he was sent back to the mother and the daughter picking rocks out of the field.

While Clo waited for Cary to return, she gathered the last of her things—a dry crescent of cheese, her father's notebook, his canvas—and a few things that were not hers—a bit of rag, a few dozen fish. Skewering the fish on the iron the old woman used to poke the fire, she held them above the coals until their scales crackled and they were crisp and pocketable. She wrapped the rag around the hot fish and dry rind.

For a long moment, she stood looking at the sketch of her mother—*Spinning for Clothilde*—studying its chalky lines. Her father's hand. Her mother's form.

She knew the old woman did not feel grief or sadness in the way that she did, but still...some part of her, some part deep beneath her apple skin, must miss her daughter. She would leave the portrait for the woman.

As she smoothed the wrinkles and placed the sketch on the old woman's table, Clo started, seeing a detail she had not noticed before. Her mother's spindle...its dark whorl, was it not the button from the cloak? She squinted. Just there in the sketch, along the side of the dark whorl, she could see where her father had left a fishy squiggle. A starry spot.

She removed the cloak button from her pocket. *Was it?* Its central hole was just the right size for a spindle. Clo squinted. It was impossible to know for sure. *Still.* She smiled. Perhaps it was.

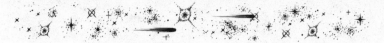

Clo placed the whorl-button carefully on top of the sketch. She would leave both portrait and stone for the old woman.

Outside, the drone of the villagers' voices rose again in the street—then faded away as they continued their search for the cat. The keening of the old woman carried over the general murmur, and the cat gargled in distress at her voice. Feeling a flash of guilt, worrying too that the old woman might hear and return, Clo tossed the beast a few fish to quiet his noise.

When Cary finally did return, he arrived with a clanging, each step down the street marked with a *ting-ka-chung*. Clo opened the door: Cary was pushing a barrow on a loose, dented wheel, and his face had swelled with exertion.

"I'm sorry, I'm sorry," he said as he *ting-ka-chung*ed his way over the cobblestones. "Everything else I've brought, but this...I couldn't bring it down the cliffs, not by myself, and this is the best barrow I could find. The box is good." His knock against the metal produced a healthy boom. "But the wheel is not. It won't roll. I'm sorry."

Clo gave a dismissive wave. "Not important." She stepped aside to let Cary enter. "I think I've found a way so we will return together. To the same time. I'm not *certain*, though." She hesitated. "I'm not even a little sure."

Cary nodded.

"I'll understand...if you don't want to risk...if you don't want to go."

"Don't you need me?"

"Y-yes, but..." Clo thought of the filament holding Cary's thread in place. She thought of her own thread and the decision she had made. "I don't even know—know for certain—where I will be when we return. And you..." She glanced away. She did not want to tell him this. "It's possible...you may end up nowhere familiar. You may fall out of the sky and into a field where a mother and daughter are picking stones. Or...maybe not even there. Maybe you'll fall into the sea again, only this time, no one would fish you out."

"I see." Cary's moons looked hollow, almost dusty. Cratered. His chin wobbled.

"If you don't go"—Clo tried to keep emotion from her voice—"you can still help me. I'm—"

"No. I am. I am going with you."

"You are?"

"I think...I'd rather...There is a chance, right? There is a chance we'll return together?"

"If I'm honest..." Clo raised her eyes to meet Cary's. "It's small."

"A chance." Cary's chin had ceased wobbling. "That's enough." He paused, considering his words. "Before you told me about what you saw in the tapestry, when I fell...I didn't know my father searched for me. I didn't know *why*, why the wings...why he'd tied them to me. I didn't remember I was

loved. And falling–I don't want to...again...but I know what I'm risking. And I know what it would be to stay." He gave Clo a small smile.

"Well." Clo nodded. "Well then." She felt her own fear rising now. "There's just one thing..."

Cary looked at Clo expectantly. She gestured for him to follow her to the tapestry. "You need to help me unweave my thread."

"Unweave your thread?"

Clo looked away to hide her agitation. She nodded.

"But...won't that...won't you–"

"I wasn't ever supposed to know my father. I was never supposed to *be*–or, at least, I was not meant to have the life I have had. My mother...she changed what was meant to happen in the world. She gave herself a thread, and then she gave my father what was left of her thread to save his life... and so that I would have a life with him. So that I would know him. But she didn't know the thread she gave him was rotting."

Clo thought back to her drowning in the grotto, to the pale cloud that had carried her across the darkness, to the soft voice warning her, *Do not let my mistakes become your own....Be brave enough to accept what I could not....* She closed her eyes. Her heart beat heavily. She still was not sure if this was the right thing.

"I think...nothing happened as she intended. I *know*

she feels she made a mistake. And my thread, the one that's there"—Clo pointed to the weaving—"I wasn't supposed to have this thread in the tapestry. I wasn't meant to be born in the world."

She held up the ball of yarn she had pulled from the cloak and handed it to Cary. "*This* is the thread my mother spun for me. If I had been born here, on the island, I think she would have given it to me so I could... *visit* the world one day. But when she decided that I should be born in the world, she couldn't give it to me. The old woman placed a thread here for me instead."

Taking the yarn back from Cary, she turned it over, feeling its fibers buzz in her palms. "Cary, I'm really not sure if what I'm doing... I'm not sure if it's right. I only know that my father's thread is rotting... and maybe..." She twisted her hands together. She could not bring herself to say what she hoped she could do. She did not know if it was possible. "Maybe if I can undo part of what should *never have been*," she said instead, "maybe I can stop his suffering."

"But what will happen to you when you pull your thread from the tapestry?"

Clo's throat felt uncomfortably tight. "I think I have to give up... everything. My... memories."

"You can't do..." Cary was aghast. "I won't *let* you do that! You would be giving up *yourself*!"

"Cary, I have to. It's the only way I can help my father."

She tried to steady her voice. "I have to choose who to help. And what to lose. To save him, I will have to lose him."

"And lose yourself! Lose all your memories! No father would want to lose his child so he could be saved."

"He would do the same for me." Clo thought of how her father had kept his suffering—his daily pain, his loss of talent—hidden from her. "He *has* done the same for me. And he won't lose me. He'll keep his memories of me." She hesitated, suddenly unsure. "Or I *think*...he might keep them. And if you help me, I won't lose him, not completely. I—*we*—can find him again. We can try, at least."

Cary started to shake his head, but Clo interrupted. "Cary, please. Listen. I'm not sure I will want to return to the world if I can't remember. I won't have a reason to. You'll need to remind me why I should. You'll need to remind me that I have a father I love. That there is a kind boy with a cauliflower nose who lifted him out of the pig straw. That the world has darkness *and* light. But right now, he's suffering. Dying. If I do nothing, he will die."

"You'll have your memories—"

"I'd rather have him."

"But you won't! You won't even know him—"

"Cary. Wouldn't you? Wouldn't you do whatever you could to save..." Clo trailed off. "You *did*. Your father. You put on wings for him. You flew for him. You tried to save someone you loved."

Cary stared at the tapestry. "I don't remember my father. I don't remember making a choice to save him. I don't remember...if I...if I loved him," he said quietly. "But I know I would help someone I...cared for." He raised his eyes to meet Clo's. "I would try to keep someone I cared for safe."

"Please." Clo fastened her eyes on Cary's. "Please help me."

The two stood in silence. Finally Cary, pushing a damp curl from his brow, cleared his throat. It was a minute before he found his voice. "Wh-what can I do?"

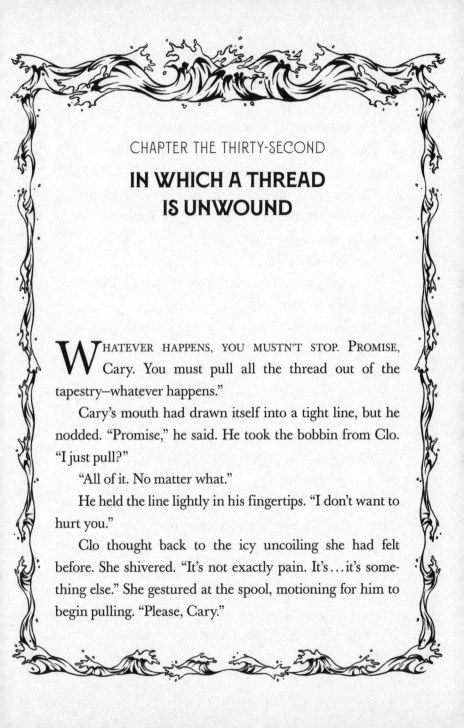

CHAPTER THE THIRTY-SECOND

IN WHICH A THREAD IS UNWOUND

WHATEVER HAPPENS, YOU MUSTN'T STOP. PROMISE, Cary. You must pull all the thread out of the tapestry—whatever happens."

Cary's mouth had drawn itself into a tight line, but he nodded. "Promise," he said. He took the bobbin from Clo. "I just pull?"

"All of it. No matter what."

He held the line lightly in his fingertips. "I don't want to hurt you."

Clo thought back to the icy uncoiling she had felt before. She shivered. "It's not exactly pain. It's...it's something else." She gestured at the spool, motioning for him to begin pulling. "Please, Cary."

Eyes questioning, he tightened the slack of the line. "Are you sure?"

Clo forced herself to nod. "Now. All of it."

Cary pulled gently, uncertainly, but, as before, the thread came away from the weaving easily.

Clo felt again an unraveling, an unwinding happening deep within her. Her limbs began to feel distant, too far to reach. She swayed, staggered.

"Are you all right?"

Clo struggled to form the words to answer. "K-keep... k-keep. Keep pulling."

"I'm hurting you."

She forced herself to shake her head. "N-no." A numbness, a cold finger, pressed into her consciousness. She felt it at the base of her skull, scraping at the matter between her ears.

"Clo—"

"Keep p-pulling. Y-you must. M-must not st-stop. You pro—...p-promised."

Memories flashed and faded as Cary pulled away her thread: she understood them, then only the absence of them, the impression where they had once been. Trampled grass.

She tried to hold on to the sensation of early morning, the smell of pines. The idea of walls, field, forest. Stone and dew. Bread. Turnips. Table. Hearth. Sunlight. Starlight.

Her father—she tried her hardest to hold on to him. She saw herself as a child, toddling at his heels. Pulling at his arm while he tried to work. Carried on his shoulders through the busy streets of town. She knew him—the shape of his hands, the unsteadiness of his step; the sound of his laugh, of his grumbling—then these memories too began to peel away. Looking for them, she found only their shadows.

The cold finger scraped a deeper hollow. "N-no…"

"Clo?"

"Prom—…*promised*," she tried to say, though she could not be certain whether her mouth had moved or whether any sound had come from it. Somewhere, far below her, Clo felt what had been her legs give way. She felt the firmness of the floor, then felt it dissolving beneath her.

"Clo!" she heard again, faint, an echo.

She was in darkness. She clung to the word *father*. At the last, she had the sensation of arms around her, of rocking, of a fragment of song; then even this was gone, and the word was emptied. She tried to form its sound—a hollow box.

"Clo!" The darkness pressed and distorted the name. *Guh-loh*.

"I—" she tried to say, but the word *I*, too, had been scraped clean. She felt its shell, its brittle edges, around her.

"Clo?"

She could not move out of the hollow form of *I*.

"Clo?" The word could not reach her.

331

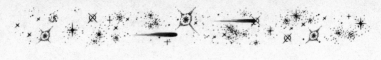

Guh-loh.

Guhl.

Guhl—y.

Something thudded against the shell that was her *I*.

It knocked, once, twice; it slipped under her.

"Girly." She felt herself lifted on a wooden slab. *Perhaps she was the wooden slab.* "Girly, once again, yer no full passage." The darkness grunted, and she found herself tossed onto something solid. "Ye ought t' know better. Ought t' know not t' go beyond."

There was a rocking. A steady wet sound. Sloshing.

"Ah—girly. 'S good thing I was out here."

More sloshing.

"Y'know, you might open yer eyes."

Darkness.

"Here." A poking, two fingers. "They're here. Try here." Again, a poking. Two pokings. "Open those."

A line of glowing pebbles.

"That's it. Give it some time."

The sloshing started again. A regular knocking—wood rolling against wood.

"I found someone out here fer you. Not ready fer my boat jus' yet, but think you were lookin' fer 'em. Last saw

'em round about–" A grunt. "Round about here." The pebbles opened. "Hallloooo! Hallloooo! Hallllooo there!"

Silence.

"Be back soon, I imagine. You might wait fer 'em."

Silence.

"Ah, girly. Ye have t' get out. I can't stay with you. Here–" Something gripped her. Moved her. "Sit here." A push. " 'S safe here."

The pebbles had a sad mouth around them.

"That's good. Wait here fer 'em."

A splashing.

"Good luck t' you, girly."

Splashing. Splashing.

Splashing.

Silence.

Something firm was beneath her. And a smell–air that carried the scent of open space. And dappled light.

She waited for a long time in the air of light and space.

She tried to use her eyes, the places where the pebble mouth had poked. Patches of bright and dark.

Gradually, the looking gave the patches form. Color. A bright speck was moving across something wide and dark and tall. A bright green speck. She watched it proceed across

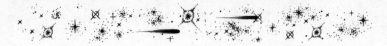

the dark expanse. She touched the dark thing: it was rough, uneven. Barklike.

A beetle was climbing a tree trunk.

She watched its progress, and in the watching, in her focus on this tiny thing, more objects took shape around her.

The tree—she was sitting beneath it. Its branches hung over her, sharp needles casting sharp shadows. The sharpness was a prickling in her mouth—the word *pine*.

All around her was empty space, as though she—and the tree—were on an island. The empty space had the quality of a field, though it was not a field. It shimmered with waves green and gold.

She sat for a long time, her back against the trunk, watching the shimmering waves.

Out of the shimmering, little by little, she became aware of a darker smudge. It, too, shimmered—a silver smear—but it moved forward, crossing the expanse, and grew slowly into a shape, thin, ovoid, that took on a form with arms and legs.

It walked with steady steps across the expanse—long, even strides—and the silver smudge resolved itself into a man. He was smiling, his cheeks flushed with health, and hailing her with a wave.

"Hullooo!" he called.

When he reached her, he sat down, placing a pack beside him on the ground. "Hello," he said again.

"Hello," she said.

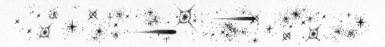

"I am so glad to see you."

"You are?"

"Yes. I've been alone here for so long."

"Ah."

"Have you been here long?" he asked after a pause.

"No...I don't think so. I can't really remember."

"What are you doing here?"

"I'm...not sure."

"I've been dreaming," the man said.

"Really?"

"Yes. Strange dreams. Wonderful dreams. But sad dreams, too."

"Sad?"

"I dreamed I had a wife. And a daughter. But I don't."

"Oh."

"I lost them."

"I'm sorry."

"I miss them. Even though they were a dream, I miss them. I loved them. They were..." He hesitated. "You look like her–my daughter. Perhaps you are part of my dream?"

"No...I don't think I am. I think I came here on a boat." She squinted at the man. His eyes were kind, his hair just tinged with silver. "You look like a father," she said. "Like you could be a father."

"Thank you. I'm not sure–in my dream–I'm not sure I was a good one."

"I'm sure you were."

"How can you know?"

"I..." She shook her head. "I just feel it. When I saw you walking, just now, I felt that you seemed like a father a daughter would be happy to see. And..." She paused, considering. "And that you would have something good to eat with you."

"I do! I do!" the man exclaimed. "Pastries. My pockets always seem to be full of them." He held up a bun studded with fruit and sparkling with sugar. "Would you like one?"

"Y-yes," she said, but when she went to take the sweet, she found her hands already full.

"What do you have there?" the man asked.

"I..." She held up her hands. They were tangled with thread, the soft fiber draped in messy coils over her fingers and wrists and arms. "Thread?"

"Lovely," said the man. He lifted a strand between his fingers. "Just beautiful. Look at the colors."

She examined it. The thread's colors shifted and swam, turned from dark to light to dark again. Had she ever seen anything more wondrous? She did not think so. But the man looked like he might need it.

"Would you like it?" she asked the man.

"Oh, I couldn't possibly."

"No, please," she said. "I'd like to give it to you. A trade for the pastry."

"No, no." He laughed. "A stale little bun that came out

of my pocket...that I...well, I think I might have taken it, stolen it even...certainly isn't a fair trade for that remarkable thread. But...I could...oh, yes! Here!" He unbundled his pack. "I have just the thing." He removed and unrolled a canvas, spreading it across their laps.

"Oh!" she gasped. "How...wonderful..."

"I am rather proud of it." The man smiled. "It's a dream I had. An unusual dream, different than my others, but I had to paint it."

She gazed at the painting. A boy was falling from the sky into froth-tinged waves. He had wings—and the feathers of the wings had come free and drifted everywhere in the air around him.

"It's not finished yet," the man added regretfully. "I couldn't decide how the boy should look." He pointed to the painting. Though the wings had been painted in exquisite detail so that even the downy lines of the feathers seemed to breathe, the boy's own features were smudged. "I had dreamed he had red hair...and a...bit of a funny nose, but that didn't seem right."

She squinted at the smudge. "Could he not be younger?"

"Yes," the man said, thinking and nodding. "He would need to be young...about your age...wouldn't he? To put on wings like that."

"And round cheeks. It seems like he should have round cheeks."

"That does seem right. So young, he'd be a bit soft."

"And could there not be...someone on the shore who sees him fall? Who helps him?"

"Would he survive? In my dream, he disappeared under the waves."

"I think he would. I feel like he would."

"Well," said the man, pointing to the cliffs in the painting. "There is room here for a person who might see him."

"Oh, yes."

His gaze traveled over her. "Perhaps that person could look...a bit like you. My look-alike daughter. That would make me happy." The man smiled, and again, he reminded her of a father a daughter would be happy to see. He began to roll the canvas. "I'll finish this for you, and then we'll trade. Your thread for the painting."

"No, no. Please, take the thread now."

"I couldn't."

"Please." She held up the handfuls of yarn. "I'll come back for the painting."

The man hesitated. "You must come back. I wouldn't feel right if you didn't."

"I will. I promise."

Reluctantly, the man took the thread from her. He held it up, lacing his fingers through the loops, and it glimmered in the light. "It really is so beautiful," he said. "Just... remarkable." He shook his head. "I still don't think I should

take it. It's too...lovely. You should not give it up. You should not be left with nothing."

"I want you to have it. And the painting...it is a fair trade."

"I don't feel it is...and I still need to finish it. I will be leaving you empty-handed."

"Not empty-handed." She gestured at his pocket. "I will still take a sweet!"

"Of course, of course!" The man took one, two, three fruit-filled pastries from his pocket.

She ate the first right away, taking quick bite after quick sugary bite. She smiled at the man through jammy teeth. "It's good," she said.

"I'm glad you like it. In my dreams, my daughter always liked pastries."

She took another mouthful. *Honey and berries and bread.* Closing her eyes, she felt the word *comfort* fill her mouth.

The man looked happy to see her happy. "You must have been hungry."

"Yes, I guess I was." Thinking about it, she added, "I can't remember the last time I ate." Licking the fruit and honey from her fingertips, she looked around for a place to store the other two buns. She found she was wearing a smock. She slipped the pastries into one of its wide pockets.

"Well," said the man, standing, "I'm glad I could give you something to eat. When I see you again, I will bring more."

"I will look forward to that."

The man slung his pack over his shoulder. "Do you think this is another dream?"

"I don't think it is. I don't feel like it is."

"You will return when the painting is finished?"

"Yes. I promise." She paused. "How will I find you?"

The man glanced around at the field that was not a field, at the shimmering waves of green and gold. "Look for me under the tallest pine," he said, and pointed to the tree she sat beneath. "In my dreams, I always met my daughter under the tallest pine." Lifting his hand, he began to walk away. "*Always*," he repeated softly, wondering at the word.

She watched him go, his figure becoming smaller and more smeary until it disappeared into the luster of the waves.

Once again, she was alone.

All about her was quiet...so quiet that she could hear the beetle still clambering up the bark, the steady scratching of its insect feet up and up and up into the needled branches.

K-k-k-k-k, its feet tapped.

Slowly, incrementally, the light around her faded. The waves of the field, growing darker, crested with silver. She watched them lift and break, lift and break and foam. The beetle continued on its path up the trunk. *K-k-k-k-k*.

The noise began to bother her. She moved around the little island, circling the tree, trying to escape the sound, but the *k-k-k-k* followed her everywhere.

Tentatively, she put her feet into the dark waves. They felt heavy and pulled against her, but with effort, she could walk through them. She stumbled stride by stride out into the darkness. *K-k-k-k* continued to echo behind her: no matter how far she walked, she could still hear the klacketing racket.

The farther she walked, the thicker and darker the waves became: they began to pull at her knees and thighs. Each step was now a struggle; she felt a sucking pulling her down. She began to fear she might sink beneath the surface. She staggered forward, panic growing. She did not know where she was going, if there even was anyplace to go. Gasping, tripping, she looked for the tree and the little island; though she could still hear the infernal tapping, she could see no land.

Suddenly, she felt something take her by the elbow. Beside her, a voice came out of the darkness. "He's so loud, isn't he?"

She turned. The nebulous profile of a woman was beside her. "Yes," she answered.

Still holding her arm, the cloudlike woman gently guided her forward. With the woman's support, it became easier to move through the waves; though still heavy and grasping, they no longer threatened to pull her under.

"Do you know me?" the woman asked.

She turned to examine the shadow. In the light of the

waves, the woman's hazy silhouette seemed etched with starlight. "Y-yes," she answered, though she could not be sure. The silver light was comforting. It felt like the encircling of arms.

"Ah. You do not." The woman sighed. "One day, perhaps."

"One day?"

The woman did not answer. "Did you see your fa–" The woman paused. "A man?"

"Yes. He was kind. He promised me a painting."

The woman's voice was shaped by smiling. "Ah. I wish I could see it. See him."

"Can't you?"

The woman shook her head. "We are on different journeys here." They walked forward in the darkness still echoing with *k-k-k-k*.

"You are brave to travel here again," the woman said at last. "Brave to travel here as you did."

"Am I?"

"You unwove your thread."

"Unweaving…I don't remember such a thing. I know I gave the man some thread."

"Yes," the woman said, and her voice was sad. "You were brave to do so."

"It seemed like he might need it."

"It was very precious," the woman said. "It held so

342

much...." She shook her head, and her voice grew even more sorrowful. "I did not intend this for you. I would never wish for you to give up so much. And he...he would not have taken it if he had known."

"Well, he did give me some pastries."

"Did he?"

"Yes." She took one from her pocket and held it for the woman to see.

"Lovely," said the woman. "Jammy?"

"Yes, very."

The woman nodded. "Lovely," she repeated. "Jammy is lovely." She raised a soft hand to point across the darkness to the shape of the tree and the island, now visible in the silver light. "Here we are."

"Oh, I left this island. The beetle was annoying me."

"Of course he was." The woman guided her onto the shore. "He is very persistent."

They stood under the tree.

The woman gazed up into the boughs. "Do you see this?" She lifted a finger where a spider dangled from a line it had stretched between two branches.

"The spider? Yes."

"Watch."

As they stood gazing, the spider moved rapidly between the branches, pinning and dropping, pinning and dropping. A web, a hemisphere of silver, began to take shape.

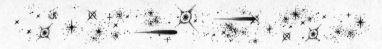

"She spins her whole life," the woman said. "Remarkable, really."

"Her whole life?"

"Her whole life. All her own." She pointed again at the spider now resting on its haunches at the end of the branch. "See how she's learned to use her thread?" As they watched, the spider spun a trail of silk out into the air. Caught by the wind, the silk whisked the spider into the darkness, carrying it across the waves. "Beautiful, isn't it?"

"Where is she going?"

"Wherever she wishes. Wherever the thread she has spun takes her." The woman pointed up into the branches where the beetle was still tapping its steady tattoo. "We ought to be careful your beetle friend isn't caught, though."

"Oh, it would be fine if he was. That noise!"

"No, no." The woman patted her arm. "You need to listen to him."

"No—that sound—it's terribly annoying. It won't let me rest."

The woman shook her head. "That is the sound of love. You will hear it....It will carry you from here, but..." The woman hesitated. "Afterward, you will not want to leave. It is easier there...where things are certain. Unchanging. It's hard to trade certainty for sorrow...." She paused. "Tell me, would you trade a pastry?"

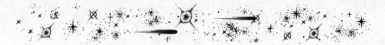

"My pastry?" She took a fruit-filled bun from her pocket and looked at it longingly. "Do you want it?"

"I do," said the woman. "But I'd like to give you something in return."

"What?"

Rummaging at the base of the tree, the woman pulled up a bulbous, shriveled root. "This." She held it out. "I will trade this for your pastry."

She looked between the shriveled, dirt-covered thing and the jammy sweet. "Um..."

"I promise you," said the woman. "This, *this turnip* is so much better. Truly. Please, trust me. I want you...I want you to have a life in the world. To shape a life in the world that is all your own. I have always wanted this for you. One day...perhaps one day you'll return to the island, and we will know each other. I would like that. But you deserve your own life first."

The smell of the root, sharp, bitter, like dirt and darkness, told her it would not taste good. But the woman...her pleading tone...she did not want to refuse her.

"Daughter. *Please.*"

That word *daughter*—from the woman's mouth—it did not sound wrong. She stretched out her hand, offering the sugared bun flat on her palm.

The woman smiled in relief. "Here," she said, pressing the tuber into the daughter's palms.

She dropped the turnip into her pocket, still uncertain. "Hmm."

"I have to leave you now," the woman said.

"Do you?"

"Yes." The woman gestured to the invisible beetle in the branches. "But listen to him."

"Must I?"

"Yes."

"Will I see you again?"

"I hope not for a long time. But... tell your grandmother I am still traveling home."

"I don't understand."

"You will." The woman stepped out into the shadowy waves. "This journey from beyond, this journey through darkness, through formlessness, is long. But I am"—she lifted a misty arm—"becoming myself again."

"But..."

"Listen to him," the woman called as she sank into the water. "Listen! He will bring you...." The waves closed over her.

For a time, she looked at the place where the woman had disappeared, at the waves that rocked steadily in the darkness. Again, the beetle's sound grew loud around her, so that even the waves reverberated with its *k-k-k-k*.

Softer, though. Not a *k*, but a *c*. *C-c-c-c-c-c*.

C-c-c-c-c-c.

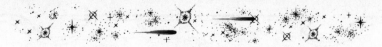

She could hear the soft, sticky hairs of its feet. *Cl,* the hairs *shush*ed against the wood. *Cl-cl-cl-cl.*

She looked up to see—the tree had grown taller. She could see neither the beetle nor the branches, just the trunk stretching up and up and up. A great shadow.

Cl-cl-cl-cl! The sound was booming through the wood now.

Cl!

Cl!

Cl!

"Clo!"

"CLO!"

"CLO!"

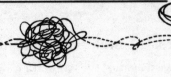

IN WHICH A POCKET HAS NO PASTRIES

"CLO!"
"CLO!"
"CLO!"

The shadow of the tree towering above her reshaped itself into the shadow of a boy. Hands on her shoulders, the boy was leaning over her, shaking her, shouting, "CLO!" over and over.

She took a deep breath and felt her lungs, which had been empty, fill.

Clo. The name felt like air in her lungs.

The boy closed his eyes, and relief softened his features. His moonish cheeks swelled and filled with light. She knew this boy; she felt she had always known him.

"Cary," she said. Her throat was dry.

"You came back," he said. "You were gone. I was worried—I thought you were never coming back."

"Yes. I was…" She tried to find a word to fit what she had been doing. "I was dreaming."

"I did what you asked," he said. "But…" His voice trembled.

"But…?"

"Oh, Clo…when you collapsed, the thread…"

She raised herself carefully on her elbows. "Yes?"

"I thought I had removed it all. Like you asked. But then I noticed it was still entangled, there, in the weaving, that only part had come free…and the rest…" He held up a handful of tangled line. "Look," he whispered.

Long gray lines of gut—blood-streaked, slimy, fishy, clumped together, breaking apart, slipping through his fingers.

"I don't know what happened." His lashes were damp. "It's all falling apart."

Calm, unconcerned, Clo took the handful of viscera from him, little pieces dropping onto the floor. She thought of the thread she had been holding in her dream, the one she had just given to the man, how it had pulsed with color and light. "Was I…" She looked up at the tapestry. "Was I trying to help someone?"

"Oh, Clo..." Cary wore a pained expression. "Your father."

"My father," she said slowly. "Hmmm." She tried to feel around her mind. She had memories of Cary, of her arrival on the island, of the old woman and the piggish cat. But when she tried to recall the *before*, even though she knew there must be a *before*, she found only clouds as thick as the fish sludge in her hands. But the clouds were comfortable. Plush and full. She did not mind that they were there.

"Clo, please." Cary pointed to the fish gurry in her hands. "Have I ruined everything?"

"Perhaps?" Clo was not sure. She was not sure it was important. She was content in her fish-clouds. "I gave someone some thread."

"Who? How did you give thread to anyone? Clo, please think. I pulled your thread....I can't have done so for nothing."

Closing her eyes, Clo thought of the kind man who had stridden through the waves of green and gold, who had given her fruit-studded pastries, who had lost his daughter. She thought of his painting—the boy with wings, a boy with wings like Cary—and stood slowly.

"Well..." She was untroubled. "Where did this come from?" She held out an open handful of fish sludge. "Can you show me in the tapestry?"

"Here." Cary touched the fabric.

Parting the warp, Clo searched in the mirror for the man to whom she'd given the thread. *There he was.* She followed the length of his line, tracing it back and back. She saw a time where it was entwined with another thread, a woman's thread—a line of rotten gut that abruptly entered, twisted in and around the man's thread, then disappeared again from the fabric. There the painter's thread was dangerously wispy, so delicate it seemed ready to break. But just before the rotting fiber left the fabric, the man's thread grew suddenly stronger, brighter: it was lonely, perhaps—hardly interwoven with any other threads—but it was vibrant, shimmering. It did not look like the tangle of fish guts she was still holding, the tangle of guts that twisted with it early on.

"I don't think anything has been ruined," Clo said, still looking at the thread. She gazed curiously at the man's recent life. *What strange days he had had.* He had been hiding beneath the straw in a pigsty. And he had been carried to a hut—and tended to. He had been feverish, delirious. A woman and her son had placed him on a pallet by their fire and had nursed him back to health, had spoon-fed him—potato soup, turnip soup, dark earth-tasting soup—and he had woken, just now; in the tapestry, he was awake.

He was digging around in a bucket; he was searching for parchment. For ink. Intrigued, Clo watched the man sketch as quickly as he could. A seascape—cliffs and waves, an expanse of sky. A boy with wings falling out of the air.

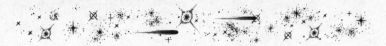

"Ah! And don't ye look well!" the mother was exclaiming. "Picture of health, y'are. Why, y' look like forty years've been taken from you! I told tha"—she nodded at her son—"th' potato soup'd do th' trick!"

The son, lanky, cauliflower-nosed, was standing over the painter's shoulder, watching him sketch. "That's a good renderin'. A good likeness of th' sea. And th' boy. I heard a story, once, of a boy did fall like that."

The painter nodded his thanks but continued his breakneck drawing.

"Do you remember, afore you fell ill, I gave th' letter and th' parcel to yer daughter," the son with the cauliflower nose was saying. "Like y' asked. She took 'em both."

"Daughter?" The painter was sketching now a girl standing on the cliff. Her hair was shorn as tight as a lamb's in spring, and she wore a boy's dirty tunic and leggings, but she was a girl all the same. "I had a dream I had a daughter...," the painter murmured.

"Ah...yer a bit confused still, then," the red-haired boy said. "Y' do have a daughter. Y' told me she was a lass with all the beauty of th' stars and sun."

"All the beauty of the stars and sun..." The painter shook his head. "In my dream...I had a wife and a daughter." He continued to sketch the girl on the cliff. She was fishing, tossing a line into the water. It was clear from the angle of her head that she could see the boy falling into the waves.

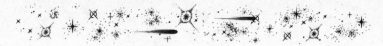

"But y' do!" the mother insisted. "The village'd watch her skulkin' round the corners. And we'd pity her—little slip o' a thing, and no mother 'n' all."

"No…" The painter rooted in his bucket again. "I'm all alone. I've been all alone."

The mother and son exchanged glances. "Well, is there anyone we can bring here to fetch you? Ye've been ill. My son found you collapsed in the pig yard. Someone must be worried."

"I need…I need a canvas," the painter said, still pawing through his materials. "I must paint this.…And the sky and sea…I can't quite…the color…I think I need to paint this outside, to get the colors just right.…"

"Yer still a mite woozy, I think." The mother put her hand on the painter's shoulder. "A bit o' bread, some more rest, maybe, ye'll be feelin' better."

"No!" he snapped, then, chagrined, softened his tone. "Something's changed.…I need to…" He put his hand over his eyes. "I haven't been able to…I was an artist…once.…" His voice shook. "Everything is cloudy. But I am certain of this. I dreamed…I promised…"

"All right, then. All right, then." The woman nodded at her son. "Why'n't tha take him on outsides, and see if the fresh air might help him."

"C'mon." The red-haired boy held out his arm. "Bring yer bucket. We'll go for a walk, and if the notion strikes,

why, y' might paint a bit then. Oh, and here!" he exclaimed, stopping by the doorway. "Here's th' wood'n matter y' told me to take from that lass, yer daughter. 'S all wilted and dried out now. She said I might sell it, but I kept it for you just in case." He handed the dried plants to the painter. "A silver coin, y' said I'd get for returning with that." A grin blossomed under the cauliflower bulb. "Bit steep for some weeds."

"Woad and madder," the man repeated, lifting the plant stalks. "Ah, yes...Yes! My pots–I need to mix some paint. And have you a kettle for water? I need to steep these roots and leaves. Yes, woad–just the blue for the sky...the boy would fall through bright air...and the cliffs...just so, madder red, where the girl would stand..."

Clo picked up the man's bobbin. The coils of yarn sparkled and shifted with all manner of color and light and shade. Here was a life that still had possibility.

"It's all right," she said slowly. "I think...I think we did what I meant to. I think it's all done."

"And will I..." Cary spoke uncertainly. "Will I return with you when we leave? Or will I be left"–he gestured to the bottom of the tapestry–"somewhere else? Somewhere in the past?"

Clo felt the fish-clouds turning in her mind. *Had she*

wanted to leave? Why? She glanced at Cary. *He wanted to leave.* His moonish cheeks were tight with apprehension.

"Well..." She touched the fabric. She thought about how the man had been sketching a boy with wings and a girl to witness the fall on the shore, how the man she had seen had promised a painting in which the boy was saved. She peered closely at the fabric—*yes.* Just there. A bubble was forming in the tapestry where the man was sketching...and a fine gold filament was spinning out, hovering inchworm-like above the spot where she had last tucked Cary's thread.... Yes, surely this, and now another filament, shimmering out, would come to hold Cary's line and anchor it there in the present, beside the cauliflower-nosed boy and the painter standing in the sunlight.

"Yes," she said. "I think he is painting you. I think his painting will hold your thread so that you could return"— she placed her fingers on the working edge—"here. Or near here, at least. I think we could return together. But..." She bit her lip, undecided. "Am I to leave? Do I want to leave?"

"You want to," Cary said. "You have wanted to leave ever since you arrived."

Clo tried to remember. Again, she could only find fish-cloud sludge in her mind. Why should she want to leave? Here life was easy. Predictable. The same gray sky, the same fish stew. The same task with the same fish-wool twisting through her fingers—everything easy and inevitable. A

life as tepid as the island's air—nothing much to feel at all. "I do?"

"Clo, yes! You convinced me! You told me there was more beyond these endless gray days."

"I can't seem...I don't remember why I would want to go. And the weaving..." She looked at it now. It seemed as though she were seeing it—the entirety of its beauty—for the first time.

Her throat tightened in astonishment and wonder. *Oh, how beautiful.* Even the holes—which had so bothered her, she remembered how much they had bothered her—seemed now a necessary part of the design. She saw their darkness against their bright edges, against the wide colors of the tapestry. Yes, from here, this balance, light against dark, suffering against joy, she understood why the woman would let the cat tear at the fabric.

It would be easy, *comfortable* even, to stay, to card the fish, to spin the thread...to stay *outside* the tapestry. To enjoy its design. To avoid the pain of being *inside* it. She didn't remember what her life had been, but she knew that to be *inside* the fabric...to be in a place where children coughed—*hee*—alone in the middle of the night...would involve grief.

Here, in her white smock, she was, finally, *comfortable.* She looked down at the expanse of material, flat and empty. She felt flat and empty and content. *Almost empty.* There was a lump in her pocket. *The pastries.*

It was not the pastries, though. It was merely her own thread, the blue thread she had unwoven from the cloak and rolled into a ball. She felt a twinge of disappointment that it was not the sweets from her dream. The memory of the imagined pastry, its jammy brightness, came rushing back. She tasted again the berries, the bread, the honey, and she felt the shape of the word *comfort* in her mouth. *Comfort.* Like the wool-stuffed bed in the next room. Like the certainty of dayless days. Like fish stew bubbling over the coals. *Yes,* here was full of comfort—as plush and easy and predictable as that pastry.

There was something else as well in the pocket. Something small, hard, round.

"Ugh." She wrinkled her nose.

A turnip. Old. Shriveled. Scarcely larger than a thumb. Almost more dirt than turnip. "Ugh," she said again.

She sniffed it. It smelled of dirt and dark and bitterness. She knew it would taste of bitterness and dark and dirt. *Why had she traded a pastry for this?* It seemed a mean trick. She thought of how the woman had dug beneath the tree, of how she had so insistently asked to trade.

But... Clo sniffed it again. The dirt... It didn't just smell like bitterness. It had—she raised it to her nose—*something else.* Not just darkness.

"Clo?" Cary put his hand on her shoulder.

Keeping her eyes closed, she inhaled deeply again.

Home. The word came to her. "Home," she whispered, to see what it sounded like.

It sounded empty—but not without meaning. She was suddenly full of longing.

Longing for what, exactly, she could not say. She had no memory of a specific place or person, and when she tried to imagine meaning in the word, she had a sense of a pallet of straw, of rats and fleas, of watery soup, of dirt and weeds. But even these ugly things—paired with the dream of the man smiling at her as she finished the pastry—felt suddenly irreplaceable. The endless gray comfort of this island felt suddenly desolate.

"Yes," she said.

"Yes?"

"*Home.* Whatever that means for us."

"Now?"

"Now."

WHEREIN NO ONE IS FISHED FROM THE SEA

CLO, WHO HAD NO MEMORY OF HER WEED-PICKING OR wall-jumping or forest-trekking days, nevertheless felt it right that she was hurrying now with Cary, a barrow balanced between them, down the cliff path. Under one arm, his bristly fur prickling against her skin, she held the cat, which squirmed and hissed and clawed at her.

"Now, now," she soothed the beast. "It's for the best."

When they finally arrived at the shore, Clo found—as she had expected—the old woman again roving the small beach and keening over the loss of her cat. Her cries bounced and echoed off the stones, so that the sea itself seemed to be wailing. The tidesman trailed the woman helplessly; here and there, a villager knelt by the cliffs, peering

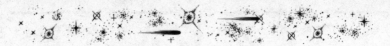

into cracks in the rocks, or stood knee-deep in the water, looking beneath the surface for the lost beast.

"Mischief! Mischief!"

Cary and Clo set their barrow on the stones.

"Grandmother!" Clo called.

The old woman did not hear her.

Clo raised her voice over the wailing. "Grandmother!"

This time, the old woman looked up. For a moment, her gaze was blank, her face a bruised apple, red and over-wrought. Then relief came flooding over her features as she saw the animal snarling in Clo's arms.

"Mischief!" She hurried across the stones. "Mischief!" Reaching Clo, she gathered the cat up and cradled him against her. He rumbled contentedly. "Oh, Mischief," the old woman crooned. "There, there. You have not been lost. Not been lost."

Clo watched the reunion of weaver and beast. The woman tickled the creature behind his ears; he nestled into the folds of her body. The cat purred, a kind of grunting. "Grandmother," Clo interrupted at last.

The old woman looked up. "Granddaughter." The word was and was not a question. "There is something changed about you." Again, the words were and were not a question. They hovered, uncertain. She peered at Clo, her eyes narrowing in her cheeks.

"Yes."

"You unwove your thread in the tapestry." Another hovering.

"Yes."

"Ah." She paused. "I did not expect this. Such a...thing to give up."

"I suppose...it was." Clo did not know now what she had given up.

"Without memories...you will wish to stay, then."

"No." Clo shook her head. "No. I want to return."

"And yet you bring Mischief to me."

"Yes."

"You know what he does. Know how wide and deep the holes he tears."

"Yes."

"You know what you will return to."

Clo hesitated.

"The weaving," the woman went on, "it is pleasant and easy. Your work—it is pleasant and easy. You would be content here. Boy." The woman turned to Cary. "Boy, your work—the nets, the fish—this is pleasant and easy. There is no grief here. The days are the same here."

"Yes," Clo said. "The days are the same here. I know it would be easy to stay. I know the world is..." She thought of the little boy coughing alone in the dark; she imagined *herself* alone and ill in the dark. "I know the world is full of suffering. But..." She thought of the way the man had

smiled at her when he came across the field of green and gold. "There's also joy. The world is full of joy. You showed me yourself—one is not possible without the other."

"And you want that? Though you do not remember, still you want it? Though you might weave it, might *see* it, still you would rather be *of* it?"

Clo wavered. "I understand how important the weaving is. How important the spinning is. But…" She thought of the way the threads glowed around the edges of Mischief's torn holes. The way they glowed where the mother had bent over her coughing children, the way they glowed where the cauliflower-nosed boy had carried the painter back to his house. "In the world, there's also care. You told me that. *Help and care are for the world.* Here…" Clo lifted her hands toward the barrenness of the island.

"In the world, your gestures—however full of care they are—will still be small, granddaughter. A handful of threads. A few bright edges. Here you might weave the whole tapestry."

"Yes. I know. A handful only." She reached and scratched behind Mischief's bristly ear. "But here I cannot help at all. Cannot care at all."

Her grandmother sighed. "You have too much of your mother in you." Shaking her head, she turned to Cary. "And you, boy? You too? After so long?"

Beside her, Cary nodded. "She helped me remember…

362

a little. I remember there is *more*. I remember I was..."
Moony cheeks bright, he glanced at Clo. "I remember I was
loved. My father loved me."

"Love," the old woman hemmed. The word was and
was not a statement. She stared hard at the flushing boy.
"Yes." She nodded. "The world is the right place for that.
The only place."

"Will you...," Clo said after a moment. "Will you
help us?"

"No," her grandmother said firmly. "As you know, it is
not my place to help. It is not even my place to hinder. I
place the threads only."

"But–" Clo held up the yarn she had unraveled from
the cloak. "Can you not help with this? Can you not place
this for me in the tapestry so I can return?"

Pinching the tail end of the thread, her grandmother
squinted at it for a long moment.

"Granddaughter, this is your own."

"Yes."

"Lovely. The fiber, the spinning is lovely. Even the
color"–she held a strand against the gray sky–"it has taken
its color from the world."

"Yes."

"A gift from your mother."

"Yes."

"You might weave it yourself."

"I do not wish to stay."

"Yes. But even so, *this*–this is yours. Your mother spun it in the world–it is *of* the world. You might weave your own life with it. All your own. It will still be mirrored in the tapestry."

"I don't understand."

"You will." Pressing the skein back into Clo's hands, the old woman turned to go. "This gift is precious. Keep it with you."

Clo tucked the ball of thread back into her pocket. "Grandmother," she called after her departing form. She thought of the old woman all alone in front of the tapestry, endlessly tapping threads into place, endlessly shaping indistinct bright fields and dark forests and glimmering mountain heights into the design, endlessly at work alone... but for the cat and his claws. She felt a flood of guilt. "I'm sorry not to stay... not to help with the work."

Still walking, the little woman waved her hand dismissively. "Ah," she said over her shoulder. "You've spun enough. I have thread enough for centuries. I have thread enough to wait for a return."

"She *is* returning, you know," Clo called up the shore. "My mother, she told me to tell you. I saw her...."

The woman and the cat were disappearing into the shadows of the cliff. "Yes," her grandmother's voice echoed back. "But that is not the return I will wait for.... When

your thread is all unraveled, when you have had your fill of joy and sorrow, you might return again. I will be waiting for you."

As the old woman's voice died away, Clo and Cary found themselves alone on the shore. All the villagers had returned up the path when they saw the cat cradled in the woman's arms; only the tidesman remained. He was standing as silently as he always did, but on the pebbles of the beach, not on his line of stones.

"Take it!" he called when he saw them looking at him. "Take it!"

"Take it?" Clo asked.

He flapped something at them. "Take it."

Clo and Cary crossed the beach to him. He flapped a little slip of something. Two little slips of something.

Cary reached out and took the slips from his craggy hand.

The tidesman nodded. "Tickets," he said. "For return. Island return only."

As the tidesman hopped, stiff-legged, rock by rock back to his post, Clo and Cary examined the slips.

"Half passage," Cary said, his eyes growing wide. He looked up at the island cliffs.

Clo ran her thumb over the words. "Half paffage."

"Someday."

"Yes."

"Or not," said Cary with a quick glance at Clo.

"Or *someday*," Clo said feeling the word grow certain. She tucked the slip of *half paffage* deep in her pocket for safe-keeping. She glanced once more at the cliffs—*Yes, someday*—before turning her eyes to the sea.

Water that is full of salt and has no edge.

No. Somewhere, somewhere else, there was another edge. Another land. "Ready?" she asked.

Cary followed her gaze. Clo saw fear flash across his cheeks, saw his moons grow papery and gray. She saw how he must have looked when he fell from the sky, but still, he nodded and raised a smile.

The thing they built from the objects they had gathered—the barrow, the wing, the bucket, the oars—could not really be called a boat. Cary, remembering his father was an inventor, blushed and fretted that Clo might expect more of him in the creation of this craft, but she did not notice his discomfort or have any expectations—she did not wish the thing to be anything more than it was—a barrow box ripped from its wheel, a thing that could float, a thing that could hold them holding the wing.

Under the tidesman's stony gaze, they pushed the barrow box into the water.

"Get in," she said when they were knee-deep.

First Cary, Clo steadying the box, settled himself into the craft beside the wing, then Clo, Cary doing his best to keep the thing upright, settled herself next to Cary. Each raising an oar, they began paddling.

The barrow wobbled under their efforts and threatened to tip or simply to spin in place. But after a few minutes of fruitless exertion, they found a rhythm, and the boxy craft began to skim across the water.

From time to time, Clo glanced over her shoulder. The island seemed to be departing from them—its great gray cliff walls shrinking into the distance. Only the ever-growing line of waves ahead gave Clo the sense that it was they—and not the island—who were actually moving.

As they drew closer to the waves, the noise began to reach them. Cary, eyes wide, stared ahead at the crashing wall of water.

He lowered his oar. "Clo..."

She realized in the trembling way he said her name that, of course, he had only ever seen these waves from a distance. He had fallen from the sky. He had been fished from the sea. He had not had to cross this line before.

"Clo," Cary said again, his voice full of urgency. The barrow pitched beneath them; they were reaching the first of the breakers.

"It's possible," Clo said. "The bosun rowed me through. I know it's possible. I remember he said it's only *a bit of time*."

"But…" A wave crested over the edge of the barrow box. Cary stared horrified at the puddle that now sloshed in the bottom of their craft. "This isn't really a boat. And I… I'm not a bosun. I'm just a net boy. Neither of us knows how to guide a boat through waves like that! We'll never make it through."

"We will." Clo tried to make the words sound certain. "And you're not just a net boy, but I don't want you paddling."

"What?"

"I'll paddle." Clo raised her voice over the roaring of the water. She took the paddle from him and placed it on the floor of the barrow. "You need to play your flute."

"What?" Again, a wave rolled over the edge of the barrow.

"Cary, the waves, I think they're…the *real* edge of this island. I think when we cross them, we cross into the world. Into the time of the tapestry. Like the bosun said, they're *a bit of time*. And I think…I think it's easier to enter the world if the fabric is not pulled so tight…if there's a pocket. A bubble." She glanced ahead at the line of watery mountains, hoping she was right. "If the fabric bubbles, I think the waves also open."

Cary stared at her, panic-struck and uncomprehending.

"Your flute, Cary!" Clo mimed the instrument. "Play it! "

Cary raised his flute from his pocket and lifted it like a question.

Yes! Clo nodded vigorously. "Play it!" she called. "Think how the tapestry bubbles, how art changes it, changes time... if you play something true"—she shouted to make herself heard—"the tapestry will bubble. The waves will open for us. Open *enough* for us. Even the bosun sang when he rowed me through. Play!"

A mountain of water had begun to grow in front of them. Clo could see foam cresting at the top.

"Play! Cary, play!"

A few wan notes *pipp*ed out of the flute. Cary's eyes, his moons were flat with terror.

"No!" Clo was truly yelling now, paddling furiously up the wall of water, but she could not even hear herself over the thundering of the waves. "Play what I saw you playing in the tapestry! The song about the warmth of the hills and the tide... or play the song I heard you play on the street that was full of sunlight...."

Clo could not hear the words, but she saw Cary's mouth form the shapes: "I don't remember!"

"You do!" The water tore violently at the paddle in her hands. They were halfway up the mountain of water. Its top had begun to curl over them. She looked desperately at the boy who was lost in his own horror of falling again into the sea. "You do! Play the song you played on the shore about the sea, the song about the starry darkness... *Anything*," she pleaded, though she knew he could no longer hear her.

"Silver fish. Wings made with wax and string. A barrow-boat. *Anything*, Cary! Anything true!"

They would not make it over the water-mountain; it was going to collapse over them. *On them*. They were falling with the falling of the wave; Cary shut his eyes. Clo pushed her paddle deep; she felt the depth of the ocean—the force of *water that is full of salt and has no edge*—wrench the oar from her: it was in her hands, then it was not. She grabbed the second paddle, but the water, gray, frothing, was all around them, over them. She saw Cary, in the moment before the collapse of froth and salt and air, put the flute to his lips: she heard a piping melody—then he was lost behind the wave. Clo gasped, struggling to breathe, to see.

In darkness, in water, she thought she saw, in what space there was to think, something yawn over them—some dark shadow, boat bottom, gloomy craft. "*Girly*," the barnacled darkness seemed to howl, "*not again*." She could not breathe, she could not see, she could not find air or light: she was lost beneath salt and terror and sea. She heard, under the roaring that had covered them, another trill, the high piping of a flute, but it could not be Cary—*we must be*, she thought in the darkness that was all water and lost air, *we must be drowning*.

We will not, she thought—the last thing she thought before the darkness became simply darkness and all the roaring became a single high-pitched piping trill—*we will not be fished from the sea*.

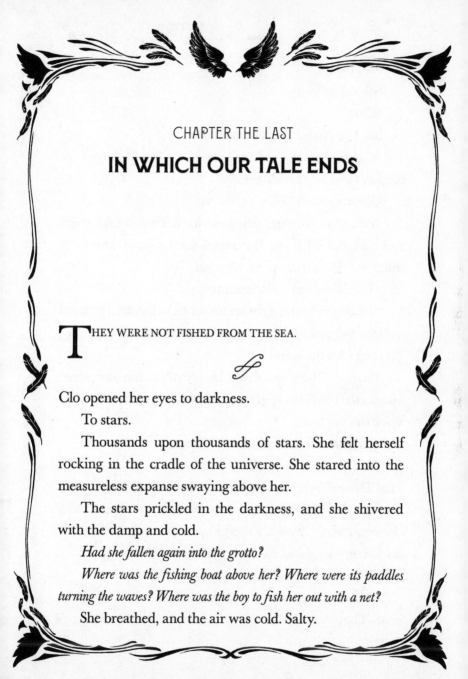

CHAPTER THE LAST

IN WHICH OUR TALE ENDS

T HEY WERE NOT FISHED FROM THE SEA.

Clo opened her eyes to darkness.

To stars.

Thousands upon thousands of stars. She felt herself rocking in the cradle of the universe. She stared into the measureless expanse swaying above her.

The stars prickled in the darkness, and she shivered with the damp and cold.

Had she fallen again into the grotto?

Where was the fishing boat above her? Where were its paddles turning the waves? Where was the boy to fish her out with a net?

She breathed, and the air was cold. Salty.

She breathed.

She was breathing.

"Clo?"

She felt a hand touch her shoulder.

"Cary?" She grasped the hand. *Yes, Cary.* She could see the form of a boy beside her.

"Are you all right?"

"I'm...I'm not sure." She considered her body. It felt wet and cold, but it felt like her own. Like she was within it. "I think so." Then, hesitating, "Are you?"

"Yes, I think so....Where are we?"

"I thought...I thought we might be in the sea. Where I fell into the grotto. Where you saved me with the net. See the stars? All the stars?"

"Stars...," breathed Cary. He tilted his chin and stared up into the swathes of light. "I had forgotten...it's so..." His voice caught.

She gestured in the darkness. "But..."

"But?"

"The stars, they're simply there. They're still; in the darkness, they're still. Before, they swam like fish, and I was sinking through them....Now...I don't know where we are. There's no fishing boat above. No one to fish us out of the sea."

"We are in a boat."

"Y-yes." They were in their boat. Their barrow-box boat. They were huddled together on its wet floor. Cary's

372

wing, waterlogged, was beside them. Clo looked again into the darkness above them and at the stars, spiny and sharp in the cold breeze. Shivering, she leaned over the edge of the barrow box. Below, too, were stars, but faint, smeared, rising and falling and fading—below was only the reflection of stars in the water.

"Cary," Clo whispered, squeezing his arm. "We *are* in a boat."

"Yes..."

"No, we *are* in a boat. We are not underwater. We made it through the waves. Cary, your flute, your song—it was enough. Oh, it's nighttime, Cary." Her voice rose. "It's nighttime. It's night!"

"Night?" Cary said wonderingly. "I hardly remember..."

"Night!" The word was full of joy. "Oh, it's night!"

They sat shivering in the darkness, leaning against each other for warmth and comfort, listening to the steady splash of water against the sides of their barrow box. *Stars*, the waves lisped against the metal. *Stars*.

"I'm cold," Cary said at last, quietly, happily, through his chattering teeth. "I can't remember when I was ever cold before."

"Yes, I am, too." Clo smiled. "But look..." She raised an arm. A thin line of gold—fine as gossamer thread—was just becoming visible in the distance, stretching across the expanse of sky and waves.

"What's that?" Cary's voice was round with awe.

"The sun rising."

As they watched, the gossamer line thickened and took on a rosier hue. The stars above grew dimmer, the sky paler—first violet, then gray, then nearly yellow, then a wash of peach, the faintest brush of blue. Finally, a sharp bright light cut the line of sea and sky.

"Oh..." Cary squinted against the light blooming on the horizon. "The sun!"

It rose steadily, becoming at last a full orb climbing the sky, its reflection marking a path across the waves. Clo felt her skin warm under its light; next to her, Cary, moony-cheeked, openmouthed, could not keep from staring at the colors of the water, at the colors of the sky.

"Color," he said. "So much color..." His skin was flushed with the pink suffusing the sky. "Clo, I had forgotten."

Your cheeks! Clo nearly exclaimed but caught herself. *Ruddy, rising moons.*

She smiled, scanning the horizon. Now that the sun had risen, she could see they were in the middle of the ocean: no land was in sight. For a moment, she felt a flash of terror—*Nothing! There was nothing to show them the way!*—but then she settled herself into the bottom of their craft and began to work. Gathering Cary's wing over her lap, she took her skein of yarn from her pocket. It was damp, and here, in

the morning light, it looked simply gray—it had none of the shifting light and colors from when she had first unraveled it—not even the steady blue of the cloak. *Gray fish-wool.* Her eyes had changed, but she knew what the thread was, what it could hold.

She began weaving the yarn through the gaps in the wing, the places where the feathers had come free. Slowly, slowly, she closed the spaces: the wing began to hold its shape again.

Cary finally pulled his attention from the sky. "What are you doing?"

"Here," Clo said, lifting the wing. "Help me hold this."

Grasping the edges, Cary held the wing upright in the center of their barrow. Around his hands, feathers trembled in the breeze. "But what are you doing?"

Kneeling, Clo continued looping the threads through the gaps, twisting and winding, patching the holes. "It will be our sail. It will bring us home." As she wove the fabric patches, the wing caught more and more of the wind; soon, Cary had to brace himself to keep it from flying away.

As the wing billowed and filled, the boat began to scud across the water. It splashed brightly over the waves, sunlight catching the water they tossed up in a spray all around them. They were sailing straight along the gleaming path the sun was still cutting in the water.

Clo squinted at her weaving. *Just gray. Fish-wool.* She

could see no images, no coughing boy, no man with sweating ox, no woman kneeling on the forest floor. But then—this, this bright splashing, this warm sunlight, this boy with plump cheeks struggling to keep a sail of feathers steady—this was all her own.

The wing was repaired enough for now—it was catching enough wind to bring them...*somewhere*. Tucking the remaining skein of yarn carefully between the feathers, Clo stood next to Cary and took hold of one edge of the wing.

"Can I help you hold it?"

He nodded. "It feels...it feels almost like..." He was pale, but smiling. "Like flying."

She felt the wind pulling at the feathers and her weaving as they skimmed across the water. They bounced lightly along the waves, the boat splashing *somewhere, somewhere, somewhere* as they crossed the expanse. Watching the waves ripple and curl around them, blue and green and gold, Clo breathed deeply: the air smelled of salt. And fish. And open sky. And damp feathers. And...*something else*. She closed her eyes, inhaling, considering.

Pine.

The air smelled of pine. Just a hint, the faintest whiff. But there it was. *Pine.*

She scanned the horizon.

It seemed little more than a shadow, so at first she said nothing; she simply watched the shadow as they sailed. But

the shadow grew larger...and wider...and its edges became raggedy and sharp. Sharp as stones. Sharp as houses. As boats. As trees.

"Is that...," Cary whispered.

"Yes." It was.

Home.

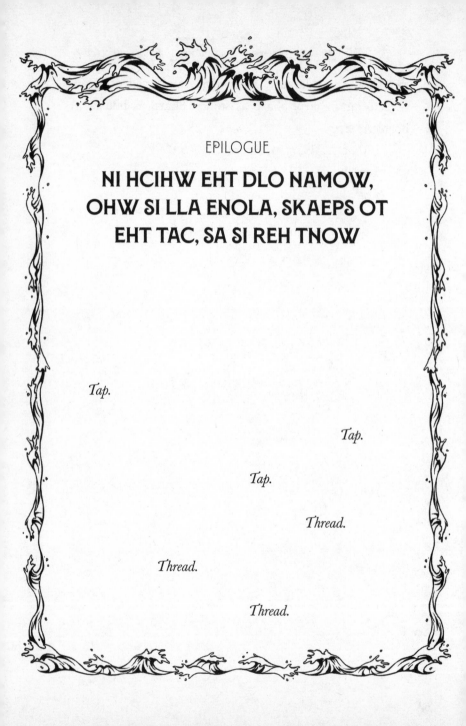

EPILOGUE

NI HCIHW EHT DLO NAMOW, OHW SI LLA ENOLA, SKAEPS OT EHT TAC, SA SI REH TNOW

Tap.

Tap.

Tap.

Thread.

Thread.

Thread.

Thread.

                                      Tap.

Thread.

"Do you miss her, Mischief?"

                                      Tap.

"You must."

                   Tap.

"How much fish she gave you."

                            Thread.

"How quiet it is without her. How much noise she brought."

Tap.

"She brought so much of the world with her. Too much."

                   Tap.

"Oh, my eyes are not so good, Mischief. But see...see here."

Tap.

"Yes, there she is. Our Clothilde."

Thread.

"Yes, and the boy, too."

Tap.

"Well, *perhaps* a boy. *Perhaps* a girl. They're nearly grown. They grow in the world, Mischief. They have days and months and years, and they change. But she's still Clothilde. You needn't worry. She keeps her hair shorn tight as a lamb's in spring. She wears a boy's dirty leggings. Boots. They live in the last of the crumbling homes. *No*, it's not fine, not at all. There are no beds stuffed with wool. There's a dirt floor and rats and they sleep on pallets of straw. They have a garden with some...turnips, I think. Some potatoes. Weeds... *no,* herbs. So many herbs. She's always poking in the dirt. Every morning in her garden. But..."

Tap.

"...*No, Mischief.* She doesn't sell them. She...oh, even you can see this. Look how the threads glow here, where you've been scratching. *That's our Clothilde. Yes.* Mixing salves and balms and tonics. She's sitting here in a neighbor's house tending to a little one's fever and spots. Look at her, all night, holding cool cloths against the child. Spooning medicine. *So much care*, Mischief. She stopped even your claws here."

Tap.

"I don't know if she thinks of you then, Mischief. She must. I imagine she must."

Thread.

"*No*, the boy, he's a...fisherman. Of course he is. Look here. He's very good with a net and pole. See how he fills the boat...the other fishermen, they are astonished by his skill. *Yes*, our fishermen would be pleased to know this. Perhaps I'll tell them."

Tap.

"Are they content?"

Thread.

"Not in the way we are content, Mischief. They are happy sometimes. They are sad sometimes. Sometimes... see here. Here they are full of sorrow. Look. This tiny woman with a crooked back and a jangling laugh has died. *Yes.* Her thread was all unwound. She was their neighbor. Friend. Clothilde and the boy lit her fire and brought her dinner when she could not help herself. They are mourning her."

Tap.

"But here, they are full of joy."

Tap.

"No, it's a small moment, Mischief. It's nothing large. Joy in the world...it doesn't have to come from something large."

Thread.

"Well, they've carried a basket of turnips and fish to the painter's house. *Yes,* that painter, Mischief. *No...* They don't *really* know who he is: he is just the painter who lives outside the town in a small house beneath a tall pine. Perhaps they feel they may have met before? *A little?* But he is their friend.

See here? His thread? The bubbles? The gossamer strands?
Oh, he is always reshaping my fabric."

Tap.

"Yes...here, they've just come for dinner. They've set the
fish to cook on the coals, and the painter has put out some
bread and cheese. *No*, he did not steal it, Mischief. He is
showing them his work."

Thread.

"What has he painted? Oh, Mischief. Such trouble this
painter causes me. And Clothilde! Look at *her* mischief
here. She's been telling him of a weaver with...apple cheeks
who sits in front of a loom all day. She's been telling him of a
great monster of a cat. And look, he has painted it! Can you
imagine, Mischief!"

Tap.

"Ah. It is a good likeness. Look at you, Mischief. Why, you
are almost piggish here. He has painted you with a great
round tum and a mouthful of fish."

Tap.

"No, that is not the joy. That is pleasant; they are pleased, but that is not the joy."

Thread.

"The joy is nothing, really. Nothing particular. It is evening. They are sitting at the table. The fire is warm, the candles bright. The fish is well cooked, the turnips soft. They have eaten, and their bellies are full. 'If I had a daughter…,' the painter is saying. He raises his glass. 'If I had a son…'"

Tap.

"*No*, Mischief. That is not the joy. Not yet. For a moment, they are all missing something they cannot remember. For a moment, they are all quiet, trying to remember."

Tap.

"But now the boy has taken up his flute.…*No*, this one is not broken, not cracked. It is new. He carved it himself. He is playing a jig, and the painter has bowed to Clothilde and invited her to dance. And they are dancing, and the boy is playing, and the room is too small for their jig—too small for their stomping and spinning. Chairs are tumbling over,

cups and spoons are rattling on the table, and their faces are bright with laughter."

Tap.

"And now the painter has taken the boy's flute...and he cannot play, Mischief, oh, he cannot play at all...but he is piping *something*, noise, just notes, and Clothilde and the boy have linked arms and are whirling about the room. And the painter is skipping and piping, and Clothilde and the boy are galloping and spinning, and the dishes and cups are clattering, and they are all laughing so that they cannot catch their breath. They fall into their chairs, still laughing."

Thread.

"The room is quiet now. They sit about the table in the quiet, warm and breathless from their dancing."

Tap.

"Their faces are shining in the candlelight. The shadows of the room are soft around them. Outside, dark is settling over the hills and fields. *Dark*, Mischief. Dark. Imagine. Like your fur...like your fur settling over the sky. But the stars are coming out...one by one...one by one, like silver

fish…and the nightjar is churring in the distance. The air carries the scent of dew and pine."

Tap.

"They are together."

Tap.

"That is their joy, Mischief."

Tap.

Tap.

"You will have to imagine it."

Thread.

Tap.

Tap.

Tap.

Tap.

ACKNOWLEDGMENTS

WHILE THE OLD WOMAN WEAVES ALL ALONE, THANKFULLY authors have an entire tapestry of people supporting them: I am profoundly grateful to my agent, Sara Crowe, for her invaluable guidance and her enthusiastic championing of this work; to Pam Gruber and Deirdre Jones, editors extraordinaire, for understanding and believing in the manuscript and for shepherding it through its revisions with wisdom and insight (how many loose threads they helped me find and tie down!); to Karina Granda, for her artful book design, and Yuta Onoda, for bringing the design to life with inspired illustrations; to Barbara Perris and Annie McDonnell, for sharp-eyed copy and production editing; to Hannah Milton, Hallie Tibbetts, Megan Tingley, Jackie Engel, Alvina Ling, Patricia Alvarado, Victoria Stapleton, Stefanie Hoffman, Natali Cavanagh, Siena Koncsol, Janelle DeLuise, and everyone at Little, Brown Books for Young Readers for standing behind this book and working so diligently to bring it into the world; to the whole team at Pippin Properties—Holly McGhee, Elena Giovinazzo, Ashley Valentine, and Cameron Chase—for their passionate devotion to children's literature; to the communities of the Upper Valley and Kearsarge-Ragged region—especially friends, neighbors, teachers—for countless acts of kindness and goodwill; to this family of friends—Sally, Peter, Bruce, Mary Jane, George, Amy, and Carol—for being the first to celebrate; to my parents, Rolande and Donald, for everything, really, but especially for a lifetime of love and encouragement and a childhood filled with books and changing landscapes (and for—once upon a time—carding and spinning and weaving wool); to my sister, Sara, for her enduring friendship and her sage advice and artistry... and for showing how much bravery is needed to risk one's memories; to my husband, Dean, for traveling with me through every page of every draft—I could not ask for anyone more perceptive or supportive by my side—and for braving even the darkest seas with me; and, lastly, to Oliver, who read it first, for being the brightest strand, for sharing music and stories and imagination, and, above everything else, for inspiring it all.

S. Walton

Christiane M. Andrews

grew up in rural New Hampshire, Vermont, and Maine, on the edges of mountains and woods and fields and sometimes even the sea. A writing and literature instructor, she lives with her husband and son and a small clutch of animals on an old New Hampshire hilltop farm. *Spindlefish and Stars* is her first novel. Christiane invites you to visit her online at cmandrews.com.